Lord Margrave's Secret Desire

SAMANTHA GRACE

Samantha Grace Publishing
Email: samantha@samanthagraceauthor.com

For my dear friends Heather and Lori. I'm lucky to have such wonderfully supportive women cheering me on from both sides of the globe.

FOREWORD

Dear reader,

The following romantic adventure is a blending of history and an author's active imagination. Aside from the main characters, the Regent's Consul and the Black Death mentioned in the book are complete fabrications. If you start researching either group or try to unearth a connection between them and the real historical figures mentioned in the story, I'm afraid you will come up empty-handed. I hope you enjoy this fictional world I've created. I welcome you with open arms.

Samantha

FROM THE DIARY OF ISABELLE DARLINGTON

April 1800

My dearest Matthew and I have been blessed with a third daughter on what could otherwise be a dreary month in England. I feared my loving husband would be disappointed when his dreams of fathering a son did not come to fruition yet again, but my worries were unwarranted. Matthew was charmed the moment he beheld his youngest daughter.

Our little darling had the most serious expression when she regarded her Papa for the first time. Matthew marveled over the wise look in her eyes. He said it was as if she had lived a thousand lifetimes before blessing our family with her presence.

As with our other daughters, he has deferred to my wishes to name her after *my angels*, as he refers to them. My beloved pretends my study of angelology holds no interest for him, but I could tell he was eager to learn our daughter's name. We shall call her Sophia in honor of the archangel of love. Matthew declares it a most fitting moniker, and I

1

could not agree more. Sophia embodies my heart residing outside of my body.

～

Christmas, 1819

SOPHIA DARLINGTON STUDIED HER TWO OLDER SISTERS' GLUM faces across the festive drawing room. With Uncle Charles away on one of his expeditions, the holiday season did not feel the same, but Sophia was determined to bring a little cheer to Hartland Manor on what should be the happiest day of the year.

She rose from her chair and clapped her hands. "Your attention, please, ladies and..." When her gaze landed on Crispin Locke, Viscount Margrave, he winked. Her heart fluttered and an uncontrollable smile spread across her face. "Ladies and *gentleman*."

Her uncle's godson inclined his head. The sunlight pouring through the window at his back illuminated his golden blond locks; he returned her smile. *An Adonis in Uncle Charles's favorite chair.*

Sophia suppressed a dreamy sigh and continued with her address. "Uncle Charles could not join us for Christmas this year, but he will always be with us in spirit. I have little doubt he would tell us to stop moping and start celebrating."

"Hear, hear!" Aunt Beatrice nodded with approval while scratching behind her spoiled black poodle's ears. "As usual, Sophia speaks with the wisdom of one thrice her age."

Sophia's heart swelled with affection for her darling great-aunt. She suspected even if she suggested they storm the London Tower, Aunt Beatrice would declare it a marvelous idea simply because it was Sophia's. "Thank you,

Auntie. We cannot forget to toast to Papa and Mama either."

Her sisters perked up at the mention of their late parents.

"Sophia is right," Regina said. "We mustn't allow Uncle Charles's absence to distract us from observing tradition. He would be disappointed if we did."

"Shall I ring for the good crystal?" Without waiting for a reply, Evangeline tossed one of Uncle Charles's old travel journals on the plush settee cushion beside her and hopped up to yank the bellpull.

The Christmas following the loss of Sophia's parents, Uncle Charles had instigated the ritual of toasting Mama and Papa to honor the memory of his little sister and her annoyingly perfect husband. Uncle Charles had ruffled Sophia's hair when he spoke of his brother-in-law, proving he held no true feelings of ill will toward his sister's husband.

Even though Sophia, Regina, and Evangeline had been mere girls, their great-aunt had retrieved the family crystal, filled the goblets with punch, and entrusted them not to break the valuable heirlooms. Sophia did not remember much about the day, but she recalled every toast since.

"Lord Margrave," Aunt Beatrice said, "my nephew keeps a bottle of claret in his study. Would you kindly retrieve it?"

"It would be my pleasure." Crispin rose from the leather wingback chair and sketched a bow. "If you will excuse me a moment, ladies."

Sophia tried not to stare as he exited the drawing room, but he moved with a majestic bearing that mesmerized her. His handsome face and striking figure had been dominating her imagination these past few months as she prepared for her upcoming London debut. She often daydreamed of strolling through Hyde Park on his arm, dancing together beneath the glittering chandeliers at Lady Eldridge's annual ball, and allowing him to steal a kiss in Uncle Charles's drawing room.

The fantasy had become her favorite escape from the dreary weather plaguing the English countryside this time of year. Nothing more than an entertainment since Crispin never noticed her—until today. Much to her delight, he seemed incapable of tearing his gaze away from her.

Of course, she had changed a lot since he last saw her two years ago. She supposed he might simply be shocked by her transformation. No longer was she the scrawny girl who hung on his every word or laughed too heartily at his tales. She was a woman of nineteen. Some gentlemen even found her fetching. At the country assemblies this autumn, she rarely had been without a dance partner.

When he disappeared from sight, she released her breath—unaware she had been holding it. The twinkle in Aunt Beatrice's eyes and slight upturning of her lips suggested she had caught Sophia ogling. A rush of heat singed Sophia's cheeks, and she turned toward the fireplace to hide her blush.

A footman entered the room, and Aunt Beatrice asked the servant to bring the heirloom claret glasses.

"Yes, ma'am."

"It is time for kisses from Cupid," Sophia announced with exaggerated gaiety and plucked a stem of mistletoe from the garland draped across the hand-carved mantle.

Upon hearing his name, the dog scrambled from Aunt Beatrice's lap and came to jump up on Sophia's skirts. She bent to scoop him in her arms and held the stem overhead.

"Merry Christmas, *mon amour.*" She affected a rather poor French accent—which coincidentally was a perfect imitation of the one she'd heard from the modiste commissioned to sew gowns for her coming out—and placed a noisy smooch on Cupid's curly head.

Regina and Evangeline laughed, rewarding Sophia's efforts toward chasing away their blues. Encouraged, she marched to the fainting couch where her oldest sister was sitting.

"Look what I found," Sophia sang out and wagged the piece of mistletoe over Regina's head.

"Kisses from Cupid? My *favorite*." Regina reached for their beloved pet and held him at arm's length in front of her. Cupid pawed the air in his eagerness to lick her face. She attempted to affect a stern expression, but her mouth twitched as she fought back a smile. "No slobbering this year. Do you hear me, little rogue?"

"The pooch only gives sloppy kisses." Crispin's voice rang out, startling Sophia. "I question his status as a rogue."

He continued to the sideboard with a slight smirk

"Come now, Margrave." Evangeline joined him at the sideboard. "I am sure you have licked a face or two in your day."

Sophia laughed at the ludicrous image her sister's words invoked, earning a playful glower from Crispin. The servant returned with a tray of heirloom glasses.

Evangeline grabbed an empty claret glass, flashed an innocent smile at Crispin, and held it out to him. "Please, may I have some?"

"Since you asked nicely..." He tweaked her sister's cheek, eliciting a pang of envy in Sophia, even though the exchange was innocent.

She retrieved the poodle from her eldest sister and approached the sideboard. "Kisses from Cupid. Who is next?"

"I respectfully decline," Crispin said. "I have a rule against kissing anything with more hair on its face than me." The full force of his smile landed on Sophia and stole her breath.

Evangeline set down her glass and held out her arms. "I never refuse a kiss from my favorite pup, not that Cupid usually gives me a choice." Hugging the dog to her chest, she placed a quick peck on his head while he thrashed in her arms, attempting to lick her face.

Crispin snatched the mistletoe from Sophia's fingers and lifted it above her head. "I believe it is *your* turn for kisses."

Her heart lodged in her throat a brief moment until she realized he was referring to kissing the dog.

"I had my turn while you were digging around in Uncle Charles's study." She grabbed for the mistletoe, but he held it out of reach just like he had done when she was a girl. She was too old to play such games. The reminder he likely still thought of her as a child stung."Keep it. I do not want it anyway." She tried to appear nonchalant, but her words sounded strained.

Evangeline carried Cupid back to their aunt and sat beside Regina on the fainting couch.

"I *will* keep it"—Crispin tucked the mistletoe into his waistcoat pocket—"if only to help you avoid falling into mischief."

Sophia's hands landed on her hips. "And who will help you?"

"There is no help for me, darling."

Tingles swept through her at the term of endearment, and she couldn't stop herself from beaming.

"Very well," she said. "You may forego the Christmas kiss, but you must participate in the annual game of hide-and-seek."

His eyes sparkled with good humor. "And if I resist, how do you propose to compel me?"

Rarely did she command his full attention; she likened it to being bathed in sunbeams. She was warm all over and feeling slightly reckless. "Some men find my charm irresistible."

"Yes," he murmured where only she could hear, "I can see how resisting you might be a challenge."

She flushed with pleasure.

"Margrave will join us." Regina left the fainting couch to collect glasses of wine for herself and Aunt Beatrice. "How could he say no? It is *tradition*."

"You know how Sophia loves observing traditions," Evangeline piped up. "You do not wish to disappoint her, do you, Margrave?"

"Of course not. I cannot abide disappointing a lady." Crispin offered Sophia his arm. "Shall we join your sisters and aunt?"

Aunt Beatrice led the toast to their parents while everyone raised their glasses. "To Mama and Papa," Sophia intoned and took a sip of wine.

"I am unconvinced any of you should be out in the cold," Aunt Beatrice said, "but if you insist on following tradition, you must don your pelisses and mittens."

Crispin gently nudged Sophia toward the door. "I promise to chase the ladies back inside before too long, madam."

He stayed to chat with Aunt Beatrice while Sophia and her sisters hurried to retrieve their warm outerwear. She lingered in the corridor outside her sisters' bedchambers, but when they took longer than usual to gather their belongings, she wandered downstairs to wait in the entrance hall.

Crispin's voice carried from the drawing room. "It seems early to be thinking about marriage, is it not? Regina and Evangeline have not made matches yet."

7

"Sophia begged for a Season last year, but my nephew and I thought it best to postpone her debut for that reason. With her twentieth birthday approaching, I have decided it is unfair to ask her to wait when her sisters show little interest in finding husbands, and I am certain Charlie would agree. Perhaps you might recommend a young man."

Much to Sophia's disappointment, his response was drowned out by her sisters' laughter at the head of the staircase. She hoped he had recommended himself.

"You are too slow, Margrave," Evangeline called as she descended the last few stairs. "That means you are the seeker."

"You have until I reach fifty." In a booming voice, he began counting. "One, two, three..."

"Ludwig!" Regina grabbed Sophia's arm and dragged her toward the front door. Evangeline scrambled after them. The footman opened the front door, and they dashed outside into the cold, laughing.

Regina released her. "We should split apart."

"Agreed," Sophia said. "I will hide close to the stables."

"Very good, and I will go this way." Regina darted toward the back of the house while Evangeline contemplated her direction a moment before heading toward the fields. The soft ground grabbed at Sophia's boots as she rushed for the stables. The pungent scent of hay and horses greeted her as she neared the building and stayed with her as she rounded it en route to the old travel coach. It would make a perfect hiding spot while providing shelter from the cold.

The carriage, which had lost a wheel and listed to one side, was hidden beneath weathered sailcloth. It had been out of commission for as long as Sophia had been alive. She didn't know why Uncle Charles hadn't disposed of it. She kicked aside a couple of rocks used to weigh down the sailcloth, slipped beneath the cover, and climbed inside the carriage, taking care not to latch the door.

It wasn't long before heavier footsteps approached the carriage. It had to be Crispin. She covered her mouth, certain he could hear the churning of her breath. The sailcloth rustled as he circled the carriage. When he began to whistle a tune and walk away, she smothered a chuckle. He had been so close and hadn't found her. She was feeling rather clever.

The carriage door jerked open. "Aha!"

She screamed and rammed back against the carriage wall before bursting into laughter. "You startled me."

Crispin ducked his head inside.

"Did I?" A wide smile eased across his face. He climbed into the carriage, slid onto the bench beside her, and closed the door.

"No!" Sophia dove across the carriage, landing halfway on his lap. She sighed and sat up. "The latch is broken."

Crispin pushed on the door. It didn't budge.

"Now what are we going to do?" She flopped back against the bench. "Didn't you notice the door was open?"

"I did, but how was I to guess the latch was broken?"

She raised her eyebrows. "Surely you saw the missing wheel."

"Again, there is no connection between the wheel and latch. It is good you are not responsible for carriage maintenance."

She playfully wrinkled her nose. "Regina and Evangeline will come looking for us eventually. I suppose I can tolerate your companionship until they find us."

Crispin sank against the seatback, smiling and appearing untroubled by their circumstances. "Your aunt said you are entering the marriage mart next Season."

"I am." She folded her hands in her lap, curious to see

where the conversation might lead. "This may be our last Christmas together. Next year you will regret not accepting your kisses. I doubt Regina or Evangeline will continue the tradition."

All traces of playfulness vanished from his demeanor, and his strong brow furrowed. "It is hard to imagine a Christmas without you."

"Bah..." She flicked her hand, unsure of what to say in return. His nearness created tantalizing quivers in her belly. She could barely think.

"Are you certain you are ready to marry?" he asked. "There is no need to rush into a decision."

"I am not rushing." She sounded slightly breathless. "I have been donning my mother's wedding gown and practicing my vows since I was nine. I am eager to find a love like my parents shared. Mama wrote about it in her diary. They adored one another and never spent a night apart."

"Your parents had a rare marriage, Sophia. I fear your expectations are too high, and you will be disappointed."

"How so?"

"I know most of the bachelors in Town." He scowled. "They are rascals, one and all. You cannot fall prey to their honeyed words."

His protest pleased her beyond measure. Could he be jealous? "Are there no respectable gentlemen left in England? That is disappointing. Perhaps I could tame one of these rascals and turn him into a good husband."

"Strike it from your mind, darling. They are unredeemable."

"I am afraid I am faced with a bit of a conundrum. I wish to marry, and the only available men are wicked rogues."

She caught her bottom lip between her teeth,

pretending to mull over the situation. Crispin's gaze dropped to her mouth, and her heart fluttered with excitement.

"Perhaps I must lower my standards, my lord."

"Most unadvisable, I say." He leaned toward her. The cramped space grew hotter—electrified. "You deserve better. You deserve someone who understands and appreciates you. Allow yourself time to find the perfect man for you."

She had found him already. Emboldened by his nearness, she slipped her hand into his pocket and withdrew the twig of mistletoe. His body heat filled the space between them.

"It is not too late to claim your kiss." She lifted the sprig of mistletoe above them. "This could be your last chance before I capture my rogue."

Her stomach churned with uncertainty; his intense hazel gaze held her frozen in place. She did not fear desire. She'd been taught passion was natural and beautiful when love was involved. Fear of rejection, however, made her hands shake.

"Sophia." Crispin's voice had grown smoky, bordering on seductive. "You deserve better than *me*."

"I am willing to compromise this once," she teased and nervously swept her tongue over her lips. He inhaled, his nostrils flaring slightly. "Time is running out, my lord."

Cupping her nape, Crispin eased her toward him, pausing to search her face as if she might change her mind. She lowered her hand to his chest, the mistletoe loosely clutched between her fingers.

"Kiss me," she whispered.

"You are too irresistible by half, Sophia Darlington."

"I warned you."

When their lips touched, victory billowed beneath her

breastbone, expanding in her chest. How long had she dreamed of this moment? He nestled his fingers into her hair, angling her head to leisurely take the kiss she had brazenly offered. She melted as his mouth teased hers—a nip of her lips, the tip of his tongue tracing the seam between them.

She exhaled. *Havers.* Her fantasy suffered in comparison to a real kiss from him.

Tentatively, she imitated his movements. A deep hum of pleasure sounded in his throat; her confidence blossomed. Parting her lips, she twined her arms around his neck to draw him closer. He dragged her against him and deepened the kiss; his tongue swept into her eager mouth.

This was no longer a polite acceptance of her offer but a claiming. She joyfully surrendered, arching into him and grasping the front of his jacket. His wine-tinged kisses and searing heat swirled around her, *through* her, intoxicating and lovely.

Her head filled with thoughts of their future. Of many more Christmases observing old traditions and creating new ones of their own. Of a lifetime of passionate kisses under the mistletoe after their children were tucked into bed. She would be his perfect companion, his helpmate, his eager lover, his Lady Margrave. *I adore you,* her heart whispered as it beat in a driving rhythm.

When he suddenly broke the kiss and eased her away, she blinked—startled and confused. She reached for him, but he gently caught her shoulders.

"Your sisters are calling for you," he murmured and caressed his thumb over her cheek.

"Oh." She was breathless. Her heart pounded in her ears. Her sisters shouted her name in the distance. Neither she nor Crispin made a move to exit the carriage. His hazel gaze, more brown than green in the shadowed confines of the carriage, bore into her. His expression was inscrutable, unmovable, as if he were made of marble.

She began to squirm under his unwavering gaze. "Aunt Beatrice has asked me to play the pianoforte after dinner. Do you have a favorite piece? If I have the sheet music, I could perform it for you—unless it is a piece I have played. I can recall the notes if I've played the piece." She babbled when she was nervous. It was a deplorable habit.

He half smiled, half grimaced. "I am sorry, Sophia. My presence is required in Town this evening, and I am unable to stay."

Her insides flinched. "But Aunt Beatrice said you would be our guest for several days."

"Yes, that was my original intent when I wrote to your aunt, but a matter of importance forces me to return to London tonight."

A lump formed in her throat. Perhaps her inexperience had been off-putting, or worse. He considered her another conquest in a long line of ladies who had been all too eager to be conquered by him. Unaware Sophia held a tender regard for him, Regina had found it amusing to share rumors of his escapades over breakfast last Season. Sophia had been sick with jealousy one moment, and hopeful the gossips were wrong the next.

He captured her chin between his thumb and forefinger and urged her to look at him. "My man of business fell ill yesterday. He is a loyal man, and I feel duty-bound to insure he is receiving the best care."

"Oh, dear! I am sorry." She laid her head against his shoulder to hide her pleased smile, lest he think her heartless. She genuinely wished his man well, but knowing Crispin wasn't leaving to enjoy the company of another woman was a relief. "Will you visit again before Parliament is in session?"

"It is unlikely." He placed a kiss on her hair before easing her from his arms. "I meant what I said about you deserving better than me. It is hard to accept Little Sophia is grown and old enough to marry, and I might have unjustly judged the other men. You will find the right husband for you, and when you do, he will be the luckiest man in England."

She scowled. Was he teasing? Did he truly believe she would be happy with another man when it was obvious they belonged together? She chose to ignore his ridiculous suggestion that he was not good enough for her.

"Uncle Charles plans to meet us in London after Easter. I will look forward to receiving you at Wedmore House."

His smile seemed pleasantly detached. "I am certain Charles will have many tales of his latest adventures. You may rely on me calling at Wedmore House to hear them. Your nose is pink from the cold. We should return to the house."

He chucked her on the chin, his unromantic gesture infuriating after the kiss they had shared. She glowered at his back as he removed the carriage window, reached for the outside handle, and opened the door. He climbed from the carriage and offered his hand as he held the sailcloth out of the way. She refused his assistance when it was her turn to disembark and stood toe-to-toe with him outside, refusing to be dismissed.

"I am aware of your reputation, Lord Margrave. Tell me, am I another one of your conquests?"

His jaw fell. "Gads, Sophia. Is that what you think?"

Her eyes stung, warning her of impending tears. She blinked to keep them at bay. "I do not know what to think. This is all new to me."

His face lost its hard edges, and his eyes lit with a soft glow. "I would never see you as a conquest. You must know you hold a special place in my heart, but that does not make me the right man for you. Promise you will never settle for anyone who cannot make you happy."

His answer soothed her hurt. There was no doubt in her mind Crispin could make her very happy, but he needed time to realize it. "I will wait for as long as it takes."

She thought her promise would placate him, but his sour frown said otherwise. *Better not to allow him to dwell on it.* "My sisters have stopped calling for me. I should return to the house before Aunt Beatrice sends a search party. Will I see you inside?"

He nodded.

"Splendid." She started toward the house and tossed over her shoulder, "Merry Christmas, Lord Margrave."

ONE

ON THE COACH RIDE BACK TO LONDON, CRISPIN COULD STILL feel Sophia's lush mouth against his and the warmth of her cheek through his glove. Faint notes of her perfume clung to his cravat. He closed his eyes, savoring the alluring scent of camellias.

Try as he might, he couldn't break the spell she had cast over him when she'd reached into his pocket for the sprig of mistletoe, her nose and cheeks pink from the cold and her topaz blue eyes twinkling with anticipation. Her subtle desire for him had been charming, her innocence endearing.

When her pink tongue had darted over her lips in preparation for his kiss, it had nearly undone him. A heady desire to take her to his bed and love her to completion had coursed through his body as he'd grappled for control. Even now, his muscles quivered as he imagined eliciting cries of pleasure from her sweet lips. Her pleas for him to do it all over again would be granted until she was sated, languorous, and gave up any dreams of belonging to another man.

He shook off the ridiculous notion. It wasn't like him to be fanciful, nor did he intend to take a wife, which would be the only way he would ever have Sophia in his bed. She was special, one of Charles Wedmore's precious angels, and Wedmore would have Crispin flogged if he disgraced her.

Hell. Crispin would save his godfather the trouble and kick his own arse. Sophia belonged on a pedestal to be cherished, adored, and protected from men like him. Fortunately, he had come to his senses and done nothing more damning than satisfy her curiosity. He expected she would forget about him soon and enter the marriage mart this spring.

"Damnation," he muttered. *That is a depressing thought.*

A chuckle interrupted his introspection. Crispin glowered at his valet sitting on the opposite bench, which did nothing to stifle Kane's mirth.

In a voice formed of steel and ice, Crispin said, "What do you find humorous?"

A shrewd smile was plastered to the younger man's face. "Do I have leave to speak frankly?"

"Have you ever practiced restraint?"

"Rarely, my lord."

"At least I can always count on you for an honest answer."

"I blame you," Kane said with a shrug. "You never taught me to tell a proper lie."

Crispin's rigid spine began to soften. Kane's cheerful disposition had a way of spreading to others in his vicinity, which was likely the reason Crispin didn't mind his presence on the long ride back to London.

"Kane, even when it would serve you well to hold your peace, you have a tendency to speak out of turn."

"It is in my nature, I think."

"I believe it is, and as I recall, this quality almost resulted in you being tossed in gaol when I found you."

Kane lowered his head and grinned sheepishly. "It was rather fortuitous you came along when you did. I do not know how you got on all those years without me."

"It is a mystery," Crispin said with droll sarcasm.

His first encounter with his valet was on Bond Street eight years ago. Upon exiting the haberdashery, Crispin literally bumped into him. Kane had been knee-deep in a row with a baron over a scrawny boy who was curled into a ball on the ground. Tears had forged muddy tracks down the lad's cheeks, and he was whimpering. It was a most pathetic sight, one so young reduced to picking pockets for scraps of food.

When it appeared Lord Nevitt intended to crack both of their skulls with his walking stick, Crispin had intervened and taken the boys into his service—a wise decision in the end. Ernest was the most loyal first footman under Crispin's employ, and Kane was... Well, he was the worst valet in England, but he made an excellent spy and partner. Crispin felt duty bound to overlook Kane's lack of fashion sense for the good of their country.

"I thought you were made of sturdier stuff," Kane blurted, "and here you are fleeing from a slip of a girl."

If glares had the ability to deliver a physical blow, Crispin's valet would be severed in half. "I am running from no one. My presence is required in London."

"Is it?" Kane cocked his head to the side. "I saw no messengers arrive during our short stay, and I had an excellent view of the stables from the servants' quarters."

Crispin's stomach churned uneasily. "You saw me with Sophia Darlington earlier?"

"If *you* are the one posing the question, the answer is

yes. As far as anyone else is concerned, I was polishing your boots all afternoon and saw nothing."

Crispin lifted his foot to inspect his less than pristine boot. "You are a terrible liar."

"Then you are fortunate Charles Wedmore is not in the country to interrogate me. Otherwise, you would be a husband and father by next Christmas."

His valet's reminder of Crispin's careless disregard for Sophia's reputation was sobering. He thought he'd checked every direction for onlookers before assisting her from the broken carriage. He hadn't looked up—an amateur mistake that would earn his protégé a lecture if he had made it.

Crispin scrubbed his hands down his face and cursed his foolishness. "Wedmore will mount my head above the mantle, and you will dance on my grave."

"Balderdash!" Kane grinned. "I will be too busy raiding your wine cellar to visit your grave."

"Your loyalty is overwhelming."

Kane laughed. "Do not pretend you are unhappy with your predicament. You've always been fond of Miss Sophia, and clearly, your feelings have grown along with her. Now you can court her properly when she comes to London for the Season."

"Wedmore will not allow it. He has done his best to shelter his nieces from his work. He expects them to marry ordinary fellows and settle into an ordinary life."

"Egads," Kane said with a groan, "what a dull and dismal prospect. How can he expect his nieces to appreciate the charms of a conventional existence when all they have known is the eccentric?"

"It isn't my place to question my superiors."

Crispin turned to stare out the window, effectively ending the conversation. Kane had a point, but Crispin doubted his godfather could be swayed. When he'd learned of Crispin's choice to join the Regent's Consul, his position had been unambiguous.

Espionage is a dangerous game, young man. I forbid you to follow in my footsteps. Tell Farrin you have changed your mind.

When demands had no effect, Wedmore tried to appeal to Crispin's sense of reason.

It is not too late for you, son. Do not make this decision carelessly. You cannot know where your path will lead in five years, or ten, or twenty. You only need to look at me to know I speak the truth. I had nothing to lose when I embarked on this life. Now I am guardian to three amazing little girls who deserve a certain future. I cannot guarantee I will be here for them, and they have lost too much already.

Charles Wedmore, a founding member of the Regent's Consul, had lost his stomach for the work. At age eighteen, Crispin had viewed it as a weakness in his godfather, one *he* would never suffer. Everyone he loved was gone, and everything he had believed about his life was a lie. He'd had nothing to lose either when he joined.

He and Kane traveled in silence for the remainder of the journey. The young man presumably slept beneath the hat he's pulled low over his eyes while Crispin relived his last moments with Sophia. They arrived in London after dark.

"I have a matter to tend to before home," Crispin said.

Kane remained slumped on the bench. "Aye, my lord."

When the coach rolled to a stop outside Ben Hillary's Governor Square town house, Kane sat up and adjusted his hat. By the curious crane of his neck, Crispin could tell he wanted to ask why they had stopped to see an old school chum on Christmas, but his valet held his tongue.

Ben must have been watching for his arrival, because he exited the house before Crispin alighted from the carriage. His friend climbed inside and sat beside Kane. He sidled a glance at the servant.

"You may speak in his presence," Crispin said. "I see you received my message. Were you able to make the arrangements on my behalf?"

Ben inclined his head. "He is waiting at the coffeehouse across from the Esterdell Hotel."

It must seem odd for Crispin's younger brother to take lodgings rather than stay at the family town house, but if Alexander had arrived at Arden-Hill unannounced expecting accommodations, it would have been an awkward reunion.

"I will accompany you to make introductions," Ben said.

"Thank you for the offer, but no." Crispin smirked. "Your wife has only of late grown tolerant of my company. I'll not have her despise me for dragging you from bed."

Ben chuckled. "You dined at our table three times last week. Eve likes you well enough, Margrave. I would even venture she looks forward to your verbal sparring."

"Alas, we have something in common. I relish her sharp-tongue. It reminds me to watch my manners."

When Ben and Eve were newly wed, Crispin had overstepped his bounds in an attempt to protect her from a danger she hadn't known existed. Understandably, the lady hadn't appreciated Crispin's meddling and put him in his place, earning his respect.

To this day, Eve and Ben remained ignorant her life had been in jeopardy, but Crispin was obligated to keep the secret since it involved a fellow spy. Fortunately, Eve was safe now, and the couple was too enamored with their infant son to fret over bygones.

Crispin wished his own past were as easily forgotten. "Thank you for making arrangements on my behalf. There was no time before I was expected at Lord Wedmore's home in Kent."

"Are you certain you do not wish for my company? Moral support never hurts."

He shrugged. "It doesn't, but my morale is not in danger."

After years of friendship, Ben seemed to accept Crispin had nothing more to say on the matter. They were men's men; they did not require a sympathetic ear. Crispin had grown up believing his mother and brother were dead. It was a lie. No amount of bellyaching over the unfairness would change anything.

"Very well," Ben said. "I will leave you to it."

With a jaunty wave, he disembarked from the carriage. Kane settled against the seatback as the conveyance lurched into the street. Crispin trained his gaze out the window again, staring into darkness and seeing his brother's neat handwriting in his mind.

Yesterday morning, as Crispin prepared to travel to spend Christmas with his godfather's family, a letter arrived from his brother. He recognized the handwriting from years of exchanging correspondence when Alexander was at boarding school in Edinburgh, and later after he purchased his commission as an officer in the 68th Regiment.

Lieutenant Alexander Locke had returned from Quebec two days earlier and taken lodgings in Town. Once the road became passable, he would travel on to Finchingfield where their mother resided with her second husband. It could be his and Crispin's only opportunity to meet.

Crispin had almost tossed the letter on the fire. He and Alexander had survived without one another's companionship for a long time. A meeting was unlikely to bridge the chasm carved out between them after decades apart. When Alexander admitted in his letter he did not relish spending another Christmas alone, Crispin's resistance had broken. It was not right for a man to feel forsaken and forlorn, especially upon his return from having served his country.

When Crispin's carriage arrived at Arden-Hill, he left Kane to unpack his belongings then continued to his destination. The Esterdell Hotel was a modest establishment compared to the rooms most gentlemen of his brother's station rented when staying in London. What did that say about Alexander? Had he grown too accustomed to the meager trappings of military life to find comfort in the luxuries available in a finer hotel, or had he accumulated debt that required him to be pennywise?

Crispin would know more once he sat down with his brother. He could always take a man's measure by looking him in the eyes.

Alexander was recognizable upon sight. Despite being the only man dressed in regimentals, he was a robust, younger version of their father with russet hair, a soft jaw, and blue eyes. The only physical similarity Crispin and his brother shared was a strong brow—a feature that caused them to look serious whether they were or not. Crispin's memory of his mother had faded over time, but he recalled he had inherited the physical trait from her.

This air of seriousness seemed to be working to his brother's advantage this evening. Alexander had been given wide berth and sat alone at one of the tables in the back of the coffeehouse. His eyebrows veered toward one another as Crispin approached.

"Lord Margrave?"

Crispin slipped onto the bench across from him. "No need to stand on formality. We are blood."

The lines of apprehension crisscrossing Alexander's forehead disappeared. "I was uncertain you would claim me as kin. We are like strangers to one another."

"I remember you," Crispin said. "Not well, but I remember you tried to eat one of my building blocks when I wanted a playmate."

"I was very young." His brother smiled and ducked his head. "I am afraid I have no memory of you, but Mother spoke of you often after you found her."

Crispin sensed his eyebrow arch in doubt and guided the conversation away from their mother. He suspected she could be a point of contention between them. "What brings you home? Has your regiment returned to England?"

His brother followed his lead and abandoned any discussion of their mother. "I am on leave. My stepfather fell ill a couple of years ago, and Mother writes that his condition has worsened. I've come home to see after him."

It seemed he and Alexander shared something else in common, a devotion to the men who had raised them. Crispin hadn't strayed far from his father's bed at the end. He smiled sadly, reminded of his father's demise.

"You are a good son. Mr. Ness is a lucky man."

Blood rushed into Alexander's cheeks, and he swiped his finger over an invisible speck on the tabletop. "I only now realized how that must have sounded. I am aware Zachary Ness is not my father, but he has no children of his own, and he has always treated me like a son. Forgive me if I've given offense."

"I am not offended. I was remembering when our father was ill," Crispin said. "You look like him."

Alexander's gaze shot up. "Do I? I always wondered..."

Crispin might not want to talk about their mother, but it seemed obvious his brother was curious about their father. For the next half hour, he shared stories about Father and answered Alexander's questions about their family lineage.

As Crispin spoke, anger simmered inside him for the

lifetime of memories their mother had stolen from him and his brother; he buried the resentment deep before it bubbled to the surface. Appreciating this moment with his brother was more important. They might not see one another again for many years.

He and Alexander had been sitting across from one another for an hour when Kane walked past the table with his hat in his left hand; he switched it to his right.

A signal.

Crispin was yanked from the pleasant cocoon that had enshrouded him as he spoke with his brother. The Regent's Consul was calling him to duty.

He sighed and stood. For a moment, he had tricked himself into believing he was an ordinary man. "I have enjoyed myself immensely, Alexander, but I must take my leave."

"I expect I will be in London for some time," his brother said, looking up at him like an eager pup. "Perhaps we could meet again? I would like to see our father's home, if it is not presumptuous of me."

"It is not presumptuous, but unfortunately, I will not be in residence much longer."

"But you've only arrived in London. What calls you away so soon?"

Evading his brother's inquiry didn't sit right with him, but he had little choice. "A mundane task. I will not bore you with the details."

Alexander held a steady gaze. "I see." His sudden cool demeanor and stiff posture suggested he didn't see at all.

Crispin wasn't attempting to get rid of his brother, but he had responsibilities that transcended familial duties. "You are welcome at Arden-Hill even if I cannot receive you," he said. "I will inform my housekeeper to provide you with a tour when you call."

The wariness in Alexander's eyes diminished slightly. "Yes, thank you, I will try to find time to call at Arden-Hill before I leave London." Alexander stood, too. "Thank you for meeting with me, my lord. It was rather sudden. Perhaps you had plans."

"Nothing important. I am glad you contacted me." Crispin began to ease away from the table before the guilt ghosting over him could take solid form. He had begun to enjoy himself, but Kane's interruption was a harsh reminder of the solitary profession Crispin had chosen. "I wish you a safe journey to your stepfather's bedside and pray for his recovery."

"You should come to Finchingfield when you are able. Mother would like to see you again."

"I will consider it," he lied. The woman had made her wishes clear years ago. She wanted nothing to do with him; he returned the sentiment.

Kane was waiting for him on the empty street. "I came by horseback."

Crispin fell into step with him en route to the mews. When he was certain no one was close by to overhear, he spoke. "What are my orders?"

"Limerick at first light. I am to accompany you. We must stop an assassin."

"One of our men or an enemy?"

Kane scoffed. "Ours. Farrin recalled his orders when the Lord Chamberlain discovered his plan."

"That must have been an interesting conversation," Crispin said. "To hear Farrin talk, he fancies himself the King's advisor."

"Or next in line for the throne."

Crispin smiled at the younger man's joke; there was a thread of truth in it. Like everyone in England, Farrin understood the rules of succession, but he was an ambitious man. The leader of the Regent's Consul would settle for pulling the monarch's strings like a puppeteer.

"There are rumors the Regent's Consul might be dissolved now that Napoleon is in exile," Crispin said. He didn't give the gossip much credit. England would always have enemies. "Farrin will have to take his pleasure elsewhere if that comes to pass."

Kane uttered a sound of disgust deep in his throat. "I shudder to consider what he might become without the rules of the Consul to temper him."

"It is a frightening prospect, indeed."

Crispin had been sheltered as a boy, but in his service to the King, he had discovered evil often lurked behind a thin veil of civility with men like Farrin. This potent reminder of the life he had chosen sobered him. He had left Sophia with no promises, because it had been the right thing to do. Still, kissing her made him feel like the worst sort of blackguard—as well as the luckiest man on earth.

TWO

My Dearest Lord Margrave,

Forgive my boldness in writing, but after two weeks without any sightings of you about Town, it has occurred to me that you might be unaware Aunt Beatrice, my sisters, and I have set up house in London for the Season.

Unfortunately, Uncle Charles remains abroad, but we anticipate his return any day. I am certain Aunt Beatrice would deem it suitable for you to call at Wedmore House given our longtime family connection. Perhaps you could call tomorrow, so we might determine what has kept each of us occupied since our parting.

I must admit, I am longing to take a turn around Rotten Row, but I have been unable to bring myself to accept another gentleman's invitation when the memory of our kiss occupies my every thought. I have grown exceedingly eager for the day I am afforded the pleasure of your company.

Yours always,
Sophia

"Hellfire and damnation!" Crispin dropped the letter on the polished walnut desk. This was a distressing turn of events.

Sophia should have forgotten about their kiss by now and set her cap for another gentleman. Instead, she was writing to him—a bachelor. He ought to march into Wedmore House to put a stop to this recklessness at once. She could not write to a man who was neither kin nor her intended without dire risk to her reputation. Was she not in possession of better sense?

A whiff of something pleasant teased his nose.

He snatched the letter and inhaled. "Camellias?" She had spritzed the paper with her perfume. As if they were *lovers*.

He rang for his valet.

Before one of his servants stumbled across the letter, he should burn it. No, he would burn it—*later*—after he read her elegantly swooping hand once more.

Kane entered Crispin's study, his posture stiff and formal as he played the role of servant whenever someone might overhear. "You rang, my lord?"

"Close the door." When the latch caught, Crispin held up the letter. "What do you make of this?"

Kane shed his awkward formality and strolled to the desk to inspect the paper. "It appears the lady has grown impatient waiting for you."

"I am not a dolt. I can see she is impatient." Crispin pushed away from the desk and strode to the hearth, agitation punctuating every step. "Why hasn't she forgotten me? She should have made a match by now. I cannot frequent Brooks's without hearing her name. She is the most sought after debutante this Season."

Kane hummed with approval. "She is a rare beauty. I am certain she will make her choice soon and settle into her new life with the lucky bloke."

"I—" Crispin crumbled the paper in his fist and forcefully threw Sophia's letter into the fire. "I want to *hit* something."

"Naturally, you thought of me?" Kane asked with a cheeky grin.

Crispin's strangled laugh stemmed from a mixture of surprise and mortification at his behavior. What had come over him? He wielded power over his passions; he was not one to be manipulated by desire or jealousy, and here he was high in the boughs over the prospect of Sophia choosing another man.

"You are my only equal when it comes to sparring," Crispin said, his humor returning in pieces. "Mrs. Throckmorton cannot block a punch to save her life."

Kane tossed back his head and laughed. "She would beat you like a rug."

Crispin chuckled picturing the head housekeeper squaring off with him, rattling the ring of keys at her waist while she taunted him for being a lovesick weakling.

"Venting the spleen might improve your disposition," Kane said. "Should I set out your sparring attire and meet you in the gymnasium?"

"Yes, that is a splendid suggestion."

The exercise might do him good. Anything to help him forget this damned gnawing need Sophia had created in him, an itch beneath his skin he couldn't satisfy. Gads, if it didn't cease once she was married and out of his reach, he might be driven to madness.

He returned to his desk. "I have a message to send round to Wedmore House before sparring."

"Aye, milord."

When Kane exited the room, Crispin pulled out a sheet of foolscap from his desk drawer and retrieved his quill to dash off a quick missive.

DEAR BEATRICE,

How pleased I am to learn you and your nieces have come to London. I regret that my duties at the House of Lords have occupied the majority of my time, and I have been unable to issue an invitation to dine at Arden-Hill. I do not expect a reprieve anytime soon, therefore, I am writing to extend my best.

Please convey my regards to Regina, Evangeline, and Sophia. I have come to understand Miss Sophia has been deemed a diamond of the first water and should have her selection of eligible suitors. May she make a wise choice and a match that is to her advantage. I look forward to celebrating the nuptials if I warrant an invitation.

Kindest Regards,
Margrave

THREE

10 weeks later

"Stay!" Crispin issued a stern reprimand that held the rambunctious black poodle at bay. Wedmore House's pampered pet lowered to his belly and rested his chin on his paws. His large black eyes glittered in the morning light spilling through the drawing room windows. Tremors racked his small body.

Then it began—the pathetic whimpering that always chipped at Crispin's resolve. The dog was a master at manipulation, better than most men of the Regent's Consul.

"I refuse to hold you," he said for the fourth time. "Cease this nonsense."

If he succumbed to Cupid's pleas for attention, he would be slathered in dog drool for his audience with Sophia, and his call was not a casual one. Hell, nothing was casual between them since he had rebuffed her.

At the time, he expected they could avoid one another until she was happily settled in marriage and forgot about him. Turns out he was terrible at predicting the future, and now he was escorting Sophia and her aunt all over London, keeping watch over them while Sophia's older sisters traveled to Athens in the company of Regina's new husband.

Hopefully, Sophia would not send him away without seeing him.

When the dog's whining grew more insistent, Crispin raised an eyebrow. "Enough."

The dangerous edge to his voice would cause a wise man to slowly back away before turning to run. Cupid was not intimidated. The little dog inched forward on his belly, pausing to blink at him innocently.

Crispin shook his head, amused. "You are relentless. Show a little patience. Sophia will be here any moment."

Upon hearing her name, Cupid leapt from the Aubusson and dashed for the drawing room door. The dog turned back when he reached the threshold, tipping his head to the side as if asking where Sophia was. His tongue lolled from the side of his smiling mouth.

"*Patience*, mutt."

Crispin admonished himself as much as the dog. He was eager to see her too, albeit for different reasons. She had befriended an actress, a duke's former mistress, and the ill-advised friendship endangered more than Sophia's reputation. Claudine Bellerose was a suspected murderess.

Equally alarming, he had learned of Sophia's solo trips to the Drayton Theatre while he was on a mission for the King. She hadn't uttered a word to him about her association with the actress, despite her having had many opportunities to confide in him over the past few weeks. Of course, any discourse he and Sophia attempted these days often ended in a row.

They argued about everything: The way in which he had

gawked at her during dinner at Lady Chattington's party. How he'd overstepped his bounds in warning her against laughing too heartily at Mr. Wittenberg's stories unless she intended to encourage the scoundrel. The time she accused Crispin of spying on her at Hyde Park, which he hadn't done. If he had been spying, she never would have seen him.

After every gathering they attended, she chided him for skulking and looming and glowering while she tried to enjoy a pleasant evening. And she was correct. He acted beastly in her presence. A seething monster stirred awake inside him every time he saw her dancing with another man—all because he had given into temptation and kissed those sweet lips that now spewed rancor at him.

It was bloody torture. He wished she would choose a husband and be done with it. Better to drive a dagger into his heart than slowly carve away at him.

A rustle came from the doorway; he snapped his head toward the noise. Sophia stood in the threshold, her attention already on the poodle bounding across the room to greet her.

Crispin rose from her uncle's favorite chair. "Good morning, Sophia."

She scooped Cupid into her arms, evaded the dog's tongue, and scratched behind his ears. The rambunctious poodle melted beneath her touch, his large black eyes glazing over almost instantly. She inclined her head in greeting, her gaze wary. "Good morning, Crispin."

His heart beat a little faster when she spoke his name— not Lord Margrave, the too impersonal designation of viscount, or the myriad of monikers she had bestowed on him this Season, but his given name.

She paused in scratching the pooch to tentatively pat a hand over her pale gold spun hair. The silky locks were piled on top of her head and adorned with a strip of muslin that was secured into place with a light blue ribbon. "I am afraid I was not expecting callers."

He should hope not at this hour, but Sophia seemed to be full of surprises. He smiled, hoping to disarm her. "Forgive me. I should have sent a note. I did not intend to catch you unawares."

It was untrue. An unprepared Sophia was more likely to be honest when he questioned her.

She wrinkled her nose. "You needn't apologize. We do not expect forewarning before you call. *Any* written communication from you would come as a shock, frankly."

In all of their arguing, she had never broached the topic of her unanswered letter. This was the closest she had come.

"Have you eaten breakfast?" she asked, changing the topic. "Should I ring for refreshment?"

Her thoughtful offer and attempt to avoid an argument warmed him inside. Nothing had been easy between them since she arrived in London, and he was to blame. She guarded her heart with harsh words and a hardened exterior, but she allowed him a glimpse of the sensitive girl he had known since they were children. He was hesitant to spoil the moment.

"Do not trouble anyone. I broke my fast earlier," he said, and following her lead, he directed the conversation even further away from the unanswered letter. "I barely recognize you in ordinary attire."

The white morning dress she wore, probably a discarded frock from one of her sisters, was the tiniest bit too long; only the tips of her black slippers peeked beneath the hem. In the ballrooms, she wore her lovely silk gowns. She commanded every eye and charmed every gentleman who stood up with her. Yet, to Crispin, she had never looked more beautiful than she did now.

"Lud, Margrave. Did you suffer a knock on the head? You are staring as if you've never seen me before."

He blinked, realizing he had been ogling. "Your gown needs hemming." *Gads.* One would think he was dull in the head with his lack of social graces, but she had that effect on him. "Nevertheless, it suits you."

Sophia sighed. "Surely you haven't come to Wedmore House to comment on my ensemble, and it is too early to begin chasing away my gentleman suitors. Get on with it then."

"If I've frightened a few men into giving up their pursuit, you should thank me. A coward makes a poor husband."

She snorted. "I did not ask for your assistance, Lord Matchmaker."

An unrestrained grin spread across his face. Sophia was a spirited young woman, although she rarely showed that side of herself to anyone but him.

Despite her lack of appreciation for his efforts, he would continue to protect her from the undesirables. He'd had years to take the measures of the men courting her this Season. They had been fellow classmates at Eton and Oxford, and later, his opponents at the gaming hells. He knew their temperaments, the state of their family coffers, and the scandals that could ruin them if they were discovered.

"No need to ask for my help," he said. "I give it freely."

She raised one elegantly shaped eyebrow. "Hurrah for me."

He laughed. Matching wits with her only made him crave more—to crave *her*—but he seemed incapable of ignoring the traps she set. "You have ruled out two reasons for my visit, Miss Darlington, and I can assure you I did not come to Wedmore House to verbally spar with you."

He met her in the middle of the room and offered his hand. "Will you sit with me, please? I would like to discuss a matter with you."

"Can it wait until later at the ball?"

He had forgotten about the Hillarys' ball. *Splendid. Another dreaded evening of watching her flirt with other men...* He was beginning to suspect she enjoyed torturing him. "I am afraid it cannot wait."

She hesitated before placing her hand in his and allowing him to draw her toward the ivory settee. The faint scent of her soap reminded him of that brief moment following a summer rain shower, when mist rose from the sunbaked earth and the air held promise. It was her signature scent, camellias.

"The matter sounds important." Sophia gracefully lowered to the settee, perching straight-backed on the edge of the cushion. She regarded him with shrewd topaz blue eyes. "Auntie is still in her chambers, but I could send for her if you are at leisure to wait."

"Do not disturb Beatrice. I wish to speak with you alone."

A pink blush swept across the apples of her cheeks, and the shimmer of her eyes filled him with an unexplainable disquiet. "I see. Has Uncle Charles written to you? Is he expected home soon?"

Crispin swallowed to ease the dryness of his throat. "I've received no word from your uncle. As far as I am aware, he has only written to your sister and aunt."

As a fellow Regent's Consul member, Crispin was one of a small number of people his godfather could confide in without risk. Yet, Wedmore had mentioned nothing about his plans to travel when they dined together the night before his departure. The secretive nature of his godfather's affairs gnawed at him. Something was wrong.

Shaking off his suspicions, Crispin claimed a chair adjacent to Sophia. Her smile faded, and she hugged the dog against her chest. He inhaled sharply as it dawned on him she might have mistaken his early morning visit for courtship, and furthermore, she might still welcome his attentions.

His chest puffed up, and the urge to abandon his good sense and join her on the settee was strong. He kept his seat. At Christmas, his behavior had been rash. He would not mislead her again.

Sophia recovered her smile, but her eyes had lost their sparkle. "I do hope this will not take long. I have plans to join Lady Octavia and her mother on an excursion to Bond Street."

He sank against the chair cushion as his warring emotions battled for domination. "Is Lady Octavia the girl that always wears pink?"

She snorted. "Octavia is no more a *girl* than I am, and she looks lovely in pink. Why shouldn't she wear it if she pleases?"

Even idle chitchat landed him in hot water.

He cleared his throat. "I was not passing judgment on your friend's choice of attire. I am trying to recall which one she is." It was difficult keeping Sophia's companions sorted when he only had eyes for her. "I have no objections to Lady Octavia, pink, or your friendship with her."

"I cannot recall asking for your approval, Lord Almighty," she said sweetly and nuzzled the little dog's head.

"I did not come here to quarrel, Sophia. I am here as a friend."

"A *friend*?" She shook her head and chuckled as if she

couldn't believe the tripe spilling from his lips. "Tell me, Lord Margrave. Does Ben Hillary welcome your friendly overtures, or am I the only chum you kiss?"

Tension seeped into his muscles, making them rigid. "I will not be goaded today. I've come to Wedmore House out of concern; I care for you."

"Of course you do, as a friend." Cupid crawled from her arms, turned a circle, and plopped beside her on the settee cushion. She casually toyed with the pooch's ears, gazing at Crispin from beneath her lashes. "I wonder if I will ever be allowed to define our relationship."

"Sophia." He pushed his fingers through his hair and sighed. This conversation was overdue, but another must take precedence. "Could we please postpone this conversation for another day?"

"When—tomorrow? Next week? When we are in our dotage?"

"I do not know. *Soon.*"

What was there to say? He had taken liberties that did not belong to him and recovered his senses too late. A small indiscretion on his part should not condemn her to a lifetime of being tied to him. She would be miserable. His work called him away for months at a time. He would be forced to lie about his destination and purpose. One day, he might not return from his travels, and she would never learn his fate. Perhaps she would believe he had abandoned her. That was no way for a lady to live, especially one who longed for a close marriage like her parents had.

Smoothing a wrinkle from his trousers, he took a deep breath and reclaimed control of the conversation. "As I relayed earlier, I am here on an important matter, and you have an appointment to keep. I would prefer to stay on task."

Sophia narrowed her eyes. He rushed on before she

concocted a new strategy to knock him off kilter. "It has come to my attention you have been frequenting a playhouse in Marylebone and befriended an actress."

Her frown turned into an amused smirk. "Spying again, Margrave?"

"Perhaps you've read one too many books of intrigue, Miss Darlington."

In fact, he *had* been spying, but not on Sophia.

The head of the Regent's Consul was missing, and Crispin had been charged with investigating the commander's disappearance. The Marquess of Hertford, Lord Chamberlain of the Household, had summoned him to the royal palace last week. Hertford kept abreast of Regent's Consul operations since the King had lost interest in his elite emissaries after Waterloo, and the Lord Chamberlain had never been pleased with Farrin's renegade leadership. Hertford wanted to know Farrin's fate and what pots he had been dipping his fingers into.

Everything Crispin had uncovered so far pointed to foul play. Farrin had last been seen in the company of two gentlemen hours before they were murdered at the London docks. In all likelihood, Farrin had been another victim, and his body became lost in the river. The commander was too meticulous at covering his tracks to have killed the gentlemen and left them to be discovered.

"London is smaller than it appears," he said. "A theatre is no place for a lady of good reputation to frequent, and an actress is not a suitable companion. Anyone could witness you entering the Drayton Theatre at off hours and believe the worst."

She sat up straighter and notched her chin. "Aunt Beatrice approves of Claudine Bellerose; I had her blessing to visit the Drayton. *You* will not decide whom I may and may not befriend, and you certainly have no say on where I choose to go."

Faith! Her place was in Mayfair; she had no business venturing outside the boundaries of safety. Why must anyone need to remind her?

His smile was tight. "If you are not mistaken about your aunt's approval, her judgment is circumspect. Are you aware there have been assaults in the area?"

"Of course I am aware. That was my reason for calling at the theatre. Claudine thought the other actresses would feel safer if they learned to defend themselves, so I taught a class on Wing Chun."

"*You?*" Crispin laughed in surprise. "You hated attending your uncle's lessons. Wedmore had to bribe you with the promise of a trinket to entice you to step one foot into the gymnasium."

She flicked a hand dismissively. "I would have attended lessons without a reward, but I was very fond of ribbons and sweets."

He chuckled and shook his head in disbelief. "A clever minx is a dangerous creature."

"I was a *girl,*" she said with a defensive edge to her voice. "It was important to Uncle Charles, so ultimately that was my reason for learning to fight. He wanted my sisters and me to be capable of defending ourselves when he is away."

"Can you, Sophia?" He scooted to the edge of the chair. "Defend yourself?"

"I can." She caught her bottom lip between her teeth, and her eyes lost their glimmer of certainty. "At least, I think I can."

Her answer was inadequate. She needed his protection whether or not she wanted it, and he would risk anything to shelter her from the type of men he encountered in pursuit of his duty to the King. There was a darker side to

London than she could ever imagine, and she was venturing too close.

"I am concerned about the company Miss Bellerose keeps." He leaned toward her and said gently, "Her benefactor was murdered."

"I heard."

"How?" Her lack of surprise caught *him* off guard. "How did *you* hear the Duke of Stanhurst and his son were murdered?"

The Stanhurst family managed to keep any mention of murder out of the newssheets, deeming the duke's and his son's deaths the result of accidental shootings. Conveniently, the magistrate who discovered their bodies had come into money and left for America with his wife and children before the account could be challenged. The entire affair reeked of deceit.

"The late Duke of Stanhurst was her *former* benefactor," Sophia said, ignoring his question. "Claudine left him, and she was fortunate to escape with her life. You should have seen what he did to her. It was deplorable."

Perhaps Sophia knew more than Crispin had credited her with knowing. "Are you implying Miss Bellerose is responsible for her benefactor's death?"

"Of course *not*, and I do not care for this line of questioning."

"She was a woman scorned, Sophia. How do you know Miss Bellerose wasn't involved?" It seemed unlikely the woman could have killed the men alone, but she'd had a protector when Crispin interviewed her at her town house last week—a large fellow that appeared capable of carrying out the deed at her behest.

Sophia crossed her arms and jutted her chin. "Claudine is a gentle soul who would not hurt anyone. That is how I know."

He opened his mouth to argue that appearances could be deceiving, but she cut him off.

"She was a guest at Wedmore House the night in question. The *entire* night." Sophia bolted from the settee, startling the dog. "You should go. I do not want to keep Ladies Seabrook and Octavia waiting, and I must change my gown before they arrive."

She swept toward the door, but Crispin shot out of the chair before she was halfway there. He captured her wrist, pulling her close before realizing his mistake. The warmth of her body crossed the sliver of space between them, heating his blood.

"She has a servant," he said softly. "Perhaps you have met him."

Sophia's breath quickened; her pulse fluttered at her collarbone. "Benny did nothing wrong either."

She knew the man's name. She definitely knew more than Crispin had expected. "How do you know this man is innocent?"

His fingers tightened around her soft bare skin, touching, memorizing the feel of her. God, he was hungry for more. The thrumming of his heartbeat in his ears wreaked havoc with his ability to reason.

"I give you my word," she murmured. "Benny is good and kind."

Her tongue dashed over her lips, leaving them moist and glistening in the morning sunlight. She drew Crispin toward her with an invisible force he halfheartedly fought to resist.

If he kissed her now, there would be no turning back. She could be his, forever. He only needed to accept her offer and claim her mouth.

And doom her to a life of isolation?

For that would be the only means of protecting her

from enemies he had made in his service to his King—men that would strike at him by taking the one treasure he valued above all others.

He released her arm and blinked, breaking free from the fantasy of having Sophia for his wife. When she reached for him, he stepped back. She persisted, placing her hand against his cheek.

"Why do you withdraw from me?" The tender concern in her voice nearly broke his will. She stroked his cheek; his eyes drifted shut. "Do you fear I no longer love you?"

Gads. He brushed her hand away, the spell shattered. He smiled to hide the unexpected agitation her words had stirred up inside him. "You are a champion at distraction, and you almost succeeded. Tell me what you know about Stanhurst's death, so I may be on my way and you can keep your appointment."

He was being harsh, but it was easier to keep his wits about him when they were arguing.

Her jaw hardened. "I have nothing to tell you."

He took another step away from her, still not trusting his power to resist her with her close. "You wouldn't lie to me, would you, Sophia?"

Fire flared in her blue eyes. "I don't have to lie to you. You do well enough on your own."

"Is that supposed to make sense?"

She sighed. "We are more than friends, Crispin. And when you are ready to be honest about *me*, perhaps I will feel free to confide in you. Now please, see yourself out."

She turned on her heel and marched toward the drawing room door.

"Sophia, wait."

"Your escort will not be required this evening," she called over her shoulder. "Good day, sir."

Her quick footsteps sounded on the stairs a moment

later. She was running from him. Crispin formed fists at his sides. The instinct to chase her up the staircase shook him. He wanted to grab her and kiss her until she had no more angry words to hurl at him. His body screamed for it. The need to taste her and stroke her soft skin rushed through his veins, pounding like horses' hooves in his ears. In five long strides, he was at the landing, his foot on the first step.

He froze.

Devil take it! What has come over me?

Cursing his foolishness, he turned and stalked from Wedmore House before he did something that could never be undone.

FOUR

"Sophia Darlington!" Lady Octavia's scandalized tone snapped Sophia out of her pensive state of mind. "Where are you this afternoon? You are not listening to a word I am saying."

"I *am* listening." Warmth washed over Sophia's cheeks at the lie. "You said the color of the ribbon matches your new gown."

"That was several ribbons ago." Octavia's smoky brown eyes, which perfectly complimented the spool of magenta ribbon in her hand, crinkled with amusement. Octavia's mother had left them alone to browse the fripperies while she shopped for a new pair of gloves. Sophia and Octavia were the only patrons in this part of the shop, leaving them to speak freely without censorship.

"Since then," Octavia said, "I've received the occasional distracted nod from you, as well as your blessing to use the ribbon to tie Lord Ramsdell's hands behind his back if he cannot keep them to himself at the ball tonight."

Sophia laughed. "I said no such thing."

"Perhaps I've embellished a bit." Her friend grinned and

tucked the ribbon back in the display before sliding her finger over a yellow one. "The idea has merit, though. Discouraging the rogue seems to have no effect."

"If you were not smitten with your betrothed," she said with a wrinkle of her nose, "I might be alarmed."

"I truly am. I cannot believe we will be wed in two weeks. Isn't it marvelous?"

Octavia's reminder was akin to a blow to the gut for Sophia, followed by a rush of guilt for feeling anything other than joy for her friend. Sophia was happy for Octavia —truly she was—but the quarrel with Crispin that morning left her tender and feeling hopeless about her own future.

"Oh, dear." Octavia's smile fell from her pretty face. "I did not intend to flaunt my happiness. I am a horrible friend."

"You are the most loyal person I know. Pay me no mind. I had a visitor this morning, Lord Margrave. I've been in a temper since he left."

Octavia clicked her tongue in sympathy. "Did you argue again? Honestly, I am beginning to believe the rogue is right. You deserve better than him. Are you certain you should not make a match with another man? You still have suitors in the wings eager to earn your notice."

Their numbers had dwindled, however. Many gentlemen were in need of a wife, and with Uncle Charles remaining abroad, the uncertainty of a match with Sophia had driven them to seek out other ladies—not that she cared about bringing any of those men up to scratch, despite her efforts to lead Crispin to believe otherwise.

"It seems unkind to encourage them when I love another." Sophia plucked a spool of ribbon from the rack. "What is your opinion? Does this color suit me?"

Octavia curled her lip in disgust. Sophia plopped the ribbon back in place. "Never mind."

"It is the color. It's hideous," her friend said. *"You* are beautiful."

"It does not matter." Sophia did not need another frippery. Crispin was immune to such trappings anyway. "With Regina and Evangeline away, I am considering abandoning this charade. I see no reason to pretend I am excited about the marriage mart, and Aunt Beatrice knows my heart is not invested in the endeavor."

She had kept the kiss and her feelings for Crispin secret from her sisters. Regina and Evangeline would never understand how she could view him in such a way. Regina had trained alongside him in Uncle Charles's gymnasium, and Evangeline had recruited him to dig through the dirt for Roman coins at Hartland Manor. To them, he was like a brother.

Sophia had been too young to be his companion. Therefore, he had remained a mystery. A world of secrets churned behind his penetrating hazel eyes, and on the rare occasion when his guard slipped and he allowed her to see a glimmer of vulnerability, her heart filled to bursting. He was much more than he allowed anyone to see. She longed to unravel him.

"I, for one, refuse to allow you to give up on love," Octavia said as she compared two spools of ribbon. "Furthermore, I do not believe you are prepared to give up on Lord Margrave either, so you will continue to attend balls, have a merry time dancing, and show the viscount what he is missing by denying his feelings for you."

Sophia smiled. Her friend was as fierce and commanding as her mother. She shrugged off her depressing musings and silently repeated Uncle Charles's mantra. *Fall seven times; stand up eight.* Or ten or twenty or however many times it took.

"You are correct, Tavi," she said. "I am not a quitter."

"Excellent." Sophia's friend dropped the spools on the counter and turned to her. "It is clear the viscount is smitten with you also. Ramsdell said the man is incapable of holding his tongue at the club. He talks of you incessantly."

Sophia snorted. "Ramsdell has mistaken someone else for Margrave. He prides himself on being the strong and silent sort."

"Perhaps, but the viscount is forever interrogating this gent or that about what you discussed during the waltz or over dinner."

"He is likely gathering ammunition to use against me. All he does is grumble and boss me about when he should mind his own affairs."

Octavia hummed as if his behavior made sense. "Ramsdell reassures me that is how a gentleman acts when he does not want to get caught in the parson's noose, but the outcome is inevitable. One feels he is in control if he is allowed to bluster a bit and make commands. It is best to allow him to believe he has the upper hand. Lord Margrave does not yet realize what he wants, but he will."

"I see." A reluctant chuckle slipped from Sophia. Her friend spoke with such authority. "You seem to have gentlemen all figured out. Did I miss a pamphlet?"

Octavia smirked. "Mama is better than any pamphlet. She advised me to show Ramsdell what *he* wanted by making myself useful to him, and she was right."

"How did you accomplish the task?"

"My uncle is allowing Ramsdell first pick of the litter from his prized hound. There is quite the list of gentlemen waiting for a pup, but Uncle Gunnar has never been one to deny me."

"Lord Margrave would not be swayed by a puppy," Sophia said. He and her great-aunt's poodle had a tumultuous relationship at best. Cupid loved Crispin, and Crispin preferred his attire free of dog slobber and teeth marks. Besides, he was not much of a hunting man. "I suspect Margrave should have his *own* pamphlet."

"Then we must put our heads together," Octavia said. "I could enlist Ramsdell's assistance at the ball tonight. Perhaps he could uncover Lord Margrave's weakness."

Crispin had no weaknesses, but Sophia did not want to appear argumentative in the face of Octavia's generosity. "Thank you, and I would happily accept Lord Ramsdell's assistance. However, Margrave will not be attending the ball this evening."

"It must have been quite the row."

"Yes, we had words"—Sophia smiled sheepishly—"and I had the last one."

FIVE

WITH A NOD FROM CRISPIN, HIS COACHMAN RETURNED TO his post at the back of the carriage while Crispin assisted Sophia's great-aunt on the steps. Beatrice gripped his forearm for balance as she disembarked from the carriage and thanked him before idly strolling toward Mr. and Mrs. James Hillary's front door.

Sophia didn't budge from her spot on the carriage bench. When Crispin proffered his hand to her, she gawked as if he was thrusting a hot poker in her direction rather than extending a courtesy.

"Shall we go inside, Miss Darlington?"

She didn't answer.

"Do you intend to treat me to silence after I volunteered my evening to play escort?"

She bristled on the carriage bench. "How dare you arrive at our door tonight," she hissed then craned her neck to see around him to the outside. Apparently satisfied no one could overhear, she continued to upbraid him. "I made it clear this morning your services for the ball were neither wanted or needed."

"Ah"—he grinned—"the cat hasn't stolen your tongue after all."

She snorted softly. "Indeed not, and if we had more privacy, you would receive the proper dressing down you deserve for disregarding my wishes."

"Regretfully, I cannot allow your wishes to dictate *my* actions. I promised your sister I would watch over you while she and her bridegroom are on their honeymoon, and I honor my word."

She notched her chin, forever challenging. "But not your unspoken word, do I understand the situation correctly, my lord?"

He sighed. The truth was irrefutable. As a gentleman, he should have offered for her hand after their kiss, but the most honorable action was to let her go. A typical woman would harbor hatred for him after he had misused her, but Sophia claimed to love him still, which made her the most stubborn woman he had ever known. Her persistence both vexed and warmed him through to the bone.

"You must know you deserve—"

"Stop! I cannot listen to this drivel one more time."

Her aunt turned back toward the carriage, catching Crispin's eye but speaking to her niece. "Sophia darling, is something wrong?"

"No, Auntie." Sophia plopped her hand in his and climbed from the carriage. Her expression softened when her gaze landed on Beatrice. "I misplaced my fan for a moment, but I have it now."

She flicked open the mother of pearl fan for proof, which only served to prove she was a poor liar. One typically did not feel the need to present evidence when telling the truth. In the line of duty, he had grown accustomed to dealing with liars and cheats. He found her lack of skill in this area refreshing.

When it seemed she might sweep past him, he linked arms with her. "The fan suits you. Do you like it?"

It had been a gift from him last Christmas, discovered at a bazaar in Valletta on the island of Malta. The iridescent shimmer of mother of pearl possessed a magical quality, reminiscent of a fairy's wing. As soon as he had laid eyes on the piece, memories of Sophia skipping through the gardens at Charles Wedmore's country estate, her laugh like the tinkle of bells, had washed over him. He'd realized she wasn't a little girl any longer when he purchased it, but nostalgia had driven him to select it.

"My lady's maid chose it," she murmured, refusing to look at him. "I barely gave it a thought."

Another poorly told lie.

"Margrave," a voice called from the drive. He tore his gaze away from Sophia to discover Ben and Eve Hillary standing with Sophia's aunt. It appeared the couple had just arrived.

"How nice of you to attend your mother's ball," Crispin said with a hint of humor and led Sophia toward the couple. "It is about time you joined decent folk again."

"I would never describe you as decent, Margrave." Ben smiled at his wife. "Would you, dear?"

"Oh, he has grown on me." Eve greeted Crispin warmly with kisses to his cheeks before extending her best to Sophia and her aunt.

"Good evening, Miss Allred." Ben accepted Beatrice's outstretched hand and placed a chaste kiss on her glove. "What a happy coincidence to cross paths with you. Eve was telling me on the ride here you are hard at work knitting blankets for the children at the foundling hospital. Did my ears deceive me, or have you finished twelve already?"

Sophia's aunt beamed at Ben. "I completed fifteen as of

this afternoon, Mr. Hillary. Your sister-in-law will send someone around to collect them tomorrow."

"How wonderful," Eve gushed. "The Mayfair Ladies Charitable Society believes every child at Woodmore Foundling Home should have a knitted blanket of his or her own, and Miss Allred has been instrumental in helping us come close to fulfilling our goal."

Sophia's aunt tittered with pleasure. "I do love a good cause."

Ben offered his free arm to Sophia's aunt. "Miss Allred, will you allow me the honor of arriving to the ball with two lovely ladies?"

"How could I refuse such a charming offer?" Beatrice linked arms with him and flashed another brilliant smile in his direction before continuing her discourse with Eve. Ben led the women inside, leaving Crispin and Sophia alone on the drive.

Muffled laughter and music spilled from the upper floor ballroom. Sophia exhaled slowly and glanced up at Crispin. When the full strength of her stunning topaz blue gaze focused on him, his heart collided with his breastbone.

"Forgive me for being surly," she said. "You should have respected my wishes, mind you, but I should not have dismissed you this morning. I do not enjoy crossing swords with you."

He chuckled, caught off guard by her apology. "I think you do, Miss Darlington, at least a little."

"Perhaps a little," she agreed. The corners of her lush mouth curved into a mischievous smile. "Nevertheless, I prefer when we get on well. As you said earlier today, we were once friends."

"I still consider you a friend, Sophia."

She shrugged and made a vague noise in her throat that did not quite sound like agreement.

"Like you," he said, "I prefer when we get along. Is it possible to start over with a clean slate?"

"That is a difficult question to answer, my lord." She tapped her closed fan against her cheek as if thinking. "I believe I am capable of allowing bygones to be bygones if you promise me a dance this evening."

Wariness crept up his spine. The wisest course would involve him politely declining, but Crispin had never followed the easiest or most sensible path—especially where Sophia was concerned.

"Very well, Miss Darlington. I would be honored to stand up with you for one dance this evening."

"Splendid, I will mark your name beside the supper dance."

Crispin flinched. The supper dance would require him to escort her to the table and dine next to her. Although the prospect was greatly appealing, it was risky. She looked exquisite this evening. Her apricot silk gown complimented her ivory complexion and made her eyes appear bluer, while snowy white lace on the bodice gently hugged her willowy body. He would have a devil of a time maintaining an air of friendly indifference throughout the meal.

Before he could form a response, she interjected, "Your glower deserves a rest, Margrave. Besides, no one else will want to claim the supper dance with you here. You've earned an alias, did you know?"

He blinked in surprise. "An alias?"

"That is correct." She flicked open her fan and whispered behind it, even though they were alone, save the matching pair of footmen at the door. "Lord *My* Grave. They say you dig holes for sport and hunt bachelors to fill them."

He laughed. "You minx, I almost believed you."

"Just because no one has spoken it aloud does not mean they have not been thinking it."

"Are you able to read other's thoughts, Miss Darlington?"

"Perhaps." She tipped her head to the side, studied him for a bit, then aimed an innocent smile in his direction. "Thankfully, it appears you cannot, my lord."

"Yes, *thankfully*," he grumbled good-naturedly. "I can imagine the creative insults you are storing away for me in that brilliant mind of yours."

"Rest assured, any insults I concoct I will make you privy to immediately."

"I am sure you will." He ushered her inside before she had a chance to charm him into a second dance.

After seeing Sophia safely delivered to her aunt's side, he excused himself to search for the card room. Having Sophia near and knowing she would always be out of his reach created a strong undercurrent of frustration he didn't relish enduring longer than necessary. He would save his strength for their dance.

At a set of massive oak paneled doors, he stopped to ask a footman for directions to the card room.

"Through here, sir." The servant tugged one of the polished brass handles and indicated he would find a game of loo in the drawing room at the end of the long corridor.

As the door closed behind him, the sounds of merrymaking and a lively violin solo diminished. Intricate gold leaf wall sconces lit his way; candlelight undulated on crimson wall coverings as a warm breeze floated through the bank of open windows to his right.

As was typical, the evening's host and hostess had selected a room far away from the ballroom to provide male guests with a sanctuary free of husband-hunters—not that Crispin ever worried about such matters. He had worked hard to cultivate a reputation as an unredeemable rake, which discouraged most marriage-minded ladies, as well as providing an effective cover for espionage. One might be shocked by how freely men of dubious morals could roam wherever they pleased without raising questions.

A floorboard creaked close behind. Reaching into his jacket for the small knife he always carried, he spun on his heel. The blade flashed in the candlelight. A lady yelped and jumped back, banging into the wall.

It took him a moment to recognize her in the dim lighting and mourning attire. Tension drained from his body. "Forgive me, my lady. I was not expecting to encounter a member of the gentler sex in this part of the house."

Baroness Van Middleburg, second cousin to Perry Walsh, the current Duke of Stanhurst, regarded him with wide eyes. To the lady's credit, having the life frightened out of her didn't dull her sharp tongue. "Is it customary for blackguards to attack innocent, unsuspecting *gentlemen* outside the card room?"

"Innocent men rarely sneak up behind me." He returned the folding blade to his pocket.

She sank against the wall; her hands were trembling. "I was not sneaking. I tried to catch you in the ballroom, but you were too quick." Perhaps the chase and fright had been too much for her.

"Do you require a doctor?" he asked. "Perhaps smelling salts?"

"Smelling salts!" Her mouth puckered. "What do you take me for, young man? I am not an empty-headed debutante prone to swooning."

This was true. As a mother of six grown sons and a daughter, she was a seasoned lady. She should have enough sense not to accost a man when he was woolgathering, not that she could have anticipated his state of mind.

He gentled his tone, thinking of Sophia's great-aunt and how she occasionally became turned around in unfamiliar places. "Are you lost, my lady? Should I retrieve your husband?"

Flames blazed in her nearly black eyes. "I know where I am, you deplorable arse," she spat. "I do *not* require smelling salts. And if you can find which harlot's bed my worthless husband is warming tonight, tell him to go to the devil and to take you with him."

Crispin fought back a smile. "Duly noted. No smelling salts required."

His mirth was like tinder tossed on a fire. An angry blush flooded her face, fists formed at her sides, and a stream of extremely unladylike insults aimed at him, his manhood, and his mother poured from her. It seemed she had inherited the Stanhurst temper like her deceased cousin. Crispin waited for her tirade to die down, his patience waning.

He interrupted. "You said you tried to catch me in the ballroom."

"I know what I *said*," Lady Van Middleburg replied with an inelegant sniff. "There is nothing wrong with my memory."

Gads! She was a cantankerous woman. Setting aside his inclination to leave her in the corridor to rant to the wall coverings, he crossed his hands at his waist and assumed a non-threatening stance. "How might I be of service, Lady Van Middleburg?"

She drew herself up to her full height and jabbed a finger toward his chest. "You can stop haranguing my family and honor my cousin's memory. Old Stanhurst was a good man, and he does not deserve to have his name besmirched by a worthless—"

Crispin held up a hand to signal she should stop where she was. "I heard what you think of me the first time, and I, too, have an excellent memory. Allow me to reassure you that I have no interest in sullying your cousin's name."

Old Stanhurst, as she had dubbed her deceased cousin, required no help in that area. He had been an infamous hothead and brutal master to his family, servants, and mistress alike.

"If you intend no harm," she snipped, "then stop coming to his heir's door and bothering the servants with your prying questions. I heard you were there again today. You are worse than the pox."

"If your cousin's heir would allow me an audience, I am sure he could satisfy my questions quite well. There would be no more need for me to make inquiries of his servants."

With a glare that would sour grapes on a vine, she took a step toward him. "What is it you want? Did Old Stanhurst owe you a debt? Have mercy and allow his family to mourn in peace."

"I had little contact with your cousin or his deceased son, and I have no desire to disrupt a grieving family. Nevertheless, I believe the current duke might have information to assist with another matter. I will speak with him."

"Leave well enough alone," she said through gritted teeth, "or you will regret being rash."

"It would not be the first time I've regretting acting without forethought, my lady." His jaw firmed. "I *will* speak with the duke."

He anticipated the crack of her palm across his cheek. Her strike was weak and her glove cushioned the blow.

"Egads," a male voice called from the direction of the ballroom.

It was the Earl of Ramsdell, and once again, Crispin had been caught unawares. He was losing his skill.

Lady Van Middleburg snarled at the poor earl before storming toward the ballroom. Ramsdell quickly shuffled aside to allow her to pass and turned to watch until she disappeared from sight. When they were alone, the earl glanced over his shoulder at Crispin.

"Dare I ask what that was about?"

"Apparently, she took issue with my face." Then because the situation was too ludicrous to believe, Crispin burst into laughter.

SIX

WHILE SOPHIA AND OCTAVIA WAITED FOR LORD RAMSDELL to do his part to advance *The Matrimony Mission*, as Octavia had dubbed her plan to bring Crispin up to scratch on Sophia's behalf, they moved toward the small orchestra of twenty. Several pairs of eyes followed their progress. Sophia's would-be suitors, emboldened by Crispin's retreat from the ballroom, hadn't given her a moment's peace since her arrival. If not for her friend's insistence that they required a moment alone, Sophia's dance card would be full already.

The musicians were taking up their instruments for the first set when she and Octavia reached the large dais. Sophia's friend sighed heavily. "At last we are afforded a little privacy. No one will interrupt us now."

From the curious stares they were receiving from bystanders, Sophia wasn't so sure. "How do you—?"

An earsplitting quadrille drowned out her question.

"Clever," she shouted. "Who could compete with this noise?"

"What did you say?"

Sophia laughed and waved her hand to indicate it was unimportant.

Her friend giggled, seeming to understand the gist of Sophia's comment. Octavia pointed toward the ceiling and yelled, "Would you look at that chandelier? Have you ever seen anything as elegant?"

"Never."

The splendor of Hillary House was without rival, if one excluded the royal palace. At least a hundred candles graced the massive gold French Ormolu chandelier lording over the ballroom. Lush gardenia garlands draped the arms, filling the room with a dreamy fragrance. But it was the teardrop crystals as big as Sophia's fists, dripping from the chandelier like tears from heaven that captured her imagination. The ballroom was magical.

"How sad the Hillarys have no more sons in need of a wife," Octavia said into her ear.

"Poor Lord Ramsdell." Sophia clicked her tongue in sympathy, teasing her friend. "Tossed aside for an elegant chandelier."

Octavia grinned. "You know I would choose Ramsdell any day, but it is an exceedingly beautiful piece. Oh, there he is!" She linked arms with Sophia to pull her toward the set of double doors Lord Ramsdell had used to re-enter the ballroom. "Let's discover what he learned from Lord Margrave."

"Now?"

"Of course now."

"I do not want to appear desperate."

"You seem nothing of the sort."

Octavia tugged Sophia's arm and whisked her along the outskirts of the dance floor to intercept the Earl of Ramsdell. One stern look from Sophia's friend aimed at a gentleman as he approached kept him at bay. Octavia was fierce like her mother—tall, blazing eyes, and descended from Norsemen—and she had mastered her father's withering stare. But as a friend, Sophia couldn't ask for a more loyal, kindhearted ally.

"Lord Ramsdell was not gone long," Sophia said. "Perhaps he couldn't find Margrave."

Octavia tsked. "Sophia Darlington, give Ramsdell credit. How difficult could it be to locate a man of Lord Margrave's stature and pleasing visage?"

"Yes well, I do not know how pleasing Lord Ramsdell might find him, appearance or otherwise. The viscount behaves like an ill-tempered headmaster with a severe case of gout and a plaque over his desk that reads, 'Spare the rod; spoil the child.'"

Octavia slowed her step to fix an incredulous stare on her. "That is an impressively detailed description. Given it a lot of thought, have you?"

Heat spread up her face. "Only a little." She hadn't been feeling very charitable after their run-in earlier nor had she found it easy to concentrate on anything else.

When Sophia and Octavia reached Lord Ramsdell, he invited them to the terrace. Octavia linked arms with him, and they headed for the bank of glass doors at the back of the great room. Sophia had no qualms about accompanying the couple since they were as good as married with a formal betrothal agreement. The earl led them to a less populated corner, leaned against the railing, and scratched his head.

"Well?" Octavia prompted. "Did you speak with him?"

"Not exactly." The earl frowned. "It seems I interrupted him."

A lump formed in Sophia's throat. Crispin's name had been absent from the gossip sheets for months. No mention of him attending scandalous parties in Marylebone or sightings of him leaving the theatre with an actress on his arm. She'd had cause to hope he had abandoned his rakish ways.

"Was he with another woman?" Sophia whispered.

Lord Ramsdell fidgeted with his cuff link, avoiding eye contact. He needn't answer. She read the truth on his face.

Her friend's brown eyes overflowed with sympathy, but just as quickly sparked with ire. "Answer her, Ramsdell." Octavia shook his arm. "What did you interrupt?"

His frown deepened and lines appeared on his forehead. "I am uncertain what I stumbled across, but Margrave was not with a woman. Correction, he was with a lady, but it was harmless—at least, harmless in the sense there was nothing to suggest I interrupted a rendezvous. I came upon him and Lady Van Middleburg engaged in conversation outside the card room."

Relief washed over Sophia, leaving her slightly weak. She sank onto one of the marble benches placed around the terrace and laughed breezily over her vivid imagination. Lady Van Middleburg was a paragon of virtue and polite manners, certainly not the type to engage in a liaison with a man almost half her age.

"Did you overhear anything useful?" Octavia asked.

"I'm afraid not. The baroness accused Margrave of harassing the Stanhurst family and demanded he leave them alone. Then she slapped him."

Sophia gasped.

"Havers!" Octavia gripped Ramsdell's hand, her face eagerly tipped toward him. "What did he do after she slapped him?"

Her betrothed shrugged one shoulder. "What any decent man would do. He turned the other cheek."

"And she slapped him again?"

Ramsdell laughed and tweaked Octavia's button nose.

"No, you adorable girl. I meant it in the figurative sense. Lady Van Middleburg stormed off in a temper when she did not get a rise out of him."

"Oh." Octavia's shoulders slumped as if she was disappointed her lust for theatrics went unfulfilled. "Well, I am sure Lord Margrave has more important matters to attend to than harassing the Stanhursts. I hope he at least denied the charge."

"He did not utter a word."

Crispin wouldn't defend himself if Lady Van Middleburg's accusations were true. Earlier, Sophia had thought he was being overbearing and overprotective when he warned her away from Claudine and the theatre, but perhaps he had a real interest in what had occurred that night at the London docks. The only question was *why*. The Duke of Stanhurst and his son, Lord Geoffrey, died from a firearm mishap. All the newssheets said it was so.

Sophia knew better, of course, and she suspected anyone with half a bucket of good sense would question the story. Two firearms misfired and hit unintended targets at the same exact moment? The scenario was ridiculous. Still, most people accepted the story for truth since it was in print. Knowing Crispin was not easily duped pleased her. She admired a man who could think for himself.

Octavia snapped her fingers in front of Sophia's face.

She blinked.

"You are doing it again," her friend said, cocking her head to the side. "Traveling to some enchanted world hidden in your mind."

Sophia chuckled. "Alas, you caught me. I was dreaming of a tart glass of lemonade."

Octavia's eyebrow arched, suggesting she did not believe her, but Lord Ramsdell came to her rescue. "I would like a glass of lemonade myself. May I suggest we all retire to the refreshment room?"

"You may, sir." Sophia accepted a hand up from him.

Her friend's gaze lingered on her; Sophia flashed a disarming smile as they headed for the refreshment room. Octavia did not reciprocate. She often voiced the suspicion Sophia was not completely forthcoming with her, which was an unbecoming trait in a best friend.

Sophia agreed friends should be open with each other, but she also believed Octavia deserved to maintain her innocence for as long as possible. Sophia's friend woke every morning secure in the knowledge good things came to good people. Her parents and siblings were alive and well, her betrothed adored her, and she felt pretty when she wore pink.

Sophia would have held on to her own naivety a little longer if she had been given a choice, but her parents had been killed in a riot when she was very young. Sometimes the world was a dangerous place.

While Lord Ramsdell collected glasses of lemonade, Octavia pulled Sophia aside. "It sounds like Lord Margrave could be involved in one of Papa's latest endeavors, although I never would have suspected they ran in the same circles."

"What do you mean?" Sophia asked.

"Do you recall I told you about the time William and I stumbled across Papa and his companions in the stables?"

Sophia chuckled. "How could I forget?"

One evening last autumn, Octavia and her younger brother had interrupted a strange gathering during a house party at their father's country estate. Lord Seabrook had been wearing a fox skin hat, complete with snout and ears, and was leading his guests in a chant Octavia later realized was part of a children's rhyme. When she questioned him in his study the next morning and refused to leave well enough alone, he had confessed to forming a secret society dedicated to the hunt.

"I must admit," Sophia said, "I fail to recognize the connection between your father's club and Lord Margrave's recent activities."

"As it turns out, my father is terrible at keeping secrets. The other evening he admitted to having joined another club when I caught him sneaking from the house." Octavia sniffed. "He told Mama he was retiring to bed, but he is a poor liar. He never retires before ten o'clock."

If he were any other man, Sophia might believe he was an *excellent* liar and Octavia had actually caught him sneaking out to see another woman. But Lord Seabrook seemed to live in fear of displeasing his wife. Lady Seabrook ruled the household without question, although Sophia had never witnessed her being unkind to her husband, children, or servants.

"I knew he was up to no good," Octavia said, "even before I spotted the hat behind his back."

"Does your father's club willfully ignore stories printed in the newssheet and harass dukes?" Sophia was only partly teasing. "Because that seems to be Lord Margrave's goal. The Stanhurst deaths were ruled an accident, so why would he bother the duke's family?"

Octavia shrugged. "Who knows what the corkbrains are up to behind closed doors? Although Papa did say they fancy themselves modern day sleuthhounds."

Membership in the secret society might explain Crispin's sudden interest in poking around in others' affairs, but the scenario didn't ring true. "Lord Margrave keeps to himself mostly," Sophia said, "and I cannot imagine him wearing a silly hat."

"Fair point," Octavia said.

Lord Ramsdell returned with glasses of lemonade and handed one to Sophia.

"Thank you, my lord."

She chatted with her companions a few moments more then informed them she was returning to the ballroom. The first few spaces on her dance card were empty by design, but her first partner would be searching for her soon.

"Ask Lord Margrave," Octavia advised before she walked away. "The direct approach is always best."

Ramsdell looked back and forth between Sophia and her friend. "What should she ask the viscount?"

"It is a secret," Octavia said with an enigmatic smile.

Sophia left them playfully bickering with one another and returned to the ballroom. Her first dance partner seemed to spot her immediately and came to claim his dance. After the end of their spin around the floor, the next gentleman was waiting to escort her back to the dance floor. And so, the set progressed, Sophia not being allowed a moment's rest before being whisked back onto the parquet floor time after time. She was having such fun, she lost track of time.

When Major Hughes joined hands with her to sashay around the floor, she caught a glimpse of Crispin standing at the edge, watching.

"Is it time for the supper dance already?" she asked the dashing officer.

"I believe so."

Sophia's gaze kept traveling to Crispin as she and her partner circled the room. Instead of glowering like usual, he graced her with a rare smile. She gasped and tripped over the major's foot. Her partner caught her around the waist when she stumbled and held her much too close.

"Steady, Miss Darlington." He slanted a smirk at her as if she had faked missing a step on purpose.

Crispin narrowed his eyes, his smile long gone. Surely, he didn't think she welcomed the man's attentions. Heat flashed into her cheeks, and she elbowed the major to create distance between them. He grunted and loosened his hold.

Crispin's piercing stare never wavered from her any time she stole a peek in his direction, even after the orchestra played the last note of the song. She lost sight of him for a moment when she and her dance partner entered the promenade, but he loomed into view as they neared the end of the line. Major Hughes must have noticed his menacing presence as well; his gulp was audible. The officer bade her a hasty good-bye and shot into the crowd before completing the promenade.

Crispin smiled again—a deliberate, predatory, satisfied arching of his lips. Suddenly, she was overcome with shyness when he sauntered in her direction. His gaze remained locked on her; her knees wobbled.

The man moved like seduction personified, his tailored black jacket skimming his strong shoulders. He took her hand as he reached her. "I've come to claim my dance." His smoky voice rolled over her, filling her with breathless excitement.

She nodded, not trusting herself to speak.

His hand in hers was firm, his step confident as he led her onto the floor. They took position for the waltz. His touch on her upper back created tingles that rained down her body, touching her everywhere. It was as if she couldn't tell where he stopped and she began. The sensation did not lessen when he led her into the first turn. They moved as one, their rhythm and timing perfectly matched.

A whiff of his cologne teased her nose; she inhaled deeply, savoring the delicious hints of mint, vanilla, and a spice she couldn't place. The fragrance was almost as bold and intoxicating as the man.

When he spoke softly into her ear, his breath caressed her neck. "Are you enjoying yourself?"

She shivered with delight. "I am." *Now.* How could he miss how perfectly suited they were for one another? It was as obvious to her as the fact that she possessed two arms and two legs. "I suspect you are not enjoying the evening as well as I am. I heard about your unfortunate encounter with Lady Van Middleburg."

He chuckled, his voice low and slightly husky. "Now who is the spy, Miss Darlington?"

"As you are fond of saying, I was *not* spying."

"True, you sent Lord Ramsdell in your stead." He winked. "Very clever move."

Pleasurable heat swept through her. "You think I am responsible, my lord? Octavia—the one who always wears pink? She is the culprit."

"Never trust a lady in a pink gown." His smile threatened to scorch her to cinders. "Quite right, Margrave. Do file that knowledge away. It might come in useful someday."

She wet her lips, contemplating whether to bring the conversation back to Lady Van Middleburg or simply bask in his pleasant mood and attention.

Crispin cleared his throat. She barreled on before she lost her nerve.

"Why have you been questioning the Duke of Stanhurst's servants?"

"Hmm... It seems Ramsdell overheard more of the conversation than he led me to believe."

"Then it is true? I had hoped the earl was mistaken." She lowered her voice to just above a whisper. "You should heed the baroness's warning. The old duke was a horrible man. I told you how he treated Miss Bellerose. I can only imagine such cruelty ran in his blood. His heir might be as corrupt as he was, and I would hate for you to come to any harm."

Crispin's strong brows rose toward his hairline. "Are you worried for *me*?"

The wonder present in his question irked her. How could he doubt her regard? She was not a wanton who kissed gentlemen willy-nilly. He was her first love—her only, for that matter.

"I wish to throttle you most of the time," she said, "but yes, I care about your safety."

"We have that in common." Slight pressure from his hand on her back lessened the distance between them. Her chest was scandalously near his. His mouth lowered toward her ear. "I would sacrifice everything to protect you."

His breath whispered across her skin. She turned her face toward his; their lips were so close. If she leaned slightly, they would touch. His eyes devoured her, as powerful as if he caressed her with his hands. Her body pulsed with awareness of him, of how glorious it must feel to be touched by him.

"You would give up *everything*," she murmured. "Your reputation, your happiness—your beloved horse?"

The corners of his mouth twitched. "Even Atlas." He drew away, erecting a blasted wall between them again. "Do you question my devotion to you and your family? Regina charged me with watching over you and—"

"Yes, yes," she said impatiently. "You promised Regina, et cetera, et cetera."

Crispin had been spouting the same nonsense ever since Regina and her new husband left for Athens with Evangeline in tow. This elevated sense of duty he claimed to owe Sophia's family seemed like an excuse to keep her close while simultaneously pushing her away. It was maddening.

"You should worry less about me," she said, "and watch out for yourself. The Stanhursts are an influential family. They could make trouble for you if they wished."

Crispin grinned. A lock of golden blond hair slipped onto his forehead; her fingers itched to smooth it back into place. "I am capable of protecting myself *and* you, Miss Darlington."

Law! He was the most unpredictable, infuriating man in the world. One moment, he was much too dire when the situation did not call for it, and the next, he laughed in the face of a serious threat.

She lowered her voice to a near whisper. "If you've set your mind to finding out what happened to the duke and Lord Geoffrey, maybe I can help."

"Are you implying your actress friend is involved after all?"

Sophia sighed; frustration seeped into her voice. "How many times must I defend her? Claudine is innocent."

"Then I cannot fathom what assistance you might offer."

She nibbled her bottom lip, torn on whether to confide in him. The actress might be blameless, but her new protector was no saint. Benny wasn't a ruthless murderer, but he'd held Sophia's brother-in-law hostage at one time. The poor man's brother had threatened to kill him if he allowed Xavier to go free.

Most men of Crispin's class would not view Benny's actions in a good light, but to Sophia and her family, he was a hero. He had saved Regina's and Xavier's lives. If all of Crispin's poking around was for sport, Sophia couldn't chance any harm coming to the sweet, simple man.

"Are you a member of Lord Seabrook's secret society?"

she blurted. "The group that fancies themselves amateur sleuthhounds? Octavia told me all about it."

Crispin chuckled. "It's not a well-kept secret if you and Lady Octavia are aware of its existence."

"Answer the question."

He opened and closed his mouth as if he considered lobbing another witty retort and decided against it. "I am not one of Lord Seabrook's sleuthhounds. Now, it is your turn to answer. What can you tell me about Claudine Bellerose?"

"There is nothing more to tell." Loyalty compelled her to discuss the matter with Claudine before revealing what happened the night Stanhurst and his son were murdered.

"I know one of the current duke's sisters well," she lied to steer him away from Claudine. "If I write to Lady Emmeline, she might extend an invitation to visit her in the country."

"Stop." Crispin gripped Sophia's hand tightly, his hold commanding but not painful. "I do not want you involved. The Stanhursts pose little danger, but I am equipped to handle any risk."

Once, her sister Regina had believed she was invincible —all because Uncle Charles had taught her Wing Chun, a method of combat created by an abbess after she observed a crane and snake embroiled in battle. A fable, Sophia was sure. Just like the one Regina and Crispin told themselves. No one could hurt them. They could protect themselves.

"There will always be someone bigger or more skilled than you," she said. "You would be wise to remember you are but flesh and bone."

"As are you, Sophia. Promise you will forget about this business with Stanhurst."

She notched her chin. "I will promise if you do the same."

"Sophia…" The music faded. The dance was at an end, and so was their opportunity to speak without others overhearing. "I wish to continue our discussion at a later time."

As did she, before too many days passed. If she visited Claudine at the Drayton Theatre in the morning, she could be back home in plenty of time to receive Crispin in the afternoon. "Call at Wedmore House tomorrow."

He inclined his head, signaling his agreement.

"In the meantime," she said, "try not to harass anyone."

"Now, Miss Darlington." His hazel eyes sparked with devilment. "How can I make a promise I might need to break?"

She pursed her lips, attempting to suppress a smile. "At least try to limit your harassment to my suitors and leave the matrons alone."

"A promise easily granted."

"My gentlemen admirers will be thrilled to hear it."

His smile was soft, bordering on affectionate. "I hope not."

SEVEN

MIDMORNING THE NEXT DAY SOPHIA ARRIVED AT THE Drayton Theatre in Marylebone. Her friend Claudine would be occupied with play rehearsal and unable to converse with her until the stage manager dismissed the players, but Sophia had time to wait.

If Crispin learned she had defied his wishes by visiting the theatre again, his hazel eyes would light with a dangerous blaze that would set *her* on fire in the most delicious manner. How tempting and wicked it would be to allow her secret to slip when he called that afternoon. A marvelous tremor of anticipation raced through her as she climbed from the carriage.

Trevor, a young footman newly hired at Wedmore House, hurried up the stairs ahead of her to open the theatre door while the coach circled the block.

"Please remind John Coachman to collect me in an hour," she said. "I am receiving callers this afternoon."

The footman nodded, his slicked auburn hair catching the light. "Aye miss, I will carry your reminder post haste, that I will."

She smiled; Trevor's eagerness to please was sweet. "You may leave me at the door. I know the way to the auditorium."

"Yes, miss."

She entered the theatre alone and paused to get her bearings in the dim light as the door closed behind her, muting the noise from the streets. Only one wall-mounted lamp burned on low wick in the lobby, but the Drayton would be transformed and lit up like a ballroom when the patrons arrived this evening.

Claudine spotted Sophia as soon as she walked into the auditorium and lifted a hand to wave. Sophia's timing appeared to be perfect. The stage manager was dismissing the players for a short recess.

"Good morning," Sophia said in her most cheerful voice.

Natalia and Rachel, two of the actresses in Claudine's troupe, greeted Sophia by name before excusing themselves to take refreshment in their dressing rooms. The stage manager acknowledged her presence with a grunt, which might have been insulting if Sophia hadn't grown accustomed to his gruff manners.

"What an unexpected surprise." Claudine's beautiful eyes lit with pleasure, more than making up for Mr. Jonas's reticence. "May I beg your pardon for one moment?"

"Of course."

Claudine retreated to the wings briefly, and Benny popped out from behind the curtain. The near giant of a man wore a wide grin, his rust-red hair damp at the temples. "Morning, Miss Sophia."

"Good morning, sir. How goes the world of theatrical performance?"

He swiped the back of his hand across his forehead and shrugged. "Don't know much about that sort of thing, miss, but Miss Claudine says I been pulling my weight real good."

"Benny is a godsend." The petite actress patted his forearm affectionately. They made quite the pair standing side-by-side. "The Drayton Theatre and *A Lady's Fate* would not be the same without him."

The debut play Claudine had authored and starred in was doing very well. It appeared the theatre doors were in little danger of closing now.

"I cannot imagine the play without Benny," Sophia said as she drew close to the stage. "You are magnificent, sir. I would venture that Aunt Beatrice and I would be lost without both of you joining us for weekly dinners at Wedmore House."

The dear man blushed to the roots of his hair.

Claudine descended the stage stairs to take Sophia's hands and place kisses on her cheeks. "We are honored to be your guests."

Dining with theatre folk was unconventional, to say the least, but Aunt Beatrice was the first to point out the family had been eccentric for generations. The *ton* no longer pretended shock. This family trait troubled Sophia at one time, but after her exposure to Society, she realized everyone had foibles. Some simply hid them better.

"Will your betrothed be back in time to join us tomorrow evening?" she asked.

Aunt Beatrice insisted anyone marrying an honorary family member was granted the same status, so Mr. Hawke, the theatre owner, attended the weekly dinners whenever his scheduled allowed.

Claudine frowned. "I am afraid estate affairs have extended Russell's stay in the country. We expect him next week."

Sophia had hoped Mr. Hawke was back in London by now. The actress would likely desire his counsel on what to do about Benny, but the conversation shouldn't be postponed.

"Unfortunately, this is not a social call," Sophia said. "Is there someplace we could speak privately? Benny, too."

Claudine's eyebrows arched high on her forehead. "Oliver's office is vacant." She informed the stage manager that she required the use of his quarters and an extended recess.

Mr. Jonas clapped his hands to gain the remaining players' attention. "Everyone worked hard this morning. We are adjourning for the day."

"He is in an unusually jovial mood," Sophia said under her breath.

Benny nodded. "He likes to be in charge, but he isn't really. Mr. Hawke is the boss."

Claudine playfully shushed him.

When they reached the stage manager's office, Sophia did not waste time coming to the point. She reported on Crispin's snooping and explained she was worried for him, given what she knew about Claudine's former benefactor, the late Duke of Stanhurst.

"I want to tell Lord Margrave what I know about the men's deaths," Sophia said. "Perhaps that will satisfy whatever curiosity has been roused. However, I cannot do so with a clear conscience unless I have your blessing."

Claudine slanted a troubled glance toward Benny. "Do you believe Lord Margrave means to harm him?"

"No," Sophia said, "he will be grateful when he learns Benny saved Regina's life."

"And what about Benny's other crime? Will he overlook your brother-in-law's kidnapping?"

"I do not understand Margrave's interest in what happened to Stanhurst and Lord Geoffrey, but I believe his inquiry is limited to their deaths. Nevertheless, it might be prudent to send Benny away for a time." Sophia smiled ruefully at the dear, sweet man who had been toiling to redeem himself. "Please understand, I do not blame you for Xavier's incarceration. You did so under duress."

A blistering blush covered Benny's face. "I was wrong for what I done, Miss Sophia. If I am to be punished, I will accept it, but I cannot leave the theatre with Mr. Hawke away. I watch out for Miss Claudine and the others."

"And a fine job you do," Claudine said, smiling with a mix of affection and sadness.

"Tell your fellow about the duke and Farrin before he gets himself into trouble," Benny said. "You have to watch out for him, too."

Sophia took the man's hand in hers and squeezed. "Thank you, Benny. If only Lord Margrave possessed your good sense..."

He beamed at her.

"Before I reveal anything, however," she said, "I will insist on Lord Margrave's promise that no harm will come to you. Is that acceptable, Claudine?"

The actress sighed. "It is Benny's choice. His theatre friends and I will stand beside him come what may."

A knock interrupted their conversation. The stage manager stepped inside his office. "Wait here," he barked to someone in the corridor.

The door swung open. "I will not be kept waiting like a —" Crispin stopped abruptly inside the threshold. His eyes flared before narrowing. "Miss Darlington, how unexpected to find you at the theatre."

An undercurrent of fury simmered beneath the surface of his calm facade. Her mouth grew dry as her heart took off at a terrific gallop.

"Good morning, Lord Margrave. Did we not agree to meet at Wedmore House this afternoon?"

"It is far from a good morning, miss."

He strolled toward her. The air became heavy with the threat of an impending storm. His fiery gaze seared into Sophia. A light sheen swept over her body, causing her undergarments to cling to her skin.

When Benny shifted to the edge of his chair, Sophia gestured for him to stay. She did not require protection from Crispin.

"It is far, *far* from good." The viscount bit out each word and stopped in front of her. His jaw bulged as he ground his teeth repeatedly. "If the morning was a good one, I would not be stumbling across you at the one place I specifically forbade you to go."

His gaze ran over her from head to toe as if he were sizing her up in preparation of tossing her over his shoulder and toting her home. Her stomach quivered with unexpected excitement. Sophia allowed herself a fleeting triumphant smile before lifting her chin defiantly.

"Must I remind you once again, sir, you have no claim on me?"

"Oh, my dear Miss Darlington," he ground out. "You are sadly mistaken. I am your family's champion."

"My family's—not *mine*."

His eyes blazed. Any hotter, and he might set the room afire. She did not protest when he assisted her from the chair and informed her friends he would call another day. She offered a hurried good-bye as he led her from the manager's office. They strode toward the stairwell at the end of the corridor with Crispin's fingers lightly wrapped around her upper arm. She could break free of his hold, but she craved his touch too much. It was never enough to sustain her after they parted.

In silence, they descended the stairs, and neither uttered

a word as he marched her past the guard stationed at the stage door and into the alley behind the theatre.

"Where are we going?" she asked as he urged her along the alley.

"I am returning you to Wedmore House."

She dug in her heels, forcing him to stop unless he wished to drag her by the arm. "Claiming to be my family's champion does not permit you to command *me*. I am an independent-minded lady. I wish to stay."

In a blink, he pressed her against the brick wall. His hands on her shoulders were gentle tethers, but she didn't dare move. How many nights had she longed to feel his lips cover hers again? She had lost count.

"You lied to me," he said with a slight growl to his voice. "You said she was innocent."

"She *is*."

His face lowered toward Sophia's, stopping only inches away. A wonderful hum swept over her, filling her ears and vibrating through her body. "How can I believe you now? The evidence is clear. You came to warn the woman."

"I-I am not a liar." Her tongue swept across her lips and stoked the flames in his nearly black eyes. His response emboldened her. "How can you ignore the evidence at your fingertips? How can you not see *me*?"

"I see you, Sophia. You've ensnared me in a spell, and I cannot look away." The husky rasp of his voice elicited a shocking pulse between her legs. She couldn't catch her breath. "I watch you with other men, charming them as surely as you have charmed me. Your cruel reminders that you are not mine are burned into my memory, to be viewed a thousand times when I am alone."

The admission stunned her. Her lips parted. If he felt as strongly as she did, why did he push her away?

"I could be yours, Crispin. I want it, too. All you must do is accept me."

His eyes dulled, and his smile was more like a grimace. "How can I make you understand? You are out of my reach."

The grip on her shoulders eased. He was retreating.

Not again! Desperate, she captured him around the neck. "I am right in front of you, you daft man."

THE LAST OF CRISPIN'S CONTROL SHATTERED WHEN SOPHIA'S lips slammed into his. He tugged her against his chest and devoured her mouth. Gone was the sweetness and wonder of their first kiss. This was passionate, consuming. She possessed him—her scent, her warmth, her erotic little moans.

He sank against her, trapping his hands between the small of her back and the bricks to keep from acting on his basest desires. At the edges of conscious thought, he recognized he couldn't take her. Not in some alley against a brick wall, him driving into her over and over, losing himself in the sweetness of her scent and the softness of her skin.

Lord help me, I want this woman, all of her. He trembled in an effort to restrain himself.

Sophia, for her part, seemed oblivious to his inner battle. A pleasing murmur slipped from her when he teased her lips apart. She sighed, opening to him; he swept his tongue into her sweet mouth.

Winding her arms around his neck, she arched into him. The temptation to explore her exquisite body beckoned—to begin at the gentle slopes of her hips and slide his hands along her waist until he was cradling her small breasts. He wanted to strip her until every silky, alabaster inch of her was bared and pleasure her until she cried his name and begged for more.

A faint reprimand echoed in his mind. *Restrain yourself, man.* The voice forged through the fog to wake his conscience. Reluctantly, he ended the kiss, but his mouth brushed her cheek and strayed to her ear to tease the button of velvety flesh there between his teeth.

"Heavens!" She had grown breathless and pliable, which made retreat even more difficult but necessary.

Sophia exhaled as he drew away and leaned her head against the wall with her eyes closed. He allowed himself to revel in her beauty in this unguarded moment. Her pink lips were swollen from his kisses, and her lashes lay like gossamer against her flushed skin.

He lovingly caressed the length of her delicate neck. Sophia was the most winsome creature he had ever encountered. Standing here with her, feeling her pulse beneath his fingertips, he understood the reason his godfather had tried to discourage him from joining the Regent's Consul.

Crispin could never provide her with a normal marriage or the family life she desired. Yet, he couldn't continue taking from her and offering nothing of himself. He was stuck in a hell of his own making.

Regret swirled in his gut. "Sophia..."

"No!" She squeezed her eyes tight and shook her head. "Unless you intend to say you love me, do not speak. You will spoil everything."

He chuckled softly. Her eyes snapped open. Ire sparked in their blue depths.

"Are you *laughing* at—?" She gasped.

Instinctively, he threw up his forearm and spun to block a blow before it smashed into his head. The dull sound of wood connecting with bone made him nauseous; pain shot into his shoulder.

Sophia screamed. He pushed her away.

Before he could get his bearings, a second hit knocked him off balance. His gaze locked on the weapon, a thick cane poised to strike again. Crispin lunged and grabbed his assailant's arm. "Run, Sophia!"

She dashed toward the stage door, yelling for help.

Crispin's opponent was smaller than him—a street rat, to be sure. Hooking his arm around the back of his attacker's neck, Crispin threw him to the ground. The gangly footpad landed on the packed dirt with a grunt. A swift kick knocked the weapon from his hand.

Bloody cane.

He couldn't decide which made him angrier, the throbbing in his arm, or knowing he was to blame for his injury.

A scraggly ruffian standing at the alley's entrance abandoned his watch and ran in their direction, screaming a battle cry as he barreled down the alley. Crispin snatched the cane from the ground and darted to the side. The dimwit ran past; Crispin smacked the battered mahogany stick across the backs of his knees. He crumpled on the ground with a loud "Oof" and skidded on the dirt, creating a small dust cloud.

The first attacker pushed to his feet and scrambled down the alley, leaving his rescuer to Crispin's mercy. He raised the cane overhead, prepared to frighten some sense into what he could now tell was a boy no older than fifteen lying on the ground.

"Run along after your cohort while you still can," Crispin said.

The whelp struggled to stand. Crispin extended his arm to offer assistance. With a disgruntled frown, the lad placed his sooty hand in Crispin's and pulled himself up. Grumbling, the urchin limped down the alley.

"If you desire honest work, call at Arden-Hill in Mayfair. Tell them Lord Margrave sent you."

The lad looked back at him warily.

"I could use a brave man like you on my staff," Crispin said.

The boy blinked and a slow grin cut across his face. "Aye, milord." With renewed vigor, he dashed toward the street and disappeared around the corner.

Sophia's scream was like a dirk driven into Crispin's chest.

He spun toward the sound and froze. The stage door flew open and the guard burst into the alley.

"Don't move," Crispin ordered, but the guard had already drawn up short.

Not ten feet away, a man stood behind Sophia with a blade pressed to her neck. Crispin's throat closed as if he was being garroted.

"Drop the cane," the blackguard barked, "and no harm will come to the lady."

The man was older and heftier than the assailants Crispin had fought off, more experienced. *Probably the leader.* He towered over Sophia, and in his clutches, she appeared more delicate than Crispin had ever realized. One wrong move, and she would break like a porcelain doll.

"Hold very still, darling."

She rolled her eyes. "Do you think me a d-dolt?" Despite her bravado, her voice quivered. It was all he could do to resist storming them and beating the blackguard unconscious.

Sweat dripped down the assailant's pronounced forehead. He darted a glance at the guard. "Stay where you are. This don't concern the likes of you."

Crispin's grip tightened on the cane. "Release her, or I will *end* you."

He eased toward the man and Sophia, calculating the odds of reaching them before she was harmed.

"You ain't fast enough to save 'er, Lord Margrave."

Crispin's heart skipped. *He knows my name. He is here for me.* Rage roared through his veins. This was his fault. Sophia was in danger because of him.

"Do not hurt her. I surrender." He held his arms out at his sides and dropped the cane. It landed with a thud. He didn't require a weapon to disable the bastard, but he couldn't make a move while Sophia was being used as a shield. "You are here for me. Let her go."

The man's low laugh grated on him. "I think I like 'er where she is. He who has the wench controls 'er man."

"He is not my man," Sophia said. "Believe me, I've tried enticing him, but—"

"Quiet," her captor snapped. His meaty fingers dug into Sophia's upper arm. She hissed in pain.

Crispin growled low in his throat and took a step closer.

"Stay where you are, Margrave. I ain't the squeamish sort. I'll cut 'er."

Sophia whimpered then began mumbling to herself. Her lips formed the same words repeatedly. Did she recite a prayer? Her face screwed up in disgust for a moment, then her silent chanting resumed. When Crispin made out the word peach, his pulse skipped.

Squeeze the peach, she was saying. *Squeeze the peach.*

Only now did he realize she had wedged her hand between her neck and her assailant's arm when he had grabbed her, just as her uncle taught her. Hope surged in Crispin. All he required was a moment's diversion.

The blackguard paid her no attention, mistakenly

assuming she posed no risk. "Listen," he snarled. "I ain't going to warn you but once. Stay away—"

"Yes, Sophia," Crispin murmured, "the fruit is ripe for picking."

Furrows cut across the man's forehead as he looked back and forth from Crispin to Sophia. She kept mumbling. "Shut your trap! *Both* of you."

Her chanting ceased; she opened her eyes.

Do it! Crispin inclined his head, the movement barely perceptible.

Her gaze hardened. In one quick motion, she stepped to the side and grabbed the man by the bollocks while the knife away from her neck.

The blackguard howled like a mezzo-soprano. The weapon clattered to the ground. She kept squeezing, showing no mercy until he released her first. He collapsed on the dirt, gasping in pain.

"Oh, my heavens! Ew!" Sophia skittered away, wiping her hands on her skirts and shuddering with revulsion. "Ew! Ew! Ew!"

Crispin and the theatre guard pounced on her assailant while he was still immobilized and moaning. If the blackguard could walk any time soon, it would be surprising. He was unlikely to threaten another lady again, of that Crispin was certain.

A stagehand exited the theatre and happened upon the scene. His jaw dropped.

"Find Mr. Jonas," the guard barked as he helped Crispin haul their captive to his feet and trap his arms behind his back. "And see the lady safely inside."

The stagehand jumped to obey the guard's command, placing his arm around Sophia's shoulders. "Come with me, miss. Have you been hurt?"

Sophia shook her head and allowed him to usher her toward the stage door.

"You are trembling like a leaf," he said. "The stage manager keeps a bottle of brandy in his quarters. A nip might calm your nerves."

"Thank you, but I am all right." She threw a quick glance over her shoulder as if she was worried Crispin might abandon her.

"I will follow," he said.

She hesitated but entered the building with the stagehand.

Crispin addressed the guard. "You will be rewarded for your bravery, sir."

"The name's Penhale," he said, "and no reward is necessary. Let's take him inside. There's rope backstage to secure him while the manager sends for the magistrate."

"In due time." Crispin didn't intend to relinquish custody of the blackguard until he received answers. As he and Penhale neared the stage door with their prisoner, Crispin shoved the man chest first into the brick wall. A grunting wheeze escaped him on impact.

"Talk," he growled into the assailant's ear. "Who sent you?"

The blackguard's lips curled, revealing several rotting teeth. "Ye'll regret treating me poorly."

"His lordship asked you a question." Penhale slapped the back of his balding head. "Answer."

The prisoner cursed them. Like his godfather, Crispin was opposed to acts of brutality for the sake of loosening one's lips, but picturing Sophia at this villain's mercy tested his convictions. Before he acted on the impulse to commit violence, he jerked his captive away from the wall and wrestled him through the backstage door.

The giant named Benny rounded a corner at the end of

the corridor and stalked toward them with Sophia and her actress friend on his heels.

"There he is," Sophia said and pointed. "*He* is the one."

Benny stopped in front of the prisoner, looming above him, and glowered as if he contemplated tearing the flesh from the man's bones. "You attacked Miss Sophia? Did your mama never teach you to be kind to ladies? Perhaps you need some learning on the subject." He rolled up his sleeves, revealing massive forearms that were the size of small trees.

The captive shrank back. A spark of pleasure ignited in Crispin at seeing him frightened when faced with a larger threat. Perhaps Benny had the right of it. The coward could use a lesson in how to treat a lady, although Crispin doubted the bigger man's teaching methods could be any more effective than Sophia's own.

Crispin couldn't help feeling proud of her bravery, and equally horrified that she had been in danger in the first place. The morning's event only reinforced the notion he should maintain his distance, but he was unlikely to convince her.

She caught his eye and her mouth turned up slightly with a coy smile.

Hell, he was no longer certain he could convince himself.

As Benny raised his fist, Sophia touched his forearm to intervene. "No doubt this brute needs a lesson in manners, kind sir, but he cannot answer questions if he is knocked silly."

Benny's fierce gaze bore into the man; he kept his fist raised. "And if he refuses to answer?"

"Then by all means, you may take matters into your hands," Sophia said, her eyes twinkling with mischief, as they did when she was putting Crispin through the paces. "I doubt the magistrate will care whether he is able to walk into a cell or must be tossed inside like a sack of grain."

The man gulped. "H-how do I know you ain't going to order him to attack if I tell you what you want to know?"

She clicked her tongue. "Benny is not a hound, sir."

Growling, the big man snapped his jaws, causing the blackguard to yelp and stumble backward. He fell into Crispin trying to escape. Crispin jerked him upright.

"Oh, dear," Sophia said and captured her bottom lip between her teeth. "I think you have upset him."

Benny snarled.

Sophia's actress friend covered a chuckle with her hand and spun away.

The blackguard was quivering.

Crispin smiled. Sophia was a master at making men squirm. Funny this hadn't occurred to him until now.

A second stagehand rounded the corner with coiled rope and handed it to Benny. While he secured the prisoner's hands behind his back, Sophia turned to Crispin. "What would you like to ask him first?"

"Perhaps we should start with him revealing who sent him."

"That does seem a logical place to begin. Perhaps we should adjourn to the stage to continue the interrogation?"

The drama she and her cohorts were performing belonged on stage, and he would enjoy every minute of the blackguard's discomfort.

"Lead the way, Miss Darlington."

EIGHT

SOPHIA ACCEPTED CRISPIN'S ASSISTANCE ON THE CARRIAGE stairs, her mind preoccupied with what they had learned during the interrogation of their attacker. She settled on the bench for the ride home and turned to thank him for coming to her aid. He climbed inside and sat on the opposite seat. Her eyes widened in surprise.

"We are traveling to the same location," he said evenly, "and you should not be without an escort."

Her manservants could see her home, but she didn't dare argue. The incident in the alley had shaken her, and she didn't want to be alone.

"What do you propose we do about Lady Van Middleburg?" she asked.

Crispin spared her a brief glance before he redirected his gaze toward the bustling street out the window. "We will take no action."

"None? You cannot be serious."

"I am."

"What? *Why*? She hired a thug to threaten you. Doesn't that strike you as a bit of an overreaction on Lady Van

Middleburg's part? You questioned the Duke of Stanhurst's servants. That is hardly a reason to resort to violence." She crossed her arms. "The baroness is hiding something by pretending to be her cousin's champion. Something personal, I think."

He abandoned his mission of broodingly staring out the window. "There is nothing odd about it. She wishes to protect her family."

"If you believe that to be true, you need my help worse than I thought."

"*You* will mind your own affairs." The ubiquitous scowl was back on his handsome face. "I will handle the matter alone."

Sophia sniffed. "As you wish, Lord Overbearing. I will mind my own affairs."

"Thank you, and my name is Crispin. You have leave to use it."

Havers! He was the most arrogant and difficult man she'd ever met, and she was hopelessly in love with him anyway. She moved across the carriage and plopped down beside him.

"You were impressive today," she said. "I had no idea you could fight like you did. You must have kept up your exercises like Regina."

His eyebrow slanted when she took his hand between hers. "What are you doing?"

"I am simply minding my affairs, my lord."

His stiff posture softened, and the hint of a smile played about the corners of his lips. "Are you certain you want me involved in your affairs? Usually, you scold me for interfering."

She laced their fingers together, their gloves creating a barrier. "I am feeling generous today. After all, you saved my life. Such bravery deserves a nugget of kindness."

A muscle in his jaw twitched. She seemed to have struck a sore spot. "You saved yourself," he said.

The sensation of cold, sharp metal pressing into her skin seeped into her memory. She snuggled against his side and forced herself not to think about what could have been. "I never would have had the courage without you."

He released her hand to place his arm around her shoulders. "You never would have been in danger if not for me. I was careless."

"How dare you take all the credit?" She tipped her head to the side and gazed up at him, teasing. "It was *my* idea to kiss in the alley, and might I add, it was amazing."

His eyebrows rose on his forehead.

"What? I quite enjoyed myself. Did you not?"

"Did you hear any objections from me?"

"Miraculously, I did not."

He chuckled halfheartedly. "At least no one of consequence saw us today. I will have your driver drop me at the next street while there is time to salvage the situation. You may return to husband hunting tonight without anyone being the wiser."

When he reached to knock on the carriage roof, Sophia planted her hand in the middle of his chest. "Move one more inch, and I will sit on you. You are going nowhere."

"Do you think sitting on me would be effective if I wanted to leave?"

She notched her chin. "Would you like to find out?"

"Maybe," he admitted with a wicked glint in his eyes that caused an excited tumble in her belly. "I will stay to argue my case, though. Sophia, it is not too late to choose another man."

She groaned. "Please, not again. I cannot listen to any more monologues about what I deserve or don't deserve.

And why do I not deserve to have what I want, which is you? Why do you insist on pushing me away?"

"Because you do not want *me*. You want a version of me that does not exist. I am not a family man. I never will be. Marry a man who can make you happy."

"According to you, that man does not exist. You've objected to every gentleman who has shown me attention. Law!" She flopped against the seat and took a cleansing breath. How could she want to throttle the man and kiss him at the same time? She decided to change her strategy. "I imagine it gets lonely in that big house of yours."

He shrugged. "I am barely there."

"See? You *must* be lonely. You cannot bring yourself to stay there, and you probably haven't been to the family seat in years."

"I am not avoiding home—either one. I have responsibilities abroad that call me away often. Fortunately, I employ an excellent man of business and land steward who keep me well informed."

She huffed. "Responsibilities abroad. What nonsense. You have wanderlust like Uncle Charles. Heaven forbid either of you should stand still long enough to take root any place. You both crave adventure."

"How well you know me, Sophia. I am an adventurer." He sounded a tad sarcastic and bitter, although she couldn't fathom what would make him so. "It wouldn't be fair to leave my wife at home alone."

"It would not, but that is the beauty of taking me for your wife. I crave adventure, too. Allow me to travel with you. Papa never left home without Mama at his side."

Even though her parents had met with a cruel end, Sophia took comfort in knowing they had been together and neither of them must live without the other.

"That is impossible," Crispin said.

"Why?"

He gently took her by her shoulders and turned her so they were eye-to-eye. "I need you to hear me and understand. Matrimony will change nothing for me. I will continue to be called away often, and you will be in that big house or tucked away in the country alone. This is the only life you will be allowed to have with me. I know it isn't what you want, but it cannot be changed. Carefully consider this before deciding you want me for your husband."

She shook out of his hold and returned to her seat across the carriage. "Well, you have given me much to think about on top of the Lady Van Middleburg situation."

"There is nothing for you to do about Lady Van Middleburg. Strike it from your mind, and I will address the matter."

"You cannot command my thoughts, Margrave. And *you* should carefully consider whether you want to leave me alone when I become your wife. No telling what kind of trouble I might get into without you around to boss me."

"Fair point." He smiled, even though it seemed to pain him. "Lanfort Castle has an old dungeon. I suppose I could toss you in shackles if you are too much to handle."

She was heartened to hear him speak of a future together, and he was only teasing about the dungeon. They were making progress.

"The shackles *must* be gold," she said. "Iron irritates my skin."

"Only the best for Miss Sophia Darlington."

"At last, we agree, and there is no one better suited for me than you."

He grumbled a bit under his breath, but he was smiling.

"Now, about Lady Van Middleburg." She met his gaze, holding it and daring him to tell her to mind her own affairs again. "I am uncertain how today's event relates to Regina and her husband's encounter with the elder Duke of Stanhurst and Lord Geoffrey, but it does not require a genius to conclude a connection exists."

Crispin's face turned to stone. "What encounter? Is this what you have been keeping from me?"

"Regina and Evangeline would be displeased with me for saying anything, but since I am the only one who must suffer your ill-temper..."

The fire was back in his eyes. When it appeared she was about to receive a scolding to end all scoldings, she blurted what she knew about the men's untimely demises.

"The duke and Lord Geoffrey interrupted Regina's wedding night at the Pulteney Hotel. Stanhurst came looking for his mistress, but Claudine was safe at Wedmore House. He had convinced himself Xavier and Claudine were having an affair."

She waved away Margrave's question before he could voice it.

"It's a much longer story and unimportant now. Regina hid while the duke tore apart Xavier's rooms. Stanhurst found nothing, but he was not satisfied. He forced Xavier to lead him to Claudine, but Xavier would never place us in danger by bringing him to Wedmore House."

"He led them to the docks."

"Yes, but Xavier didn't murder the duke or his son. The murderer is a man named Farrin. I do not know if it is a first or last name."

Crispin's eyes flared slightly while his expression remained unchanged. It was enough to rouse her suspicion.

"Do you know this Farrin fellow?" she asked.

"The name is familiar, but I cannot place him. Who is he?"

Sophia didn't know whether she believed him, but he

had no reason to lie. "Farrin is a thief for hire with a special interest in antiquities. He sent Xavier into Wedmore House to steal a map from Uncle Charles."

"Your sister married a thief?"

"No, *Farrin* is the thief. Xavier was trying to earn his freedom."

"Freedom from—?"

She held up a hand, interrupting. "Again, this detail is unimportant. What matters is Farrin murdered the duke and his son, and the blackguard would have killed my sister and her husband if Benny hadn't acted the hero."

"Where is Farrin now?" he asked in a quiet voice. "The magistrate did not take him into custody. By all accounts, no crime was ever committed. How did Farrin escape punishment?"

"He didn't, exactly." She took a deep breath to calm the butterflies fluttering in her belly. Crispin was a reasonable man. He would understand. "Please believe me, Benny did nothing wrong. He tried to save Farrin even though the blackguard didn't deserve mercy, but it was hopeless. Farrin drowned in the Thames. I expect the watermen will discover his fate eventually."

The muscles in Crispin's jaw bulged several times while his penetrating stare agitated the butterflies inside her. The silence became unbearable. "Do you have nothing to say?" she asked.

"You've kept this secret for weeks. When I asked you what you knew about Stanhurst and Lord Geoffrey, you held your tongue."

"I understand you are unhappy"—she licked her dry lips —"but I was respecting my sister's wishes. You have a tendency to take charge of situations, and Regina needs to be in control. You know this about her. She did not want Auntie to know either."

"You are not Regina. I appealed to *you*. I trusted you to be honest with me."

"I know." A lump formed in her throat; she swallowed around it. She couldn't hold his gaze any longer and stared at her lap.

She could pretend her reticence had stemmed from a promise to keep her sister's confidence or blame it on a desire to protect Benny, but both were partial truths. She had kept Crispin in the dark, because it had felt like justice. *Tit for tat.* He pushed her away; she closed him out.

"I am sorry," she murmured. "If I could have foreseen the consequences... But how was I to know you would have an interest in this matter?"

"You believe I have no interest in your welfare or that of your sisters?"

Her head popped up. "No, I have never questioned your loyalty to us. Your interest in the duke is surprising. Please, forgive me for not being forthcoming. I would never forgive myself if Lady Van Middleburg's man had harmed you."

The planes of Crispin's handsome face lost their hard edges, and his chest deflated as he exhaled. "I do not hold you responsible for today. This was my doing. You saw first hand the danger involved, so I will ask you to leave this alone."

While she understood his wishes, she could not agree, and they were nearing Wedmore House without being any closer to solving the problem of Lady Van Middleburg. Sophia didn't trust the woman would be satisfied with today's outcome, and her actions proved she shouldn't be underestimated. "Who do you think Lady Van Middleburg's associates are?"

Crispin drew back. "How do you know she has associates?"

"A lady cannot hire thugs without assistance. She would risk being recognized and her reputation would suffer. How would she even know where to find men of sullied character?"

"Sound reasoning. You have given me a good place to turn my attention."

She sighed, happy he was accepting her help. The carriage was slowing. "I feel I must repeat my apology for not being forthcoming earlier. You have my word it will not happen again."

He reached across the space; she placed her hand in his. "Thank you, Sophia."

It wasn't until he saw her settled at Wedmore House and took his leave that she realized he hadn't given the same promise of honesty.

Law! He'd even sidestepped her question about why he was poking his snout where it didn't belong in the first place. Perhaps she must resort to sitting on him after all.

NINE

A<small>FTER SUNDOWN THAT EVENING,</small> C<small>RISPIN WAS SAVED A CLIMB</small>
to the second floor balcony when he discovered an
unlocked window at the Duke of Stanhurst's town house.
He marveled at the duke's lackadaisical approach to
security as he slipped inside undetected. One would expect
a double murder in the family to urge one into securing the
premises, but that was not the case at Walsh Place.

If he were to offer Stanhurst advice, he would start with
a discussion of the household staff. Their habits left the
duke vulnerable to thieves and all sorts of men of unsavory
character. Two days earlier at the Covent Garden market,
Crispin had encountered a chatty young kitchen maid
under the duke's employ. He had walked away from the
meeting with knowledge of the household routines, the
duke's dining schedule for the week, and much of the
servants' gossip.

As he inched toward the main staircase with his boots in
hand, the faint sound of conversation emanated from the
hall below. The servants were sitting down to supper. On
the evenings that the duke was away, the butler demanded

every house servant arrive to the table at the appointed time. According to the maid, the butler commanded the household like a captain would a ship. Everything had a place, routines never varied, and tardiness was punished.

Knowing he would not be discovered any time soon, Crispin did not rush on the stairs. He reached the landing and veered toward the duke's quarters in the South wing. Once, he'd caught Stanhurst peering at him from a window in this part of the house, even though his servants had insisted the duke wasn't in residence.

The second door Crispin tried led to the duke's bedchamber. He let himself inside. A small fire burned in the hearth, chasing away the chill of evening and casting long shadows in the room.

Stanhurst's valet would come above stairs in two hours to turn down the bedding and light a lamp, allowing Crispin to search the room at his leisure. Hell, he might even help himself to the decanter on the side table before retiring to the adjoining bedchamber to await the duke's return.

He dropped his boots on the thick carpet and approached the table to ascertain if the duke preferred brandy or scotch. Crispin's father used to say one could tell a man's character from his choice of spirits. Since the meeting with his brother months earlier, he had been cataloguing memories of his father. Perhaps some part of him hoped for another opportunity to share them with Alexander, although their awkward parting almost guaranteed Crispin's brother would not seek him out again.

Their sire had been a great father. Even when he had lain in his sick bed, his only concern had been for Crispin.

Wedmore will see that you want for nothing. I have his word he will watch over you when I cannot.

All Crispin's life, his father had seen to it that he receive the best of everything, and Alexander would have enjoyed the same advantages if their mother hadn't taken him away. The stables had been stocked with the highest quality horseflesh. Crispin's early education came from the most prestigious tutors. Even his godfather had been chosen to better him.

In his younger days, Charles Wedmore had been a superior sportsman, something Crispin's father's weak heart had never allowed him to be. Everything Crispin needed to know about being a man, he had learned from his father's oldest friend.

Crispin removed the silver stopper from the decanter to examine it closer. It was engraved with the Stanhurst ram and the Latin words *fortis in arduis.*

"Fortune favors the brave," he murmured.

The duke was not upholding the family motto by hiding behind his servants. Perhaps he would redeem himself tonight and prove he was braver than he appeared.

Crispin poured two fingers into a glass and sampled the liquor. *Brandy.* A man averse to taking risks, his father would say. Crispin would test his father's theory when he had Stanhurst in front of him.

Sophia's observation that Lady Van Middleburg had required a man's assistance to hire ruffians was astute. Perhaps Stanhurst was that man; perhaps he was not. With Sophia safe at home with her aunt, Crispin had all night to persuade the duke to talk.

Sophia had begged his discretion when they had arrived at Wedmore House earlier. She didn't wish to worry Aunt Beatrice unnecessarily by telling her about the attack, especially since Sophia had escaped the ordeal without injury. Crispin had agreed to keep quiet for the moment on one condition; she must claim a headache and beg off attending the opera that evening.

He did not condone lying to her kin, but the account might lead to questions about what she had been doing in the alley, and Sophia deserved time to decide if she truly wanted to become his wife. She was young and idealistic, but she was sensible, too. Once she realized a union with him would not be as she dreamed, she would likely reconsider.

"Devil take it," he muttered as a slow burn invaded his gut. He abandoned the brandy and took a turn around the room, his mood irritable now.

He learned all he could from the duke's belongings then grabbed his boots from the floor and retired to the adjoining bedchamber to await Stanhurst's return. The valet came at the appointed hour. Crispin tracked his movements by sound: the thud of another log on the fire, the squeak of wardrobe doors, and eventually the closing of the bedchamber door and footsteps fading in the corridor.

The duke arrived home a short while later. Outside the adjoining bedchamber door, he told one of the servants he did not wish to be disturbed. "I will ring if I require assistance."

"Aye, Your Grace."

Crispin waited until the rustling sounds coming from the duke's room ceased before creeping toward the adjoining door. It opened on a well-oiled hinge, making no sound.

Stanhurst was sitting in the brown leather chair with his back to him; a book lay open on his lap. Crispin left the door ajar and slipped into the room. He took care with his steps, having learned which floorboards to avoid when he had explored the room earlier. He stopped a couple of feet from the duke.

"At last, you are in residence, Your Grace."

Stanhurst startled and dropped the book. It landed with a thump on the carpet.

Keeping the duke's hands within sight to make certain he didn't reach for a weapon, Crispin rounded the chair, pointing his own firearm at Stanhurst. The duke's frigid gray gaze swept over him.

"You are a determined man, Lord Margrave. I cannot decide if I find your tenacity impressive or vexing."

"No need to play coy. I am certain it is the latter." Crispin sat on the chair opposite the duke and lowered the pistol to his lap without relaxing his guard. "You have been avoiding me, Stanhurst."

"And yet, here you are." The duke hadn't blinked since Crispin sat. "I surmise you are not one for subtle rebuffs."

"Subtlety has never been my preferred method of communication. It requires more effort than it is worth." He leaned back in the chair and propped his ankle across his knee. "Security is lax around here. You should speak with your servants. No telling what manner of vermin might find their way inside."

Stanhurst's stony expression didn't alter. "As you have demonstrated. Will that be all? You interrupted me at an especially interesting place in my reading."

Crispin read the title on the book spine. *A Treatise on the Mathematical Principals of Architectural Symmetry.* "Doubtful, but like you, I would rather be otherwise engaged this evening. I will be brief. What do you know about your father's involvement with a man called Farrin?"

No flicker of recognition crossed Stanhurst's face. "A man with only one name?"

"That is what he calls himself. I suspect it is an alias."

"I do not make a habit of mingling with men who require an alias, and I have never heard of him."

The duke's measured calm was impressive. He would

make a worthy foe if they were equally matched, but they were not. Crispin's training afforded him an advantage.

"I was under the impression your father and brother knew Farrin well," Crispin said. "They entertained him at Claudine Bellerose's town house on several occasions."

Stanhurst sniffed and proudly looked down his regal nose at him. "I've devoted the last five years to running the family estate and tending to my sisters while my father pursued his own interests. I did not keep abreast of his personal affairs."

"You cannot deny you are familiar with your father's mistress. You gifted her with the deed to the house in Marylebone after his death. One might surmise you were paying her to keep your father's secrets."

Stanhurst scoffed. "My father had no secrets. Everyone knew of his obsession with the actress. I can assure you from the wariness in which I am regarded at every gathering, no one has forgotten about his cruel treatment of her either. I presented Miss Bellerose with the deed to put this nasty business behind me. Is all this sneaking around and questioning my servants on behalf of Miss Bellerose? Did she put you up to it?"

Crispin leaned forward, his arm casually draped across his thigh. "Your father had a man kidnapped once—to punish him for trying to help Miss Bellerose escape England. Were you aware of that little secret?"

"N-no." Crimson rose in the duke's face; his calm faltered. "Is this true?"

"My source is reliable."

The duke exhaled. "Damnation. If this rumor makes the rounds, no father or mother will allow their daughter in the same room with me. I will never find a suitable wife."

"A wife?" Crispin drew back. "Your father and brother were murdered, and your concern is with making a marriage match rather than finding their killer. One might wonder if you had a hand in their deaths."

Stanhurst nailed him with a withering stare. "One would quickly discover I've not been to London in over a year, and I was fond of my brother, if not our sire."

As the duke surmised, Crispin had discovered that fact during his investigation. Stanhurst was not a suspect, but neither did Crispin care about solving the murders. His mission was to determine Farrin's fate. Nothing more.

"I inherited a failing estate from my father," Stanhurst said, his frankness a surprise. "Bringing his murderer to justice will not change my situation. Any concern I have has been reserved for my younger sisters."

Crispin recalled hearing that upon Old Stanhurst's death his eldest son had become guardian to five girls not yet of marriageable age. He hadn't given it much thought at the time. "Do not tell me you covered up the murders to protect your sisters' marriage prospects."

Stanhurst squared his shoulders, challenging him with his stance. "My sisters' chances of making a good match would be difficult enough given our father's reputation for being hot-tempered. The pitiful dowries he set aside for them will make it impossible. My title is the only currency I possess to secure their futures. Is there no one in your life you care enough to protect?"

Crispin weighed the likelihood of this man playing a part in placing Sophia in danger today; his fingers tightened around the stock of the pistol. "I would not be lying in wait for you if I cared for no one."

Stanhurst scoffed. "It seems you've developed a liking for Miss Bellerose after all. Tell my father's paramour she has received all she will from me, and I am not amenable to extortion. I will ruin both of you if you further sully our family name with this preposterous tale of kidnapping." He bent forward to retrieve his book from the floor. "I want you to go."

"I am not here on the actress's behalf. She is a stranger to me. I've come to gather information about Farrin. What business did your father and brother have with him? I want to know the reason he killed them."

Stanhurst's breath rushed from him as if he'd been struck in the gut. His mouth open and closed while he searched for his voice, or perhaps the correct words. "How —how do you know this man murdered Father and Geoffrey? The magistrate said they probably surprised smugglers."

"There were witnesses that night. I cannot tell you their names."

The duke's complexion was pale, but he drew himself up in the chair, his spine seemingly fashioned from iron. "Where is this man now? He will be brought to justice."

"Farrin is dead. He will give you no more trouble." Crispin arched an eyebrow. "Did you believe him—the magistrate?"

"He seemed cocksure of himself." The duke swallowed hard. "I had my doubts, but the magistrate provided reassurance that my father and brother were innocent victims."

"You had doubts. Elaborate."

"How does this concern you?" Stanhurst ran his steely gaze over Crispin; he paused on the firearm. "My brother was a frequent patron of the Den of Iniquity. Father covered his gambling debts more than once. If you hold Geoffrey's vowels, you have come here in vain. I will not honor his debts."

Crispin ignored the duke's insinuation. It was best to allow him to draw his own conclusions about his interest in the Stanhurst family.

"Lady Van Middleburg waylaid me at a ball last night," Crispin said. "Your cousin warned me to leave you alone."

"Good Lord! Ida did not have my blessing to speak with you."

"Your cousin acted alone?"

"I've never mentioned you to her, which means someone on my staff has been whispering in her ear." Stanhurst's jaw hardened. "I will question the servants and firmly put Ida in her place when she calls. She calls every day, so I expect her tomorrow."

That was excessive by anyone's standards. Crispin's suspicions were roused even more. "What does she want when she calls?"

Stanhurst blinked as if the question was odd. "To offer her sympathies, of course."

"She offers her sympathy every day?"

"She is family and wishes to help. Do you find this unusual? She offers to sort Geoffrey's belongings, but I've ordered her to leave my brother's chambers untouched. I will complete the task"—Stanhurst's eyes misted and he roughly dashed away the dampness—"in time."

Crispin looked away. He refused to feel a kinship with this man. Sorting through his own father's personal items after he was gone had been hard. He'd been numb for the wake but felt every scrape over his raw heart when the time came to face the task. He had been avoiding the master's chambers for months. The sight of the room without his father had left him adrift. It was too quiet, too cold. Nevertheless, he had completed the task then buried the memory of his father like he'd buried any thoughts of his mother and brother all those years ago. It was what his father would want.

Crispin shook off his sudden irritation and sharpened his focus on what brought him to the duke's home. "Could

Lady Van Middleburg be searching for something in your brother's chambers?"

"Such as a snuffbox or our grandfather's gold watch?" The duke shook his head, his laughter humorless. "The lady is meddlesome, not a thief."

"More like an aspiring boss of the underworld."

Stanhurst's brow wrinkled. "Pardon?"

Crispin didn't fully trust the duke's claim of ignorance, but neither was he in a position to prove Stanhurst was lying—yet. He rose from the chair, the firearm dangling by his side. "No heiress will come within thirty feet of you if I discover you were your cousin's accomplice in the attack on me this morning."

Stanhurst's jaw fell.

"You appear genuinely shocked, Your Grace." Crispin's smile lacked humor. "You might have a future on the stage."

He left Stanhurst gaping in his chambers and saluted a befuddled maid as he passed her in the corridor. In principle, his mission was complete. Farrin was dead and posed no threat to the Crown, but Crispin's meeting with the duke left him with too many pegs that didn't fit holes.

In the morning, he would inform the Lord Chamberlain of Farrin's fate, but his investigation was far from complete. Lady Van Middleburg's plot to scare Crispin away reeked of desperation, and he intended to uncover what she was attempting to hide.

Coded Message sent to Mr. Theodore Wolfe's rented rooms in London:

zhxmmv xcvkpgp iru oedl ctcv ncc mv ffko kq xal fjomepmgn. xjtp eq sgl ctc lrxi alewl jiqq fl.

Deciphered Message

Gather Garrick and make your way back to the beginning. Tell no one you have heard from me.

Farrin

TEN

AN OIL LAMP BURNED LOW IN THE WINDOWLESS BOARDING house kitchen, hiding the dust and spider webs collecting in the corners. Jewel usually kept a tidy house—aye, spotless—but these days, fastidiousness was the least of her concerns. Nursing her man back to health required her devotion and tireless efforts, not to mention the better part of a bottle of gin.

The gin was for Farrin's lingering cough. Jewel never touched spirits, not after seeing how possessed by drink her husband had become before his death. He had been a mean bastard while sober. He was a brute when he was deep in his cups. The only good deed he ever performed was bringing Farrin into her life.

She flicked a nervous glance over her shoulder where Farrin's two men were seated at the wide plank table waiting for him to come below stairs. They had arrived at her door at sunrise, just as Farrin predicted, and they were as intimidating as she remembered—especially the dead-eyed one staring a hole through her. A shiver snaked up her spine as she turned back toward the fire to ladle porridge from the iron pot into a bowl.

Like Farrin had done for her husband, he raised had Garrick and Wolfe from the gutter. They were loyal like dogs, and well trained, but only a flimsy veil existed between civility and wildness for these gutter rats.

Farrin strolled into the kitchen like he was the King himself as she was carrying a bowl to place in front of the dead-eyed one. Her chest swelled with pride at belonging to such a regal man. Her mama said she would never amount to anything, and Jewel hoped the witch was rolling over in her grave now.

Farrin was a man of importance and great influence—the man who advised King George and held Napoleon's fate in his hands. She'd had no idea how powerful he was until he lay delirious in her bed, spilling his secrets.

She delivered the bowl of porridge to Wolfe and hurried to dish up a serving for Farrin as he took his place at the head of the table. The hair on the back of her neck stood on end. Garrick was still watching her.

"You trust her?" he ground out.

She bristled at the insinuation. Farrin was her world. She would sooner cut out her tongue than betray him, but she said nothing in her defense. She knew better than to argue with her guests. When Farrin had set her up with the boarding house, she made promises. She only accepted the boarders he sent her way. She never uttered an unpleasant word against them. If she saw or heard anything, she always pleaded ignorance.

Garrick's insult was too hard to ignore, however, and she aimed a scowl at him when she slid a bowl in front of Farrin. Her lover grabbed her arm above the elbow and jerked her forward. She cried out when her knee banged into the table; her mouth gaped. Hunched over the uneven plank top, she was eye level with Farrin. A blistering heat invaded her cheeks, and she darted a glance toward his men. Wolfe crammed porridge into his mouth like a ravenous dog, not allowing the outburst to interrupt his breakfast.

Farrin smiled benevolently and pulled her closer to place a kiss on her forehead. "I trust her." His voice was still raspy from the lung fever he'd caught from falling into the River Thames. A weaker man would have died, but *her* man had regained most of his strength. She reflected his loving smile.

"Leave us, my pet," he said.

"Aye, my lord." Her deference was to his position of power rather than his birthright, although she suspected he was higher born than he led anyone to believe. His manners were more refined than any of the men under his service.

She slipped from the room but didn't go far. If he later asked if she overheard his conversation with his men, she would deny it, and he would believe her. He always did.

Farrin coughed and cleared his throat. "What news do you bring from the streets?"

"No one knows what happened to you," Wolfe said in his usual cheerful manner. Whether he was discussing the weather or gutting a rabbit, his disposition remained the same. "There are rumors you might be dead. Garrick and me, we started to believe it until your message came."

"Gossipmongers are morbid creatures."

"Aye, and some of them have the Lord Chamberlain's ear it seems. Viscount Margrave was summoned before him last week, and now Margrave is asking questions about Old Stanhurst and his boy."

As usual, Wolfe carried the conversation while his

cohort probably fantasized about the death and dismemberment of his enemies. Garrick was a beast. *And how dare he question my loyalty?*

"Has Margrave learned anything useful?" Farrin asked.

"Not yet," Wolfe said, shaking his head. "The Stanhurst family went to great lengths to cover up what happened to the duke and Lord Geoffrey. Margrave will get no cooperation from the current duke."

"I expect his investigation will prove thorough," Farrin said. "I trained him well."

Jewel peeked through the hole in the wall between the pantry and kitchen. Garrick's heavy brow dropped lower over his frigid eyes as he stared in the direction of her hiding place. Her heart stopped. *He sees me.*

The brute didn't sound the alarm. "Let me at Margrave; he'll not be a problem."

"Killing Margrave won't do nothing," Wolfe said reasonably. "The Lord Chamberlain will find someone else to do his dirty work. It is the witnesses that pose a problem."

Jewel eased away from the hole and leaned her head against the wall. Her heart continued to batter her ribs. If Garrick told Farrin she was spying on them, he would be disappointed. Still, she couldn't leave her hiding spot without the floorboards creaking, and there was a chance Garrick hadn't seen her at all. *Pray God, please let it be true.*

"Wolfe is right," Farrin said. "Margrave is harmless as long as there is no one left to talk. The map Xavier Vistoire and Wedmore's niece found was a fake, but they saw what happened at the docks."

The mysterious map again.

In Farrin's delirious ramblings, he had begged Jewel to bring it to him. She tried to tell him she knew nothing about it. He became agitated and berated her for her stupidity. He'd said in the wrong hands, he would be marked for death.

To calm him, she had promised it was safe. It had worked, too. He'd grabbed her hand, showered it with kisses, and thanked her for rescuing him from the gallows.

Gallows, indeed. Jewel's man was not a criminal. He was a patriot, the leader of the King's secret detachment. Ambitious men often tried to overthrow those in power. Farrin had told her so many times. She would bet her life an envious man was trying to cast the blame on Farrin for something he did not do—probably this Margrave fellow— or Charles Wedmore. *The devil's spawn,* Farrin called him during the worst of his illness. A decent man would have no such moniker.

Unable to resist temptation, she put her eye to the hole again.

"Vistoire and the girl stumbled across something, though," Farrin said. "Vistoire thinks the map leads to the Black Death."

Garrick cursed under his breath.

Farrin formed a fist, opening and closing his fingers like he did when he was thinking. "Wedmore might have kept a record of his investigation. It breaks the first tenet of the Regent's Consul, but he is a renegade. Always has been. He did not request permission before setting off in pursuit of a suspected traitor. Why would he observe the rules of the Consul?"

The conversation made little sense to Jewel. Perhaps Garrick and Wolfe were confused, too. Neither man had an answer to his question.

"No cause to worry yet," Wolfe said. "Unless Wedmore's niece met with the Home Office before she left, she won't be talking to anyone soon. No telling where she and her bridegroom are or when they will return."

Farrin narrowed his eyes on Garrick. "What does he mean?"

"Vistoire and his bride took a honeymoon trip," Wolfe answered and shoveled another spoonful of porridge into his mouth. "Took one of the sisters too, the one with all those curls. Reminds me of my younger sister."

Garrick glared at him; Wolfe stopped yapping and swallowed. The scar that ran from Garrick's temple to the corner of his mouth twitched. When he spoke, his voice was grating to Jewel's ears, like a hoe scraping against rock. "An informant at the docks saw Mr. and Mrs. Vistoire and Wedmore's middle niece board a ship bound for Port Le Havre. The youngest niece and his aunt stayed behind."

Farrin drummed his fingers on the table and studied his men. "You *allowed* them to leave."

"We had no word they were going," Wolfe said with a defensive edge to his voice. "But now that we know you're alive and what to do, we will be watching for them to come back."

Garrick sneered. "There's a problem with the aunt and young one that can't wait. Margrave has been escorting the women around Town. If the old lady or girl knows anything, they might start yapping if they haven't already. I can take care of 'em. It would be my pleasure."

Wolfe recoiled. "You *want* to kill an old lady and a girl? What is wrong with you? Did your pa beat more than the pretty outta you?"

Garrick called him a bastard.

"Enough!" Fire flared in her man's eyes, his anger forging a blade that would mercilessly strike down his enemies. Jewel had seen his temper in action many times. In his boxing days, she would sneak to the fights to watch him obliterate his opponents. He had never been a large man, but his anger—when unleashed—became a giant, crowding the ring and sucking life from the air.

"Not just the two women. Margrave must go, too." His leer stole Jewel's breath. In that moment, he appeared as the devil incarnate. She wanted to run from this stranger, but her feet were rooted to the floorboards. "Wedmore signed their death warrants when he betrayed the Consul. He will pay for his treachery."

"With interest," Garrick growled, glee dancing in his cold eyes.

Wolfe's Adam's apple bobbed. For once, he appeared concerned. "Eh... wouldn't it be better if we left before Margrave figures out the truth? An execution's not a pretty matter for men like Garrick and me."

Garrick scoffed. "I ain't dying. Hell don't want me taking over."

"No one will be spared my wrath," Farrin snarled. "*Everyone* must be eliminated—even that bloody yapping dog. We will divide and conquer then meet at the designated place once the targets have been eliminated. Garrick will leave at once; Wolfe and I will follow tomorrow."

Jewel's heart leapt into her throat. Nothing frightened her more than losing Farrin. If he left her and never returned, what would become of her?

"Has there been any word of my brother's fate?" Farrin asked. "I hope he is starving on the streets, the ungrateful idiot."

"The Duke of Stanhurts' former mistress has taken Benny in," Wolfe said. "Gave him work at a small playhouse. I heard he even has a part on stage."

Garrick grunted. "Benny will get what's coming to him, too."

Farrin made no comment. The conversation turned to

more people she didn't know, and Jewel's mind was too troubled to pay attention. When Wolfe pushed from the table with his bowl to fill it again, she made her escape from the pantry.

She was above stairs bent over the bed to change the linens when Farrin found her. He alerted her to his presence when he slipped his arms around her waist. She jumped then laughed when he pulled her close to nuzzle her ear.

"I've loved you well, Jewel."

She smiled and sank against him, secure in his arms. "I have loved you more."

His gentleness was in sharp contrast to the fierce anger she had seen blazing in his eyes a moment earlier. He was always gentle with her. She had been foolish to fear him. He would come back to her. He loved her too much to abandon her.

She had no ties to London, or anywhere else. Her parents, siblings, and husband were long dead and buried. She only had Farrin, and he was all she needed. She wasn't stupid enough to ask him to take her with him, however. He would know she had been spying if she did, so she would wait until he sent for her, and she would leave the boarding house to fall into ruin for all she cared.

He kissed her cheek. "Run along to see Wolfe settled in his chamber while I rest." The sharp smack to her buttock was delivered in affection.

"Only Mr. Wolfe? Doesn't Mr. Garrick require a room?" she asked, feigning ignorance.

"Garrick offers his regrets, but he was needed elsewhere."

"Of course." She smiled, cognizant that questions would not be welcomed. "I will see to Mr. Wolfe and look in on you in a moment."

In truth, she was relieved Garrick wasn't staying under her roof. She couldn't sleep with him in close proximity for fear he might steal into the chamber she shared with Farrin and cut their throats as they slept. When she had voiced her concerns to Farrin once, he reassured her that Garrick and Wolfe would never raise a hand against anyone without his command. He was being naive. Men did many things when their superiors were not watching.

The kitchen was empty when she returned to the kitchen to grab an empty bucket for water to fill the washbasin she kept in Wolfe's chamber. She hoped he took the hint and cleaned the stink from his body. His name was fitting, because he smelled like a wild animal.

At the sink, she pumped water into a bucket until it was half-full and toted it upstairs. She was pouring it into the plain white pitcher when a feral stench assaulted her nose. She gagged a little as she turned to find Wolfe standing an arm's length away. Like Farrin, he walked on silent feet.

She nodded toward the basin and a sliver of lye soap she had left in a dish. She saved the good soap Farrin gave her for herself. "I'll retrieve a cloth, and you can have your privacy."

When she tried to step around him, he moved into her path, blocking the way. His bushy eyebrows drew together. "I knew your husband since we was boys. He never treated you right. I always thought you deserved better."

"Thank you," she said with a brief dip of her head. She didn't know how to curtsey like a real lady, but she had watched the ladybirds at Covent Garden and emulated their manners as best she could. With their pretty dresses and gentlemen patrons, they were as close as she would ever get to being in the presence of a lady.

"I'm real sorry, Jewel."

She scoffed, dismissing his sympathy. Her husband had

been dead to her for a long time before she saw him buried. Besides, it had been years since she had become a widow. It was silly to offer condolences now. "As I said, I'll be retrieving that cloth. Then I should look in on your commander."

She attempted to skirt around him again. He lunged; his meaty hands closed around her neck. The shock made her gasp. She couldn't catch her breath as his fingers cut off her air.

"You shouldn't have been listening in the pantry. I don't like killing no women. Sorry, Jewel. I'm sorry."

He kept muttering his apology and telling her that she deserved better while pinpricks of darkness slowly stole her sight. As she clung to the last scraps of awareness before fading into nothingness, she had one final thought. Wolfe wouldn't raise a hand against her without Farrin's command. The man she loved with every ounce of her being had ordered her death.

ELEVEN

Two days after the brush with Lady Van Middleburg's ruffians, Sophia and her great-aunt strolled arm-in-arm through their neighborhood. Happy blue skies made one forget there had been a morning rain shower, complete with window-rattling thunder.

A breeze rustled the lace trimming Sophia's bonnet. She glanced at her aunt, assessing if she was still spoiling for a fight.

"It turned out to be a pleasant afternoon," Sophia said. "I expect the Mayfair Ladies Charitable Society meeting will be well attended today."

"Yes," Aunt Beatrice agreed. "It is a shame Lady Van Middleburg is the hostess. I had more than I can stomach of that woman yesterday."

When the baroness had called at Wedmore House to collect the blankets Aunt Beatrice knitted for the foundling hospital, she took one look at Auntie's hard work, wrinkled her regal nose, and refused the donation. She deemed Aunt Beatrice's work too substandard, even for orphans.

"Pay her no mind, Auntie. One must have a heart to understand generosity."

Sophia did not elaborate. Aunt Beatrice knew nothing about the assault behind the Drayton Theatre, and Sophia wished to keep her in the dark. Like Crispin, her aunt would demand Sophia keep her distance from the baroness, which was quite impossible. Today's charitable society meeting afforded Sophia the perfect opportunity to search the Van Middleburg town house.

"The baroness is a prickly one to be sure," Aunt Beatrice said. "Her lady's maid probably has to let out her skirts to accommodate the quills protruding from her bum. Her drawers must be full of holes."

"Auntie!"

Aunt Beatrice laughed. "I will be biting my tongue all afternoon. Allow me this single moment of pleasure to imagine the old porcupine struggling to use the chamber pot."

Sophia playfully arched an eyebrow in censorship. "Do you truly intend to bite your tongue? Your current discourse leaves me with doubts."

"I will behave—"Aunt Beatrice's smile was everything mischievous—"if *she* does. I do not suffer fools in silence, dear girl."

"I am aware." Sophia leaned her head against her aunt's in a show of affection. "You make me proud to call you kin."

"Not nearly as proud as I am of you and your sisters." Aunt Beatrice sighed with contentment as they crossed the street and headed west. "Have I ever told you that you are my favorite?"

"You have, Auntie." Sophia smiled brightly. "I've heard you tell Regina and Evangeline that they are your favorites, too, but I know you only mean it when you say it to me."

"My clever girl, how dull London would be if you had

travelled to Athens with your sisters. I would be quite lost for companionship if I were alone."

Sophia's great-aunt loved her and her sisters equally, but she realized that she possessed a special place in Auntie's heart. As soon as Aunt Beatrice had arrived at Wedmore House with her trunks to mother her and her sisters, Sophia became her shadow. She was still her aunt's constant companion.

"You know I would never leave you alone, Auntie. When we take our honeymoon trip—"

"*We?*" Aunt Beatrice's thin eyebrows rose on her wrinkled forehead. "Have you selected a suitor?"

Sophia nearly choked as she realized her mistake. It was premature to discuss her future with Crispin when no firm agreement existed between them. He would offer for her hand in time, once he realized he needed her, and she must remain patient.

"I meant to say *I*. When I take my honeymoon trip, I would never dream of leaving you behind. There is no we— no gentleman, that is. You and I make a we." Sophia cleared her throat. "Oh, look! We have arrived."

Aunt Beatrice groaned, her attention diverted toward the Van Middleburg town house looming two houses away. "The trip was shorter than I anticipated."

"We could circle back later if you need more time to prepare," Sophia offered, praying her aunt wasn't having second thoughts. She couldn't attend the meeting alone.

"There isn't time. The meeting will be called to order soon."

With a determined nod, Aunt Beatrice marched toward the front door to grasp the brass knocker and gave it three hard raps. The door slowly swung open. A butler in black greeted them and ordered a footman standing by to lead them above stairs. When they entered the first floor drawing room, several ladies glanced in their direction before continuing their conversations.

Sophia gestured toward the refreshment table. "Would you like to take refreshment? I will fill a plate for you."

Aunt Beatrice screwed up her face, which Sophia took as a refusal.

Amelia Hillary, steadfast patroness of the Mayfair Ladies Charitable Society, approached with a stunning smile aimed at Sophia's aunt. "Miss Allred, how lovely of you to attend this week's meeting. I was unsure if you would grace us with your presence, and I am pleased to see you have."

"I am always happy to support the charitable efforts you sponsor, " Aunt Beatrice said. "May I introduce you to my great-niece, Sophia Darlington?"

"Yes, of course, it is a pleasure, Miss Darlington."

Mrs. Hillary was too kind to draw attention to Auntie's memory troubles. Sophia had been present when the lovely woman called at Wedmore House yesterday afternoon to apologize for the deplorable treatment Auntie had received and to humbly accept her gift for the orphans. In addition, Mrs. Hillary and Sophia had crossed paths many times this Season and were acquainted.

"Lady Norwick and I paid a visit to the foundling hospital this morning," Mrs. Hillary said to Aunt Beatrice. "The children were overcome with excitement over your gifts. I am in possession of a letter I transcribed expressing their gratitude. I intend to read the children's sentiments aloud during the meeting. Perhaps you would like to hear what the children had to say now?"

"How marvelous!" Aunt Beatrice beamed at the charity's founding patroness. "I would like that very much. Sophia darling, will you excuse us for a moment?"

"Of course, Auntie." She glanced at her dearest friend,

who was seated on a tufted plumb bench in a corner of the room. "It appears Lady Octavia arrived before us. Perhaps she would appreciate a companion."

When Mrs. Hillary whisked Aunt Beatrice away, Sophia approached her friend. Octavia sat with her arms crossed and a mutinous frown on her otherwise fetching face. Her dour demeanor lessened marginally when she spotted Sophia.

"Oh, dear," Sophia teased as she reached her friend. "Did your mother scold you and send you to the corner?"

Octavia's dark brows dropped low over her eyes. "Mama had the good sense to stay home. She sent me with Amy." She pointed toward her married older sister at the far end of the drawing room where she was playing cards with three other ladies. "Any time spent in Lady Lovelace's company is punishment enough."

"That widow is a menace," Sophia agreed.

Lady Lovelace was an unredeemable coquette who was never discouraged from flirting with a man by anything as frivolous as a betrothal. She had been buzzing around Octavia's intended like a bee gathering nectar ever since the pending nuptials were announced. Lord Ramsdell paid her no mind, but Sophia's friend took umbrage, and rightfully so.

Octavia scooted to one side of the bench and patted the place beside her.

Sophia sat. "What has she done now?"

"She said my gown reminds her of small pox," Octavia grumbled as she grabbed a fistful of pink dotted skirts and shook them.

Lady Lovelace truly was a shrew.

"Pay her no mind." Sophia dispensed this advice a lot when discussing Lady Lovelace, but she didn't know how else to handle women who viewed every other female as her sworn enemy. "She is only jealous because you wear the pattern so well."

Octavia shrugged as a begrudging smile quirked her lips. "I look marvelous, do I not? Madame Delannoy is a genius."

"You look lovely. Even I am envious and I *adore* you."

Octavia giggled, her good nature restored. "Thank you."

"Thank you for attending," Sophia said. "You must know I wouldn't have asked you to endure the widow's company under normal circumstances."

"Your message indicated it was important."

She nodded. "I need you to cause a distraction."

"Now?" Octavia sat up straighter, interest sparking in the depths of her eyes.

"After everyone arrives. Would you mind too much?"

"Not in the least. It would be my pleasure." An impish smile played across Octavia's lips. "I love a good distraction."

Sophia laughed and squeezed her friend's hand in gratitude and affection. She never had to explain herself to Octavia. She was the type of loyal person who would dive head first into the Thames without question if done in the service of a friend.

Octavia's gaze seemed to follow Lady Lovelace as the widow made her way to a small table laden with a platter of sandwiches, cakes, and fresh fruit. Octavia's eyes narrowed; she puckered her lips.

"Are you certain you are all right?" Sophia asked.

"I *will* be."

Following her friend's example, Sophia asked no questions. Octavia was likely plotting a wickedly marvelous distraction, and she did her best work alone.

Sophia linked their arms to drag her friend from the bench. "Neither of us are wallflowers, Lady Octavia. Let's stop hiding in the corner before someone mistakes us for one."

Sophia spotted Aunt Beatrice seated in the middle of a long sofa between Mrs. Hillary and Lady Norwick. The best friends had seen to Auntie's comfort by propping a feather pillow behind her back and retrieving refreshment for her. When Aunt Beatrice spoke, Lady Norwick tossed her head back and laughter exploded into the air. Sophia smiled, feeling reassured Aunt Beatrice was in good company and could do without her for a while.

Sophia and Octavia stopped to exchange pleasantries with the other guests as they took a turn around the room. After a few minutes, Octavia whispered in her ear, "The time is nigh."

She chuckled over her friend's dramatic delivery of words. "Do your best, soldier. Make your brothers proud."

"Be quick about whatever it is you are doing. I do not know how long I can cause a commotion."

Octavia pasted on a bright smile and strolled toward the refreshment table where her nemesis was stuffing a watercress sandwich into her mouth.

"Lady Lovelace," Octavia called. "You have, uh—" She waggled her finger at the widow then pointed to her own teeth.

"Pardon?" The lady plopped the plate she was holding onto the table and dabbed at her mouth with a lacy handkerchief.

"There is nothing on your lips," Octavia said. "Your trouble is *there*—in the front."

Octavia's loud conversation began to capture attention, and the ladies stared in her and Lady Lovelace's direction.

Red washed over the widow's face. "Are you teasing me? Is this retaliation for what I said about your gown? I meant it as a compliment."

"How could I take your earlier observation as anything other than a compliment?" Octavia appeared very innocent when she batted her long lashes. "The color of small pox is the latest fashion."

A couple of ladies standing nearby snickered.

"Unlike you, Lady Lovelace, I am trying to be helpful. This *is* a charitable society, or have you forgotten?" Octavia flicked her hand as if swatting flies. "If you wish to converse with others with something hideous between your teeth..."

"Hideous?" Lady Lovelace rushed to the other side of the room to peer into the looking glass. "Where? I see nothing in my teeth."

Baroness Van Middleburg grabbed her guest's shoulder to turn her away from the mirror. "Allow me to look. You cannot see a thing without spectacles."

Lady Lovelace sputtered. "That is *you*. I-I do not wear spectacles."

"Oh, stop resisting and open your mouth." Their hostess tipped her head to the side when the widow flashed her teeth. "Yes, Lady Octavia is correct. I see something."

Lady Lovelace whipped back toward the mirror. "Where? I see nothing."

The other guests—minus Aunt Beatrice and her companions—crowded around the widow for a turn at examining her teeth.

"It's the start of a rotting tooth, I think," Lady Corbin said.

Lady Lovelace cried out in despair.

Octavia raised her glass in Sophia's direction and mouthed, "Godspeed."

As her friend approached the widow to render her own opinion, Sophia snuck from the room and almost collided with a footman carrying a tray of sandwiches.

"Pardon me, miss." A crimson blush inched up his neck and face.

"No, no, I should have been watching where I was going." She dropped her head and feigned a shy smile. "Could you direct me toward the water closet?"

"Turn left at the end of the corridor. It is behind the door across from his lordship's study."

She looked up, her eyes wide. "I do hope Lord Van Middleburg is not disturbed by the noise. The Mayfair Ladies Charitable Society can cause quite a ruckus when we set our minds to it."

The footman chuckled uneasily, as if he was unsure it would be appropriate to find her comment humorous. "Lord Van Middleburg is at his club today, Miss. You needn't worry about disturbing him."

How convenient. "Thank you. I am greatly relieved."

Since the study seemed like a logical place to start searching, she set off in that direction. She didn't encounter anyone else in the corridor, and a quick peek into the study confirmed it was empty.

"Havers," she mumbled when she stepped inside and pulled the door closed behind her.

Lord Van Middleburg's private area was a mess. Books and papers covered the entire surface of his desk and two side tables. Even one of the chairs held a stack of books. It was daunting enough to make her want to run in the other direction; she considered it. What little time she had to search for clues would be spent sifting through the baron's belongings. Still, Lady Van Middleburg might be the mastermind behind the attack, but she had required someone's assistance. Sophia wagered on her husband being that man.

She ran a quick glance over the books stacked on the

side tables and chair as she made her way to stand in front of the desk. A closer view of the mess dashed her spirits.

She sighed. *Where to start?*

There were more books than papers, so she began with the opened post left discarded on his desk, fighting the urge to organize as she worked. As it turned out, her worries about wasting her time were justified. She found nothing of importance in the papers. It would have been wiser to seek out and search Lady Van Middleburg's chambers, but Sophia wouldn't have enough time now. Her absence would be noticed before too long.

Halfheartedly, she moved on to the books, not expecting to make any great discoveries. The abundance of tomes around the room suggested Lord Van Middleburg was an avid reader, but his treatment of books left much to be desired. Pages were bent at the corners, some were ripped, and others showed evidence of past meals. Evangeline, her bibliophile sister, would be scandalized by the man's abuse.

Sophia reached for a black leather-bound book that had been left open and placed face down on a stack of papers. Turning it over, she noted the cracked spine and carefully flipped through the loose sheets.

3 August, 4 August, 5 August.

Each page of the book was dedicated to a day of the month. Times and locations had been scribbled across the pages in barely legible handwriting. Perhaps it was an attempt by Lord Van Middleburg to keep organized, although the task usually fell to a gentleman's secretary.

At first, it appeared nothing out of the ordinary was written in the book—a meeting with a banker here, a lecture there—but as she looked back a few months, she began to notice a pattern of late night appointments occurring in early spring.

Midnight – Griffin. Simply designated with the letter G or letters BG at times.

She knew no one by the name of Griffin, but Lord Van Middleburg's book suggested they were well acquainted.

"What are we going to do about the wool in your ears?" a man asked from the doorway.

Sophia jumped. "Margrave," she said with an edge of irritation when she recognized his voice. She spun to face him. "Do not sneak up on me like that. What are you doing here?"

He returned her glower and closed the door. She hadn't heard it open. "I could ask you the same."

"I am a member of the Mayfair Ladies Charitable Society. I was invited. You were not."

He sauntered toward her, appearing as calm as he would strolling through the park while her heart was still thrashing in her chest from the scare. "We agreed you would leave Lady Van Middleburg to me. I could have sworn you heard me, but now I must question if your ears are stuffed with wool."

She sniffed indignantly. "They are *not*, Lord Ludicrous, and I agreed to nothing of the sort. How did you make it past the butler?"

"There was no butler manning the terrace door, and Lady Van Middleburg's servants are preoccupied."

"You walked inside without permission?"

He arched an eyebrow. "It was more practical than dancing." As he reached the desk, he held out his hand. "Whatever you have there, I will take it. You should run along before someone finds you snooping."

She rolled her eyes and passed the book. She would leave when she was good and ready. "It appears to be Lord Van Middleburg's schedule. Heaven only knows why he seems to keep it himself rather than entrusting his secretary with the task."

Crispin thumbed through the pages. "Perhaps he has something to hide."

"Such as a regular rendezvous with a man named Griffin?"

He looked up from the book, curiosity brightening his eyes and stoking her excitement. She might have found a real clue.

"The baron hasn't met with the man in four weeks," she said, "but prior, it was a weekly engagement. Here, let me show you."

She reached across him to turn the pages. The back of her arm brushed his chest; he inhaled sharply. She pretended not to notice his reaction to her touch, but satisfaction swelled inside her. When she reached the appropriate page, she pointed out the words.

"Midnight, Griffin. The times and days change, and sometimes he designates the meeting with the letters BG, or simply G. What do you make of it?"

Crispin's brow furrowed as he flipped the pages, presumably verifying her claim about the baron's recurring engagement. "Griffin is likely a place rather than a person. There is a tavern located on the South side of London with the name Ye Olde Black Griffin—BG—but it is not the sort of establishment gentlemen of means frequent."

She smiled. "Yet, you are familiar with it."

He glanced at her briefly before returning his attention to the book. "I have frequented a number of places most gentlemen wouldn't dare to tread."

"You've intruded on a ladies' gathering. No need to state the obvious."

He stifled a grin; his gorgeous hazel eyes sparkled. Their color was as changeable as he was.

"I must admit, I expected a lecture when I saw you standing in the doorway," she said.

"Indeed?" He arched a blond brow. "I was under the impression lecturing was a poor use of my time. You pay me no heed in the end."

"There, there." She patted his forearm as if to comfort him. "Do not take it personally, my lord. I am much too independent-minded to blindly follow *anyone's* direction."

"You are a vexing woman, Sophia Darlington. Yet, I find myself uncommonly pleased to find you here today."

A genuine smile broke through his control. The world around her brightened, and she recalled the reason she had always been drawn to him. Her memories of Crispin as a young man were quite nice, like the time he had tracked Cupid to a fox den when the dog went missing. He and the poodle fell in a bog on the way home and had returned smelling like boiled eggs and Hades, but Crispin had been laughing. He had always found the humor in even the worst of situations in those days. It did her heart good to realize that part of him still existed.

"I rather like this mellow version of you, Crispin."

"Do not grow accustomed to it," he teased. "There is a meeting on Van Middleburg's schedule for tonight. I should follow the baron and see which of us is right. Is Griffin a man or a tavern? Do you care to place a wager?"

"Not unless you take me with you." She smiled sweetly. "To keep you honest, of course. You could say anything you like to win the bet, and I would be no wiser."

"Your faith in me is touching." He closed the book. "Neither of us will follow Van Middleburg, I think. All we are likely to uncover is the name of the baron's mistress."

"Ew! No, thank you."

"Once again, we are of like mind."

She nibbled her lip, considering the proximity of the

attack in the alley with the baron's upcoming rendezvous. Perhaps Crispin's queries into the Stanhurst murders had brought him too close to discovering a secret Lord and Lady Van Middleburg wished to keep hidden.

A scandal? If so, it must be a terrible one for the baron and baroness to sanction violence. Sophia didn't seek skeletons in others' closets, but the Van Middleburgs had thrown down the gauntlet when they had deemed Crispin an enemy.

"We shouldn't dismiss tonight's meeting out of hand," she said. "Lady Van Middleburg was desperate to keep you from talking to her cousin. What if there is a connection between her attempt to frighten you into leaving the duke alone and this meeting? You must admit the timing is suspect."

"If you had found *Lady* Van Middleburg's schedule, I would be more apt to agree. Her husband has done nothing to rouse suspicion."

"Law," she huffed under her breath. "Do not pretend to be a dullard. I am not fooled. It is common knowledge husbands and wives come together to protect one another from outward threats, even if they despise each other behind closed doors."

The corners of Crispin's mouth twitched. "You are too clever for your own good, Sophia. I suspect this quality will be to your detriment."

"I am not afraid. You will protect me while coming to rely on my brilliance."

"You have everything planned. Should we join that amateur sleuthhound club you mentioned?"

"Perhaps we should see this mystery to its conclusion before making any rash decisions."

He laughed, and it was the most beautiful sound in the

world. He sobered too soon, however, and his serious mask slipped back into place.

"There is no real danger in Van Middleburg's study, and you have been helpful. Nevertheless, I must see this mystery to its conclusion alone. It is too risky to involve you."

He missed the point of a partnership. Life was filled with rutted lanes, but traveling with one's helpmate made the journey meaningful. Her mother had repeated this sentiment many times over in her diaries, and Sophia had taken it to heart.

"I could use your assistance now, however," Crispin said.

She blinked in surprise. "Of course. What can I do?"

"Return to the drawing room." He took her by the shoulders, turned her toward the door, and gave her back a gentle push. She dug in her heels and glowered at him over her shoulder.

"I want to be of *real* assistance, Margrave."

"You are." His voice was kind and his gaze soft—one might even say admiring. "I need you to keep the baroness occupied while I search her chambers. Only you are able to walk into the drawing room without creating an uproar. I need you."

"You are not fobbing me off?"

"I promise, I am not." He flashed a smile that made him breathtakingly handsome and left her too pliable by half. "*Please*, darling?"

"Oh, very well," she murmured, "if you promise to come to Wedmore House this afternoon with a full report of what you find in the baroness's chambers."

"I will call later."

Mollified, Sophia crossed to the door and peeked into the corridor. Finding it empty, she slipped from the study and returned to the drawing room. She joined her aunt on the sofa and attempted to pay close attention as Amelia Hillary addressed the assembly, but her mind kept wandering.

Where is Crispin now? I wonder what he has found in Lady Van Middleburg's rooms.

Unfortunately, the opportunity to learn of the fruits of his search never arose, because he never arrived at Wedmore House. At half past ten, disgruntled and submersed in self-pity, Sophia trudged upstairs to ready for bed. He had claimed he needed her. *He said please.* And she had been too blinded by a smile as exciting and uncommon as the sighting of a rare bird to realize he'd only wanted to get rid of her.

The sound of a carriage coming down the street jolted her from her doldrums. *It is him.* Sophia hurried to the window to tug the curtains aside. The carriage drove past.

"Law," she mumbled.

The red-tipped glow of a cheroot in the square caught her eye. Lord Kellerman was hiding from his wife again, sneaking outside for a smoke and a nip of brandy from his flask. She didn't know who she felt sorry for more—the henpecked husband or his deceived wife.

Is that how life would be for her and Crispin? Him filling her head with whatever she wished to hear while he did exactly what he wanted without her being any wiser? She dropped the curtain into place with a disheartened sigh then retrieved her mother's diary. It always brought her comfort, and Sophia needed the hope her mother's words instilled more than usual tonight.

Around midnight, she extinguished the light and checked the street once more for any sign of Crispin. All was quiet, but oddly, Lord Kellerman was still in the square, puffing away on another cheroot. The glowing red tip was like a warning signal, flaring brighter as he inhaled.

Gooseflesh rose on her arms, and a sense of foreboding descended over her. Everything was not as it should be.

Sophia shook off the ridiculous notion and returned to bed. She had never been one to engage in fancy, and she refused to start now. Nevertheless, the feeling of unease lingered long after she crawled under the covers.

TWELVE

DRESSED IN DARK WOOL WORK CLOTHES, CRISPIN LOUNGED in a dark corner of Ye Olde Black Griffin, blending in with the dock men who had crowded into the tavern after their shifts. The best disguises made one into another face among the masses, but the soot rubbed into his skin would be a devil to scrub clean. Fortunately, his valet would understand. Filth clung to Kane, too.

A serving wench slammed two tankards of ale in front of Crispin before bustling away to serve another table. He passed one to Kane. The younger man took a long draught before sighing with pleasure. "This rot tastes like heaven. Almost makes wearing these disgusting clothes worth it."

Crispin chuckled and took a drink. He and Kane smelled like dead fish and a month of hard labor, but one could not be choosey when purchasing the clothes off another man's back.

"I wish Sophia was as easy to appease," he said, not daring to address her formally in present company. No one appeared to pay them any notice, and he wished to remain invisible. "It will take more than a stout ale to make her forget I did not keep our appointment this afternoon."

Finding a serving wench at the tavern willing to talk had been more challenging than he'd anticipated. There had been no time to return to Mayfair before meeting Kane at the small set of rooms the Counsel kept for sanctuary nearby.

Kane slanted a grin in his direction. "Don't look to me for advice about your troubles between the sheets. You'll have to discuss that with your woman."

"Bugger your advice," Crispin grumbled in good fun. "That is not the nature of my troubles."

"If you say so..." Kane teased. "Why not offer her a reason to forgive you? Toss her a morsel of whatever we learn tonight. Nothing too sensitive, but something that tells her you value her contribution. After all, we wouldn't know about any of this if she hadn't found what she did."

Crispin couldn't deny Sophia had a unique ability to notice what others didn't. Would the pattern in Van Middleburg's schedule have been noticeable without her pointing it out? He would like to think he would have seen it himself, but he doubted it. Perhaps his protégé was correct. He should thank her for her aid and solicit her thoughts about whatever information he and Kane gathered this evening.

Crispin bounced his knee, mulling over what it could mean if he shared a small piece of his work with her and built on her insights. The prospect was slightly intoxicating.

"When Sophia was younger," Crispin said, "she would ask her sisters to choose a page from a book of their choice, glance at it once, and then recite word for word what was on the page. Her memory is amazing. Have you ever met another person with that capability?"

Kane dropped his head back and loudly groaned toward the ceiling. "Please stop blathering on about how wonderful she is and marry the girl. Can a man not savor his drink in peace?"

Crispin laughed. "Sorry to disturb." He spotted the woman he'd spoken with earlier serving a table across the room. Nodding discretely in her direction, he said, "I hope her information is useful. She demanded a heavy enough purse."

"Made you pay handsomely, aye? You are losing your touch."

Crispin shrugged, indifferent to Kane's teasing. He hadn't attempted to charm the serving wench. His head had been too full of Sophia, his body too hungry for her to pretend he wanted another woman. The innocent brush of her arm against his chest in Lord Van Middleburg's study had wrecked his rationality—although he would rather bite through his tongue than admit the affect Sophia had on him.

Weakness is for cowards. His father's voice echoed in his memory, snuffing out his jovial mood.

The tavern door whipped open, admitting a warm gust of stench from the streets as Baron Van Middleburg entered. Crispin signaled Kane, a quick tap of two fingers to the chin. They slouched on the chairs, sinking into the shadows. The baron was late. Half an hour ago, his associates—all men of the merchant class—had gathered in a private room in the back.

Over the rim of his tankard, Crispin observed the baron's progress through the crowd. Van Middleburg spoke with no one and walked with his head down. Perhaps he feared being recognized, but the tavern's patrons barely spared him a glance. Crispin, on the other hand, refused to look away.

"Someone of his rank does not socialize with men beneath him," Kane mumbled. "He is up to no good."

Crispin agreed, but he kept his own counsel. Van Middleburg wasn't the only member of nobility involved in whatever this was. When he had questioned the serving wench earlier, she recalled a younger man accompanying the baron to the tavern until a couple of months ago. Her description of the man matched Lord Geoffrey. Crispin expected Lord Geoffrey's older brother to walk through the door any moment.

After a quarter hour passed with no sign the Duke of Stanhurst would be joining the others, Crispin abandoned his watch. "Let's discover what this meeting is about, shall we?"

Kane quirked an eyebrow, grabbed Crispin's tankard, and dumped half the contents on his chest. "Ready."

"You never take half measures on anything."

His valet-turned-colleague shrugged. "What would be the purpose? Either do it right or save the effort."

"A sound philosophy, indeed. Perhaps you could apply it in your valet duties."

Kane snorted. "You could hire a *real* valet."

"I could," Crispin agreed, "but it sounds like too much trouble."

In reality, he was content with Kane. He might not perform his duties to the standards expected of a distinguished valet, but he also never complained—no matter the state of Crispin's attire when he returned home.

He allowed the younger man to assume the lead, unobtrusively following in his stumbling wake. To an observer, Kane appeared to be a drunken fool. For Crispin's purposes, he became the distraction.

Kane tripped and banged into a table as he neared a

guard stationed outside the door to the private room. Ale and wine sloshed onto the battered tabletop.

"Watch yer bloody step," a man seated on the bench growled.

Kane turned around, wobbling, and made a lewd gesture in his direction. Crispin sighed. This could only go badly for the whelp.

The man, who was built like a bull, slammed his fleshy palms against the table and lumbered to his feet. "Come a little closer and do that again."

Kane looked back at Crispin with dulled eyes. "Bollocks."

Under normal circumstances, Kane could defend himself handily without suffering a scratch, but to do so now would ruin his cover. Laborers did not fight like a Regent's Consul man, which meant Kane would leave Ye Olde Black Griffin with a few more lumps than he had when he had arrived.

His opponent raised his brick-like fist. Kane winced, steeling himself to take the hit, but Crispin couldn't allow him to return home with a pulverized face. He drove his shoulder into the man's back and shoved. Caught by surprise, Kane's opponent pitched forward and tumbled on top of two men sitting at the table. The fellows' companions sprang to their aid and tugged on the bullish one's arms, which served to anger the larger man even more. Shouting ensued and soon fists were flying.

Crispin ducked a punch that came his way, then pulled Kane from the fracas while he still had all of his teeth. More men joined in the fighting, and the guard stationed outside the private room left his post to grab a man's arm before one of the serving wenches was struck with a tankard by accident. Sobbing, she turned into the guard's chest, and he ushered her from the tavern.

"A brawl was not part of the plan," Crispin yelled over the racket.

"No half measures, remember?" Kane grinned. "You asked for a distraction. I have delivered."

The door to the private room flew open. One of the merchants stood at the threshold. His jaw dropped; his skin paled. He slammed the door, and Crispin was certain he turned the lock. With the tavern's male employees occupied with breaking up the fight, and the serving wenches hiding under tables or behind the bar, no one seemed to notice Crispin and Kane approach the private room.

The tavern wench Crispin had spoken with earlier reported the owner had commissioned a secret room to be built next to the private dining room for easy listening. Nothing occurred behind closed doors without his knowledge—usually. He had been called to his ailing mother's bedside in Hampshire, and he was not expected to return before the end of the month.

Crispin located the false panel in the wall, and he and Kane slipped inside the narrow room. It was dark except for scant light filtering through the wall where the planks didn't quite meet one another. The voices next door were as clear as if he shared a table with the men. They were arguing, speaking over one another until one cultured voice rose above the rest.

"Do not be alarmed, sirs. Allow me to reassure you our agreement remains intact."

"It is the baron," Kane whispered.

Crispin agreed with his deduction. Baron Van Middleburg had been the only peer to enter the room.

"Balderdash!" one of the men said. "Our agreement was with Lord Geoffrey, and he is dead. I refuse to extend further credit. This ill-advised venture ends here tonight."

Several voices rose in agreement.

"You cannot withdraw your support now," Van Middleburg snapped. "The wheels have been set into motion. Likely, our emissary has already engaged the group. If we do not keep our covenant and pay what is owed when the deed is done, they will come to England to collect."

The baron's detractor scoffed. "Do you expect us to believe a group of Egyptian ghosts will come to England to exact revenge? You are cracked, sir."

The other men laughed and derided the baron. Encouraged, his opposition proceeded with his argument.

"Lord Geoffrey probably made up the tale to swindle us out of our riches. I wager there is no Black Death."

Crispin's gut clenched.

"You are wrong," Van Middleburg said. "Lord Geoffrey's source is well-connected in the British government, a man of unique power."

The mysterious connection was unmistakably a Regent's Consul man. After Napoleon's invasion of Iberia, a fellow Regent's Consul spy had uncovered evidence an advisor to the Emperor had hired the Egyptian mercenaries to quash the rebellion by murdering rebel leaders. Their deaths created an uproar and strengthened the resistance instead.

In an attempt to deflect blame from the new King of Spain, the advisor had arranged for the assassinations of his own enemies among Joseph's cabinet, but it was too late. The Spanish refused to give up the fight.

The Consul had been tracking the Black Death's movements ever since, although they lost sight of the group from time to time. The mission to study the Black Death was surreptitious, sanctioned by the Counsel's leader but hidden from the Regent. Farrin had insisted sharing knowledge of the group and their work for the French would create panic in England.

Besides, the Prince Regent had been more interested in building and redecorating his palaces in an effort to wage a war of prosperity between himself and Napoleon than he was in the actual war. Even Charles Wedmore had conceded this was true and vowed to keep the secret.

"Without the assistance of Lord Geoffrey's connection," Van Middleburg said, "our aims would be unachievable. His strategy has carried us to this point, and there is no return. We must forge onward."

Another naysayer joined in the attack on the baron. "Where is the mastermind now? Why does he not address the board himself?"

A rumble of discontent circled the room. A few men spoke up, demanding Van Middleburg bring the contact before them so they might judge the man's qualifications.

The baron cleared his throat. "I've never met the man in question, and my wife's cousin did not share his name. That was the condition for his assistance. I am certain everything is all right, and he will find me when it is time to make the final payment."

Loud grumbling ensued, but the baron's original nemesis called for quiet.

"Surely, you've corresponded with Lord Geoffrey's American contact," he snipped. "You must know *his* name."

"Er, not exactly," Van Middleburg murmured, "but his identity will be known shortly. We have the matter in hand."

The room exploded with shouts and curses at this revelation. When it seemed unlikely Crispin and Kane would learn anything of further use, they exited the hidden room and used a back door to leave the tavern. They avoided conversation on the walk back to the sanctuary.

In the dank two-room hovel, Kane set about stirring the embers in the hearth and adding kindling until a small fire crackled in the fireplace. He swung the kettle over the flames.

"Why would a handful of merchants and a baron need the services of mercenaries?" he asked.

"I do not know." Crispin crossed to the washstand to pour water from a pitcher into a chipped basin and grabbed a cloth and a bar of lye soap. He didn't wait for the water in the kettle to warm to begin scrubbing away the soot on his face and hands. He needed to think. The cold sharpened his senses.

Kane plopped into a chair by the hearth and tugged off a boot. "Van Middleburg is right, isn't he? If the men do not honor their debt, the Black Death will come for them."

"Yes."

The Egyptian warriors would make the battles with the Norsemen of the ninth century look like child's play. The Black Death were formidable warriors, because no one ever saw them coming. The ability to slip in and out of any camp undetected, leaving behind nothing except dead bodies, had earned the group their moniker. They were a plague on their enemies, and their employer's enemies alike.

Kane dropped his boots on the floor and shrugged out of the oversized coat he wore. "Will you inform the Lord Chamberlain?"

"I must."

The younger man whistled. "I do not envy you the task. When Hertford learns His Majesty's men have kept knowledge of the group's existence from him, he could recommend locking you all in the tower."

"And where will you be while I am wasting away in a cell?"

Kane smiled. "I have always been fond of the master's chambers. The bed appears comfortable enough."

"Do not count your chicks before they hatch, whelp. I will not be imprisoned, and neither will our colleagues. We are the only ones likely to be standing between England and death."

Crispin folded the cloth and left it on the washstand before sitting at the small table close to the fire.

"This was Farrin's doing," he said. "He kept His Majesty in the dark, and he orchestrated this deal with the Black Death. It had to be him. He was with Lord Geoffrey the night of his murder. They dined in secret at Claudine Bellerose's home many times over the last few years. What I cannot fathom is why. What were they plotting, and why did it end in homicide?"

"Maybe Miss Darlington knows more than she realizes. Question her. She has already shown an interest in helping."

Crispin scowled. "Sophia has told me everything. She is of no further use."

"But—"

"I will not hear any more." Crispin shoved away from the table to change in the back room.

To think he had considered confiding in her, allowing her to dip her toes into the dark waters where he was often submerged. He had lost his damn senses. If the Black Death was involved, Sophia must be kept as far away as possible.

Tomorrow.

"I will send her to the country with her aunt where she will stay until I come for her," he said from the other room.

"The lady might have something to say about your plans for her."

"I do not care," Crispin snapped. "I will hear no more arguments or nonsense about having no sway over her. She is *mine*—mine to protect—and if she gives me grief, I will remind her this is exactly what she wanted."

Kane popped his head through the doorway; his smiling reflection was captured in the looking glass. "I hope you plan to revise your marriage proposal before speaking with her."

Heat climbed into Crispin's face, and his collar felt too tight. "I was not intending to propose to her with those exact words."

"Smart thinking," Kane said and tapped two fingers to his temple. "She might have you tossed out on your arse otherwise. Ladies like romance. I could tutor you if you like."

Crispin chuckled. "Thank you, but I am capable of romancing a lady on my own."

THIRTEEN

SOPHIA PACED ALONGSIDE THE MANICURED HEDGES bordering Lord and Lady Seabrook's closely cropped lawn of their country home. The ground was still soft from yesterday's rain and gently grabbed at her boot heels as she walked. A large crowd had turned out for the Seabrooks' garden party, despite the half hour ride from London. It seemed everyone and their second cousins had turned out for the event—everyone except the one person Sophia was eager to see.

Blasted Margrave!

Impatience expanded inside her, tightening her chest. She walked faster in an attempt to outrun the urge to scream in frustration. She had anticipated cornering him at some point today to demand he answer for not calling at Wedmore House yesterday. Instead, she was left waiting again.

"His vanishing act has grown too tiresome," she said to Octavia. "I do not know how much more I can tolerate."

"I...understand. Will you *please* slow down?" Octavia's

distressed voice jolted Sophia to the present; she stopped abruptly to attend to her friend.

"Oh, dear! Are you all right?"

Octavia's face was bright red, and her chest heaved with each breath. "Just...a little...winded."

"I am so very sorry. Please, come sit while you catch your breath."

Octavia nodded. "Splendid...suggestion."

Sophia took her friend's arm and led her to a bench beneath a willow tree. Sometimes she forgot other ladies were not accustomed to vigorous activity. She walked with her aunt daily, and before Regina married and set off on her honeymoon, she had often coaxed Sophia into sparring with her. Sophia was no match for her older sister, but she never would have heard the end of it from Regina if she had not put forth adequate effort. A turn about the lawn was easy in comparison.

When they reached the bench, Octavia plopped down and heaved a sigh. She stared in the direction of the tents her parents' servants had set up around the vast lawn.

"Forgive me," Sophia said and sat beside her friend. "I was preoccupied and lost a sense of how fast I was walking. Would you like a glass of lemonade? I will retrieve one for you."

Before Sophia hopped from the bench to visit the designated tent, Octavia grabbed her wrist. "It is still early. Lord Margrave will make an appearance. He accepted mother's invitation."

Sophia hoped so. "Every time I believe our relationship is advancing, he disappears."

Octavia narrowed her eyes; her mouth scrunched into a tight circle. "I am beginning to suspect the viscount stays up at night plotting ways to drive you insane."

Sophia laughed at the absurd thought of Crispin

standing before a large battle map of Mayfair, complete with toy suitors, carriages, and horses. "I am perfectly sane, and Lord Margrave has better ways to occupy his time."

"I suppose most gentlemen do," Octavia said with an indignant huff. "Business keeps Ramsdell away today. I hope it is very dull, and he is filled with regret for abandoning me."

"I am certain your betrothed finds everything dreary compared to you."

Octavia smiled coyly and smoothed a wrinkle from her skirt. "That *is* my aim."

Sophia changed the subject before her friend returned to criticizing Crispin. She might be incensed with his behavior, but she did not like when others found fault with him.

"It was kind of your mother to plan a party," she said. "From what I understand, the gentlemen deserve a day away from London to clear their minds."

"Yes, Papa comes home every night from the Lords exhausted. I overheard him telling Mama the situation does not look promising for the Queen." Octavia lowered her voice to a whisper. "One of her servants testified she paid an unsavory man to dance for her."

"Unsavory?"

Octavia leaned closer, her breath quickening. "He did not wear a stitch of clothing. Can you imagine? The patronesses of Almack's will faint dead away if the scandalous tale reaches the assemblies."

"Indeed."

Most ladies did not possess the same fortitude as Sophia's friend, who repeated the salacious rumor without the hint of a blush.

Octavia sat up straighter. "Speaking of scandals..."

Sophia swiveled on the bench to follow her friend's line

of sight. Several guests had yet to venture beyond the terrace, foregoing lawn bowls or archery in favor of conversation. Her eyebrows rose in surprise when she spotted a tall figure lingering at the fringes of the crowd.

"The Duke of Stanhurst has come," Sophia said. "He hasn't attended a large gathering since the accident."

"*Accident.*" Octavia snorted softly. "I would not be surprised if it was murder. Papa said the old duke had many creditors and made enemies with his erratic behavior. Someone had a debt to settle. I would stake my reputation on it."

"Please, do not." Sophia's friend was surprisingly close to the truth, and fortunately, too astute to speculate on the Stanhurst deaths within earshot of anyone who was not a confidant. "Does your father know you like to eavesdrop?"

Octavia sniffed. "No, because I am very good at it. Do you want to know what I overheard, or would you prefer to lecture me for my bad habits?"

"I never lecture." Sophia would like to take the highroad and not fall prey to gossip mongering, but curiosity overrode her honorable intentions. *A thread of truth binds every rumor,* her mother had written in her diary. Perhaps Sophia could learn something useful to pass along to Crispin. "You mentioned a scandal?"

"Word has it Stanhurst is desperate for a wife, one with a large dowry. He offered for Lady Mary's hand last week, and her father chased him away with a fire poker."

Sophia frowned. "If that is true, it says more about Lord Pitkin's character than the duke's. Why shouldn't His Grace be in want of a wife? He will need an heir, especially now that his brother has passed."

"I suppose." Octavia tipped her head to the side, presumably studying the dark-haired duke. "I cannot deny he is handsome, but the devil has been known to use attraction to his advantage."

"Stanhurst is not the devil." That did not mean he was innocent of any wrongdoing, however, and Sophia was not one to ignore an opportunity. She grabbed Octavia's hand to pull her from the bench. "Come, be a gracious hostess and challenge the duke to a game of lawn bowls."

"Yes, let us get the story from the horse's mouth. What a marvelous idea!" Octavia shot to her feet and nearly dragged Sophia toward the terrace.

They weaved past the other guests as Octavia marched up to the duke. Sophia's friend lifted her chin, boldly holding his chilly silver gaze. "Your Grace, Miss Darlington and I are in search of competitors for lawn bowling. Will you join us?"

A spark of warmth flickered in his eyes. "You wish to challenge *me* to lawn bowls?"

"Did I not address you directly, Your Grace? You are the only duke in attendance."

Sophia cringed at the rudeness of Octavia's response, but the duke's mouth twitched with the hint of a smile. "You are direct, Lady Octavia. I appreciate a lady who does not mince words."

"I assume you accept the challenge."

Stanhurst inclined his head. "With pleasure."

"Very well, you require a second." Octavia spun on her heel, tossing her mahogany hair, and marched away, leaving Sophia alone with the duke.

He smiled. "Did the lady challenge me to a duel or a game of lawn bowls?"

Despite her best intentions, Sophia returned his smile. He seemed unaccountably tolerant of her friend's cheekiness. "It is often difficult to discern Lady Octavia's intentions, but rest assured, her father keeps the blades and firearms locked away."

Stanhurst chuckled. He was friendlier than she had imagined when catching glimpses of him across the ballrooms, but she would not draw conclusions about his character based on one exchange.

"An enigmatic debutante. How intriguing." The duke studied Octavia speaking to a servant at the edge of the bowling green. His smile widened. "If you will excuse me, Miss Darlington, it appears I must enlist a second."

While the Duke of Stanhurst searched for a partner, Sophia joined Octavia. Her friend accepted a bowl from a footman and tested its weight. "This size will do."

"Yes, milady."

"The duke seems to find your surliness appealing," Sophia said.

Octavia snapped her head toward her, her face a mask of horror. "Are you teasing? You must be."

"I am not. He called you intriguing."

"Intriguing? I was a *shrew*." Octavia shook her head. "Good heavens, do you think he fancies taming me?"

"I cannot say—"Sophia approached the footman to select her own bowls for the game—"but you might change your tack when he joins us, as a precaution. Lord Ramsdell will not welcome competition for your affections."

Octavia scoffed. "The Duke of Stanhurst is not a contender. I am already promised to my kind, honest, and gentle Ram."

"That does seem for the best."

In general, Sophia did not judge a man by his father's actions, but an association with Stanhurst warranted prudence. There was a reason the saying 'like father, like son' came into existence.

"I only wished to prepare the duke for candid questions if he chose to join us," Octavia said.

"I cannot imagine he is under any delusions now."

"Perfect." Sophia's friend playfully wrinkled her nose. "It appears I did not frighten him away, and he has recruited Lord Leo."

Stanhurst and a lanky young man walked toward them, closing the distance with equally long strides.

"His sister married Marcus Fletcher recently," Octavia said. "I read the announcement in the Morning Times."

"I heard about Mr. Fletcher and Lady Adele from my friends at the Drayton Theatre."

Octavia pushed out her bottom lip. "Your life is much more exciting than mine."

Sophia had no chance to comment before the men reached them. Her friend welcomed Lord Leo and suggested they begin the game. The men encouraged Octavia to be the first to roll the jack, but she deferred to Sophia.

Taking the small white ball from her friend, Sophia approached the mark and threw the jack underhand. It rolled approximately one hundred feet before drawing to a stop.

"Excellent form, Miss Darlington," Lord Leo said. "I might be out of my element."

"As am I," the duke agreed.

Octavia spared Stanhurst a brief glance before tossing the first bowl and trying to come closest to the jack. Everyone else followed suit. Stanhurst was reticent throughout the match, concentrating on each shot before he took it, despite Octavia's prying questions about his search for a wife. Sophia abandoned her plan to interrogate the duke about Lady Van Middleburg. The idea had been silly and ill considered.

Where the duke was quiet, Lord Leo was the opposite. He was a gregarious young man who threw himself into the competition with gusto and made everyone laugh with his antics. Eventually, Octavia seemed to give up her mission to loosen the duke's tongue and began to enjoy the game.

"Watch this," Lord Leo said before tossing a bowl underneath one leg. When it rolled up to the jack and gave it a kiss, Octavia cried foul. He and Stanhurst were too occupied with celebrating to give her complaint credence.

The duke appeared to grow more comfortable with the company after Octavia stopped hounding him. His guard relaxed and a playful side emerged. Sophia's wariness of him began to fade. Crispin would put no stock in her intuition, but she trusted it without fail. Stanhurst was not the type of man to conspire to harm another person.

Octavia and Sophia lost the first match by a point and challenged the men to another game. They were nearing the end of the second match when a tingle began at the back of Sophia's neck; the wispy hairs there stood on end. She turned, looking for the source of her disquiet but found nothing out of the ordinary. A small group of ladies played battledore and shuttlecock in the open grass, swinging their rackets and squealing, whether they missed or not.

Couples strolled with arms linked through the gardens while the ladies' parasols lent shade and a false sense of privacy. Even the older men had found an activity to occupy them—sipping brandy and playing cards in one of the smaller tents.

"It is your turn, Miss Darlington," Lord Leo said.

Shaking off the sense she was being watched, she grabbed one of her bowls. She misjudged her strength and tossed it too hard. The bowl flew past the jack to land in the shallow ditch.

Lord Leo clucked his tongue in mock sympathy before

strutting toward the mark to take his turn. As he took aim, Octavia sidled up beside her and whispered, "Look who has arrived at last."

Sophia arched her neck to look behind her. Crispin was striding across the emerald lawn, his gaze fixed on Sophia. A pleasurable heat engulfed her, and she lost some of her appetite for scolding him for missing their appointment yesterday.

He looked amazing.

His hat sat at a jaunty angle that made her fingers itch to sweep it from his head and muss his golden blond hair. A demure waistcoat of cream hugged his lean torso, and a dark blue jacket stretched across his broad shoulders. Bronze trousers skimmed his long, sculpted thighs and encased his narrow hips in a way that caused her to blush.

"Gads," Octavia mumbled. "Is he always ill tempered?"

"What?" Sophia blinked. She had become too spellbound by the sight of his muscled form to recognize the bulging muscles in his jaw. "Oh, dear."

Stanhurst sighed. "That murderous glower is directed at me, Miss Darlington. The viscount and I exchanged words the other night."

When Sophia's eyes flared in surprise, the duke offered a reassuring smile.

"Allow me to handle Margrave." He stepped in front of her, shielding her with his body. "Good afternoon, Lord Margrave. We are in the middle of a match. You will need to enlist a partner if you wish to compete in the next game."

In the brief silence that ensued, Sophia thought she heard the sound of Crispin's teeth grinding. "Miss Darlington," he said with exaggerated politeness while pointedly giving the duke the cut direct, "might I request an audience with you?"

Sophia peeked around the duke. *Law!* She had never seen his face that particular shade of red. "Now, my lord?"

"Yes, Miss Darlington." Crispin extended his hand. "If it pleases you..."

His smile was tight and dangerous; butterflies stirred in her belly. She had seen him truly angry only once—behind the alley. Moments before he had returned her kiss with a hunger that had ignited a passion inside of her she didn't know how to extinguish. She would follow him anywhere.

"I would be delighted—"she placed her hand in his and allowed him to draw her away—"if Lady Octavia, His Grace, and Lord Leo do not mind a delay in our game, of course."

All three gave their blessings, although they appeared perplexed by Crispin's brazen request to steal her away. Sophia was not. She expected to receive another lecture about leaving the investigation into Stanhurst to him.

They would quarrel.

She would point out her obvious advantage at gaining access to the duke, her being of marriageable age and Stanhurst being in the market for a wife.

Crispin would bluster.

She would challenge him.

And if she was lucky, he would kiss her again.

Crispin was already escorting her away.

"I will return momentarily," she called over her shoulder.

"You will not," he ground out.

She bristled at his cocksure attitude. "We are in the middle of a match."

"Lady Octavia will find another partner."

Sophia deemed the matter unworthy of an argument. She would do as she pleased, just as she always did.

He led her toward the hedge maze, and they walked

along the outside, remaining in sight of the other guests. He effortlessly matched her brisk pace. "Where is your aunt? She should be watching over you."

"Aunt Beatrice remained in London. Lady Seabrook is my chaperone, and there is nothing inappropriate about playing a game of lawn bowls."

He aimed a censorious glower in her direction. "I am more concerned by the company you are keeping."

She ignored his disapproval and commented on the pleasant breeze. Blue cornflowers and white daisies swayed in the meadow ahead, while large beech trees oversaw the dance from their perch on a hill.

"I warned you to stay out of this business with the duke and his kin," he said.

"True, we've had this conversation a few times, but we never seem to reach the part where you explain *your* interest in the duke's business. Do you hold a vendetta against him? Does he owe you a debt?" She aimed a teasing smile at him. "Did he look cross-eyed at you at the club?"

Crispin grunted, apparently not appreciating her attempt at levity. "You cannot believe I care how anyone looks at me."

"I do not know what to think, Crispin. You are guarded about everything. I have questions, and if I am unable to elicit answers from you, my options are limited. I could hazard wild guesses or attempt to learn what I can when an opportunity is presented, which is what I did today."

"While I appreciate the gesture, I am capable of managing on my own," he said. "I always have."

Her throat grew thick with emotion. When would he realize he wasn't alone in the world? He never had been. Even when he had despaired over the loss of his father, her family was there to welcome him into their fold. He would always have her.

She drew to a stop and turned to face him. "I could be an asset if you would allow it. You've known me most of my life. You are aware of my talents, and you must realize how I long to be your confidant. Please, allow me to be your helpmate. Did we not get on well yesterday in Van Middleburg's study?"

Crispin's jaw softened; he wrapped her hand in his strong warm ones, cradling her fingers between his palms. "I recognize your gifts, Sophia, and under different circumstances, I would be a fool to decline your offer. However, you are more hindrance than help in this situation."

His words slammed into her; her breath stuck in her lungs. He was still talking, but she couldn't focus as his revelation echoed in her ears. She was a hindrance. While she had been attempting to make herself indispensable, he'd found her to be a nuisance.

"It is best for you and your aunt to return to the country," he said. "You will be safe, and I will be free to fulfill my duties without worry. Once this matter is settled, I will join you at Hartland Manor to hear your answer."

"An answer?"

"As to whether you wish to become my wife. The separation will be a test—"

"Stop!" Sophia jerked her hand free. "Stop talking, you blathering addle pate."

He gaped. *Splendid!* She had shocked him into silence.

Anger welled inside her, expanding her chest. "Must you spoil every moment of intimacy? I offer my heart to you, and you respond with insults? I am a hindrance, a nuisance?"

"I didn't say nuis—"

"*Crispin!*"

He sighed and crossed his hands at his waist. "Please, continue."

She blinked to prevent the prickling at the backs of her eyes from transforming into furious tears. He was sorely trampling on her patience.

"I will not be sent away. *Ever*. You—"she jabbed a finger in his direction—"should consider if you want a wife capable of forming her own thoughts, because that is what is in store for you if we marry."

Spinning on her heel, she marched toward the meadow.

"Where are you going?"

"We need a separation *now*, before either of us say something we cannot retract."

"Your great-aunt and uncle have overindulged you," he called to her back. "Most gentlemen would find it disagreeable."

What was wrong with the blasted man? It was as if he put effort into being abrasive. She growled in frustration and walked faster.

FOURTEEN

CRISPIN WAS NOT LIKE *MOST MEN*. HE FOUND NOTHING disagreeable about Sophia. She recognized her value. She commanded respect. She spoke her mind without diffidence. It was arousing as hell.

Unfortunately, these admirable qualities also made protecting her more difficult than necessary. Her independence was a hindrance under the circumstances, and he was a bloody fool for speaking the truth.

He sighed and watched her storm away without attempting to stop her. He had mucked it up between them —again. For too long, he had relied on tactlessness to encourage others to keep their distance. It had been easier to protect his country's secrets when no one was interested in sustaining a relationship with him, but for a moment, he forgot he no longer needed to drive Sophia away.

As the distance between them grew, he followed at a sedate pace, respecting her wish to be free of his companionship for a while and mulling over how he could make amends. Her light blue dress matched the wild flowers surrounding her in the meadow. The overgrowth slowed her progress. She seemed to be headed for the trees on the hill. Perhaps she would allow him to sit with her in the shade, and he would share a truth that had been repeating in his heart for days.

I love her.

He had tried to deny it, but the evidence was too plentiful to ignore. She was in his thoughts, continuously—upon waking, during his morning ride through Hyde Park, at various moments throughout the day. He had fallen for Sophia Darlington and could not imagine life without her, nor could he fathom how to give her the marriage she deserved.

Several yards from the foot of the hill, her skirts became snagged on a thistle. Her grumbling carried on the air. He smiled. A lifetime of passionate battles with her would never be long enough.

She bent forward to gingerly pluck the prickles from the muslin; a strand of silky hair slipped from her bonnet. Crispin caught himself before he called out an offer of assistance. Helping one another was a sore subject today.

A movement on the hill caught his eye. A rider and horse appeared from behind the largest tree, the full branches having hidden both from sight. The hair stood up on the back of Crispin's neck.

"Sophia?"

Perhaps detecting his wariness, she jerked up her head and met his gaze. His heart quickened; his muscles tensed.

The rider extended his arm. Sunlight glinted off metal.

"No!" Crispin lurched toward her as the firearm discharged. A blinding flash and boom ripped through the air. The rider yelped; the pistol plunged to the ground. It had exploded in his hand.

The horse reared, but the shooter kept his seat. Shouts came from the manor house. The rider calmed the horse then spurred it down the hill. Massive hindquarters sent the animal barreling toward Sophia.

Crispin dashed through the field to reach her, crashing into her before the horse's hooves ran her into the ground. Twisting midair, they landed hard with him underneath her.

He gulped, trying to regain his breath after having the wind knocked from him. Wide blue eyes stared down at him.

"Are you—hurt?" He gasped between words.

She scrambled off him. "No, are you?"

He didn't know. The rage thrumming through his veins numbed him to pain.

The rider spun the horse around and kicked its sides. Crispin jumped from the ground and hauled Sophia to her feet. Men from the party were rushing the field, yelling.

He reached for the small pistol tucked in his boot and shouted to Sophia. "Run toward the house."

She ran, the cumbersome growth slowing her. The rider turned the chestnut gelding to give chase. Crispin raised the flintlock, set the hammer, and fired. The ball slammed into the man's shoulder. He jerked on impact, losing his grip on the reins and falling to the ground. The brave steed stayed by his side as if he'd been trained for battle. The blackguard struggled to get his feet beneath him.

Dropping the spent pistol, Crispin sprinted across the meadow. The chestnut tossed his mane and flared his nostrils as Crispin gained ground. The man staggered toward the gelding, but the horse danced out of reach. Crispin was nearly on top of them.

The man snagged the bridle and captured the dangling reins. His foot hit the stirrup. Crispin lunged and snatched a handful of the man's jacket to unseat him. Quick as a snake striking, a blade bit into his forearm. Crispin lost his grip. The rider kicked him in the chest, and Crispin saw his face for the first time.

Garrick.

Another well-placed boot caught Crispin in the jaw. His head snapped back and he crumpled on the ground. Farrin's henchman spurred the horse into a gallop as a shot zinged overhead. Man and horse had become a shadow on the horizon by the time Lord Seabrook reached him. The Duke of Stanhurst accompanied him and was carrying a rifle.

"Was that you?" Crispin asked Stanhurst, assessing if a second assailant might have fired the shot. Farrin's men often worked in tandem.

The duke inclined his head.

"Thank you," Crispin said.

Stanhurst offered him a hand up, and Crispin accepted his help.

"We heard a gunshot," Seabrook said. "Did the addle pate not see you and Miss Darlington in the vicinity?"

"I expect not," Crispin lied.

Sophia might not realize she had been the intended victim, and he didn't wish to frighten her any more than she already had been. He would get her to safety as soon as possible.

"Probably one of those drunken fools from the tavern," Lord Seabrook spat. "Young rabble-rousers have been causing all sorts of trouble lately. It is time to put a stop to this nonsense."

Seabrook held his hand out to reclaim his rifle from the duke then stalked in the direction of the manor house, barking orders to a footman to find the magistrate and bring him to the house.

Stanhurst hung back with Crispin, who had earned a limp during the scuffle. "You lied to Seabrook," the duke said. "I was watching from the lawn. The blackguard was aiming for Miss Darlington. Why would anyone wish to harm her?"

"I do not know, but I intend to find out." Stiffly, he climbed the hill to retrieve Garrick's firearm. Stanhurst jogged ahead, snagged it from the ground, and brought it to him.

"It is a pepperbox." The duke sounded genuinely shocked as he handed the multi-barrel pistol to Crispin. "He truly intended to kill her."

"I know," Crispin ground out.

Once Sophia's safety was insured, he would track down the bastard and make him pay. He headed toward the spot where he had discarded his own firearm.

"What manner of demon would harm an innocent young woman?" The duke had grown ashen. Perhaps he was imagining one of his sisters in a similar predicament. A twinge of sympathy dulled the edge of Crispin's fury. It was a blow the first time one recognized men like Garrick existed, men with no honor or care for women, children, or beasts.

"It is beyond comprehension," Crispin said.

He did not devote time to understanding how one became a damned soul, and focused instead on how to stop him.

Why would Farrin's man make an attempt on Sophia's life? She had mentioned a map the other day, a map Farrin had been desperate to retrieve. His personal guards followed his commands alone. Between the two of them, Wolfe and Garrick didn't possess enough smarts to be anything more than guard dogs. The facts added up to one disturbing possibility.

Farrin is alive.

"The man's name is Bert Garrick," Crispin said as he located his pistol.

"It is good you recognized him. You must tell the magistrate when he arrives."

"He will never find Garrick." Unless Crispin's shot had done more than graze him, and he suspected it hadn't given the thug's ability to fight to escape.

He glanced at the duke. Stanhurst's color was improving. Crispin was no longer concerned he might faint, so he did not soften his words. "I would watch over my shoulder if I were in your position. Garrick is employed by the man who killed your father and brother."

Stanhurst stopped in his tracks. Crispin kept walking, his limp easing up the more he moved.

"Why would I be marked as a target?" the duke asked. "I had no dealings with the blackguard."

Crispin scoffed. "Do you believe Miss Darlington did?"

"Of course not." Stanhurst caught up to him in a few long strides. "You obviously know more than I do. Explain yourself." The duke's haughty mask was firmly in place again.

"Your brother's past dealings place you at risk. Lord Geoffrey was involved with dangerous men when he died, as is your cousin and her husband. From what I have gathered, Farrin was probably your brother's partner. If your brother kept incriminating evidence—and it seems your cousin believes he did, since she has been angling to access his chambers—Farrin will find out, if he hasn't already. He does not allow potential problems to exist."

The duke's eyes darkened. "I am aware."

A young man, the fourth player from Sophia's lawn bowls match, trotted out to intercept them, cutting short the conversation.

"Lord Margrave, on behalf of Miss Darlington, I've been

charged with informing you that she wishes to return to her aunt. Lady Seabrook has ordered the carriage to be readied, and she will see Miss Darlington home presently."

"Excuse me." Crispin brushed past the messenger. Sophia was not leaving his side.

FIFTEEN

CRISPIN CUT ACROSS THE LAWN, HURRIED UP THE TERRACE stairs, and stalked through the house. He located Sophia standing outside by the drive with her friend. Lady Octavia had her arm around Sophia's shoulders, offering the comfort he desired to give.

Lord and Lady Seabrook had retreated to a spot several feet away. The marchioness was whispering furiously. "What should I tell her aunt? She entrusted me with the girl."

"Tell her the truth," her husband said.

"I do not know what the truth is."

Crispin closed his ears to their argument and focused on Sophia. Her eyes were rimmed in pink as if she had been crying, but she offered a brave smile when he approached.

"Miss Darlington, may I see you home? I could speak with your aunt on your behalf."

"Absolutely not," Lady Seabrook snipped, her face pinched with disapproval. Her husband stood by in silence. "I must honor my duties as chaperone. It was a misstep to allow you and my charge to walk the meadow without me."

She softened her tone and gazed at Sophia with much more affection. "You should have requested my permission, Miss Darlington. It can be viewed as unbecoming for a lady to disregard propriety. Others talk and reputations become tarnished. You must promise to be more cautious."

Sophia blushed and lowered her gaze. "I promise."

Annoyance tightened Crispin's chest, even though he suspected the woman's intent was not to embarrass Sophia. Nevertheless, she had, and he could not allow Sophia's character to be questioned.

"I am at fault for what has occurred," Crispin said. "I did not deem it necessary to request your blessing prior to escorting Miss Darlington to the meadow."

Sophia peeked at him; her brows angled toward each other.

He smiled reassuringly. "Do you wish to tell Lady Seabrook, or should I?"

She shook her head as if trying to clear her mind. "I have no—"

"No preference? Yes, very well," he said brightly. "I will be the bearer of good tidings."

Lady Octavia dropped her arm from around Sophia's shoulders and peered at her with narrowed eyes. "If there are good tidings, why am I only now hearing about it?"

Crispin answered on Sophia's behalf. "We had agreed it was premature to make a formal announcement, since Miss Darlington's guardian is out of the country. However, under the circumstances, it seems prudent to lift the veil of secrecy. Miss Darlington and I have an agreement. She has consented to become my wife."

Sophia's eyes flew open wide; her friend gasped.

"I am honored and humbled," he added, holding Sophia's gaze.

Lady Seabrook sniffed. "I would offer my best, but since

you appear to not have the Earl of Wedmore's blessing, I will refrain—unless of course, you do not believe you require *his* blessing either."

"Uncle Charles will grant his permission," Sophia murmured.

"Whether he does or not remains to be seen, young lady. You may not travel alone with Lord Margrave until you have his blessing." The Seabrook's carriage turned onto the drive and approached the front of the house. "However, it would be wise to travel in the company of a man, I think. Lord Seabrook must remain behind to speak with the magistrate. Would you make the journey in our carriage, my lord?"

"Of course. Allow me to speak with my driver, and I will return shortly."

Crispin located his carriage and retrieved two flintlock pistols and holsters he kept in a compartment beneath one of the benches. His driver was under orders to return home and bring Kane to Wedmore House.

When Crispin returned, the ladies had boarded the carriage. The seat beside Lady Seabrook was vacant. He climbed inside and sat across from Sophia. Her gaze locked on the firearms strapped around his waist. She paled.

"I have armed myself as a precaution," he said. "No need to fret. The danger has passed."

Her smile was tremulous. "I am not worried."

They were lying to each other, but it seemed the best course of action for now.

He would be honest about what they were facing once they had privacy. She deserved to know. If Farrin had ordered his men to eliminate her, neither would stop hunting her, which meant Crispin would have to find them first.

Lady Octavia chattered continuously on the bumpy

road to London, while Sophia remained somber and kept her face turned to the window. His stomach began to churn with uncertainty when she seemed to sink deeper into introspection, no longer responding to her friend's conversation.

Sophia had always been the girl who detected the promise of sunshine behind every rain cloud, sought out rainbows, and unearthed the lesson in every setback. Her silence was uncharacteristic and worrisome.

He shifted on the bench, restless and longing to reach across the carriage to take her hand, to provide her with real comfort—to promise he would protect her, for he could not bear life without her. He needed her to remind him there was goodness and joy on the other side of darkness.

Perhaps she sensed him watching her, because she turned her head. She inhaled sharply. "Are you bleeding?"

"Oh?" He inspected his sleeve and noted a darker blotch surrounding the rip in his jacket. The dull ache in his forearm had been forgotten in his concern for Sophia. "It is a flesh wound. It does not bother me."

Lady Seabrook huffed and dug into her reticule. She produced a handkerchief. "You should have spoken up, Lord Margrave. I hope you do not continue this bad habit once you marry. A wife must be kept abreast of all developments. How else is Miss Darlington to take good care of you?"

He accepted the handkerchief, although he felt he had no choice with her shoving it into his hand.

Sophia's full pink lips turned up slightly. It was the first hint his girl was still in there.

When they arrived at Wedmore House and the butler informed Lady Seabrook that Sophia's aunt was unavailable, the marchioness issued a breathless chuckle.

She seemed pleased to be relieved of the task of reporting on the day's events.

"Please make certain Miss Allred understands I did not take my duties lightly," she said to Crispin.

"I will explain you had nothing to do with today."

Once the door closed behind them, Sophia removed her gloves and bonnet to surrender to the butler. Crispin followed suit. A slight tic of the man's eyebrow was the only sign the state of Crispin's crushed hat caught him by surprise.

Sophia gestured for Crispin to follow her. "Mr. Tillman, please have a basin and supplies to dress a wound brought to the sunny drawing room. Lord Margrave has cut himself."

"I will see to it at once."

As he turned to do her bidding, Sophia added, "We will need the salve Joy mixes, too."

"Yes, miss."

She led Crispin toward the small family drawing room where guests were rarely invited.

"You mustn't say anything to Aunt Beatrice about what happened today." She spoke quietly, confidentially. "Dr. Portier reports her heart remains strong, but at her advanced age, he advises my sisters and I avoid giving her any frights."

"He dispenses that advice to everyone. I believe some parents even bribe him for the speech to keep their offspring out of trouble."

Sophia drew back. "Does he? That cannot be true."

"It is. I heard it when I was a youngster."

In Crispin's case, however, the advice had been appropriate. An abnormality with his father's heart at birth had bothered him all his life. A fright could have easily sent his father's heart racing too fast or stopped it beating all together. The good doctor had made a point of drawing Crispin aside when his father was dying to reassure him that his father's condition was not Crispin's doing. The doctor's reassurance had been unnecessary. Crispin hadn't blamed himself. He had been a good son and accomplished every goal his father had set for him.

"Sit by the window," Sophia said. "We need light to dress your wound properly."

Crispin obeyed and sat in the gold brocade chair by the large floor to ceiling window. Light spilled into the room, illuminating the exotic mural covering every wall. A peacock roosted above the doorframe, monkeys created mischief swinging from vines, and a majestic tiger with a satisfied smile sprawled across a large rock, bathing in the sun. The room was whimsical and bright, as if it had been decorated with Sophia in mind.

She busied herself with clearing the small table next to the chair of a treasure Wedmore had brought back from one of his journeys. While Sophia's uncle was a Regent's Consul man, his status as an antiquarian allowed him to spy without rousing too much suspicion. Wedmore was consumed with digging for old bones and broken pots. Crispin did not share his godfather's passion.

"Your aunt will need to be informed of what happened today," he said.

"I know she will hear about it eventually. I am sure Lady Seabrook's garden party will be the topic of conversation for several days. We have a quiet evening at home planned. I will tell her tonight, or perhaps over breakfast tomorrow." She came to stand in front of him and sighed. "May I ask you to remove your jacket?"

"Any time you like." He smiled and shrugged off the ruined article of clothing.

A pretty blush dusted her cheeks as she reached for the

silver lion cufflink at his wrist. She peeked at him from beneath wispy lashes. "You led Lady Seabrook to believe we are betrothed."

"Has a misunderstanding occurred? Did we not discuss marriage when we departed the theatre?"

She caught her bottom lip between her teeth and wiggled the cufflink free. "We did not reach an agreement. As I recall, you were resistant. You suggested I should find another husband."

When she attempted to pull away, he captured the tips of her fingers. Her skin was as luxurious as the finest silk. "Sophia." Her name was a sigh of longing from his lips. "My resistance has never been to you."

"Your letter insinuated otherwise."

She pulled her hand from his light touch and moved to stand before the window. His pulse surged in alarm. She made herself an easy target without realizing. He came up behind her to wrap his arms around her waist and drew her away where she would be safe from view.

He kissed the soft spot behind her ear, unable to resist the alluring scent of her fragrant skin. Her perfume had been haunting his dreams. He would catch the scent on a breeze, following it with anticipation of finding Sophia. He always woke before he reached her.

"Not the letter I never sent," he whispered.

She grew pliable in his arms and sank against his chest. "You receive no credit for a letter I never read."

He nuzzled her cheek. "But I poured out my heart."

"It must have been a very short letter."

He laughed and placed a smacking kiss on her cheek.

"Ahem."

Crispin and Sophia sprang apart at the masculine sound of a throat clearing. Two footmen stood at the threshold with the supplies she had requested. If she was embarrassed to be caught in an embrace, she hid it well.

"You may place everything on the table and leave us."

The servants set themselves to the task then slipped from the room. Crispin returned to the chair and rolled up his sleeve. "I can clean my wound. It is not a sight for a lady."

Sophia snatched the cloth from the table and dropped it in the basin, then saturated it with water from the matching pitcher. "You do realize Aunt Beatrice cannot see a thing anymore and refuses to acknowledge it. I have tended many bumps, scratches, and minor burns. I am not squeamish."

"How silly of me." He smiled and reclined in the chair. A gentleman would request the assistance of a servant, but said gentleman would then miss the pleasure of Sophia's gentle ministrations. "I submit to your capable care."

Fortunately, the knife had only left a shallow slice in his forearm, and the bleeding had stopped a while ago. Sophia created a lather with a brick of lye soap then gently scrubbed away the dried blood. When she seemed satisfied, she returned the cloth to the basin.

"Joy's salve will heal the wound, but I am afraid it smells awful." She pried the lid from a small jar and a wave of garlic assaulted his nose. "She swears the wild garlic is necessary for healing, but I think she likes that no one wearing it can sneak up behind her and catch her napping."

"You are jesting, I hope."

She smiled. "I am, although I would not begrudge her a rest if it would not upset the other servants. She was the only above stairs maid for many years. Joy has earned her position as lady's maid, in my opinion, and the advantages the job entails."

After she covered his cut with the smelly concoction,

she wound a cloth bandage around his arm three times and tied the ends together.

"You may remove the bandage tomorrow. If you would like me to apply more salve, you may call in the afternoon. Aunt Beatrice and I have plans to visit the lending library in the morning." She stood upright; her hands landed on her hips. With a decisive nod, she said, "That should stay in place if you refrain from tackling any more ladies today."

In her own surroundings, she seemed like her usual self. He hated to disrupt the sense of order that had been restored, but he must. He stood, pulled his sleeve over his bandage, and urged her to sit in the chair. "Do you have injuries? I could summon your lady's maid if any require tending."

"I am all right." She brushed her hands over the dried mud and grass stains on her skirts and frowned. "My gown suffered worse. I hope it can be salvaged."

"I am relieved you were unharmed." He lowered to one knee, so he was eye to eye with her. Her lips parted. "We should talk about the shooter."

"Oh." Her shoulders slumped forward. "If you intend to lecture me for storming off, please save it for another time. This has been a trying day already."

He took both of her hands in his. "I never mean to scold you, Sophia. I recognize you have a mind of your own, and I greatly admire your ingenuity and independence. But now, I need you to trust and obey me without question. You and your aunt are in danger. Go to your chambers and gather what you need for a few days. Wake your aunt and have her do the same. We are leaving Wedmore House at once."

Sophia laughed. "This is the worst proposal in history."

Proposal? Faith! He *was* down on one knee.

"If you want to run off to Gretna Green," she said, "you

needn't employ a ruse. I have not been coy about what I want, but frankly, your change in attitude toward marriage is perplexing. I hope this is not a result of misguided loyalties. I am sure Regina did not expect you to marry me to keep me safe from ridiculous young bucks kicking up a lark in the country."

"Today's incident was not the act of a drunken fool."

She flicked a hand dismissively. "I suppose *you* know more than Lord Seabrook. He said it was one of the local gentry. The village has been inundated with buffoons."

"I wish that were true, but I recognized the man in the meadow."

"Oh?"

He took a cleansing breath. "The other day you mentioned a man named Farrin tried to kill your sister and brother-in-law before he fell into the river. I believe he survived. The man—the shooter—he works for Farrin."

She blinked several times as if they spoke different languages. "You denied being acquainted with this Farrin fellow. How can you possibly know the man from the meadow serves him?"

"I *know*," he said. "I was not forthcoming that day, and I am sorry."

"You lied? Why did you lie?" She blanched. "He tried to kill my sister. If you knew he was alive, you should have said."

"I didn't know until today, Sophia. I have much to explain, and I promise I will tell you everything as soon as we are in a safe location."

He would be breaking his vow to the Consul, but the Consul had involved Sophia. She deserved to know the truth.

"Wh-where will we go?" Her complexion appeared

bloodless, and her hands had grown cold. "Will we be safe at Hartland Manor?"

"Farrin will expect you to retreat to one of your uncle's properties. I cannot take you home, but I promise he will never guess where you have gone."

Wherever the hell that might be. Farrin knew the location of every sanctuary across England, and Crispin's own properties would be no safer than Wedmore's.

They were interrupted by a soft knock. The door had been left ajar. Crispin peered over his shoulder at the butler filling the doorway. "Yes, what is it?"

"Your *valet* has arrived, my lord?"

Crispin released Sophia's hands and stood. "Show him in."

The butler bowed his head then walked away stiffly.

"Why is your valet at the door?" Sophia asked.

"I sent for him." He smiled grimly. "Kane is more than he seems."

She leaned back in the chair, crossing her arms. "As are you, Lord Mysterious. As are you." She appeared none too pleased with this realization.

SIXTEEN

A YOUNG MAN IN HIS EARLY TWENTIES SWEPT INTO THE drawing room and stopped abruptly when his gaze landed on Sophia sitting in the gilded armchair. She resisted the urge to cover the stains on her skirts or smooth a hand over her disheveled hair.

"Miss Darlington," Crispin said, "may I present my valet, Kane?"

"You may." Sophia offered a tentative smile, unclear on how she should address a man who was more than he appeared.

Kane mumbled a polite greeting and moved to stand with his hands crossed behind his back and his stance wide. The poor man appeared as uncomfortable with the unconventional introduction as she was.

She eased from the chair, her legs trembling slightly. "Perhaps I should go above stairs to pack. Where should I tell Aunt Beatrice we are going?"

"I haven't decided." Crispin pinched his forehead, rubbing his fingers back and forth as if attempting to erase the worry lines. She had never seen him in such a state. She was attempting to act brave, but earlier events and the revelation that the man who had tried to kill Regina was alive and wanted Sophia dead were beginning to take a toll. She wished she could retreat to her chambers, lock the doors, and never come out.

She licked her dry lips. "Once you have chosen a destination, please send for me. I will approach Aunt Beatrice after a decision has been made." She started for the door.

Crispin extended his hand. "Please, I would like you to stay. Your help would be appreciated."

If he had asked for her assistance earlier that day, she would have been overjoyed. Now she wondered if he acted out of guilt. From the steadfast way in which he had studied her on the return trip to London, and the uncommon care he took with his words, she suspected he blamed himself for their brush with death. He was very similar to Sophia's oldest sister. Regina and Crispin seemed to see themselves as modern day Atlases, responsible for bearing the weight of the world on their shoulders.

Despite her reservations about his motives, she consented to stay. She assumed a seat on the settee closer to the door and rested her hands in her lap. "How may I be of assistance?"

"Do you have any ideas on where to go? Perhaps there is a relative from your father's side of the family willing to take in you and your aunt?"

Slowly, she wiggled her mouth side to side as she thought about the Darlington family line. She and her sisters had no contact with their father's kin, and she couldn't be certain she would be remembered, much less welcomed into their homes. Besides, it did not seem right to bring her troubles to anyone else's door.

"How difficult would it be to find us if we imposed on my father's family? After all other possibilities have been exhausted, would Farrin not think to follow that trail?"

Kane darted a wide-eyed look toward Crispin.

"Garrick made an appearance at Lord Seabrook's estate today." Crispin pushed up his sleeve to reveal his bandage. "It was not a friendly call."

"Hellfire!" The young man flinched and smiled bashfully. "Uh...pardon me, miss. I should have stated I am surprised by this distressing turn of events, for Lord Margrave and I were under the impression the gent was dead."

She tipped her head, studying Kane with a growing sense of curiosity. He did not speak like a man in service or behave like a valet, not that she was acquainted with any other valets. Uncle Charles has always insisted he didn't require help stepping in and out of his pants or tugging on his boots.

"She is correct." Crispin paced the length of the room. "After Wedmore's properties, Farrin will search mine, and eventually, he will expand the search to anyone with a connection to her."

Sophia drifted into her own thoughts while the men discussed possibilities. Her life no longer made sense. She had done nothing to warrant this madman's attention, so why would he want her dead? Crispin had to be wrong. He thought he had recognized the man, but he was mistaken.

"Take her to your brother," Kane said.

Sophia sat up straighter, attentive again. "When did you acquire a brother? I thought you were an only child after your mother and brother passed."

Crispin glowered at the valet.

"You might abhor the idea," Kane said with a shrug, "but it is a reasonable alternative. Miss Darlington is as close to you as family, and yet she is unaware you have a brother. Devil take it, *I* knew nothing about him until Christmas." His face flushed. "Pardon me again, miss."

Sophia waved away his apology. She appreciated his candor if not his coarse language. Crispin had always held back pieces of himself. A peek at what he kept behind the impenetrable wall fascinated her.

"Aside from a few letters, I've had no contact with Alexander since we met Christmas Day," Crispin said.

A weight lifted from her heart. After his rejection, she has been plagued by speculation. Had he left her on Christmas to enjoy the company of another woman? Had her inexperience repelled him? Had she imagined the spark between them?

"Is it true your mother died?" Sophia piped up, lagging behind the men in conversation.

"A lie." Crispin bit out the words, his hazel eyes stormy. "She lives with her second husband near Finchingfield."

"Oh." She wanted to delve into that emotional treasure trove, but it seemed best to wait for another time.

Kane cleared his throat. "Your mother retired from Society a long time ago, and your brother never joined. Likely, they have been forgotten. Take Miss Darlington and her aunt to your mother's home and request your brother's protection."

"I refuse to ask for that woman's assistance."

"You would not be asking for *her* help. You have a brother."

"No!" Crispin resumed pacing, his strides quicker and more agitated. Sophia and Kane exchanged a helpless glance and remained silent. When Crispin seemed to deplete his anger, he stopped stalking the room. His skin had a slightly greenish tint. He clenched and unclenched his fists.

"Faith," he muttered. "Tell your aunt we will be visiting my mother. It should not come as a shock. Beatrice is aware she lives."

Sophia startled at the news. "I see."

How odd her aunt had been able to keep a secret this big. Sophia excused herself to go above stairs to prepare for travel. She felt it prudent not to ask if his mother would receive them.

"Do not tell the servants where we are going," Crispin called.

"Yes, my lord."

Joy was waiting for her in her chambers. A clean gown was laid out on the bed.

"Aunt Beatrice and I will be traveling with Lord Margrave. I am under orders to pack enough for a few days."

The lady's maid returned the clean gown to the wardrobe and retrieved one suited for travel. "Where is your destination, miss? I am uncertain what I should pack."

Sophia trusted Joy beyond a doubt. "I know you can keep a secret. You mustn't tell the others."

"Never. I will always protect your secrets, miss."

"Lord Margrave and I are to be married." She felt strangely absent of emotion when she made the announcement. Perhaps none of this was real, and Crispin would reveal their sudden betrothal was a ruse, necessary until she and Aunt Beatrice were tucked away somewhere out of sight and mind. "We are on our way to Gretna Green."

Sophia trusted *Joy*, but many of the housemaids were new to Wedmore House. In the event that someone was listening at the keyhole and worked for the enemy, she wanted to throw the hounds off the scent.

"Lord Margrave is a lucky gentleman." Joy's smile did not reach her eyes. "May I speak freely, miss?"

"You may," she said warily.

"Is it wise for your aunt to accompany you to Scotland?"

Sophia exhaled, relieved. Servants of different households talked with one another. If Joy had heard unflattering gossip about Crispin, Sophia trusted her maid would speak up, even if she didn't wish to hear it.

"I could not bear to marry without Auntie in attendance; she would never forgive me if I did."

Joy clucked her tongue. "Yes, Miss Allred would be difficult to console, the poor woman. With all of her chicks out of the nest, I am afraid she will not know what to do anymore. At least promise not to take Cupid with you. Lord Margrave is likely to leave the little beast on the side of the road."

Sophia laughed. "He would never be so cruel, but I prefer to keep my future husband happy and comfortable. Will you look after Cupid?"

"He will be the most cared for pooch in London."

"Thank you, Joy."

After Sophia changed into her travel gown and her lady's maid brushed out her hair and pinned it up, she visited Aunt Beatrice's chambers. Her aunt was awake after her daily lie down, but Cupid was still snoring at the foot of the bed. Aunt Beatrice looked up from her knitting, her eyes large behind her spectacles. "Come in, dearest. Tell me all about Lady Seabrook's garden party. Did you enjoy yourself?"

"It was interesting." Sophia closed the door behind her and leaned against it. "Auntie, I have something to tell you."

Her aunt lowered her knitting needles. "What is it, love?"

"Joy will be in to pack your belongings soon. We are

going on a journey, but I have promised not to reveal our destination until we are in the coach and outside of London. Lord Margrave has asked me not to ruin the surprise."

"Oh!" Aunt Beatrice tossed her knitting in her basket. Cupid jerked awake. "Oh, my! Is this what I think it is?"

Sophia shrugged, playing coy.

Her aunt lowered her voice to a whisper. "Are we *eloping?*"

Sophia smiled. "I cannot say anything, Auntie. Please do not make me break my promise."

When Aunt Beatrice squealed and clapped her hands, Cupid leapt from the bed and ran to jump on Sophia's skirts, pawing to reach her. She scooped him in her arms and showered his furry head with kisses. "Joy will look after our precious boy while we are gone. Margrave has asked that we travel light. He wishes to leave as soon as possible."

"Well, I hope he does not insist I leave my knitting behind. I am making a baby blanket for Regina and Mr. Vistoire."

"Auntie! They are newlyweds."

"I see it is time to have the talk." Aunt Beatrice winked.

Sophia laughed. "You are well aware I understand procreation." Sophia had peppered her aunt with questions since she was a young girl, and Aunt Beatrice had always been forthcoming with her answers. "Knitting a baby blanket while the bride and groom are on their honeymoon might seem a bit overeager."

Aunt Beatrice sniffed. "It is time for the sound of little feet in the house again. I will start a blanket for you and Lord Margrave next."

"That is premature, Auntie, and I never said we were to be married."

"Of course you didn't, dearest." Aunt Beatrice smiled like a cat cornering a mouse. "I will make certain his lordship knows you never uttered a word about eloping, or all the babies you will give him."

"Dear heavens, *no!*" Sophia groaned and buried her face in her hands, knowing her aunt was likely to do the opposite of what she promised.

Aunt Beatrice laughed.

Fretting over her aunt's loose tongue proved unnecessary, however. Once Crispin saw her and her aunt settled in his travel coach, he informed them he would be following on horseback until it was time to change horses.

The carriage shuddered away from Wedmore House to Cupid's waves, courtesy of the lady's maid who cradled the little black poodle against her chest and moved his paw. Sophia waved, too, and prayed Joy and all the servants under Uncle Charles's roof would be safe.

Crispin had put her mind somewhat at ease when he reported meeting privately with the butler while she was overseeing the packing her belongings. Mr. Tillman would hire men exclusively from a list Crispin had provided to begin patrolling Wedmore House that evening. Crispin said their presence would discourage intruders. Despite Sophia's objections, he insisted on assuming responsibility for the expense of additional staff.

Aunt Beatrice pulled the blanket she was knitting from the basket on the bench beside her. "Why do you suppose Margrave is on horseback instead of joining us? Did you quarrel? I have never seen such passionate rows in all my life." She wiggled her eyebrows comically. "It bodes well for a happy marriage bed."

Sophia shook her head in disbelief at her aunt's single-mindedness. "Auntie, I hope you do not intend to hound me for children the whole way. Otherwise, I will switch places with Crispin. You can pester him for a while."

Aunt Beatrice sniggered. The clicking of her needles was comforting and familiar.

"You know he likes his exercise. We are not quarreling."

Sophia rested her head against the seatback and smiled, but inside she was trembling. Although he hadn't stated it outright, Crispin was concerned about another attack. He followed on horseback, so he could more readily launch a defense.

"It is a long way to Gretna Green," Aunt Beatrice said as she furiously worked the knitting needles. "Perhaps I will have enough time to make a baby blanket for Evangeline, too."

"I never said we were heading for Gretna Green. Crispin wants me to meet his mother before we marry."

The knitting needles ceased clicking. Aunt Beatrice regarded her with a wary glimmer in her eyes. "Oh? We are on our way to see his mother?"

"I am sure it must come as a surprise, Auntie. After all, we believed she died many years ago."

"Did we? It is hard to remember sometimes." Aunt Beatrice chuckled, stuck out her tongue, and made a silly face. "Too many hard knocks to the head, perhaps."

Sophia suspected her aunt might be blaming her faulty memory to avoid further questions, but Auntie *had* grown more forgetful over the last several years. It was possible she did not remember Crispin's mother was alive. Or perhaps she had wished to protect Crispin from further heartache by keeping the secret, which only made Sophia adore her aunt more.

When they reached the first coaching inn, Crispin pulled her aside. "We have too far to travel. I will find lodging for us before nightfall."

Sophia nodded. She had no choice except to trust his judgment. Whatever he had become involved in was beyond her capabilities, and she could never be of any real help. As he had claimed, she was a hindrance. The realization scraped her heart raw.

SEVENTEEN

"You have requested the key to Lord Geoffrey's chambers, Your Grace?"

Perry Walsh, Duke of Stanhurst, took a gulp of brandy for fortification and turned to face the head housekeeper. "I did. I want access now."

Mrs. Quince bowed her head. "As you wish, Your Grace. If you will follow me." She selected a key from the ring at her waist and exited his chambers, politely acknowledging his valet as she slipped past him where he stood inside the threshold.

Perry and the housekeeper walked in silence along the narrow corridor. Mrs. Quince paused at Geoffrey's door. "On your command, no one has entered the room. Are you certain you do not want a maid to set everything to order first?"

"Open the door."

"As you wish, Your Grace." Red blotches splattered her neck and cheeks. With her gaze downcast, she wiggled the key into the keyhole. The lock gave way with a clank that echoed in the empty corridor. Father had sold everything, even the thick Aubusson he and Mother had received as a wedding gift.

Before the housekeeper could scurry away like the frightened mouse she had become under his father's employ, Perry apologized for his surliness. "I must view my brother's chamber as he left it, and I need to do this alone."

Mrs. Quince smiled timidly. "I understand. You will not be disturbed."

"Thank you."

Perry stepped inside, and the housekeeper closed the door, forcing him to face the evidence of his failure as a brother. Geoffrey's room was almost as bare as the corridor. It had been stripped of anything of beauty or value, leaving only a bed, desk, a battered Chippendale chair, and an empty bedside table. He should have seen his brother was in trouble, but Perry had been keeping his distance. His father's obsession with the actress had been mortifying, and the gossip circulating about his father's cruelty had sickened him.

Stop!

Shrugging off a mantle of guilt and fury, he crossed the room to throw open the drapes. A blinding afternoon sun thrust through the leaded glass panes. He shaded his eyes with his hand and turned to survey his brother's private space. If there was anything incriminating in the room, it should be easy to find. He approached the desk and yanked open a drawer.

His brother's diary and two letters were neatly stacked inside. They were addressed to Geoffrey but did not identify the sender. The seal was unbroken on one of the letters, and neither included the usual markings associated with postal delivery. Had it been hand-delivered?

He broke the seal and scanned the page. It was filled with numbers. An acidic burn seeped into his belly.

Dropping onto the chair, he dug out the second letter to compare. The handwriting on the front matched. Again, the page was covered in numbers, grouped in threes. His mouth grew dry.

It is encrypted.

He couldn't be certain—*God, please let me be mistaken*—but another explanation evaded him. Unease spread through his limbs. Men with nothing to hide did not receive letters in cipher. Margrave's accusations echoed through his mind.

Geoffrey associated with dangerous men. His past dealings place you at risk.

As a younger man, Perry had been reckless and believed himself invincible. His life had been his to risk. Now, too many people relied on him for their own survival—his sisters, the servants, tenant farmers. He was not his father. He did not abuse nor neglect those entrusted to his care. No one threatened what was his.

Grabbing the letters and his brother's diary, he strode from the room. In his own chambers, he jotted a command on a piece of paper and rang for a footman. He thrust the paper in the boy's hands.

"Take this to Baroness Van Middleburg. Do not delay."

"Yes, Your Grace." He rushed out the door, seeming to sense the urgency.

Perry was in his study reading his brother's journal when his butler announced his second cousin's arrival. "Show her in."

Ida swept into the room a few moments later. Her face was screwed up with worry. He stood but did not leave his desk to greet her.

"I came as soon as I received your summons," she said. "What has happened? Has one of your sisters fallen ill? I do hope none of them have come down with a chill. It has been a wet summer, and young girls can be careless."

How dare she pretend to be concerned? Perry glared. "Sit."

"Mercy, the news must be terrible." Her hand fluttered to her chest, and she took a seat on the window bench. "It is all right. I am strong enough to accept whatever has befallen us. I am here to support you."

"Us," he scoffed. "There is no *us*, Ida. Do not insult me with your play acting."

She drew back, appearing genuinely caught off guard. He wagered she was. She had probably believed she had him hoodwinked, and he had been, but no more. He gathered the letters and walked around the desk to approach the window bench.

"Are these what you hoped to find in my brother's chambers, Ida? That *is* the reason you offered to sort through his belongings, is it not?"

Color drained from her complexion; the brackets on either side of her mouth deepened. She appeared stricken. "I-I only wished to help."

He held out the letters, shaking the sheets of paper when she didn't accept them immediately. "Take them."

A shadow of irritation crossed her face, but it disappeared just as quickly. She reached for the letters and examined them, first one and then the second. Her mouth opened and closed several times. "I am at a loss." When she glanced up, puzzled grooves were carved across her brow. "What is this?"

"What is wrong, cousin? Didn't Geoffrey teach you how to decipher? Perhaps it was a secret kept between my brother and your husband." Perry took the letters and shoved them into a pocket inside his jacket.

"None of what you are saying is making sense." She gently took his hand; her large brown eyes overflowed with confusion and compassion. "Forgive me for overstepping my bounds, but I only meant to help you in your grief. I loved your father like my own brother. I cannot close my eyes to your suffering. Dear boy, I am worried you are not well."

His certainty began to falter. Margrave could have been mistaken about his cousin's involvement. Ida had never shown an inclination for ill will toward anyone. If anything, her behavior was consistent with how she had always been.

When his mother died, Ida had stayed at the family home for weeks to comfort his sisters. Was it truly odd that she would offer her support now in the wake of his great loss? His brother and father had been murdered. How did one cope with such tragedy alone?

"Perry." She squeezed his fingers. He snapped to attention. "Will you please allow me to send for the doctor? He will give you something for your nerves."

He pulled free of her grip. "I do not require a tonic for nerves. I crave the quiet of the country and my sisters' company. I am going home."

It would be a brief trip since his presence was required at the Lords, but he needed time alone to study Geoffrey's diary and search for meaning in his brother's words. His younger brother's life had been stolen. Perry wanted to know the reason.

He returned to the desk to collect the diary then headed for the door, eager to dismiss his cousin and order his staff to ready his travel chariot.

"I am sorry to have bothered you. You are obviously as ignorant of Geoffrey's activities as I was. Thank you for responding to my summons promptly."

Ida wearily pushed up from the bench when Perry offered to escort her to the front door.

"Would you like me to take the letters to Lord Van

Middleburg?" she asked. "I cannot say my husband will be able to shed light on the mystery, but if it will bring you peace of mind..."

"That is unnecessary. I will decipher the letters eventually, or find someone who can." He walked her to the front door, kissed her cheek, and bade her good-bye.

She frowned. "Are you leaving for home today? You will not arrive before nightfall."

"I need respite. This house..." He couldn't explain, and she wouldn't understand. His father's presence was everywhere. It was suffocating. Perry feared he might become as mad as his father if he stayed another night.

Ida sighed. "I suppose I am wasting breath trying to persuade you to wait until morning."

"You are."

"Very well. I wish you a safe journey."

Perry escorted her to her husband's carriage then informed the butler he would be returning to the country. He and his servants, two postilions on horseback and his valet in the rumble seat, set out for home within the hour. He pulled his brother's diary from a leather bag. With at least an hour of daylight remaining, he started reading from the beginning again. The first entry was from three years ago.

Geoffrey was gone, but reading his words brought him back to life in that moment. His baritone voice filled Perry's head as he devoured the pages; he turned them quickly so as not to lose the thread of the memory. Geoffrey's first entries had been wry and humorous. Perry chuckled over antidotes about mutual friends, family members, and the occasional busybody or bore they often had encountered in London.

One such tale was about an arrogant and braggadocios man he had met at the faro table at one of the gaming hells.

Geoffrey heard rumors the man was King George IV's lap dog. When they shared a drink later that evening and Geoffrey had posed the question about the gossip, the man had insisted he held power beyond anything Perry's brother could imagine. He boasted of his importance as the head of a select group of spies, independent of the Home Office, who answered directly to the King and did his bidding.

Setting aside the possibility he is most likely cracked, I find it difficult to believe this feral gent is capable of being tamed by anyone. Ambition oozes from his pores, overpowering in its stench. If his claims are true, it smells like opportunity.

Geoffrey hadn't explained his meaning.

Later that summer, Perry's brother wrote about falling in love. *Something rather extraordinary occurred today,* his entry began. An Italian opera singer had caught his fancy, and the romantic attachment seemed mutual. Page after page detailed their love affair. Perry's brother spouted poems and was clearly smitten. Unfortunately, two and a half years ago, the passion that had burned brightly between them was snuffed out when a more important and wealthy benefactor offered his protection.

After the failed love affair, Geoffrey's diary became a dumping ground for vitriol. He railed against men like Perry who had inherited their rank through no accomplishments of their own. Geoffrey vowed to make something of himself in order to win back the heart of his one true love, and free himself from their father's influence.

Perry closed the book. He no longer recognized his brother in the hateful words. Their contacts had become brief and infrequent over the last two years. Geoffrey had offered various excuses for avoiding the family seat. His behavior made sense now. He had been hiding from Perry. Understanding his brother's actions did not bring solace.

Grateful for sunset, Perry tucked the diary back in the bag. He could pick it up again when he had daylight to read by and a good night's sleep behind him. When he and his servants arrived at the first coaching inn to change horses, the quarter moon hung in the distance, and the sky held the muted pink remnants of a day gone. Perry's servants made fast work of changing out the horses. He wished the postilions a safe ride back to London before continuing his journey with the hired men and horses.

He estimated little more than an hour remained until the traveling chariot would turn onto the lane leading home. His sisters would be sitting down to dine when he waltzed inside and caught them by surprise. He was sure to be bombarded with many questions about the Season and his search for a wife. He wished he had something valuable to share.

He closed the louvred blinds, slumped on the bench, and extended his legs. He was dozing off when shouts jolted him awake. The carriage rumbled to a stop.

The shouting continued. Perry opened the blind to peer out the forward window, but the carriage lights blinded him. He opened the door to stick his head outside. "Who is causing that commotion?"

"I think it is highwaymen," his valet said from the rumble seat; his voice quivered.

"Damned nuisance," Perry grumbled and dropped back against the seat, leaving the door open in anticipation of the blackguards coming to demand payment. "Do not resist. They will be on their way soon enough."

He had been aware of the risks involved with night travel when he set out, and although he carried a firearm on the road, there was no sense in anyone coming to harm over a few pieces of silver. Everything of value was locked in the safe at the town house. He was digging a small purse from his jacket pocket to appease the thieves when a deafening blast rang out.

What the devil?

A horse squealed. The carriage jerked forward and stopped. One of the postilions yelled commands, attempting to gain control of the team. A flash, then another bang followed. A man cried out, perhaps one of Perry's.

He dove onto the carriage floor, his large frame bent at impossible angles in the small space. He groped for the pistol at his waist. The coach violently lurched, throwing him against the rear bench. The firearm slipped from his hand.

"Your Grace!"

His panicked valet jumped, wisely abandoning his post as the carriage shot down the dark road. The door slammed then flung open again. Perry braced his arms and legs to keep from being tossed around the interior. The wheels bumped over ruts, became airborne, then crashed down with a shudder.

He struggled to climb from the floor and lost ground when the conveyance careened around a curve. The door flew open and was ripped from the hinges as the carriage sideswiped a tree.

Loud whoops came from behind, closing the distance rapidly. Perry felt around for the pistol, but it was gone. The sounds of men giving chase grew louder. What did they want? They had met with no resistance. His men had been ready to stand and deliver.

The crackle of timber splintering wrenched his heart and filled him with dread. The sound crescendoed until it ended with a loud snap.

I am going to die.

The carriage veered off the road, racing down an incline

and hitting ruts. Perry was thrown in the air and came down hard again. His head smacked against the cushioned wall. One of the front wheels rammed into something unmovable, and the back of the carriage kicked up, tumbling end over end. Perry lost all sense of where he was as he was knocked around like a billiard ball bouncing off the rails.

When the carriage stopped rolling, it tipped and landed on its side. Perry was on his back, staring at the moon through the missing door. All was quiet, as if even the crickets and frogs were out of breath.

He lay there drawing in gulps of air and taking inventory of his aches and pains. His head throbbed. Thankfully, he could move his arms and legs. His back was tight, and something uncomfortable was wedged beneath him. It was his leather satchel. Pushing to a seated position, he wiggled the bag out from under him and debated what to do now.

The horses were gone. The postilions were gone. Even the highwaymen seemed to have abandoned the chase. He was alone and had no idea in what direction was home.

"Damnation." He half spoke, half groaned the curse.

Shifting to his knees, he planted his hands against the sides of the carriage and attempted to stand. Someone clambered onto the carriage and filled the doorway, blocking the moon.

A faceless man snarled. "I'll be takin' those letters, Yer Grace."

Perry gritted his teeth and sank back to the ground.

Damn you, Ida. And damn Margrave for being right.

Perry lifted his chin in defiance. "I've no notion of what letters you reference, but let this be a warning. If you persist in this matter, I will see you hanged."

The man sniggered. "The lady sees ye put 'em in your

pocket. Don't matter none if theys bloody when she gets 'em."

The sound of a hammer cocking reverberated in the closed space. All the air was sucked from the carriage. He was really going to die. Powder exploded with an earsplitting bang.

Perry jerked.

There was a thump on the ground outside.

A few more gunshots echoed in the distance.

Someone yelled, "Run!"

"Yes, run, you cowards," a man taunted. "Run away."

As their footfalls rapidly faded, Perry patted his body, shocked to realize he was free of extra holes. How had the blackguard missed at that range? Someone was rounding the carriage. A long, low whistle carried on the air.

"Damn shame," a voice muttered. "It was a fine carriage."

"Who is there?" Perry called. "Announce yourself."

"Your Grace, you survived. I must admit it seemed improbable for a bit."

The man stepped in front of the forward window. Much to Perry's relief, the lamps had been extinguished in the tumble rather than setting the carriage ablaze, but he couldn't see anything beyond the man's shadow as he knelt beside the carriage. Perry had the strange sense the man was smiling at him through the window.

"The name is Kane." The man's tone was cheerful, friendly. "Lord Margrave sent me. Let's get you out of there, shall we?"

"A man is still out there. He has a pistol. He intends to murder me."

Suddenly, his rescuer's voice was like steel. "Not any longer, Your Grace."

EIGHTEEN

Sophia lay in the dark, staring at the ceiling and listening to Aunt Beatrice's deep, rhythmic breathing. It was late, and the inn had grown silent soon after she and her aunt retired. They were one of two parties taking lodgings at the remote location.

When she was certain her aunt was in a deep enough sleep, she slipped from the bed and donned a cloak, tugging the hood over her head to cover her loose hair. She sensed Crispin sitting outside the door of their room, although he made no noise. The sliver of light underneath the door was dimmer than when she had climbed into bed, as if a shadow fell across the threshold.

In stocking feet, she tiptoed toward the door. Crispin swung his head in her direction when she stepped into the inn's corridor and closed the door with a soft snick. He was sitting with his back leaning against the wall. His legs were casually drawn up with his arm draped over a knee. No surprise registered on his face. As she suspected, he was guarding her and her aunt. Her pulse raced a little faster. He had reassured her that they were safe.

"Am I keeping you awake?" he murmured.

Sophia shook her head. He scooted to make room for her on the pallet he had laid in the corridor. She sat beside him, struck by how uncomfortable his night would be at his post.

"Are you certain posting watch outside our door is necessary?" she asked.

"No one followed us from London, but I prefer to stay close."

His body heat warmed her side, and she longed to feel his arm around her shoulders and to be held close to his heart. "You must be exhausted after all that time in the saddle."

He smiled as if he found her concern amusing. "I am accustomed to riding, but I am a little fatigued."

"If the danger has passed, you should go to bed." She glanced at the door. She should return to her own bed before she did something foolish, like throw herself on him and break into an ugly sobbing jag. It had been that sort of day.

"I will sleep in the coach tomorrow." He reached for her hand and turned it palm up to trace the fine lines with his fingertip. A pleasing tingle spread up her arm. "If worry is keeping you awake, rest assured I will keep watch over you all night."

In the past, Sophia would have argued she was capable of protecting herself by applying common sense and avoiding dangerous situations. The incident at Lord and Lady Seabrook's estate had shattered the false sense of security she had created to keep her fears at bay. Without warning, the world had become a frightening, unpredictable place. Sophia had no control over anything, including her own body. A tremor traveled through her.

Crispin looked up from her hand; his strong brows lifted toward his hairline. "Are you chilled?"

Before she could answer, he wrapped his arm around her and drew her against his chest. She laid her head on his shoulder, closing her eyes as she inhaled his familiar scent. Tears wet her eyes as relief enveloped her. He was a cup of chocolate on a dreary day, a thick quilt on a cold night, her safe harbor when she felt adrift.

"I thought I could be your helpmate," she mumbled. "I feel stupid. I did not want to believe I was a hindrance to whatever you are doing, but—"

He shushed her. "Stop."

His gentle rebuke was softened when he captured her chin. Lifting her face, he pressed his lips to her forehead. She closed her eyes to stem fresh tears. Crying would make her a bigger burden, and she didn't require his strength to withstand this hardship. She had her own supply of fortitude, if only she could find where it was hiding.

"I was frustrated," he said. "I regret uttering the word."

"It is true, Crispin. I am no match for these men, and now you are risking your life for me. I never should have meddled. I should have stayed away from the theatre like you wanted, and I never should have entered Lord Van Middleburg's study. What if something happens to Aunt Beatrice? How would I ever forgive myself?"

"No harm will come to you or Beatrice. I will not allow it." He lowered his voice to a near whisper. "You are not responsible for what has occurred. I am sorry you have been ensnared in this mess. You have done nothing wrong."

She swallowed around the huge lump in her throat.

"This must be confusing, love." His mouth was close to her ear, and the caress of his warm breath against her neck elicited a tantalizing shiver to race through her. "I promised you an explanation, but first I must have your word you will never repeat what I am about to reveal—not to *anyone*. Not your sisters, Lady Octavia..."

She nodded. "Or Auntie, I understand. I vow to never repeat a word."

"I would invite you to my room, but I do not want to leave your aunt unguarded. It is a lengthy story."

She stretched to place a kiss on his cheek then snuggled into a comfortable position. His concern for her aunt sealed her fate. She was hopelessly in love with him. "I have no place to be." Or anywhere she would rather be, even if it meant sitting on an uncomfortable plank floor.

"You asked how I know Farrin and his men. It is best to start at the beginning, I think."

She loved the low deep rumble of his voice. It reminded her of thunder in the distance with her snug and safe in her bed.

"After I buried my father, the time came to assume the responsibilities attached to the title. I was seventeen, but my father began preparing me for the viscountcy at a young age. He also made efforts to foster the relationship between your uncle and me. Father trusted Charles to guide me when he was no longer around to do so."

"Your father must have loved you a great deal to prepare you as he did," she said. "How sad he must have been to realize he was unlikely to know you as a man."

"I have never given it much thought, but I suppose it must have been difficult for him. He spoke candidly about his illness. I cannot recall a time when I did not know his heart was defective. He did not dwell on it, though. My father was in good spirits most of the time. He had this booming laugh that echoed throughout the house. I can still hear it sometimes." He chuckled softly, and she felt tension melting from his muscles.

"After my father was away from home, his laughter

would herald his return. Some of the servants had known him since he was a boy, and they felt comfortable joking with him. All of them seemed to enjoy his jovial nature. I would run to greet him, and he would make a fuss over how much I had grown, even if he had only been gone a few days."

Sophia smiled. "He sounds lovely. I wish I remembered him."

"He was fond of you and your sisters, although he had no notion of how to talk to any of you. You did not seem bothered by his silly questions, though. When he asked how many fish you had caught for your supper that evening, you giggled and set him straight about ladies' activities."

"Now that you mention it, I vaguely recall that conversation." She laughed. "Didn't he make a show of demanding the servants take away my plate?"

"Yes, he had a grand time teasing you. Father admired your spirit. He said someday you would hold some poor gent's toes to the fire, and he would become a better man for it. I think my father would be pleased to know I *am* that man."

Sophia's mood sobered. "You must be less pleased with recent developments, considering you never intended to marry."

"I am relieved."

She drew back to ascertain if he was teasing. "Relieved?"

"I never would have exposed you to this part of life, but I am grateful to have a door opened that I believed was barred to me." He held her gaze; his hazel eyes darkened. "I have never desired anyone more, Sophia. The longing to be with you hasn't lessened since we parted at Christmas. You have no idea how it ripped me apart to see you with other men."

"I do know the feeling." Her nose tingled with warning

that tears might be coming despite her iron will. "I devoured the newssheets for any mention of you, and the prospect of finding your name linked with another lady's left me queasy."

"There has been no one since you, darling." He pushed the hood from her head and slid his hand to the back of her neck, beneath her hair. Warmth spread down her back. "I want you. No one else can ease the ache in my heart."

When he touched his lips to hers, the urge to cry was overwhelmed by elation. She leaned into his kiss. Her heart overflowed with tenderness, and a tiny sob escaped her. He drew back; his brows veered toward each other.

"Have I frightened you?"

"Never." She gently hooked her hand behind his head to draw him back. "Please, kiss me. I have an ache in my heart, too."

Her admission elicited a fire in his eyes. He captured her mouth with a husky growl. Sophia parted her lips, welcoming him. His tongue teased hers, encouraging her boldness. She tentatively caressed his bottom lip. With a hum of approval, he angled her head and deepened the kiss. She wiggled to get closer, and he pulled her onto his lap to straddle his firm thighs. Sophia arched into him. He buried his fingers into her hair as she matched him kiss for kiss. Her breasts became fuller and heavy.

Being in his arms felt like coming home. Everything was right and as it should be in those moments of becoming lost in one another. There was no danger or secrets—no denial, no distance. She was part of him, and he was part of her. *We are equals.*

The thought dragged her out of the haze. It was a lie. She was far from his equal. That had become clear earlier in the day. Even though he had tried to ease the blow by denying she was useless to him, she knew it to be true. She broke the kiss.

He smoothed his hands over her back in slow sweeps, placed a peck on the tip of her nose, and smiled. "You are too distracting by half, minx. If you keep batting those blue eyes at me, I will never finish my story."

Attempting to hide her sudden bout of melancholy, she returned his smile and exaggeratedly fluttered her lashes. "My apologies, my lord."

"You are not sorry in the least." He kissed her lips once more before settling her beside him on the pallet. She melted against him, secure in his affection for her, if not her place in his world.

"Are you sure you are not too tired?" he asked. "You've had much to take in today."

"Curiosity will keep me awake all night. Please, finish your story."

He cleared his throat. "After my father's death, his man of business reviewed the accounts with me and provided detailed summaries on the work in progress on my father's land. One day he handed me the key to my father's safe. It was located in his chambers, which I had been avoiding. It seemed like an invasion, but I knew he expected me to take the reins and remain strong. The safe could have held something important that needed my attention. Your uncle accompanied me into the master's chambers for moral support, even though I assured him I needed no help."

"Hmm... Why does that sound familiar?"

Crispin chuckled. "He did not accept my refusal for help either."

"I am sure he meant well." *I did.*

"I was glad for Charles's presence when I discovered my mother was alive and well."

"I can only imagine. The news must have come as a shock."

"I'd had no hint my father kept secrets, but he hired an investigator soon after she ran away. The man tracked her and my brother to her family home in Scotland. It appears my parents exchanged letters after the investigator located her. Father had held on to hers."

"Do you think he still loved her?"

"I cannot say. I only read her letters, so I do not know what he thought or felt. She did not love him, though. She accused him of abandonment and unforgivable cruelty, and reminded him that she had fulfilled her obligations to him. She had provided him with an heir and a spare, even if he had no love for my brother."

Sophia swallowed a sad sigh. Her mother's diary had been full of praise and admiration for Sophia's father. Her parents had been inseparable. The animosity Crispin described was foreign to her.

"My mother's letters viciously attacked him," he said, "and she threatened to make him as miserable as she had been as his wife if he forced her back to England. Her words showed her to be an unkind and petty woman, but your uncle urged me not to judge her harshly. He said one never knows what occurs in a marriage unless he is one of the parties sharing a bed."

"Uncle Charles probably stole that advice from Plato or some other ancient and wise man."

"A wise *woman*," Crispin said.

"Oh?"

"Your Great-aunt Beatrice gave Wedmore the same advice when he learned my mother left my father. Your uncle was incensed on Father's account."

"They were close friends, weren't they?"

"Since they were boys. I did not heed your uncle's advice

for long. He suggested I avoid contact with my mother until after I grieved for my father. Wedmore said grief could obscure my view, but not only had I learned of my mother's actual fate, I had a brother I did not know. I needed to hold her accountable."

"I cannot imagine my life without Regina and Evangeline."

"Neither can I," he said. "I was fortunate to have the lot of you when I visited your uncle, but I grew accustomed to being an only child at home. Still, I required answers. I couldn't fathom the reason our mother left me behind and took my brother, or why my father had not brought Alexander home after the investigator found them."

He grew quiet for too long. Sophia sat up. His face was blank, even his eyes seemed void of emotion. She hated being unable to ascertain his true thoughts or feelings, which she had to admit was more often the case than not.

"What happened when you went to your mother?" she prompted.

His mouth set in a grim line. "She was no longer in Scotland. Her parents, my grandparents, told me she had remarried and moved to a home near Finchingfield. She was a widow for less than a month."

"Oh." A proper response evaded her.

"My grandparents were welcoming and insisted I stay with them while I was in Scotland. I told them I had taken lodgings at an inn. I started for home the next morning. After I returned, I confessed to your uncle what I had done. I told him I wanted to see my mother in Essex. He advised against it but assumed I would ignore his counsel again, so he agreed to accompany me this time."

"And did you find her?"

"I did. She was alone when your uncle and I arrived.

Alexander had remained at his school in Scotland, and her husband was away collecting rent. She asked me to leave."

Sophia gasped.

"My mother did not want her husband coming home early to find me. She was content with her life and saw no benefit to becoming acquainted after so many years had passed. She said I would be a man soon and lose interest in knowing her. It would be wasted effort on her part."

Sophia was too stunned to speak. His mother had abandoned him as a child and rejected him as a young man. Was it any wonder seeking help from her was abhorrent to him?

Crispin continued his story. "I reassured her I had no interest in her. I only wanted to meet my brother. I swore I would never arrive on her doorstep again."

"Now, you must go back on your word, because of me." Sophia sighed. "I am so very sorry. Is there anywhere else we can go? Would your grandparents provide us refuge?"

"If they were alive, they would take us in without reservation. I returned to visit my grandparents a year later, and we exchanged letters until Grandfather became too ill to write. Against my mother's wishes, he told Alexander about me."

A rush of hot irritation washed over her skin. "Alexander did not know he had a brother?" *Law!* Crispin's mother deserved a proper scolding for her behavior and a good shake. Sophia squared her jaw; her stubborn streak reared its head. "We do not require your mother's assistance. We will manage on our own. Perhaps we should join Regina, Evangeline, and Uncle Charles in Athens."

"I cannot leave England, and I will not allow you to go without me." He raised an eyebrow, playfully goading her. "And do not offer the argument that I have no authority to boss you about."

She sniffed, pretending to be indignant even though she had no plans to be separated from him either. "You still have not proposed to me, Lord Presumptuous."

He grinned. "An oversight I will correct someday."

"What is wrong with *now*?"

"I want to make the moment special, darling."

He kissed her, stealing her breath when he gently caught her bottom lip between his teeth, holding it captive briefly before releasing it to tease her mouth with the tip of his tongue. She surrendered to the kiss with enthusiasm. Every moment felt special with Crispin, and she didn't require a formal proposal. She simply enjoyed bantering with him.

He ended their kiss before she was ready. She hid her disappointment by nuzzling his neck and resting her head on his shoulder.

"As much as I detest the idea," he murmured, "my mother's home poses the least amount of risk for being found."

"Well, I will prepare myself to have the door slammed in our faces."

"We will not be turned away. My mother's husband has become bedridden, and Alexander is man of the house now. He will provide sanctuary."

"What if your mother objects?"

"I do not anticipate she will. She began writing a couple of years ago to request another meeting."

"Have you been corresponding with her, then?"

"No," he said. "I have accepted the nature of our association and think about her as little as possible. It is for the best."

"Of course." Now was not a time for platitudes or observations on how *she* would travel halfway around the world for one more conversation with her own mother. Her experience was not his.

Her love for her mother had been permitted to flourish; it lasted beyond death, like all true loves. Abandonment and rejection prevented Crispin's bond with his mother from ever taking seed. How could any woman not recognize how lovable he was?

She wrapped her arms around his waist and held him, wishing she could absorb the hurt he must have suffered. "Where does Farrin fit into your past?"

"He is an opportunist. After I saw my mother and returned to London, I became bitter and was spoiling for a fight. Your uncle tried to talk sense into me, but I accused him of aligning himself with her and began avoiding him. Farrin found me at my worst."

"What do you mean? What did he want with you?"

"He recruited me to work for him."

Sophia cried out in shock. "Like that man who tried to kill us?"

"No, he wanted me for a different job." He hesitated. His muscles bunched beneath her hand resting on his chest.

"I gave my word, Crispin. Your secret is safe with me. I promise to never repeat what you share with me."

His voice dropped to a whisper. "He recruited me to be a spy."

She bolted upright to look him in the eyes. "For *whom*?"

"For England, silly." He chuckled and the hard-knotted muscles under her palm began to loosen. "Who did you think?"

"I do not know. That Farrin fellow does not strike me as a friend to England."

"You are not the only one questioning his loyalties, which is how I became involved with investigating the Stanhurst murders."

He briefly told her about Farrin's rank among the spies and how his disappearance had raised an alarm, especially after witnesses placed him outside the Pulteney Hotel in the company of old man Stanhurst and Lord Geoffrey the night they were murdered.

"I cannot tell you more, even though I would like to confide in you," he said. "I beg your understanding."

"Say no more." *Mothers rising from the dead, spies, murderers...* She didn't know if she could digest anything else now.

"What does Uncle Charles have to do with any of this? Farrin was set on possessing one of Uncle Charles's old maps, or perhaps it was a new map leading to his next dig. My sisters and I were never quite certain, but we believe the map has something to do with a fabled group called the Black Death."

"Are you sure?"

"Well, no. Farrin never told Xavier what was on the map, but Evangeline found writings about the warriors in Uncle Charles's journal. He had locked it away in a desk drawer, so we surmised he wished to protect his research."

Crispin smiled. "Evangeline is back to picking locks, is she?"

"You must know she is very stubborn about giving up such skills. Evangeline believes Uncle Charles is searching for the ruins of their civilization to prove the group actually existed. Farrin did indicate someone hired him to steal the map—probably a competing antiquarian. His interest was certainly piqued when Xavier lied about finding the map and mentioned the Black Death."

"A plausible deduction on your sister's part."

Sophia narrowed her eyes. "Why does your tone indicate it is *implausible*? What are you not telling me?"

"Farrin is lying about the reason he wants the map."

"How do you know?"

"Intuition," he said and shrugged. "And something I

overheard at the Griffin. I cannot say more, because I do not know how the pieces fit together."

"I see." She yawned. The excitement of the day was catching up to her. "Perhaps I will sleep in the carriage tomorrow, too."

"I expect Beatrice will become suspicious if neither of us can keep our eyes open. You should return to bed before she wakes and realizes you are gone."

"Soon."

Sophia snuggled closer to his side and closed her eyes to savor this rare moment of shared intimacy. It felt as if he had finally opened a door between them, and allowed her access to his thoughts and feelings. What if she surrendered to sleep only to wake and realize this had all been a dream?

"I want to be with you a little longer," she murmured.

"A little longer," he agreed and placed a kiss on her hair.

NINETEEN

As Crispin's coach passed through the gates to approach the Georgian style home where his mother resided, he was struck by how practical and plain the structure was compared to the manor home she had forfeited when she left his father. This realization caused an odd stirring beneath his breastbone.

"How quaint," Sophia's aunt mused when her feet touched the drive. "It appears your mother married beneath her station." Beatrice had always spoken her mind but rarely did so with rancor. He took her comment as an observation rather than an insult.

Crispin extended his hand to Sophia to steady her descent from the carriage.

He smiled as he caught her eye. "Perhaps my mother married for love."

Both women linked arms with him, and they approached the front door.

"It is clear Mr. Ness did," Beatrice said. "It is a fine enough estate to wish for an heir, and he married a woman unlikely to produce one."

Crispin was saved from having to consider her remark when the front door swung open. An older woman in gray fustian, keys at her waist, and a snowy white cap peered at them, wide-eyed and mouth agape as if she had never seen another human.

He cleared his throat. "Lord Margrave and Misses Allred and Darlington to see Lieutenant Locke."

She blinked but otherwise didn't move.

"Mrs. Poindexter"—a male voice came from inside —"move aside and allow my brother entrance."

"Oh!" The housekeeper scampered out of the way. Alexander was standing behind her, grinning like a fool.

"You answered my invitation. How marvelous. Please, come inside."

Crispin couldn't help smiling in return. He hadn't expected an enthusiastic welcome after the way they had parted at Christmas, even though they had exchanged letters recently.

"Mrs. Poindexter, prepare a plate of sandwiches and tea for our guests. I will show them to the drawing room myself."

"Yes, sir." The servant curtsied before bustling from the foyer.

Alexander looked expectantly, awaiting introductions. Crispin's chest puffed out when he presented Beatrice and Sophia. "My betrothed."

Those two words were pleasing to say aloud. He expected the strangeness would disappear once the fantasy of making Sophia his wife became reconciled with reality. His brother offered his congratulations and requested the honor of escorting Beatrice to the drawing room. "You must be tired from your journey, Miss Allred."

"It was no hardship, sir."

"Either way, I will have Mrs. Poindexter prepare

rooms for you so you may retire at your leisure." Alexander looked over his shoulder. "You are staying, brother?"

"If you are able to accommodate us."

"Of course." Alexander continued toward the drawing room with Sophia and Crispin trailing behind. "We've no lack of rooms, although I have been told guests are rare. Mrs. Poindexter will carry word of your arrival to Mother. She is tending Father."

Crispin stiffened at the mention of seeing his mother. Sophia placed her free hand on his forearm and squeezed gently, reassuringly. He thawed under her touch.

In the drawing room, Sophia and her aunt were encouraged to sit on the plump velvet sofa where they would be most comfortable while Crispin and Alexander were left with two hard-backed chairs opposite them.

Alexander proved to be a gracious host—engaging and solicitous of the ladies. It took no time to win Beatrice's approval.

"Have you set your heart on marrying any particular lady, Lieutenant Locke?" she asked. "I would like to introduce you to my niece Evangeline when she returns from her trip abroad, unless you are expected to return to your regiment. I cannot have my darling girl carted off to the wilds of Canada."

Alexander smiled. "I am in England to stay, miss. I have sold my commission to care for my mother and father."

"How splendid! You must visit us at Hartland Manor when it is convenient."

Sophia took her aunt's hands between hers. "Auntie, Evangeline would not approve of your ambush on Lieutenant Locke."

"Your aunt does me great honor, Miss Darlington." Alexander smiled at Beatrice. "I should be pleased to make your niece's acquaintance. If she is half as charming as you, I expect we would become fast friends."

The conversation flowed effortlessly until refreshment arrived. Alexander requested the housekeeper notify his mother of their guests' arrival before addressing Sophia. "Miss Darlington, would you pour for us?"

"It would be my pleasure, sir."

Crispin appreciated how well his brother was getting on with Sophia and Beatrice. He only hoped his mother would be as pleasant when she joined them for tea. He needn't have given her reception a thought. Half an hour later, the housekeeper returned with his mother's regrets.

"Mistress Ness is unable to leave Master Ness's bedside, but she sends a message." The servant passed a folded piece of paper to Alexander.

Alexander frowned, took the unsealed message, and unfolded it. "Thank you. Have rooms been prepared for our guests?"

"Yes, sir."

"Very good. See to it their belongings are carried to their chambers."

The housekeeper bobbed her head and scuttled away.

As Crispin's brother stared at the paper, his smile returned. He dropped the letter on the side table between them. "Mother requests an audience in her sitting room after she has seen to Father. She will be prepared to receive you in an hour."

Her invitation was met with mixed feelings on Crispin's part. If she intended to express her displeasure at his unannounced arrival, he preferred not to have an audience. However, a pull from somewhere deep inside of him wished to have Sophia by his side when he faced his mother. Perhaps it was his innate desire to protect Sophia that made him stronger when she was near, or perhaps it was something more. He felt capable of any task when she looked at him in faith. He never wished to disappoint her.

After everyone took refreshment, Mrs. Poindexter was summoned to show Sophia, Beatrice, and Crispin to the rooms that had been prepared for them. Sophia's aunt looked like fruit wilting on the vine after their long journey, and she leaned on Crispin as they ascended the stairs.

"If I must make this climb again tonight," she said, "I will need to be carried like a bride on her wedding day. Will I be forgiven for taking dinner in my chambers this evening?"

"My brother will understand." Crispin couldn't be sure his mother would join them at the table either.

"I will carry word to the cook, Miss Allred," the housekeeper said.

Crispin was placed in a chamber across the corridor from Sophia, and Beatrice was given the larger room next to her niece.

The housekeeper left them to get settled and promised once more to arrange for a dinner tray to be carried to Beatrice that evening.

Crispin escorted Sophia's aunt into her chamber and found a comfortable chair for her by the hearth. Despite the warmer weather, Sophia's aunt had been complaining of the cold most of their journey. He set about building a fire to keep her comfortable while Sophia unpacked her aunt's valise and turned down the counterpane.

"Shall we put you to bed, Auntie?"

"Will you sing me a lullaby, too?" Beatrice chortled. "What attentive parents you and Lord Margrave will be someday. I hope it will be sooner rather than later. I am not growing any younger."

Sophia ducked her head as a crimson blush rushed into her cheeks. "Enough of that sort of talk, please."

Crispin pretended he hadn't heard Beatrice to save his betrothed further embarrassment. Offspring were not his priority. Sophia would expect him to give her a child at some point, but until he hunted the men trying to kill her and found a way to be released of his obligation to the King, he was not eager to bring an innocent into the world.

"I can manage on my own, dearest," Beatrice said. "Run along and have a lie down yourself. You've been yawning all day."

"I believe I will." Sophia approached her aunt to place a kiss on her cheek. "The bell pull is next to the right side of the bed, and your sewing basket is on top of the chest of drawers. I will look in on you later, but ring for a servant if you need me sooner."

"Leave me." Beatrice made a shooing motion with her hands, but tenderness shone in her watery eyes.

Crispin and Sophia exited the chamber together; Crispin pulled the door closed.

Sophia tipped her head and smiled coyly. "May I receive an escort to my chambers?"

"By all means, Miss Darlington. I cannot have you becoming lost along the way, now can I?"

He crooked his elbow, and she lightly placed her hand on his arm. Once inside her chamber, he walked to the window to check the lock and view. There were no trees close enough to allow someone to enter through a window, and the side of the house appeared to be free of trellises to climb or other means of stealing inside. He would walk the perimeter after the appointment with his mother to be certain.

Sophia moved to the high dresser and began removing pins from her hair while checking her reflection in the looking glass. He abandoned his inspection to allow himself a brief moment of indulgence. Her slender fingers worked deftly, assuredly, as if she had dressed her own hair many times. Champagne colored locks tumbled down her back with the release of each pin. She caught him staring at her in the looking glass and smiled.

"Your brother did not seem the least bit agitated by our unannounced arrival."

"His military training would have taught him to hide his surprise, but I believe his pleasure in receiving us is genuine."

She released the last pin and turned away from the looking glass as she combed her fingers through her hair. "I hope he feels the same once he learns the reason we have come. You will tell him, will you not?"

"Yes. I am certain no one followed us from London, but he should know what circumstances have brought us to his door."

If Alexander turned them out after the revelation, Crispin would take the ladies to one of his father's smaller properties and summon Kane to watch over them.

"How long must we hide?" she asked.

"I do not know. Not long." He opened his arms, and she slipped into his embrace.

Yawning, she sagged into him and rested her cheek against his chest.

He brushed a kiss to the crown of her head and inhaled her sweet scent. How she still smelled like camellias after two days of travel was a mystery. "You should try to sleep while I speak with my mother."

"I wish I could accompany you. Is it strange that I want to see a woman I have never met groveling? I assume that must be the reason she has requested an audience with you."

"My mother is not the groveling type."

"I am holding out hope she has seen the error of her

ways," she said. "Otherwise, dinner will be very awkward with me staring daggers through her."

"Perhaps she will take supper in her chambers, too."

She huffed. "Well, that could only be seen as an insult. You have brought your betrothed to present to her."

"Sophia, I am afraid you might not enjoy a relationship with my mother like other ladies share with their mothers-in-law. Is that a possibility you are willing to accept?"

She tipped her face toward him. An attractive pink flush painted her cheeks. "Am I allowed to keep you even if I cannot earn your mother's admiration?"

He smiled. "I am yours, darling, whether you keep me or not."

"A day will never come when I will not want you." She lifted to her toes and pecked a kiss on his lips. "If there is time, please come back. I would like to hear about your tête-à-tête, so I know what to expect at supper."

"I promise to prepare you, even if we are late to the table."

"Splendid."

When she kissed him like she had at the inn, his desire flared to life. He would much rather lay her on the small bed behind her and explore all the ways he could make her sigh with pleasure. Unfortunately, he had already agreed to the meeting.

He reluctantly released her. "I should go."

"I know, and as much as I would like to entice you to stay, I am tossing you out." She turned him around and gave his back a gentle push. "Hurry, before I change my mind."

Crispin encouraged her to crawl into bed like her aunt had suggested and left the room to face his mother. Over the years, the hurt had faded and had been replaced by apathy. He would not invest any hope on his mother. The tone of her letters over the past two years hadn't suggested she felt any regret. They were filled with excuses and references to Alexander's wishes for reconciliation between them. She had never indicated she wanted it for herself.

He followed the housekeeper's directions to his mother's sitting room located in a smaller area of the house, away from the bedchambers. The door was ajar, and he glimpsed his mother perched stiff-backed on a floral patterned Queen Anne chair. It had been thirteen years since he had last laid eyes on her. Her golden hair had become a little darker, and her face gaunter, but little else about her appearance had changed. She was still a handsome woman, slender, with mercury eyes and a severe slash of a mouth that made her appear perpetually displeased.

Her expression remained impenetrable as he entered the room; she gestured toward a chair opposite her own. "Please, have a seat." Her voice was restrained, almost brittle.

"Good afternoon, Mother." He lowered into the chair she indicated. "Alexander informed me your husband is ill and has been for some time. I am sorry for both of you. It must be difficult to witness his decline."

The lines at the corners of her mouth soften marginally. "Thank you. It has been trying. I do not like to leave Mr. Ness's side for long. Perhaps you will allow me to come to the point of this meeting sooner rather than later."

As expected, there would be no pleasantries exchanged. "By all means, speak freely. I am not one to come between a husband and wife."

"Mr. Ness's illness will take his life eventually, and I find myself in a precarious position." She patted and smoothed her skirts; her frigid facade showed signs of cracks. "Regretfully, I was unable to gift my husband with an heir. Mr. Ness has always treated Alexander as a son, but an entail on the estate prohibits Alexander from inheriting. The estate will go to Mr. Ness's distant cousin, and I find myself fretting over my future."

Of course, she needs something from me. Sophia would be disappointed his mother hadn't initiated a reconciliation, but Crispin was not surprised. "Am I to assume your husband spent the settlement you received upon Father's death?"

"Mr. Ness would never be so cruel as to leave me penniless."

"Unlike my father, who you claimed abandoned you and forced you to live in squalor. Odd that you were the one to abscond to Scotland, and he was accused of abandonment."

"You know nothing," she snapped. Her cheeks bore scarlet stains. "You were a *child*. You were never privy to the truth."

"Very well, enlighten me." He crossed his ankle over his knee and willed himself to maintain his calm. "I am no longer a child, and I am capable of understanding many situations. Tell me what occurred between you and Father."

She pursed her lips and sniffed. "Why should I bother? You set your mind against me years ago. You always favored your father over me. You never loved me."

This conversation was deteriorating quickly, and he had no patience for her dramatics. "If not an income, what is it you want from me, Mother? Speak up so we might conclude our business."

"There is no dowager house," she said, "and the modest income I will receive will hardly keep me in decent lodgings. I require a place to live."

His eyebrow arched in doubt. "You wish to reside at Lanfort Castle?"

"Good heavens, no! I would rather make my bed in a stable than return to the family seat. Everywhere I look, I will be reminded of your father. I want the dowager cottage."

"I see." He formed a steeple with his fingers. "Is this the only reason you requested an audience—to request use of the dowager cottage?"

"It is a pressing issue, Crispin. I can hardly think of anything besides my beloved husband's illness, and what will happen to me after his demise. What more did you expect?"

He laughed under his breath and shook his head in disbelief at her gall. "Nothing, Mother. I have learned to expect nothing from you." Unwinding his body, he pushed up from the chair. "I have no use for the cottage. Take it. I hope you find contentment there. I must go."

As he reached the threshold of the sitting room, she called to him. "Is it true you have brought your betrothed?"

He turned to face her warily. "I am traveling with my betrothed and her great-aunt. I would like to make introductions when you join us for supper this evening."

"You must dine without me. I cannot possibly leave Mr. Ness's side."

Only when it suits you.

"I expect there will be time to make her acquaintance once I am settled into the dowager cottage," she said. "What arrangements will you be making for when she becomes a widow?"

"*When* she becomes a widow? Are you plotting my demise?"

"G-good heavens, no!" His mother sputtered. "How could you ask such a thing?"

"You needn't be concerned for Sophia, although I suspect your real concern is for yourself." His smile was strained. "I will make alternate living arrangements for her in the unfortunate event I am no longer around to see to her needs. I would not dream of asking her to move into the dowager cottage with you. I cannot inflict your companionship on her."

An outraged cry burst from his mother; she bolted from the chair and retreated to the window. She stared at the landscape, dabbing at her eyes with a pristine white handkerchief.

"Nothing I do or say is ever correct in your eyes. *Nothing.* Even as a young boy, you hated me, and now you have grown into a cruel man—cold and horrid like your father. He hardened you against me like I always knew he would. Thank God, I was allowed one son to love me. At least I know I can count on Alexander to take care of me in my old age."

He directed his gaze toward the ceiling, digging deep inside for patience. There was none left. She had depleted his reserves. "I am beginning to think the only true victim in this scenario is Alexander. He has my sympathies."

Crispin stalked from the sitting room before she attempted to draw him back into this madness. She had shown him a mercy when she had turned him away all those years ago. He would choose to be grateful.

TWENTY

THE NEXT MORNING SOPHIA WAS BREAKING HER FAST ALONE in the dining room when her aunt bustled in with her parasol and bonnet. Sophia glanced up from her task of spreading butter on a warm bun.

"You are awake earlier than I expected, Auntie."

Aunt Beatrice harrumphed. "I should think so, considering I slept through supper last night. Why did no one wake me?"

"The housekeeper attempted to rouse you when she brought a tray to your chambers. You told her to stop being a nuisance."

Her aunt's eyes rounded. "Was that Mrs. Poindexter caterwauling like an old barn cat? Ma'am!" She drew out the word, long and plaintive. "If I could have reached my boot, I might have lobbed it in her direction."

"It is rather fortunate you did not. I already feel we might not be welcome, and harassing the help would not win us any favor."

"Not welcome? Lieutenant Locke was a gracious host when we arrived. What did I miss at supper last night?"

"Nothing, I am afraid. Crispin's mother did not join us."

Aunt Beatrice clicked her tongue sympathetically. "Dearest, you cannot view her refusal as an affront. Mr. Ness must be very ill to have kept her from making your acquaintance, but I am certain she will adore you once she is able to steal away for a moment to speak with you."

"I hope you are right about her receptiveness, Auntie."

Sophia traced the edge of the gilded teacup handle, recalling Crispin's stoicism when he informed her that his mother would not be venturing below stairs last night. She had turned her back on her first-born—even after she knew his father was gone and Crispin was alone—but she couldn't venture from her husband's side for a moment to dine with the son she had abandoned. How could Sophia not take offense over the slight to the man she loved?

"I expect we will have our chance to become familiar when Crispin's mother takes up residence at the dowager cottage," Sophia said.

"I do not wish any harm on Mr. Ness, but I cannot help but think this is a step in the right direction. I am pleased Lord Margrave's mother is attempting to repair the rift between them."

"Yes, I suppose it is good news." *If it were true...*

When Crispin had escorted Sophia to her room after dinner, his report of the meeting with his mother had been terse and lacking in detail. Sophia had attempted to draw him into conversation, sensing he might have unresolved feelings after seeing his mother again, but he had cut the evening short. A lack of sleep the night prior had left him weary, so he placed a kiss on her forehead and bade her good night.

Sophia had crawled into bed rather unsatisfied. Although Crispin was not one to dissect his emotions—or even admit he had any—she had hoped the intimacy they had shared at the inn would last.

She pulled the chair beside her away from the dining table and invited Aunt Beatrice to sit. "You must be famished since you missed supper. Here, you may have my bread and I will butter another one."

Her aunt waved off her offer. "I am setting off on my morning stroll. I will eat later."

Crispin would not approve of Sophia or her aunt venturing off without him, although frankly, his displeasure was not as strong a deterrent as the memory of almost being trampled at Lord and Lady Seabrook's party. A country stroll had lost its appeal.

"The gentlemen are occupied at the moment," Sophia said. "Perhaps you could postpone your morning constitutional?"

Crispin and Lieutenant Locke were cloistered in their stepfather's study to discuss the danger that had driven them to flee London. She prayed Lieutenant Locke would allow them to stay. Dragging Aunt Beatrice around the countryside searching for safe haven would be wearing on her, not to mention the worry it would cause the poor dear. Surely, it would not come to that, but Sophia couldn't fault Crispin's brother if he determined the risk was too great.

"I cannot see how the gentlemen's activities are any of my concern," Aunt Beatrice said, "but it does warm the heart to hear they are getting on well. There is no relationship quite like the one shared between siblings. What would you have done without Regina and Evangeline?"

"I haven't a clue." She didn't want to imagine it. Her older sisters were her closest companions, and she missed them terribly—especially now.

"Do you want to join me in exercise, dearest?"

"Crispin asked that we not wander outside without him or Lieutenant Locke," Sophia said. "The men have been meeting for some time. I am sure they will be in for breakfast soon."

"Poppycock!" Aunt Beatrice smacked the end of her unopened parasol on the parquet floor. "I will not wait around for an escort. I have been walking on my own for seventy-five years and doing a damn fine job of it. I certainly know my way around a country lane without a man's assistance."

"I really think we should wait for Crispin."

"*You* wait. I am going alone and taking this." Her aunt snatched the buttered bun from Sophia's plate and marched from the room, barely avoiding a run-in with a potted fern.

"Gads," Sophia mumbled. Her aunt had trouble navigating *indoors*. Without Sophia's guidance, she might step in a hole and twist her ankle or stumble into the pond.

"Auntie, wait!" Sophia wiped her hands on the napkin draped across her lap, discarded it on the table, and chased after her. When she caught up to Aunt Beatrice in the foyer, she linked their arms. "I have changed my mind. A walk sounds lovely, but I left my bonnet above stairs. Will you share your parasol?"

Her aunt handed her the parasol then bit into the buttered bun, beaming triumphantly. She was quite the schemer when she wanted to be.

"We should stay close," Sophia said as they exited the house. "We would not want to become lost."

"You are beginning to sound like Regina. I have never known you to fret about anything."

Sophia sighed wistfully and drew her aunt closer to her side. "Perhaps because I am missing my sisters more than usual today."

"I miss them too, dear girl."

They strolled toward the back of the house where Sophia had spotted a pond from her bedchamber window. "Can you imagine Uncle Charles's reaction when Regina and Evangeline surprise him in Athens? Do you believe he will take to Xavier?"

"Regina is happy," Aunt Beatrice said. "Charlie would not kick up a fuss, even if he and Mr. Vistoire did not get on well. Without a doubt, he will be thrilled about your match with Lord Margrave." Aunt Beatrice stopped and turned to face her. "I cannot predict when your uncle will return to England, and you have another year until you reach your majority."

"I do not relish a long betrothal, Auntie, but there is nothing to be done about it. I require his permission to marry."

"Only if you remain in England." Aunt Beatrice captured Sophia's cheeks between her gloved hands; her eyes sparkled. "Let's not return to London. Gretna Green is not so far away that we could not reach it in a week. An elopement would be so very exciting."

Her aunt's suggestion was tempting, but Sophia's pragmatic side had always been stronger than her whimsical one. "Do you recall how tired you were after our two-day journey? I will not ask you to spend a week in a carriage. When we leave here, we will return to Hartland Manor to await Uncle Charles's return. It is for the best."

Aunt Beatrice grunted in disapproval and dropped her hands to her sides. "You are not asking anything of me, and I could bear the travel to see you happily settled like your sister. It would do my heart good."

"I know it would make you happy. You have always wanted what was best for my sisters and me, and *we* think it is best to keep you tiptop. After all, who will dole out childrearing advice if you are not here to do it?"

"Bah!" Aunt Beatrice rolled her eyes. "You think I do not recognize your tricks, Sophia Anastasia Marietta Jane, but there is nothing wrong with my mind."

"I am well aware, Auntie, and I learned all my tricks from you. What a splendid teacher I had." Sophia hooked her arm with her great-aunt's and led her toward the pond. "Shall we look for toads along the shore?"

As Sophia hoped, the mention of toads reminded Aunt Beatrice of days gone by when her niece and nephew—Sophia's mother and Uncle Charles—hunted tadpoles and dug along the muddy creek bank at home. Sophia loved hearing stories of her mother's childhood, and Auntie was the only person left who recalled the details that brought Sophia's mother back to life.

Reminiscing served two purposes. It was entertaining for both, and it distracted Aunt Beatrice from realizing they were simply strolling back and forth along the shoreline. With the house in full view, Sophia felt less skittish about walking without Crispin.

A steady breeze shivered the leaves of an old oak. The tree stood sentry at the pond's edge, stretching its knotty limbs toward the water as if intending to scoop some with its spindly fingers. A birdsong came from somewhere above them.

"The countryside is beautiful," Sophia murmured.

Aunt Beatrice hummed in agreement.

Nestled among the reeds, a rowboat lay bow up on the bank. It was weathered, paint-chipped, and cocked to one side as if it had crawled ashore and flopped down for a long nap. Ripples stirred the pond's surface. It was alive, perpetually in motion.

Aunt Beatrice pulled her shawl around her shoulders and rubbed her wrist across the tip of her nose.

"Are you growing chilled?" Although Sophia was

comfortable, her aunt didn't have much flesh on her to keep her warm. "Perhaps we should return to the house."

Her aunt did not protest when Sophia changed their course and led her in the direction of the front drive where their walk had begun. As they rounded the corner of the boxy structure, two riders appeared on the horizon. Sophia's heart hesitated, stumbling against her breastbone.

They've found us. Her fingers tightened on her aunt's arm.

"We need to go." She quickened her step, urging Aunt Beatrice to hurry. Her aunt was spry and had no trouble keeping pace. That did not stop her from complaining, however.

"What has gotten into you, Sophia? You are like a hound with its tail on fire."

"Someone is coming up the lane," she said, injecting as much cheerfulness as she could into her voice. "Lieutenant Locke must be expecting visitors. We should let him know they are arriving."

Aunt Beatrice pulled free of Sophia's hold and turned to gaze down the lane. "I do not see anything. Is it a carriage?"

"It is two men on horseback." Sophia reached for her aunt's arm, but Aunt Beatrice twisted away.

"You are acting strange. Since Lieutenant Locke is occupied, we should greet his guests."

"Come inside, Auntie"—Sophia snagged her around the shoulders and guided her toward the front door—"before you catch a chill. We will greet the guests when they arrive at the door."

"Yes, that does make more sense." Aunt Beatrice stopped resisting and returned to the safety of the house.

The housekeeper must have heard the door closing, because she walked into the foyer with a quizzical lift of her eyebrows. "You were outside, ma'am? I did not hear you leave the house."

"And why should you?" Aunt Beatrice asked with an edge of irritation. "We are not in the habit of creating a racket wherever we go."

Sophia smiled to soften her aunt's words and closed the parasol. "Two men are approaching the house. Will you inform the lieutenant?"

Mrs. Poindexter nodded once and bustled toward the back of the house. She was gone only a moment before Crispin and Lieutenant Locke stormed the foyer.

Aunt Beatrice startled and clutched her chest. "Lord almighty!"

"Take your aunt to Mr. Ness's study," Crispin said. "Do not leave until I come for you."

Sophia did as he ordered, grateful Aunt Beatrice didn't kick up a fuss.

"What is all this commotion? I have never seen anyone so agitated over guests. One might think it is God himself arriving by chariot."

Sophia shrugged. "It must be someone of importance, although it is hard to compete with the Almighty."

She and Aunt Beatrice were not kept in suspense long. When Crispin came to collect them, the Duke of Stanhurst accompanied him.

"That is rather a letdown," Aunt Beatrice mumbled.

Sophia came forward to greet the duke. "How unexpected to see you here, Your Grace. Do you know Mr. and Mrs. Ness?"

Stanhurst placed a brief kiss on her glove. "I have come to see Lord Margrave. His valet said I would find him here on holiday."

"Kane acted as his guide," Crispin explained. "You spotted the two of them on horseback. They are alone."

Something was amiss, but Crispin's calm demeanor eased her worries.

"Your Grace, may I present my great-aunt, Beatrice Allred?" she asked the duke.

"I would be delighted." As Stanhurst exchanged pleasantries with her aunt, Lieutenant Locke entered the study.

"A room is being prepared for you, Your Grace."

"Oh?" Stanhurst swung his head toward the doorway. "There is no need to trouble your staff. I do not intend to stay. I only wish for a brief word with the viscount."

Lieutenant Locke widened his stance, filling the doorway with his muscular form. "I insist you stay as our guest." Clearly, it was not a request.

The duke's mouth opened briefly before he snapped it shut. A muscle in his jaw twitched.

Aunt Beatrice cleared her throat. "Well, gentlemen. It seems you have business to settle, and I have a baby blanket in my chambers that will not knit itself. If you will excuse me..."

Lieutenant Locke stepped aside to allow Aunt Beatrice to exit the room.

Crispin cocked his head, meeting Sophia's gaze. "A baby blanket?"

"It is a gift for my sister and her new husband," Sophia said.

"Regina is expecting?"

"She is *not*." Her laugh was breathy. "At least, she was not when she left on her honeymoon."

His brows sank low over his hazel eyes, but he didn't question her further.

She offered a strained smile to the other gentlemen in the room. "I believe I will follow in my aunt's footsteps and

allow you privacy." She curtsied to the duke. "Good day, sir."

Crispin's valet was standing in the foyer with his hat in hand when she passed through on her way to the staircase. "Did Lord Margrave leave you holding your hat?"

The dark haired valet grinned, deepening the divot in his cheek. "I have been ordered to consider what might have happened if Stanhurst and I had been followed."

"Were you followed?"

"No, miss."

"How can you be certain?"

"I excel at cloak and dagger games."

She stepped forward and held out her hands. "This is not a game, is it, Kane?"

He sobered and passed his hat. "It is not, Miss Darlington, and I would not have brought the duke here unless I was certain we were not followed. Margrave is more than my employer. He took me off the streets and provided me with a home and a purpose. I will protect him with my life."

"I see." His admission appeased her. She turned away to hide her smile as she placed his hat on the entry table. "Follow me. You can consider your actions in the comfort of the drawing room and keep me company while the gentlemen speak alone."

Kane was telling her about the Duke of Stanhurst's troubles on the road outside of London when a woman with dark golden hair and stormy eyes swept into the room. Stopping a few feet inside the doorway, she skewered them with a glower to rival any Sophia had ever seen from Crispin. There was no mistaking her identity. Sophia was staring at Crispin's mother.

Kane stood in deference. "Good day, ma'am. May I offer you this chair?"

"Considering the chair belongs to my husband, you may not." She lifted her slender nose, gawking at him in disgust as if he were a bug in her soup. "You *may* remove yourself from my drawing room."

Sophia rose from her chair, too. "We are sorry to have disturbed you, Mrs. Ness. If I may be bold and introduce myself, I am—"

"Where is that *man*?" Crispin's mother's voice was sharp like a hammer striking a nail. She swung her head side to side, searching the room. "Drat, he is not in here," she mumbled to herself.

Kane cleared his throat. "Are you referring to the duke, ma'am?"

Her eyes narrowed on Crispin's valet. "Why are you speaking to me? I do not know you."

"This is Kane, ma'am," Sophia said. "He serves your eldest son."

The woman sneered. "The help should be seen and not heard. Where is your master? I would speak with the viscount now."

The way she spoke of Crispin as if he were a stranger and demeaned Kane riled Sophia's temper. "Your *son* is in Mr. Ness's study, and *I* would thank you to speak civilly to his valued man. Surely, you have not forgotten my future husband's generosity in granting you permission to make use of the dowager cottage."

Crispin's mother appeared unaffected by Sophia's reprimand. She twirled on her heel without a word and stalked from the drawing room.

"Should we go?" Kane asked Sophia.

"I am not budging." She plopped in the chair to emphasize her commitment to her rebellion. "I expect this will not be our last row, and I do not wish to leave my future mother-in-law with the impression I will be an easy adversary."

Kane chuckled and resumed his seat. "You brought Margrave to his knees, Miss Darlington. His mother does not stand a chance against you, although I do not expect his lordship will ask you to endure her companionship more than necessary. He has done his best to avoid her until now."

"I can see now how unpleasant this must be for him." Tenderness coursed through her, causing her eyes to well with tears. She wished Crispin would allow her to comfort him—after all, he was facing this hateful woman that he had relegated to his past in order to protect Sophia—but he had appeared to be made of stone last night when she questioned him about their private audience.

Mrs. Ness's angry voice carried through the walls. "Who gave permission for you to invite all these people into my home? I want everyone to leave. Get *out* and take that horrible, impertinent girl you have chosen for a wife with you."

"Mother, what has come over you?" Lieutenant Locke attempted to soothe her. "Are you unwell? Has something happened to Father?"

"No, no. There has been no change, but I do not like admitting strange men to the house."

"Crispin is not a stranger. He is your son," the lieutenant said gently but firmly. "Allow me to present the Duke of Stanhurst. We are honored to receive him as our guest. If Father was well, he would come below stairs to welcome His Grace properly. Father has always been known for his hospitality."

Sophia couldn't understand Mrs. Ness's muddled response, but it seemed Lieutenant Locke had the right touch when it came to calming her. She was no longer shouting. Mrs. Ness told the lieutenant she trusted him to know what was best. A few more words were exchanged, and Crispin's brother offered to accompany her above stairs and look in on his stepfather.

A door closed and shortly, silence descended over the downstairs. Kane caught her eye. "That was not the reception I expected, but it is refreshing to be disparaged to my face rather than behind my back."

Sophia smiled. "You mentioned Margrave rescued you from the streets, but you strike me as an educated man. What is your story?"

"The tale of my reduced circumstances is dull," he said with a shrug, "but my father was a vicar. I was orphaned and had no one to take me in as a ward, so I traveled to London to find work. Your betrothed stumbled across me picking pockets a year later and set me back on a path toward respectability."

"You are a *spy*."

"For my King." Kane grinned, showing his dimple again. "Is there a more noble profession?"

Crispin entered the drawing room. "Keep the duke occupied," he said to Kane.

"Yes, sir." The younger man left Sophia and Crispin alone.

His frown caused her mouth to grow dry. Before he reached the chair his valet had vacated, she blurted, "I apologize for antagonizing your mother, but she was behaving insufferably."

Crispin paused. His heated gaze ensnared her; she was unable to look away. His eyes were the most interesting combination of colors—a deep brown at first glance, but much more complicated than they appeared. Hints of green and silver were only noticeable when one was bold enough to meet his stare.

"I assume my mother was unpleasant," he said, "and you put her in her place. Perhaps she should be the one apologizing."

If Sophia's quarrelsome encounter with his mother hadn't put the glower on his face, one other possibility remained. "I tried to discourage Aunt Beatrice from going outside, but you know how strong-willed she can be."

Calmly, he lowered onto the chair and held out his hand. "Come here, Sophia."

"What? Come where?"

"*Here.*" He patted his knee.

She crossed her arms. While she had agreed to abide by his rules as long as there was danger, a quick decision had been required today. Aunt Beatrice couldn't be allowed to wander off alone. "If you have something to say, I can hear you from where I am sitting."

"Perhaps I do not wish to talk." His eyes glittered with something fierce. Her stomach fluttered. "Come to me."

Her resistance was short-lived. She was out of her seat and approaching him before realizing she had made a decision. When she extended her hand, he trailed his fingertips over hers. Lovely shivers skated along her skin, settling in her chest with a tingling ache.

"I neglected to make something clear earlier." His husky voice elicited a shocking pulse between her legs. She pressed her thighs together as warmth climbed into her cheeks. He must know how he affected her, how badly she wanted him to touch her in ways no proper lady should imagine.

"How careless of you, my lord."

"Very careless"—he continued to caress her hand, tracing the lines crossing her palm—"and I intend to correct the oversight." He grasped her hand and tugged her onto his lap. She squealed with surprise as her bottom landed on his knee.

"Crispin!"

He wrapped one arm around her waist and cradled the back of her neck. "I cannot bear another moment in the same room without touching you." He nuzzled her cheek. "What have you done to me?"

"I do not know, but I refuse to undo it." She reached for the end of his cravat, toying with it as she gazed at him from beneath her lashes. "Is that all you wished to say? I thought you were going to call me on the carpet."

"Make no mistake, Miss Darlington. That was my intention, but I find you have grown even more irresistible after locking myself in the study all morning. I will save the scolding for later."

"How delightful. I will attempt to contain my excitement."

He chuckled before nipping her mouth. She inhaled sharply and leaned into his kiss, but he pulled back with a teasing grin. "Or perhaps I will take you over my knee and teach you a lesson."

She snorted softly. "You wouldn't dare."

"Wouldn't I?" He placed another peck on her mouth.

"You know what I think, my lord?" She twined her arms around his neck and smiled. "You have no intention of laying a hand on me."

His jovial manner subsided. "Never in anger, darling," he said solemnly. "I will never hurt you. You have my oath."

"I know you, Crispin. I require no oath."

"Yet, I give it to you." He slid his hand along the curve of her waist, stopping just below her breast. "However, I cannot promise to keep my hands to myself when we are wed. I hope you will not ask it of me."

She exhaled unevenly. Would he think her too bold if

she admitted the truth? She wet her lips and decided to assume the risk. "Quite the opposite, I think. I am eager to enjoy the benefits of marriage."

"Gads," he groaned and urged her to climb off his lap. "Perhaps it would be best to send you to your seat. I have something to discuss that cannot wait."

She lowered her head, embarrassed to have spoken of her desires. "Of course," she mumbled. He escorted her back to the chair she had claimed earlier. Once she was seated, she arranged her skirts around her, avoiding eye contact.

"Sophia?"

"Hmm...?"

He leaned forward in the chair and waved to capture her attention. "Will you look at me, please?"

Heat singed her face. She reluctantly lifted her gaze.

He relaxed against the chair cushion. "It appears you noticed my own eagerness. Forgive me. I did not intend to embarrass you, or myself."

"I do not under—" The accidental lesson in male anatomy she had received when she'd stumbled across a piece of Greek pottery at Wedmore House flashed through her memory. Of their own accord, her eyes sought out his lap. They widened. "Oh!"

"*Sophia.*" He laughed, seemingly unbothered by her curiosity, despite the gentle rebuke. Not a trace of a blush colored his face, and he made no move to hide his arousal. She laughed too.

"I am sorry, but what did you expect? You must have realized I would look."

One side of his mouth inched up. His eyes appeared greener, as they tended to do when he was happy or amused. "A change of topic is in order, I think. Otherwise, I will forget the reason I sought you out."

A rush of pleasure washed over her knowing he was just as affected by her as she was by him. It boded well for a happy union like her mother had written about in her diary —like Regina had found with Xavier.

"I would like to ask for your help," Crispin said.

"Of course. If I am able, I am willing."

"Thank you." He inclined his head in acknowledgement. "Did Kane tell you the duke was involved in an accident?"

"He said Stanhurst's carriage was run off the road, and a man tried to murder him."

Crispin grimaced. "I see he was thorough."

"As he should be. If the duke's ordeal has anything to do with my own, no detail should be spared."

"Should your aunt not be afforded the same consideration?"

Sophia shook her head. "It will distress her too much. I cannot allow it."

"You do not give Beatrice enough credit. She is stronger than you realize. Telling her the truth will make the task of keeping her safe easier, and she deserves to know."

"Aunt Beatrice is *my* concern. Regina left her in my care, and I will protect her as I see fit."

Crispin's jaw firmed. His brows lowered over his eyes. She steeled herself for battle, but he did not engage. "The duke recovered letters belonging to his brother," he said, "but they have been written in cipher. I would like you to study them and render an opinion."

She blinked, completely thrown by his request. "I—I have no knowledge of ciphers. I am not sure how I can be of assistance."

"You are capable of seeing patterns others do not. I wish you to help determine if the author of the letter used a book cipher or created his own."

"What is the difference? May I see the letters?"

Crispin reached into his jacket and retrieved a folded piece of paper. "There are more in the study. Stanhurst recovered a stash from his brother's chamber at the manor house."

She accepted the paper he extended and unfolded it. "There are no words."

"If Lord Geoffrey and his letter writer used a book cipher, the numbers represent the page, line, and word of a book they have in common. It would be the simplest method, although one must know which book they used to decipher the messages."

"And if he created one of his own?"

"Numbers represent letters of the alphabet. Often multiple numbers are used for the same letter, and others are null. They represent nothing."

Sophia took a cleansing breath. The task sounded complicated but possible.

"Once you determine which type of cipher is used," he said, "I will endeavor to decipher the messages."

"Are you unable to study the letters and make a determination?"

"I could, given time, but I expect you will be faster."

Her chest burst with pride and pleasure. Men rarely saw beyond her beauty and recognized her gift, and if they did, they often found her abilities disquieting. Once when she was a child, she and Aunt Beatrice overheard a footman call her unnatural. Auntie had dismissed him at once and reassured Sophia of her specialness.

You are blessed, dearest. Never allow anyone to tell you otherwise.

She smiled at Crispin. "I will start on the letters today. Would you like to retrieve them while I wait?"

"In a moment, but there is another matter I need to

discuss." He adjusted his position on the chair. "Tomorrow I am leaving in search of Farrin and his men."

Her heart plummeted. "No! Why must you go? You said no one followed us."

"It is only a matter of time before they discover our whereabouts. My carriage would not have escaped notice, and eventually, one of Farrin's men will speak with the right person."

"You said we would be safe here."

"For a time, but we are being hunted." His gaze darkened, frightening in his intensity. "I am the hunter, Sophia. I must find them first."

"No, we need you here."

"You will be safe. Kane will remain to keep watch over you."

She huffed in frustration. Why must he risk himself? "Send a message to the Consul—to whomever is in charge. Tell them what you've learned and set them on Farrin's trail."

"I do not know who to trust. Farrin could have corrupted others, and I cannot risk placing a larger target on your back by revealing what I know." He winced slightly and rubbed his temple. "Frankly, I haven't much to tell. We know he murdered the Stanhursts, but the only witnesses are out of the country, and we have no proof of any other wrongdoing."

"Farrin tried to rob Wedmore House. How is that aboveboard?"

"Sophia, I cannot accuse a man of a crime without evidence."

She pushed from the chair and paced the length of the carpet, frantic to find an argument to dissuade him from pursuing these murderers. She stopped in front of him and threw her hands out at her sides. "*I* am a witness. Allow me to make the accusation."

He frowned. "Did you see Farrin break into your uncle's home? Did you see one of his men?"

"No, of course not. Farrin sent Xavier."

"Your sister married the trespasser. Your credibility will be called into question."

She stopped pacing and faced him; her hands landed on her hips. "I am your betrothed. I forbid you to go."

"It does not work that way, darling."

"And why not? You make demands of me."

A half-smile tinged with regret spread across his face. "The burden of responsibility falls to me. It is my lot. I will not fail in my duties."

Her lips parted, but she had lost her voice. She wished to help him carry part of his burden. She had expected that to be her role in marriage, but doubt had eked into her bones in the meadow, threatening to change her into someone that she feared she would no longer recognize. She had been useless to him.

I am the burden.

A sob welled at the back of her throat. She covered her mouth to catch it and fled the room.

TWENTY-ONE

CRISPIN STOPPED HIMSELF WHEN HE LEAPT FROM THE CHAIR to give chase. Sophia glided through the doorway and disappeared from sight. Her life had been flipped sideways. Perhaps she needed time alone.

Or maybe I should go to her?

Why must he always feel as if he were standing on shifting ground when it came to her? With a sigh, he returned to the study where Kane was keeping guard over Stanhurst.

Crispin did not trust easily. Every instinct screamed for him to treat the duke as an enemy, even though Stanhurst's actions made it difficult to classify him as such. The duke could have destroyed the letters without anyone being wiser. He hadn't. Instead, he was bringing them forward at considerable risk to himself.

If the letters proved to be an act of treason and the duke's father was a willing culprit, Stanhurst could be stripped of his title and lands. Even if Lord Geoffrey was the only guilty party, the scandal could make the duke and his sisters into pariahs. Stanhurst's face had been pale and grim when he had acknowledged the possibility earlier.

It is my moral obligation to bring this to light. What is a man if he has no loyalty to King and country?

The duke's stance had earned a sliver of respect from Crispin. When he re-entered the study, Alexander was leaning against the desk while Kane and the duke lounged on adjacent chairs. His protégé chatted amiably with Stanhurst. Perhaps he had become too comfortable.

The duke snapped his head toward Crispin; his attention was focused. "My duty has been dispatched. I require a horse, and I will be on my way."

Crispin met his brother's shuttered gaze across the room. Did he imagine they knew each other's minds with only a glance?

"I insist you stay as our guest, Your Grace," Alexander said.

The duke frowned. "But your mother—"

"She was distraught over her husband. She has asked me to extend her apologies and invite you to stay."

"I have sisters." Stanhurst stood. "They need my protection. I promised to meet them in Lancashire."

Alexander crossed his arms. He was unmoved by the duke's appeal. "It seems your cousin wants *you* dead. Maybe your sisters are safer without you."

Stanhurst exhaled as if he had been punched in the guts.

Kane glowered. It was clear he had grown fond of the duke during their short association, not that Crispin was surprised. Saving a life often tethered men together and formed a steadfast friendship that might take a lifetime to build under ordinary circumstances.

"I am sure my brother did not intend to be harsh," Crispin said and silenced Alexander with a firm glance. "The truth is often cruel, however. Lady Van Middleburg knows you are in possession of the letters. She arranged for your demise, knowing your sisters would be without a protector. We must assume she has no great love for your sisters and would not oppose eliminating them as well, if necessary."

The duke's swallow was audible.

"Allow me to go to your sisters in your stead," Kane said. "If you pen a letter, I will deliver it and stay on to protect them until this rotten business is behind you. No harm will come to them. I give you my oath."

Stanhurst looked from man to man. "Are you one of them—all of you?"

"If you are asking if we are in partnership with your cousin," Crispin said, "the answer should be obvious."

"Your man saved my life. I realize you are not aligned with Lady Van Middleburg." Stanhurst's lips thinned. "In my brother's diary, Geoffrey mentioned a group of spies answerable only to the King—the Regent's Consul."

Crispin scoffed to hide his surprise. Had Kane said or done something to lead the duke down this path? "What did your brother have to say about this Regent's Consul?"

"He met the leader at a gaming hell a few years ago, and they struck up a friendship after a time. Geoffrey described him as ambitious and hinted he was unhappy playing the King's lap dog."

Kane flashed their private symbol for Farrin, a brief flick of his pointer and little finger. *Devil's horns.*

Crispin answered in sign. *Maybe.*

"Where is your brother's diary now?" he asked the duke.

"It was in my saddlebags. Ask your brother."

"His belongings were taken to his chambers above stairs," Alexander said.

"I want to read it."

Crispin's brother nodded and summoned a footman. He gave orders to retrieve the duke's saddlebags.

"You may keep the diary," the duke said, "but you may not hold me against my will."

"I will not stand in your way, Your Grace." Crispin stepped aside and fanned his arm toward the door. "There is the exit. However, if you leave, I cannot guarantee your safe passage to Lancashire. You will be on your own."

The duke raised his narrow nose. "I will take my chances. No one will catch me off guard again."

"I do not expect they will. Whether you can defend yourself against a band of men eager to draw your blood, I cannot say." Crispin turned to Kane. "How many riders ambushed the duke on the road?"

"I counted five, more or less. It was dark."

The muscles in Stanhurst's jaw knotted. "Under the circumstances, perhaps you would lend me your man. Kane, I will see you rewarded once I am reunited with my sisters."

Crispin held his tongue. In matters of this nature, he did not attempt to influence Kane. The younger man would be risking his own life. He should have complete authority to make his decisions.

Kane cleared his throat and signed, *trust.* "You are right about Lord Margrave and me," he said to the duke. "We are Regent's Consul men. Lieutenant Locke is not, but he knows about us. We can speak freely in his presence."

Stanhurst's eyes flared slightly, revealing his surprise. Perhaps he had been casting for answers without believing he would get a bite.

"What you have done is brave," Kane said. "You have much to lose, but you came forward without hesitation. I promise, I will do everything possible to protect your sisters if you will entrust the task to me. You must know I am capable."

The duke's lips twitched.

Crispin took a step toward him. "Your contribution will not be overlooked, Your Grace. His Majesty will be left with no doubts as to your loyalty, and no one else will ever question how your brother and father died. I will take the secret to my grave."

"As will I," Kane and Alexander said in unison.

Stanhurst sighed. His obstinate stance softened marginally.

"I believe our country is in danger," Crispin said, "and you may be the only one who can help discover the origin of the threat. Have you ever heard of a group called the Black Death?"

"I take it you are not referencing the plague." The duke's voice was flat.

"I am not." Crispin gestured toward the empty chair. "You should sit. This is a long story."

"Then I believe a brandy is in order." Stanhurst sat while Alexander poured him two fingers. Crispin declined a glass when his brother offered and claimed a place on the sofa. Alexander joined him.

"The Black Death is the name given to a tribe of fearless warriors from the Egyptian peninsula," Crispin said. "Membership is handed down as a birthright, and both boys and girls undergo training at a young age. Per legend, the tribe's beginnings can be traced back to Ahmose, I."

"Should that name mean something to me?"

"Not unless you have studied Egyptian history."

"I have not."

"Ahmose, I was an 18th dynasty pharaoh who restored Theban rule over Egypt. The pharaoh enlisted these highly skilled warriors to expel the Hykos from the lower delta."

The duke frowned. "Again, this is meaningless. Is there a reason you are educating me on Egyptian history? I see no correlation between these long dead warriors and whatever trouble my brother fell into."

"The exact relationship is unclear, Your Grace," Kane said, "but there is one. Lord Margrave could omit the history, but I think it is necessary to truly understand the gravity of our current situation."

Stanhurst looked back and forth from Kane to Crispin. He sharply inclined his head. "You may continue, Margrave. You have my attention."

"Thank you." Crispin attempted to curb his irritation, but it leached into his voice. "After Egypt fell to the Romans, the tribe retreated to the mountains and lived undisturbed for centuries. Their existence would likely have remained undiscovered if not for the Crusades."

"A period of which I have some knowledge," the duke said.

"You were unlikely to have read about the tribe. Historians reached a consensus and declared the group was nothing more than a fable, a trick of Erminhilt Osterhagen's feeble mind." Before Stanhurst could ask another question, Crispin supplied the answer. "Sir Osterhagen was with the Order of Saint John."

"Rivals to the Knights Templar."

"Yes, Osterhagen's actions dealt serious blows to the Templars. After a particularly bloody battle, he became separated from his order. He wandered in the mountains for weeks, lost. Some reports claim he was dead when the tribal women found him, but he was not. They carried him to their village and nursed him back to health.

"While Osterhagen regained his strength, he witnessed the warriors performing inhuman feats. He had never seen such vicious and cunning fighters, and he took it upon himself to negotiate with the tribal chiefs on behalf of the Vatican. Osterhagen left the village at the end of his convalescence with an agreement that would earn him a position of power in the Church. He promised gold in exchange for the tribes assistance fighting the Knights Templar."

"He did well for himself, eh?"

"The alliance changed the course of the war. The Egyptians could steal into any camp undetected and leave behind no evidence that they had ever been there."

"Aside from the bodies of their targets," Kane added. "Each victim bore a mark of death on their foreheads, but the marks were conspicuously missing from other victims that fell while trying to protect their masters."

"Some believed the acts were committed by traitors in the camp," Crispin said. "The Black Death became a legend in time, but they are real. The Regent's Consul became aware of the group's existence during the war with Napoleon, but there has been no recent talk of the Black Death until last week. It seems your brother and Lord Van Middleburg enlisted a group of merchants to hire the warriors."

The duke cleared his throat. "For what purpose?"

"We don't now," Kane said, "but we need to find out. With your brother's death, the merchants' confidence has grown shaky. They are threatening to withdraw their support, which would be disastrous."

Creases appeared on Stanhurst's forehead. "I do not understand. Wouldn't it be to everyone's advantage if the deal was dissolved?"

"Under normal circumstances, yes," Crispin said, "but your brother and his cohorts already sent a man to hire the mercenaries. Half of what is owed will be paid before the job, as a show of good faith. The warriors will expect the remainder once the task is completed."

"And if the merchants withdraw their support?"

"Black Death will come to England to collect," Kane said, "and from the tales I have heard, we do not want them descending on England."

A storm brewed behind the duke's eyes. "I cannot fathom what sort of mess Geoffrey created. What did he hope would come of this?"

"We believe your brother's correspondence holds the answers," Crispin said.

"I have given you everything I found, and I have no knowledge of deciphering. I do not see how I can be of any more use. Allow me to reunite with my sisters."

Crispin acknowledged his cooperation. It had required no small amount of bravery to come forward with what he had discovered. "You may know more than you realize, Your Grace. As I said earlier, I will not stop you if you insist on going, but you must accept that your choices could have far-reaching consequences for England."

"Your cooperation," Alexander said, speaking for the first time since sitting down with the duke, "could be an opportunity to clear your name. It must be difficult to leave your sisters' care in the hands of another man, but Kane is trained for this type of work. Wouldn't your sisters be safer with him?"

"I will leave at once," Kane said. "They will not be unprotected. You have my word."

Silence descended over the room. Stanhurst plowed his fingers through his hair, grimaced, and made another pass with his hand.

"Damnation," he muttered at last. "I cannot see I have much choice. My loyalties lie with the King. Tell me how I can be of use."

After Stanhurst retired to his chamber to compose instructions to his sisters, Crispin's brother detained him.

"There is something I must show you," Alexander said. "It is unpleasant business, but I believe you deserve to know the full truth about our parents' marriage. Perhaps it will explain our mother's behavior toward you, although it does not absolve her."

Crispin's brother approached the desk by the window and retrieved a stack of yellowed papers. They were tied together with stiff string, as if they hadn't been read in a long time. He extended the packet to Crispin.

"Mother kept our father's letters, too," Alexander said. "I am afraid his words do not flatter him. If you do not wish to read them, I understand. Your memories of him paint him in a much better light. I thought you should know they exist, though, even if you choose to destroy the letters without opening them."

His brother extended the packet to him, and Crispin took it with confidence that nothing contained in the writings would alter his opinion of his father.

He was wrong.

TWENTY-TWO

SOPHIA WAS NO LESS DISTRESSED OVER CRISPIN'S DECISION TO pursue Farrin and his men when she came below stairs that evening than she had been upon learning of his plans. Nevertheless, she pasted on a smile to mask her upset, offered a bright greeting when she entered the drawing room prior to supper, and apologized for being late. Aunt Beatrice, Crispin, Lieutenant Locke, and the Duke of Stanhurst had arrived before her.

"There you are, dearest." Aunt Beatrice took Sophia's hands in her own and kissed her cheek. "We were discussing if we should wait on supper. I thought perhaps you were taking a tray above stairs like Mrs. Ness."

"No, ma'am. Forgive me for delaying everyone."

"Forgiveness is yours." Lieutenant Locke came forward with a jaunty smile and lifted her hand to kiss the air above her knuckles. His stomach grumbled; he laughed as red stole into his cheeks. "Even as my appetite protests the delay."

Sophia chuckled. She must admit to being relieved Mrs.

Ness chose not to dine with them after the unpleasantness that morning, but she hoped her absence did not signal a turn for the worse for Mr. Ness. "How is your stepfather this evening, sir?"

"There has been no change, Miss Darlington, but his rest is peaceful now. He is no longer struggling to catch a breath."

Sophia's heart felt a little heavier, given their host's troubles. She really should have practiced restraint with Crispin's mother. She must be very worried for her husband. "I am sorry for Mr. Ness's troubles, and I hope he remains free of suffering."

Sophia caught Crispin staring at her and quickly averted her gaze. Despite his assertion that she needn't apologize for arguing with his mother, Sophia's conscience insisted otherwise. She had formed an opinion of her future mother-in-law long before the conflict, and she suspected that opinion had colored her judgment. Like it or not, marriage to Crispin came with a difficult mother-in-law. Life would be easier for everyone if she and Sophia learned to tolerate each other.

"Are you well-rested now, dearest?" Aunt Beatrice asked.

"I feel much better, thank you."

Sophia had secluded herself in her chambers all afternoon on the pretense of needing to recover from their travels. Instead of sleeping, she had sat at the window seat to contemplate alternatives to Crispin's plans and had come up with no viable alternative. Everyone at Mr. and Mrs. Ness's home would be in danger if Farrin and his men were allowed to come to them. Crispin must find the blackguards first. She needed to trust in his abilities.

As he had proven during the attack behind the theatre,

he was capable of defending himself. This knowledge gave her little peace, however. A whisper at the back of her mind refused to be quiet. *You have everything you want; it cannot last.*

She ignored the fatalistic pest and accepted Crispin's escort to the dining room. The duke was partnered with Aunt Beatrice and preceded them to supper. Lieutenant Locke, absent a dining partner, followed in their wake.

A dark mood emanated from Crispin as he took his place across the table; a gloom seemed to settle over the room. The wall coverings appeared more dingy than she recalled from the morning, and the air trudged thickly through her lungs.

To ease the awkwardness, she attempted to initiate conversation at the supper table. "Did you find your sisters well when you were home, Your Grace?"

The Duke of Stanhurst's head snapped up. He seemed startled to be addressed. "Er, yes. I was home only briefly, but everything was as well as could be expected."

Sophia smiled in sympathy. She felt a kinship to the duke and his sisters, having lost both of her parents too. "I imagine this must be a difficult time for everyone. If you would find it appropriate, I would like to write to your eldest sister to extend an offer of friendship. I understand she will be presented next Season. Perhaps having a friend to correspond with prior to her coming out will make the prospect feel less daunting."

"That is kind of you, Miss Darlington. Emmeline would be pleased by your offer, I am sure."

The duke returned to cutting the chicken on his plate into small pieces that she suspected he wouldn't eat. He had only pushed the carrots around his plate since he was served.

The poor man. It must have been harrowing to be driven off the road and almost shot by highwaymen. Even more disturbing had to be realizing his assailants were working for his cousin. Was it any wonder he had lost his appetite?

Aunt Beatrice picked up the conversation and questioned Lieutenant Locke about his post in Canada. He regaled them with humorous accounts of his time with his regime, lightening the mood during the supper hour. Sophia caught Crispin studying her throughout the meal, and even though she had come to accept his decision to leave in the morning, she couldn't bring herself to offer the reassurance he likely sought.

After supper, Lieutenant Locke suggested they retire to the drawing room for a glass of claret and cards. Aunt Beatrice eagerly accepted the invitation and hooked her arm with the Duke of Stanhurst's before she directed him from the dining room.

"Convey our regrets to the duke and Miss Darlington's aunt," Crispin said to his brother. "I promised my betrothed a breath of fresh air after supper. If we go now, we can watch the sunset."

Her eyes rounded in surprise at the boldness of his lie, and her stomach turned uneasily. She didn't wish to argue with him, not when he would leave her before sunrise.

"There is an abandoned groundskeeper's cottage if you follow the footpath," Lieutenant Locke said. "The weeds have gone to seed in the flower garden, but the view is pleasant."

Crispin came round the table to help her from her chair. "What do you say, Miss Darlington?"

She darted her tongue across her dry lips. "It—it sounds lovely."

"To the groundskeeper's cottage it is." Crispin linked his fingers with hers and drew her from the dining room. They walked in silence along a narrow corridor toward the back of the house and exited through a battered exterior door. Outside, darkness was creeping into the sky, erasing the last traces of pink and purple.

Sophia ran her hands up and down her arms to ward off the slight chill. "We've almost missed sunset."

He drew to a halt, shrugged out of his jacket, and draped it around her shoulders. She snuggled into it and inhaled, savoring his masculine scent clinging to the fabric. He dropped his hand to the small of her back. "How do you feel about star-gazing?"

"I like it very much." Sparks radiated from where his hand lay lightly above the curve of her bottom. "I think I would enjoy anything as long as we are together."

He frowned. "I suspected you were still upset with me. You refused to look at me at supper."

"I saw you. I am always aware of you. Sometimes, it feels as if there is room for no one else."

"What do you mean? Do you think I have no room for you?" His voice assumed a defensive edge that forecast a stormy evening ahead if she did not change course.

"That was not my meaning." She hugged herself as she struggled to explain how he affected her. "I am sensitive to you, to your moods. When you are angry or worried or distraught, I feel it. The air around you vibrates, and I can feel it deep in here." She pointed at her chest and slid her hand down to her stomach.

One side of his mouth inched upward—sardonic and doubting. Fire whooshed in her ears.

"I cannot explain it well," she snapped. "You think I am a fool."

When she would have stomped away, he gently captured her chin with his fingers and tipped her face so they were eye-to-eye. "You are not a fool, Sophia, except when it comes to loving me. I am sorry for being difficult."

He kissed the tip of her nose, her cheeks, her chin. Each touch of his lips cooled her temper. She smiled and arched her neck as his mouth sought out the sensitive placed at the base of her ear and travelled to the hollow of her collarbone.

"Who said I love you?" she teased.

He laughed and hugged her, placing a smacking kiss on her shoulder. "Let's find the groundskeeper's cottage. I want to teach you what I know about ciphers to make your task easier."

"Oh, Lord Margrave!" She fluttered her lashes dramatically. "You really know how to romance a lady."

He winked. "That is just foreplay, darling. Wait until I teach you tracking skills."

"How splendid! I am beside myself with anticipation."

With both of their good humors restored, they kissed once more, a small peck to make-up. They set off across the field toward a rusted iron gate marking the start of a well-worn path with his arm around her shoulders. The gate had been left propped open, its purpose unfulfilled.

The path curved around a grove of trees. A light winked through the undergrowth. Sophia skidded to a stop. Her heart slammed into her ribs. "Is someone there, ahead?"

"No, it is no one," Crispin murmured. "I have prepared a surprise for you."

"A surprise?" Delight infused her words. "What have you done?"

His eyes glittered in the fading light. "Come and see."

He took her hand and urged her along the path. When they rounded the grove, a cozy white cottage came into view. The windows glowed with warm light, and a thin trail of smoke rose from the chimney.

"Is this the groundkeeper's cottage?" she asked. "Lieutenant Locke said it was abandoned."

"It is. The groundskeeper moved closer to his family after he received his pension. This evening, it is ours."

An excited fluttered originated just beneath her breastbone. She couldn't guess at what awaited her inside the cottage, and it was a strange and wonderful feeling.

"Did you plan this alone?" she asked.

Crispin shrugged, but he looked pleased. "I needed something to keep me occupied. Otherwise, I would have been banging down your door."

She laughed. "I wouldn't have minded, although it is not my door."

"I thought you disliked when I behave in an overbearing manner."

"Only when you employ it to keep me at a distance."

"Do I do that?" He didn't sound surprised by the accusation.

She squeezed his hand to ease any sting her words might have carried. "Or perhaps you simply take pleasure in bossing me about."

"It is a thankless job," he said with mock gravity, "but I put forth my best effort."

"Mm... You are very good at it, too."

As they approached the cottage, a small wooden fence and an overgrown garden came into view. Elongated rectangles of light from the cottage's windowpanes illuminated the freshly cut path leading to the front door.

Crispin stopped on the stoop outside. "Close your eyes."

"Your valet better not be inside ready to jump out and scare me."

His stern brows dropped. "Close them, or no surprises for you."

"Very well," she said with an exaggerated huff and

squeezed her eyes tightly shut. "You are too commanding by half, my lord and master."

A quiet growl reached her ears; she chuckled. Crispin took her arm and carefully guided her through the front door. The night's chill vanished when the door closed behind them.

"Open your eyes, minx."

Sophia did as he ordered and blinked the room into focus. Her breath caught. The room was unexpectedly beautiful for a former bachelor's quarters. Large crimson cushions and thick quilts had been spread on the floor in front of the fireplace, and lanterns were placed around the room to illuminate the warm golden yellow of the walls. A vase of wildflowers, a plate of biscuits, and a claret jug with two cut crystal glasses sat on the smallest dining table Sophia had ever seen.

"You've thought of everything."

"I had a little help," he said. "Mrs. Poindexter seems to have a talent for creating a love nest. Do you think she has experience?"

"Love nest!" Sophia laughed, delighted by the direction the evening seemed to be headed. "I thought I was in for boring—I mean, *stimulating* lessons."

"Hmm... I am sure that was your meaning." He tweaked her cheek. "Do not allow the romantic ambiance to trouble you. I promise, I did not lure you here under false pretenses, but I couldn't very well tell the housekeeper I wanted a private place to teach my betrothed how to play cloak and dagger."

She mumbled, "How disappointing." She removed the jacket and handed it to him. Her happiness dimmed as she thought of his upcoming mission. "You and Kane speak of your work as if it is a game. I have seen first hand the type of men you will be facing. How can you be so cavalier?"

He approached the dining table and draped the jacket over the back of a chair before grabbing the jug of wine. The sterling silver top glinted in the lamplight as he filled the first glass. "Uncertainty and fear cannot be entertained. One risks losing focus, and distractions can be fatal."

Her throat squeezed tight. How detached he sounded, as if the sensible parts of him that *should* fear danger had been stripped away.

He glanced up. "Would you like a claret?"

He didn't seem to notice her inability to speak and poured a second glass. When he carried it to her, she accepted his offering. The scarlet wine matched the lush pillows on the floor.

Turning his head, he followed her line of sight. "I do not expect you to sit on the floor. Take a seat on the settee."

The culmination of his carefree attitude and commanding manner sparked her ire. She took a gulp of wine before placing the glass on a side table, found a large pillow, and plopped down on it. It was silly, this minor act of rebellion, but she felt somewhat better for refusing to allow him control over where she sat.

He held his place and took a sip of wine, studying her over the rim of the glass. His eyes were darker in the dim light, like Turkish coffee—shimmering and hot. "I believe you take pleasure in defying me, Miss Darlington."

She notched her chin, sensing the unspoken truth. "I think you enjoy it as well, my lord."

His nostrils flared slightly. She had surprised him; her heart shuddered with excitement. "Did your governess fail to teach you that obedience is a virtue?" he asked mildly.

"She did not teach *blind* obedience. I suspect you would be disappointed if she had."

A slight smile from him emboldened her. He *did* derive

some pleasure from being challenged. She would stake her reputation on it.

Like Crispin, she would not allow herself to become distracted by worry over the consequences of her behavior. He took risks, so would she. She slid from the pillow and reclined against it, striking a pose like a Greek goddess on the pottery pieces she had ogled over the years.

"You have grown too accustomed to having your way, Lord Margrave." Her mouth tingled with the memory of Crispin's kiss. She drew a finger over her lips to ease the sensation. "Perhaps the novelty of opposition arouses you?"

Without speaking, he set his glass beside hers, lowered to his hands and knees, and prowled toward her like a great cat. She swallowed hard; it was loud in the quiet. She was out of her element, yet thrilled by his attentions. When he loomed above her, she refused to look away even as her inexperience engulfed her body in heat.

One side of his mouth inched up higher than the other. "You are innocence and boldness in equal measures, darling. I find the combination irresistible." He touched the tip of his finger to her temple and slowly—achingly—trailed it along the swell of her cheek to the corner of her mouth. "I cannot decide if I should tame you or encourage your willfulness."

She smiled and turned her head slightly to kiss his fingertip. He curled it, evading her lips, teasing her. She captured his wrist, her slim fingers creating a fragile shackle she dared him to break. He willingly remained her captive.

"I think you know which would please us both," she said. "Do not pretend you desire a timid wife in your bed."

He did not seem the least bit offended by her unladylike talk. "What do you know of a man's desires, vixen? Have you been discussing delicate matters with your older sister?

I wonder if her husband knows the Darlington Angels keep no secrets from one another."

It was true Regina had been forthcoming when she and Evangeline questioned her about her wedding night, but Sophia's certainty about Crispin's wants came from observation.

"If you desired a docile woman, any number of widows would be willing to fulfill the role. None have caught your eye."

He cocked one dark blond eyebrow.

"I have heard them gossiping about you. The ladies fantasize about being..." She looked away in sudden shyness. Repeating what she had overheard while holding his gaze required more bravery than she possessed. "Th-they want to be... *ruled* by you... in the bedchamber."

He sank to his haunches so he was kneeling beside her. Her fingers still loosely circled his wrist. Curiosity got the better of her, and she glanced up. Raw desire emanated from him. His skin heated beneath her hand; color rose in his face.

"Perhaps," he said in a husky voice that caused a thousand winged fairies to flitter in her lower belly, "the only woman I wish to rule is you."

Law! Did she want to be ruled? Her will had always been strong, and she knew with certainty she did not appreciate high-handedness any other time. *But this...*

The prospect of Crispin commanding her in lovemaking was deliciously arousing. Before logic could ruin her fantasy, she pulled his hand toward her mouth and placed a kiss on the heel of his palm.

He exhaled, his eyes as dark as midnight. "Sophia." His voice was heavy with warning. "It was not my intention to seduce you."

"I believe you," she murmured, "but perhaps I wish you had."

When he offered no more protest, she pushed to a seated position, untied the sash around her waist, and presented her back to him. Shivering with anticipation, she looked over her shoulder. "Will you help with my gown?"

His lips parted; not a muscle moved. The silence dragged on until she teetered on the edge of giving up and slinking away in humiliation.

"Faith!" He reached for the first fastener on her gown and hurriedly released each one. A soft ripping accompanied the last few, and he roughly shoved the bodice from her shoulders. The blue muslin fell limply around her waist. Her breasts swelled above the ruffle of her chemise, plumped by an embroidered pink corset. He bracketed her waist with his hands, tracing the slopes and stopping below her breasts to return to her hips.

"Beautiful," he murmured.

She blushed with pleasure. She had chosen her new undergarments at the start of the Season with him in mind. It seemed her pin money had been wisely invested.

He leaned forward to touch his lips to her shoulder. "Your fragrance calls to me in my dreams," he whispered, his breath tickling the back of her neck.

She sighed and dropped her head to the side to invite further exploration. He seemed happy to accept and placed kisses from her shoulder to her neck while she released the fasteners along the front of her corset. When the garment fell away, Crispin tossed it aside and dragged Sophia onto his lap.

She gasped. Her bottom rested on his thighs and her back was pressed against his chest. She adjusted her legs so she was straddling his knees. "You surprised me."

He eased her skirts high on her legs and nuzzled her ear

while his fingers grazed the slit in her drawers. "I think you like surprises."

She moaned in agreement as his hand made another sweep over her feverish skin.

"Do you touch yourself here when you are alone, love?" His voice was raspy like gravel being crushed beneath one's boots.

Fire licked her body. If she answered honestly, would he be pleased or disturbed? She was still a virgin, but she had always been curious about lovemaking and had never been made to feel ashamed for asking questions or reading books not meant for a lady's eyes.

"Sometimes," she whispered, capturing one of his hands and raising it to cover her breast, "I pretend it is you touching me."

His jagged breath churned pale strands of hair that had slipped from her coiffure and caressed her neck. "God's blood, Sophia. How can I be expected to resist you?"

"Don't, please." She lifted her arm and hooked her hand behind his neck. "I cannot bear to be disappointed tonight."

He captured the lobe of her ear with his teeth and gently tugged. His hands covered both breasts and kneaded them through her thin chemise. "You will never be disappointed again."

She murmured her approval and buried her fingers into his hair, holding him close. His beard was growing in; it rasped against her shoulder, lightly branding her.

He tugged her chemise to her waist and bared her breasts to his touch. Her nipples became little pebbles between his fingers as he plucked them. She moaned softly and shifted on his lap, brushing against his erection. He tensed and groaned under his breath.

She wiggled again, relishing her affect over him.

"Be still," he ordered.

She slanted a teasing look over her shoulder. "Or what?" She released her hold on his neck and snaked her hand between their bodies to further test her powers. He grabbed her forearm above the wrist, trapping her arm behind her back. His hold was firm but not painful. She suspected she could break it in an instant if she tried.

"You are not allowed to touch," he said as he lightly pinched her nipple again.

A delicious pulse beat between her legs. "Why not?"

"I did not grant permission, and you must do as I say, darling."

She snorted softly. "I did not ask for permission, and I do as I wish, my love."

When she attempted to touch him with her free hand, he released her arm and tossed her tummy first onto the pillows. She bounced on the soft landing and laughed.

"You rat!" She propped up on her elbows and smiled at him over her shoulder.

He grinned in return and tugged her gown and chemise over her hips and down her legs. Her petticoat and drawers followed, but he left on her stockings. She bent her knees and crossed her ankles in the air, so he could remove her slippers. Once her feet were free, she tried to push up from the floor, but he planted his hand on the small of her back and playfully swatted her bottom.

She squealed in surprise, even though the sting was minimal. "Crispin!"

He winked. "Stay where you are and take your pleasure like a good girl." For good measure, he smacked her other cheek.

"I will, I will. No more, *please!*"

She believed in putting on a good act, and he did seem to be enjoying the show. His eyes were as black as midnight, and the outline of his arousal was unmistakable through his trousers.

He circled his hand over the fullest part of her derriere. "See that you do, minx."

With his knee, he nudged her legs apart to kneel between them and slid his hand over the curve of her bottom. She sighed and sank into the pillow when his fingers slid between her thighs brushed her curls. He caressed her intimately with tenderness and an expertise that elicited more sighs of pleasure.

When he slipped a finger inside her, she buried her face into the pillow to muffle her moans. He returned to stroking her, his fingers gliding over her sensitive flesh and circling her secret pearl until she grew restless with need. She writhed on the quilts, wanton and unashamed.

"Crispin." His name was a whispered plea.

He allowed her a reprieve and flipped her on her back, trapping her arms above her head. She didn't protest, because *he* was above her, bracing his weight on his arms. His breath came out in ragged exhales; his eyes seared into her. She arched her neck to kiss him, but he remained just out of her reach. She growled in frustration.

"Kiss me," she demanded.

He smiled. "Yes, my love."

Lowering his head, he placed the sweetest kiss on her mouth. His lips gently nipped at hers; his tongue lovingly brushed against hers. They shared one breath, their hearts racing together. She could feel his own pounding against her breast. *Lord, help me.* Love swelled in her chest as the backs of her eyes began to sting. When he drew back, she blinked to keep her tears from slipping onto her cheeks.

"Pr-promise you will come back to me," she whispered.

He kissed her softly once more. "I swear it to you." His eyes glimmered in the firelight, and the edges of his strong jaw had lost its sharpness. "I love you, darling. Do you not know what is in my heart? Nothing will stop me from returning to you, and no one will take me from your side again. This madness will be behind us soon. Have faith."

The prospect of a future with this man she loved with every breath—the only man she had ever wanted to love her, too—overwhelmed her. Tears fell on her cheeks.

Crispin released his grip on her arms, eased away, and sank to his knees. He held her hands and helped her to a seated position. "You are crying," he said, as if she might be unaware she was leaking like a cracked teacup.

She sniffled and swiped the back of her wrist over her eyes. "Yes, thank you. I thought the dampness might be rain."

He did not respond to her attempt to lighten the mood. The concerned V between his brows appeared carved in stone. "Tell me what is wrong." He buried his fingers into her hair, his thumb caressing the rim of her ear. "Have I upset you?"

She swallowed and shook her head; a watery smile broke across her face. "Quite the opposite. I am happy."

He exhaled and mirrored her smile. "Tears of joy?"

"Of course! What did you expect? I was convinced you would desert me in the country as soon as we married."

He smiled ruefully. "You believed no such thing, love. You were determined to change my mind. This stubborn feature gives you away every time." He lightly chucked her on the chin. "And you *did*—change my mind."

"Did I? How?"

"It has become clear you can find trouble wherever you go. I dare not leave you to your own devices. I have no choice except to keep you close."

She wrinkled her nose, secretly pleased with his teasing. The strain of the last few days melted away. "Well, Lord

Observant, have you realized I am the only one not wearing clothes?"

"That did not escape my notice, darling." He spread his arms to his sides and cocked an eyebrow. "Set to work. I suspect you have wanted to put hands on me for sometime —at least around my neck."

Her gaze lowered to the bulge in his trousers. She suspected he would prefer her touch elsewhere, but she was not so bold as to say so. Smiling, she reached for his cravat to untie it. Her hands began to shake and grow clumsy in her haste to strip away the last of the barriers between them—not just the physical barrier posed by his clothing, but the unseen ones that had been holding her at a distance.

He covered her hands to still them. "Sophia, are you certain?"

A moment's hesitation washed over her. The wave receded. She locked gazes with him. "Make me yours," she murmured.

The smoldering fire was back in his eyes. He took over disrobing himself, yanking the knot free. He discarded his waistcoat and ripped the shirt over his head. Her breath froze in her lungs. A thick jagged scar was just above his nipple, a pale slash across a spectacularly muscled chest. It was an old injury but too close to his heart. She could feel her throat growing tight. *What if this is the only time I will have to love him?*

"What if this is good-bye?"

"Stop," he commanded. "Look at me."

His tone snatched her away from the abyss. She obeyed. His expression was earnest and fierce. "This is *not* good-bye, do you hear me? If you want to be mine, I will gladly make it so, but let me be clear. Tonight will be the first of many times I will have you beneath me."

His promise hit her with the force of a gale wind. Her stomach swooped with excitement.

He gentled his tone. "Have you changed your mind, darling? Is this what you want?"

She tipped her head and gazed up at him. "Not exactly."

He flinched.

A wicked smile spread across her lips. "I do hope to have *you* beneath *me,* sometimes."

TWENTY-THREE

"DAMNATION," CRISPIN MUTTERED AS LUST SHOT THROUGH his veins. It roared in his ears and made him hard as a bloody iron rod. The thought of Sophia astride him caused him to burn for her in a way he had never experienced.

He tugged off his boots and released the front fly of his trousers.

"Come here." He caught her hips and tugged until she was lying on her back on the covers. He hovered above her, his gaze raking over her. She was perfection in his eyes—pale hair like moonlight, ivory skin unblemished, firm breasts like ripe peaches begging to be tasted. Her hips flared at her waist, and she had been blessed with a generous arse he found irresistible. God help any man who tried to take her from him.

Hooking her thumbs in his waistband, she pushed his trousers low on his hips and squeezed his bum. She smiled, appearing proud of herself.

"Do you want to play, vixen?"

"Maybe." Her smile widened and her blue eyes crinkled

at the corners. Sophia was mischievous to the bone, and he loved her all the more for it.

Shifting his weight, he caught her wrists, and pushed her arms above her head again. "Leave them there, while I have my way with you."

The stubborn little chin jutted toward him. He lightly nipped it, grazing it with his teeth. She inhaled sharply, and the playful mood shifted.

He released her wrists and trailed the back of his fingers down her arms and along her sides. Her chest rose and fell steadily, her breathing deeper and quick. When he brushed the sides of her breasts, her nipples hardened. Unable to resist, he caught one between his teeth and gave a gentle tug. She closed her eyes, lips parted with a sigh. He licked a circle around the bud, taking it in his mouth when she began to grow restless.

As he lavished her with the attention that she desired, she tunneled her fingers in his hair. He allowed her to touch him. The forbidden always carried the sweetest reward. Her nails lightly scratched his scalp before passing over the back of his neck and across his shoulders. She drew lazy circles on his back, sending sharp pulses down his spine and into his cock.

He kissed a path down the middle of her torso and the small swell of her belly. Catching her beneath the knee, he raised her leg and began a new trail of kisses starting at her knee. He traveled down the inside of her thigh to taste where he had touched her.

"Oh," she said on a breath when he lovingly swept his tongue over her. He smiled and did it again. Her scent was an intoxicating blend of camellias and arousal that banished all thought from his mind, other than driving their pleasure. As he loved her with his mouth, her throaty moans grew louder and longer with each pass of his tongue. She came with an astonished cry, arching her back and gripping the quilt as the waves overtook her. Spent, she collapsed against the floor.

"Oh, my heavens. I have never—" A small jubilant laugh slipped from her.

Crispin lifted to his elbows. "You have never?"

"I forgot. My mind has been turned to porridge."

He couldn't help grinning in triumph. At his core, he was a man, and pleasing his woman tapped into something primal inside him. "You have never reached completion?"

She shook her head, smiling lazily. He moved to lie beside her, wrapped his arm around her, and rolled to his back. She rested her head on his shoulder. Now that she was satisfied, he wanted to allow her a moment of clear headedness before she gave her innocence to him.

She toyed with the sparse sprinkle of hair on his chest. Her touch made him throb. He clenched his jaw, fighting the urge to ignore honor and bury himself in her.

"Does it feel the same for men?" she asked. "Completion?"

He hugged her and placed a kiss on her hair. "I cannot say with certainty, but men derive the same pleasure."

"I see," she murmured. "In the same manner?"

"I do not understand the question."

"There is a drawing at Hartland Manor, from the Far East. It is a man and a woman seeking pleasure from one another."

Sometimes he forgot about her unconventional upbringing. Slowly, she slid her hand over his stomach, pausing to glance up at him. He smiled, encouraging her exploration. When her fingertips touched his cock, her light touch was too much. He caught her hand. She looked at him, startled. "I like it firmer," he said.

The lines on her forehead disappeared. She knelt beside

him, tugged his pants down his legs, and tossed them aside. When she took him in her hand, she seemed more confident. He showed her how to stroke him, and closed his eyes, surrendering control. She was unskilled in pleasing a man, but her earnest efforts only increased his tenderness for her. When she bent forward to place a kiss to him, he ended her experiment and flipped her to her back. He was not ready to allow her that much power over him.

She cradled his face and kissed him, her lips parted. He brushed the tip of his tongue across her top lip and slowly entered her. She tensed, sucked in a breath, and held it. He withdrew an inch, his muscles straining to keep his instincts to take her at bay. "Breathe, darling."

She exhaled, smiling sheepishly.

He kissed her temple, her cheek, the tip of her nose. "Does it hurt too badly?"

"It is bearable," she said as she caressed the small of his back; her fingers feathered over his arse. "I want to be yours, Crispin."

With a low groan, he captured her mouth and drove into her to get past her discomfort. She cried out softly and nipped his lip. He drew back in surprise, aroused as hell. He forced himself to hold back, gently sinking into her again.

Twice more, he withdrew and slid inside her. She held his gaze, flames flickering in her eyes as her body squeezed around him.

"You are mine, too," she said fiercely. "I want all of you."

His control shattered, and he surrendered everything. He gave his heart, soul—his body—everything to her. When he reached his climax, he buried his face in her hair, helplessly caught in the throes of passion. He remained close, drawing in her scent as his breathing began to return to normal. Her perfume would always remind him of this unguarded moment of happiness and deep sense of satisfaction.

"I love you," he whispered in her ear.

"Mm," she murmured and hugged him. She did not return the sentiment.

~

CRISPIN PUSHED OFF HER AND RETRIEVED HIS PANTS. THE rigid set of his shoulders caused Sophia's stomach to turn. It was silly, this superstition she hadn't realized she shared with her oldest sister, but it tied her tongue. Logically, she realized saying she loved him would not tempt fate or bring him bad luck when they were apart, but on a deeper level, she couldn't disregard the belief easily.

She sat up to hug him from behind and place a kiss on his back. He stood to pull his pants over his hips and fastened the front fall.

"Crispin," she implored.

"We have work to do."

He snatched her dress from the ground and held it out to her. When she refused to take it, he laid it beside her then grabbed his boots and shirt. He sat on one of the ladder-back chairs at the table after pulling the white shirt over his head.

Sophia ignored her gown lying on the floor, draped the quilt around her, and joined him at the table. Instead of assuming a seat, however, she came up behind him to rub his shoulders. His muscles were tense. He bent forward, out of her reach, to jam his foot into one of the boots.

"I love you, too," she blurted. "I am sorry. I should have said it when you did."

"It is not a sentiment to be spoken lightly." He tugged on his other boot. "I understand if it is too soon."

"Too soon?" Sophia snorted. "I have been waiting for you to come to your senses since Christmas. I love you, you stubborn man."

He sat up quickly and swiveled on the chair, grabbing the rails. His biceps flexed, visible through the thin material of his shirt.

"Crispin, could you truly believe I would give myself to anyone else? You are the only man I have ever loved." She leaned forward to kiss him softly on the forehead. When she drew back, the worry lines had vanished. "Even with everything we are facing, I have never been happier."

A soft light emanated from his eyes. "Neither have I."

She rounded the chair; he turned with her, watching. When she sat on his lap, straddling his legs, she nearly lost the quilt. Crispin caught the edges of it and drew it around her shoulders. She held the corners and wrapped her arms around him so they were both cocooned in the fabric.

"I only hesitated, because it is something we never say to each other when Uncle Charles is preparing to leave us. It is a tradition between him and Regina, really. Evangeline and I are passive participants. They attempt to outwit fate by wishing bad luck on each other. It is a silly practice, but I only now realized I place some faith in it."

He pulled her closer. "You wanted to keep me safe by hiding the fact you love me?"

Her face heated. "I said it was ridiculous."

"I find it sweet." He nuzzled her cheek then whispered in her ear. "I secretly love you with all my heart. Do not tell anyone until we are reunited. I would not wish to tempt fate."

She smiled. "It will be our secret until we are ready to share it."

He placed a brief kiss on her lips. "You had best don

your gown, or I will want you again, and we will never rejoin the others."

She allowed him to ease her from his lap. She was a little sore and not quite ready to be loved again so soon. She found a washbasin and mirror in the small bedchamber. Once she washed, she released the side of her hair that hadn't fallen during their lovemaking and attempted to create a simple knot with the pins she found hiding among the pillows.

"Will you help me with my gown?" she called.

Crispin appeared in the doorway with her undergarments and gown, anticipating her needs. Once she was set back to rights, they returned to the seating area hand-in-hand and sat on the settee. He passed her a glass of claret. She took a sip and smiled.

"Teach me, wise one. What is it I must know about deciphering?"

He provided an overview of the different types of ciphers, including King Charles I's personal code. "I do not anticipate Lord Geoffrey was versed enough in ciphers to have created his own. Stanhurst did not find anything suggesting he created his own alphabet, and it would be difficult to memorize, except for someone with your skills. The duke said his brother always struggled with his lessons, so it is safe to assume he was not as gifted as you."

His praise warmed her heart. Crispin never made her feel as if all she had to offer was beauty. Sophia paid little attention to such shallow measures of a person, but she had been bombarded with compliments on her appearance since she joined Society. In the beginning, she was flattered, but she quickly grew tired of the fawning.

"The Consul employs a Vigenère cipher—a code word that creates a polyalphabetic substitution method."

"We can discard that one, since the letter is written in numbers," she said.

"Precisely, therefore, I suspect he and his mysterious correspondent were using a book cipher. A common title that would not appear out of place left lying about."

"Did Lord Geoffrey keep a book with the letters?"

"The duke does not recall seeing one. Perhaps you can help him remember or uncover something in Lord Geoffrey's diary that would be useful." He loosely laced his fingers with hers. "We may not have the luxury of time, Sophia. If you can decipher these letters, we will be closer to discovering what Lord Geoffrey and his associate were plotting."

"I understand. Stanhurst and I will begin work in the morning." She took a sip of wine, her mind hitting upon a forgotten memory. She placed her glass on the small table next to her side of the settee. "I think I might know where Farrin and his men have gone. I cannot be sure, but after my brother-in-law was abducted, he was held at an abandoned farmhouse north of London. Benny—you recall the large man at the theatre?"

"I remember."

"Yes, well, Benny lived there from the time he was a child. He said after the caretaker and his wife died, Farrin started using the house as a prison of sorts. He and his men interrogated captives in the cellar—and worse, from what I have been able to gather. Do you think Farrin and his men might have returned to the farmhouse?"

"It is possible," Crispin said. "North of London. Did your brother-in-law say how far?"

"I am afraid not, but Claudine will be able to provide the exact location. Benny is the rightful heir to the property, and Claudine's betrothed has engaged a solicitor to sort out the mess. You should start your search at the Drayton Theatre."

"Excellent suggestion." He placed his arm on the back of the settee; she scooted closer to rest her head on his shoulder.

"At dinner this evening, you seemed troubled," she said. "Were you thinking about what is ahead of you?"

"I am prepared for Farrin and his men." He swallowed hard, hesitating as if he required a moment to gather his thoughts. Sophia waited patiently.

"I acquired distressing information earlier today," he said at last. "About my father. He and my mother corresponded several times after she left us, and she saved the letters. Alexander thought I should know of their existence, even if I chose not to read them."

"Did you?"

He nodded. "Part of me wishes I had not. It is hard to reconcile my memories of my father with the callous man revealed in the letters. I always knew him as a kind and proud father, but he possessed a darker side I never saw."

There was a thread of vulnerability in Crispin's voice. She raised her head and shifted her body on the settee to better attend to him. He cleared his throat, his Adam's apple bobbing.

"He accused my mother of adultery and claimed Alexander was not his son."

Sophia's eyes widened.

"His reasoning was irrational. Alexander was born sickly, but I never suffered any ill effects as an infant and child. My father convinced himself that the differences between my brother and me proved she gave birth to another man's child, which is ludicrous. Alexander bears a striking likeness to our father, and Father was sickly all his life. If he had doubts about paternity, they should have extended to me."

"You resemble your mother," she said. "I imagine he could see it, too."

"I suspect looking at Alexander was akin to seeing his own reflection in a mirror, and my father did not think kindly of himself. Your uncle once told me that Father saw in me the lad he had longed to be. I did not understand what Wedmore meant at the time, but it became clearer as I grew older. He crowed about my accomplishments to anyone willing to humor him." He grinned. "I was not taught to be humble. I have been told it is an unlikeable quality."

"By lesser men, I am sure," she teased and reached to play with the hair brushing his collar.

His smile spread, reaching his eyes. Cognizant that she might have unintentionally distracted him from talking about his father, she redirected the conversation. "Your father's accusation obviously bothered you."

"Not as much as his response to her request to be allowed to keep Alexander until he was weaned. He said he had no use for either of them, and it was just as well she had taken Alexander when she ran away. He told her to keep my brother. As far as he was concerned, he had only one son, and he did not want her by-blow bringing illness into our home."

Sophia gasped. "Poor Alexander! Do you think he read that part?"

"I imagine curiosity led him to read every word." Crispin frowned. "I could not put away my mother's letters when I discovered them, even though I believed they were full of lies. For a long time, I hated her for dying. Then I hated her for leaving me. I do not know what to make of this new knowledge."

Sophia was not prepared to easily forgive Crispin's mother for treating him poorly, but she would not discourage him from making whatever peace he could with his past. "Will you tell her you know about your father's letters?"

"I do not know if I will have the chance," he murmured. "She seems eager for me to go."

Sophia's heart cracked open and bled. She tossed her arms around him and held him tight.

"If you wish to talk with her, my love," she whispered, "your mother will see you." Sophia would make certain of it. She would never stay quiet while he was hurting.

When she and Crispin returned to the house, Alexander and the duke were deep into a game of chess in the drawing room, and Aunt Beatrice had retired for the evening.

"I should look in on Auntie," she said to Crispin. "If I am welcome, I will rejoin you in a moment."

Crispin lifted her hand and placed a kiss on her fingers. "You are always welcome, darling."

He entered the drawing room, and she slipped upstairs. When she knocked on Crispin's mother's bedchamber door, she was slightly surprised when Mrs. Ness answered. She had been spending most of her time at her husband's bedside, but Sophia had decided to take a chance.

"Miss Darlington. I thought Alexander was at my door."

Crispin's mother drew her wrapper around her body. Her eyes were sunken and dark circles marred her skin. The fight she had shown earlier seemed to have drained from her. Her icy exterior had a small crack, and Sophia glimpsed the lonely, broken down woman underneath. Her anger toward Crispin's mother lessened to some degree.

"Please forgive me for disturbing you, ma'am," she said then cleared her throat. "May I ask after Mr. Ness? How is he faring this evening?"

The older woman's bottom lip quivered before she gathered control of her emotions. "Mr. Ness is resting. Alexander insisted I allow the maid to sit with him and ordered me to sleep. I find I cannot."

Her brows sat low on her forehead—two thick slashes above watery eyes. Suddenly, all Sophia could see was the resemblance to Crispin, and her heart softened a bit more.

"We did not begin our association as I had hoped," Sophia said, "and I must accept a fair share of the blame. I am afraid I judged you before we met, and for that, I am sorry. It is my fervent wish for us to get on well. You and your sons deserve harmony after all this time, and I do not intend to make the task more difficult than it already is."

Mrs. Ness's mouth softened. "I did not give you reason to question your judgments."

"It was still unkind of me to challenge you this morning. I hope we can start anew, and perhaps form a friendship in time."

"I have no friends," Crispin's mother stated.

There was no emotion connected to her words. Sophia had no way of knowing if her overture of friendship was being rejected or looked upon with favor. Perhaps there was no hidden meaning at all.

"Well, if we *were* friends," Sophia said, "I expect you would graciously accept the advice I am about to offer."

One of Mrs. Ness's eyebrows angled up. "Advice, Miss Darlington?"

She barreled on before she lost her nerve. "Your eldest son is leaving tomorrow, and the business that calls him away is dangerous."

A spark of what Sophia decided was alarm flickered in Mrs. Ness's eyes.

"Please, do not allow Crispin to depart believing you care nothing for him. He is your *son*. You must feel some affinity with him. If he does not return, do you want the last words exchanged between you to be cross?"

Mrs. Ness's nostrils flared. "Thank you, Miss Darlington. If you will excuse me, I believe I will be able to sleep after all." She closed the door, ending their conversation.

Sophia sighed. *At least she did not slam the door in my face.* Feeling like a failure, she looked in on Aunt Beatrice, who was deep in slumber, then trudged downstairs to join the men.

TWENTY-FOUR

THE NEXT DAY CRISPIN'S BROTHER ARRIVED AT HIS bedchamber door. "Mother has requested an audience before your departure."

Crispin grimaced and stepped into the corridor, closing the door behind him. Sophia had found her way into his bed early that morning, and he did not wish to announce their newfound intimacy to the household—even as he wanted to crow to the world that she was his.

"How did our mother take the news yesterday?" he asked.

"As one would expect, with a stiff upper lip." His brother smiled kindly. "It is strange, seeing so much of Mother in you."

"I am uncertain she would agree," he muttered, reflecting on how their father had denied the similarity between him and Alexander. "Do you expect she will ask me to take Sophia and Beatrice elsewhere?"

"She did not give that impression, no," Alexander said. "She seemed sympathetic to their plight and mentioned she

288

had been afraid her father might turn her away when she setoff for home with me."

Crispin cocked his head. "Grandfather did not strike me as the type of man to turn away his own flesh and blood."

"He had been pleased to see her well-settled in marriage, and he liked our father. What should I tell Mother?"

"Tell her I accept, and I will be along in a moment."

"Very good." When Alexander was out of sight, Crispin opened the bedchamber door and slipped inside, closing it behind him.

Sophia was sprawled on the bed on her stomach, her hair nearly as light as the pillow beneath her head. She had kicked the covers, and a smooth expanse of thigh was exposed. Crispin's body stirred. He was tempted to shuck his clothes and crawl under the covers with her again, but duty called. He had a long journey back to London, and the sooner he found Farrin, the quicker he could return to her.

Still, he couldn't resist one more touch of her luxurious skin. He approached her side of the bed and slid his hand under the covers to caress her from the small of her back to the base of her neck. She moaned softly and stretched. When her eyes opened, she smiled sleepily.

"Good morning, darling." He kissed her shoulder.

She mumbled what he assumed was a greeting.

"My mother has requested to see me."

Her eyes flew open wide, then she immediately squinted against the bright morning light spilling through the window. "What time is it?" she asked.

"Time for you to return to your room unless you want the maid to find you." He kissed her once more and offered her a hand up. She sat on the side of the bed, refreshingly unashamed of her state of undress. She was beautiful and seemed aware of the fact without being vain.

"Will you find me after you see your mother?" she asked

and rubbed her eyes. "I am curious to know what this is about."

"As soon as I leave her, I will find you." He dug under the covers and unearthed her night rail.

While she pulled it over her head, he recovered her wrapper and found her slippers under the chair. "I liked having you in my bed," he said. "I am uncertain I can wait for your uncle to return before I am allowed to have you there permanently."

"Aunt Beatrice thinks we should elope to Gretna Green." She donned her slippers and stood to shove her arms into the wrapper. She tipped her head and smiled at him. "I would not be opposed, although I am still waiting for a proposal."

He gathered her in his arms. "Is there any question I want to spend the rest of my life with you? I love you, Sophia. I cannot imagine how I would survive if you refused me now."

She lifted to her toes, twined her arms around his neck, and pecked a kiss on his mouth. "My answer is yes."

"Yes?"

"Yes, I will marry you." She smiled, leaving her arms draped around his neck. "It was not the proposal I expected, but it is the only one I need."

"You are all *I* need, darling." He hugged her, lifting her feet off the floor and placing a noisy kiss on her cheek.

When Sophia was ready to return to her room, Crispin stepped into the corridor to insure the area was clear. No one was mulling about, and he signaled Sophia to hurry. She shot across the corridor and softly closed the door behind her.

Crispin's mother was in the sitting room where they'd had their first conversation. He felt guarded as he approached her, even though he had been pleased to hear she seemed amenable to providing a refuge to Sophia and Beatrice.

She waved a hand toward an empty chair. "I understand you are leaving for London this morning."

"That is correct." He sat even though he wished to stand.

"Will you be gone long?"

"I hope my task will be quick, but I cannot predict the amount of time required."

"I see." She fidgeted with a loose thread from the chair's upholstery. His fingers tightened on the arm of his own chair. She seemed as uncomfortable with mindless talk as he.

"I read the letters my father sent you," he said, impatient to have this business behind them. "He did not treat you or my brother well. Please accept my apology and allow me to make amends on his behalf. I will speak with my man of business about restitution for you and Alexander, and you may reside in the dowager cottage as long as you wish, unless you prefer the use of another property. Alexander will have access to our father's estate and the privileges associated."

She blinked, staring at him blankly. After a while, her silence became oppressive. He smiled grimly and stood. "I thank you for allowing my betrothed and her kin to stay. I will return to collect them as soon as I am able."

He turned on his heel and stalked toward the door.

"I played tin soldiers with you," she murmured.

Crispin stopped. His back was to her. He didn't move a muscle, fearful of spooking her.

"Y-your father... He hired a nurse before you were born. She was there, standing by while I labored. I was given a brief moment to admire my beautiful boy before she tore you from my arms."

Her voice broke. Silence filled the space between them. She sniffled.

His nostrils flared as a surge of protectiveness flowed over him. *This woman—my mother—is a wounded dove.* She had hidden her scars behind anger and detachment, but he heard in her voice what he had been unable to see while looking at her.

Slowly, he turned toward her. Her chin trembled; she swallowed hard while fighting against the tears welling in her eyes.

He had always thought his strength came from his father, but he saw now his iron will had been forged in the womb. His ability to lock away hurt was inherited from her.

"I remember," he said softly, kindly. "When my nurse was asleep, you carried me from my bed. The tin soldiers were in a wooden box in your chambers."

The planes of her face lost their hard edges. "Your father did not allow me to see you alone, but when he was away, I would risk angering him. You never complained when I woke you. No matter the time, you had a smile for me."

As an adult, he had only looked upon her with scorn, but once, he had loved her in a way only a mother could be loved.

"I haven't been kind to you," he said, regret tingeing his words. "Even when I arrived on your doorstep years ago, I was spoiling for a fight. I should have been happy to learn you were alive, but I was furious. I owe you an apology."

"No, I *left* you," she said with a fierceness he recognized in himself. "I deserved your rage, and I was furious with myself. In my mind, you stayed that happy little boy. I didn't want to face the truth of what I had done, so I did not. If you feel guilt or shame, release it. I do not want or need it."

He nodded once, accepting her proclamation with finality. They could forget their past and move forward. Their ability to close the door was a gift in this instance.

"I still have them," he said. "The tin soldiers."

Her eyes widened. "They were my father's. Did your father tell you they belonged to your grandfather when he was a boy?"

Crispin shook his head. "He was unaware I had them. When you and Alexander were gone so long, I stole into your chambers and pulled out the box. I found a hiding spot for them once I learned you were not returning. I wanted to keep a part of you, I think."

"Crispin, I—" She gulped and paused to take a breath. When she lifted her gaze, her eyes glimmered with sincerity. "I wanted to take you, too. Your father never would have allowed it, but I wanted you."

The last of his anger crumbled, and while he did not quite feel love for her as he once did, he looked on her with hope that a bond might form between them in time.

"Mother, I am returning to London today and must request a favor. My leaving is difficult for Sophia. I have not always treated her in a way that garnered her trust, and she fears I will not return. Please, will you show her kindness in my absence? She is the love of my life, and I intend to spend the rest of my days by her side. She is as much a part of your future as I am, assuming you want a relationship with me."

"I do. I want it very much." She caught her lip between her teeth as if contemplating whether to speak. Making up her mind, she said, "Alexander told me about your troubles, the reason you have brought your betrothed to stay."

"Yes, we discussed it, and I agreed you should know. He said you granted your permission. Otherwise, I would have found somewhere else for Sophia and her aunt."

"I have regretted turning you away for many years. I will not do it again." She laced her fingers together and settled her hands in her lap. "What you are doing is dangerous, is it not? These men you are hunting are killers."

"I am prepared," he said. "Charles Wedmore trained me well."

"I see." She sighed. "Do not worry about Miss Darlington while you are gone. She and her aunt are welcome as long as they need shelter. I wish you Godspeed, and I will pray for your safe return."

"Thank you, Mother. I *will* return."

Nothing would keep him from coming back to Sophia. Love did not make one weak as he had believed. It provided a man with a reason to live.

TWENTY-FIVE

Sophia became listless after Crispin bade her farewell. Instead of moping in her bedchamber, however, she broke her fast then went in search of the Duke of Stanhurst. She had a task to complete, a promise to fulfill, and she would not disappoint Crispin.

When she stepped outside, she spotted the duke standing at the pond's edge. His back was to her, his eyes seemingly trained to the mist rising from the water's surface, which allowed her a moment of unrestricted observation. He cut a dignified figure—tall, broad chested, and robust—but the slight rounding of his shoulders spoke of the burden he carried alone.

"Good morning, Your Grace," she called.

He snapped out of his trance and lifted his hand in greeting. "Miss Darlington, I wondered when you would seek me out. I thought you might be abed still."

"It appears we are both early risers."

The duke tossed a stone he had trapped in his fist into the pond and met her in the middle of the lawn. "All the better. I am eager to solve the riddle of my brother's letters, so I can reunite with my sisters." He held out his arm to offer his escort. "Shall we?"

Sophia linked arms and walked back to the house with him. Crispin's brother invited them to use his stepfather's study and promised to accompany Aunt Beatrice on her morning stroll when she came below stairs. Sophia didn't expect to see her for a few more hours. Auntie rarely rose before eleven o'clock. The duke excused himself to retrieve his brother's personal effects and met her in the study several moments later.

She had claimed the chair behind the desk. He approached.

"What would you like to see first?" With the letters in one hand and the diary in the other, he held his arms out at his sides, moving up and down as if comparing their weights.

"Lord Margrave believes your brother and his correspondent used a book cipher. It is an easier method for a beginner." She slanted her head. "Do you think your brother had experience with these sorts of tasks?"

Stanhurst winced. "I hope not. Otherwise, I have been a fool for longer than I thought."

"You are not a fool, Your Grace. When loved ones wish to hide secrets, we are usually none the wiser. They know us too well, and the places where we will never think to look."

"Thank you. Whether that is true or not, I feel marginally better about my ignorance. Geoffrey and I were close until a few years ago, before he began inhabiting the gaming hells. I tried to guide him toward more noble pursuits, and he accused me of being a stick-in-the-mud. I suppose I was, but I could see he was losing control of himself."

Sophia offered a sympathetic smile. How difficult it

must be to lose a sibling to the evils of excess. If Regina or Evangeline lost their way, she would be as conflicted as he.

"If it is any consolation, Your Grace, London would be better served by more sticks-in-the-mud like you."

A warm glow filtered into his eyes; he perched on the edge of the desk. "You may address me as Stanhurst, or Perry if you do not find the familiarity too off-putting."

She sat up straighter, and the friendly smile slid from her face. Use of his Christian name would be too familiar by half. "Perhaps I will feel like the fool after saying my piece, but I believe it is better to be forthcoming and avoid misunderstandings whenever possible. I am promised to Lord Margrave, and I am well-pleased with the match."

"I am aware of your attachment, Miss Darlington," he said kindly. "Even if I were not in danger of being stripped of my lands and station, and I was still in a position to court a charming young lady such as yourself, I owe the viscount my life. If he had not sent young Kane to watch over me, I would not be here today. Stealing his betrothed would be a deplorable way to show my gratitude, would it not?"

"It would indeed." The rigidness in her spine eased and her icy demeanor began to melt. "Forgive my impudence, Your Grace."

"There is nothing to forgive." He left his perch on the desk and lowered into the chair opposite her. "I thought it would be easier to have a conversation if you did not feel compelled to toss in 'Your Grace' every now and again. I cannot help but think my father is standing behind me when someone addresses me in that manner."

"I see," she murmured, ashamed of assuming the worst when his world had been turned topsy-turvy in a matter of one tragic night. "That does make sense. For the sake of efficiency, you may address me by my given name." Then because she was uncertain he knew her name, she added, "It is Sophia."

"Very good, *Sophia*." He held out the letters and diary again. "Have you decided where you would like to begin?"

She drummed her fingers against the desktop, considering her approach. "I understand your brother was not an industrious student?"

"This is true. Yet, he was ingenious when it came to shirking his duties."

She reached for the diary. "I think we should start here. Perhaps it holds clues that will point us toward whatever book title he might have used to decipher the messages. Lord Margrave said there were no books with the letters."

"That is correct."

"You found them in your brother's chambers. Were there any books in his rooms? Maybe on a bedside table?"

"No, none, his rooms were sparse. I expect he lost most of his personal effects at the gaming tables."

She folded her hands on top of the diary. "With your permission, I would like to study your brother's writings alone. Do you recall him reading any particular book or having a favorite?"

"He preferred activity to reading quietly." The duke frowned. "I would have noticed him with a book, and nothing comes to mind."

"It might be helpful to create a list of Lord Geoffrey's preferred activities. If he carried a book that supported one of his interests, it would be less conspicuous for a man who never read for pleasure."

"Very well." He drew the pot of ink closer and picked up the quill. "I need paper."

Sophia retrieved a sheet from the second desk drawer she checked and slid it across the desk. While the duke thought about his list, she began paging through Lord Geoffrey's diary.

The initial entries were mundane. He had written of his travels on his Grand Tour. Where he slept, the dishes he ate, which streets he walked down, the shops he visited. In Geneva, he crossed paths with an old school chum, and they broke bread together several times before the friend sailed to America where he had made his home.

Lord Geoffrey seemed envious of his friend's ability to increase his fortune during the war. The man had carved out a place of his own, free of his father's influence—a task Lord Geoffrey found daunting, if not impossible. His own father was an overbearing and cruel man who controlled the reins by refusing to settle an annual income on Lord Geoffrey.

The reading was rather dull until he returned to England and became smitten with a singer at Drury Lane. Soon after, his language blossomed, and the pages were littered with flowery words written in ode to his new lover. The tone changed, however, when his relationship with the woman began to sour. He was obviously still in love with her, but her caginess had roused his suspicions.

Without warning, she lacks a tongue to praise. What have I done to displease her? His phrasing was odd—antiquated—but his foreshadowing had been masterful. Lord Geoffrey's singer chose another lover a few days later. Pages upon pages of rage aimed at his former lover and her new benefactor followed. His ranting was illogical at times and frightening others, but always poetic.

"Was your brother a poet?" she asked.

Stanhurst glanced up from his list. "As far as I am aware, no. Why?"

"He developed a bit of a flair for the written word after he met Madame Zicari." She turned back two pages and read aloud. "'My sinful lust awards me pain, a vulgar scandal stamped upon my brow. How does a heart go on when mine is slain?'"

The duke narrowed his eyes. "It seems out of character for Geoffrey to have taken up poetry, but we were distant toward the end, as I indicated." He placed the quill aside and leaned his elbows on the desk. "There is a familiar ring to his words. Are there any other examples?"

"A few lines stood out. Let me find them." She thumbed through the pages. "'She is an angel in another's hell. I am determined to free her and wage war on this bloody tyrant.'"

Crispin's brother entered the study as she quoted Lord Geoffrey. Lieutenant Locke grinned. "Are you plagiarizing the Bard of Avalon, Miss Darlington?"

"Shakespeare!" The duke snapped his fingers. "I *knew* the words had a familiar ring, but they are not quite right, are they?"

Sophia held up the slim leather bound book for Crispin's brother to see. "I am reading aloud from Lord Geoffrey's diary. Is he quoting Shakespeare?"

"Not verbatim, no," Lieutenant Locke said.

Stanhurst frowned. "Dare I hope plagiarism was Geoffrey's only transgression?"

He did not expect an answer, so Sophia and the lieutenant did not supply one. She placed the diary on the desk and smoothed her hands over the pages. "Your Grace, are you sure there were no books in your brother's bedchamber? Perhaps a copy of *Romeo and Juliet* or *Hamlet?*"

"The lines are from sonnets," Lieutenant Locke said. "As a student, my classmates and I were assigned to take turns reading aloud from *Shakespeare's Sonnets.* After the tenth reading, we were bored beyond measure, but we had one hundred and forty-four left. It was a grueling assignment."

Sophia's gaze flickered toward the duke. "Do you recall seeing a volume of *Shakespeare's Sonnets* anywhere in your house in London? Perhaps Lord Geoffrey kept the letters and book separated to guard against suspicion."

"It is possible there is one in the library," Stanhurst said. "I have never searched for the book, so it does not stand out in my memory."

She closed the diary and addressed the lieutenant. "Would your stepfather have the book in *his* library?"

Lieutenant Locke gestured to the nearly empty shelves in the study. "This is the extent of his library. He reads the Bible and not much else."

"Is there any way to get our hands on *Shakespeare's Sonnets* without returning to London?"

"Possibly," Lieutenant Locke said. "The Earl of Freyshore keeps one of the largest libraries in the county. If he owns the book, I am certain he will allow me to borrow it."

"How soon could you call on the earl?"

"I will ride to his estate today and return by late afternoon. Once I see to my father and mother, I will depart."

"I could go in your place if you do not want to leave your parents," Stanhurst said.

"Thank you, Your Grace, but I promised to keep you here until my brother returns."

Stanhurst recoiled. "Am I a prisoner?"

"A *prisoner*? No! Nothing of the sort." The duke's question seemed to fluster Lieutenant Locke. "I would never assume that authority."

She reached across the desk to place her hand over Stanhurst's. "You mustn't place yourself at risk. It is best to stay in hiding until this matter can be put to rest."

His scowl communicated his displeasure. "I have been deemed a coward."

"That was not my meaning," Sophia said. "Your testimony alone will ensure your cousin is held accountable for attempted murder. If you are not alive to bear witness, Lady Van Middleburg will escape justice. Think of your sisters' welfare. Who will care for them if you are gone? A murderess?"

Mention of his sisters seemed to lessen his suspicion about why he was being asked to take refuge in the country, but his frown stayed firmly in place. "Ida will pay for her treachery," he said through gritted teeth.

"As will Lord Van Middleburg," Sophia agreed. "Lieutenant Locke, how might I be of help to your mother in your absence? If she would allow it, I could sit by your father's bedside while she rests."

"Thank you, Miss Darlington. I will encourage her to accept your help. She can be stubborn, to her own detriment."

Crispin shared the characteristic with his mother, but somehow the two had reached a truce this morning before he left for London. A happy warm glow infused her.

"I almost forgot my purpose for interrupting," Lieutenant Locke said. "Your aunt is taking her breakfast in her chamber, and she has requested you see her when you are available. I told her you are playing chess with Stanhurst."

"Am I winning?" she asked.

"Of course you are, Miss Darlington."

"Excellent!"

The lieutenant chuckled when the duke turned his scowl on her, although the spark of amusement in Stanhurst's eyes suggested his foul mood was improving.

Sophia was pleased. The duke could be a bit

intimidating when he was angry. "I will accompany Aunt Beatrice on her stroll while you see to your parents. Would you care to join us, Your Grace? Lord Margrave has asked us not to leave the manor house without an escort."

"It would be my pleasure." Stanhurst's mouth set in a firm line. "If I may point out the obvious, Lieutenant Locke could be going on a wild goose chase. We cannot be certain the letters are a book cipher. I suggest we turn our attentions to the letters themselves while Locke is gone. I do not wish to waste time."

"I understand your concern," she said, "but my guess is based on reason, and it is all we have for now. I cannot imagine your brother meant for anyone else to read his diary. More than likely, he is guilty of unwitting imitation rather than plagiarism."

The duke crossed his arms and leaned back in his chair. "Explain."

"If Lord Geoffrey frequently consulted the sonnets while deciphering, he might have incorporated the phrases into his writing without realizing. It cannot be an uncommon phenomenon. I catch myself imitating Lady Octavia's mannerisms and favorite phrases after we have spent the day together."

Stanhurst nodded slowly. "I see the direction of your thoughts. Perhaps you *have* set us on the right path."

"That is my hope."

"I would still like to study the letters in Lieutenant Locke's absence, but after your aunt's daily constitutional."

When the meeting with the duke and Lieutenant Locke concluded, Sophia looked in on Aunt Beatrice. She found her aunt sitting in a chair by the window, whistling a happy tune and working on the baby blanket she had started for Regina and Xavier.

"Good morning, Auntie." Sophia came forward to kiss

her smooth pale cheek. "Or should I say good afternoon? You slept longer than usual today."

Aunt Beatrice stopped the needles long enough to glance up at her. "It appears you could have used a few more winks yourself, dearest. You have bags under your eyes like you were up all night."

"Thanks, Auntie," she said flatly and chuckled. Aunt Beatrice was blunt to a fault, but Sophia found her tendency to speak frankly more endearing than bothersome. "Crispin was called back to London, but he does not expect his business will keep him away for more than a couple of days."

"I do hope it is nothing serious, although it is probably for the best if he is gone a couple of days." A mischievous smile spread across her aunt's face. "You should take advantage of his absence to rest. I expect many more sleepless nights are in your future."

"You know about last night?"

Aunt Beatrice winked. "I cannot see, but my ears work well enough."

"Law!" Sophia groaned and buried her scorching face in her hands.

Her aunt cackled. "I heard you knock on his door, dearest; nothing more."

The reassurance did nothing to lessen Sophia's mortification.

"You have no reason to feel embarrassed." Aunt Beatrice sighed and a dreamy softness transformed her face. "You and Lord Margrave are young and in love. I ask only one thing of you."

"Yes, Auntie?"

"Never allow the spark to extinguish. You will reap the rewards if you tend your marriage with the same care and attention you would a fire in the hearth."

A wave of tenderness swept through her, filling her heart. Sophia laid her hand on her chest to contain the feeling before it slipped away. "You dispensed the same advice to Mama on her wedding day. I read it in her diary."

A dreamy softness transformed her aunt's face. "Isabelle and Matthew made a rare love match when they found one another. She hoped you and your sisters would have what she found with your father. Her wishes are coming true, I think. She would be happy for you, Sophia."

"I wish I could have known her like you did, Auntie, but it was not to be." Sophia smiled tenderly and kissed her aunt's cheek once more. "Thank you for being a wonderful mother in her stead."

Color rose in Aunt Beatrice's face; she beamed up at Sophia. "It has been my greatest honor, dearest."

Her words were not empty. Her great-aunt had loved Sophia and her sisters from the moment she had laid eyes on them, and she had never allowed them to forget it.

"Lieutenant Locke has business with the neighbor," Sophia said, "so the Duke of Stanhurst has agreed to join us on our walk. Will you be ready soon?"

"Yes, in a moment." She stuck the knitting needles into the blanket to keep her work from unraveling and placed everything in her basket. "About that baby blanket... Do you have a color preference?"

Sophia laughed. "Auntie, you are relentless."

TWENTY-SIX

CRISPIN ARRIVED AT THE MEWS IN MARYLEBONE AT DAWN the next morning, impatient to set off for the old farmhouse where Farrin had kept Sophia's brother-in-law hostage. After a punishing ride to London yesterday, Crispin had intended to continue on to the farmhouse, but his departure was delayed by a meeting with the Lord Chamberlain.

Hertford was demanding Crispin provide indisputable evidence Farrin was guilty of treason before he would even consider approaching the King. The man had hammered his point until Crispin had been tempted to walk out of his office. Unfortunately, he missed his opportunity to speak with Sophia's actress friend until after curtain close last night.

"Good morning, milord," a male voice called as he stepped into the stables.

"Benny."

Crispin nailed his unwanted companion with a disgruntled glower. He did not require a partner, but he had been left with little choice. Unless he agreed to allow

306

Benny to accompany him, the location of the farmhouse would remain a secret. Crispin could uncover the information eventually, but time was not a luxury he could afford. Even now, he worried Farrin and his men were already on the move and would find Sophia and her aunt before he found them.

Mr. Hawke, the theatre owner, had accompanied the bigger man to the mews and offered his own greeting.

Crispin nodded once to acknowledge him then spoke to Benny. "I thought you would change your mind about joining me."

"I did not change my mind." Benny frowned. His mouth was a muted reddish purple, as if he wore lip rouge. "You said Miss Sophia and Aunt Beatrice are in danger."

"They are safe with my brother," Crispin said, "and I intend to keep them that way. If you cannot keep pace, I will leave you behind."

"I will not lag behind."

Mr. Hawke met Crispin's eye. "The farmhouse is east of Harlow in Essex. It was abandoned when the solicitor went to the house last month."

"The cow found a new home, too," Benny said.

The theatre owner smiled fondly at the bigger man. "Benny cared for a cow when he lived at the farm. She wandered to the neighbor's after he was made to leave."

"I see." Crispin eyed his companion, tempted to send him back to the theatre now that he knew the location of the farmhouse.

"I won't let Tommy hurt Miss Sophia and Aunt Beatrice," Benny said. "They are kind to me."

As if sensing Crispin's desire to leave Benny behind, Mr. Hawke said, "He will only follow if you go without him, and he can be an asset. He knows his brother's habits and the farm's layout."

Crispin's resistance began to yield. "Very well, but it will not be an easy ride. How are you in a saddle?"

"I don't fall," Benny said.

Crispin's lips twitched with a reluctant smile. He signaled the groom to retrieve the horses he'd arranged for last night before he'd returned home for a few hours of sleep. Mr. Hawke walked outside with him and Benny while the groom led the horses to the mounting blocks.

The theatre owner passed a pair of saddlebags to Benny. "Godspeed, gentlemen."

"Good-bye, Mr. Hawke." Benny moved to the mounting block and climbed onto the saddle. "Please tell Miss Claudine and Miss Rachel not to fret over me. I will be home soon."

"I will, and I would be remiss in my duty if I did not convey their wishes for you to be cautious." Mr. Hawke waved before departing.

As Crispin and Benny rode toward the outskirts of town, Crispin slanted a look at his insistent companion. "Who is Miss Rachel?"

"My friend." Benny's round face turned as red as his lips. "She is real pretty and nice." The bigger man appeared smitten, and an unexplainable hope that the woman returned his affection sprang up in Crispin.

"She sounds like a lovely friend," he said.

"She is. I only had one until I came to London. Now I have a whole lot." Benny looked him over from head to toe. "I think I like you, too. I promise not to let Tommy hurt you."

"You do realize I am capable of disabling a man with a quill, don't you?"

Benny's broad forehead wrinkled. "Did you forget a firearm?" He pulled open his jacket to reveal two holstered flintlock pistols. "You can borrow one of mine."

"Thank you."

Crispin looked toward the heavens and shook his head, smiling slightly. Sophia's actress friend had attempted to explain last night that Benny's pure heart did not understand sarcasm, but Crispin hadn't believed it until now.

Patting his side, he pretended to find his own pistol. "I remembered to pack it. No need for that quill after all."

The worried wrinkles disappeared from Benny's face. "That is good. Tommy, Wolfe, and Garrick always have firearms. A quill is a poor weapon against a pistol."

"Excellent point. You call your brother Tommy. Why?"

Benny shrugged. "It is his name. He gets real mad when I forget, but he cannot hear me now, so he won't yell at me."

No doubt, the poor man had suffered Farrin's wrath a time or two. The Consul leader was not known for his patience or mercy, and he took umbrage at the smallest mistakes.

"Why did your brother change his name?"

"I think he doesn't want anyone to know his real name."

Crispin chuckled under his breath. "That makes sense. I thought Farrin was a family name."

"It was Tommy's boxing name. He never let me attend a match, because I had to help at the farm."

"I heard he was a pugilist at one time. He was the King's favorite."

And still was, according to the Lord Chamberlain. King George IV, during his reign as Regent, had recruited Farrin to the Consul after watching him fight in a boxing exhibition. He had admired Farrin's tenacity in the ring and ability to match him drink for drink after the fight. The King's opinion of Farrin would not easily be swayed. Therefore, Crispin had promised to return with proof to support any accusation he would pose against Farrin. The letters Sophia was working to decipher held the answers he needed. Crispin was certain of it.

"Tommy came to help on the farm for a while," Benny said brightly. "I liked working in the field together, but he hated it. He said we would work ourselves into an early grave or starve unless he did something to improve our lot."

"Is that the reason he became a boxer?"

"I don't know. He always liked fisticuffs. Maybe he wanted to hit someone."

The prize money was simply a bonus.

"He came home real mean like Garrick and Wolfe," Benny said. "I wished he never came back."

"Are you certain you will be able to stand up to him if there is a fight? He is still your brother." If Benny cowered in Farrin's presence, Crispin might not be in a position to protect him.

A crimson blush swept over the bigger man's face, and his eyes blazed. "He has hurt too many people. I won't let him harm Miss Sophia or Aunt Beatrice."

"I believe you," Crispin said, and he did. He changed the subject. "You probably know every nook and cranny at the farm. Tell me how the house is laid out."

Benny obliged. Once he had recited all the rooms in the farmhouse, Crispin inquired into outbuildings and the surrounding area. He had a good mental map of their destination by the time they left the city and urged their horses into a trot.

Benny proved to be a decent traveling companion. He was not graceful in the saddle, but he offered no complaints. When they changed horses, he only spoke when asked a question and mounted his fresh horse when given the command. His reticence provided Crispin with ample time to formulate a plan for when they reached the farmhouse.

Their final stop was at the coaching inn at Harlow. He and Benny ate a small meal, and Crispin questioned the barkeep, his wife, and two older men who were identified as local farmers. He learned that he and Benny were the first strangers to stop in the village for a week, but a lamp had been spotted burning in one of the farmhouse's windows a couple of days earlier. Otherwise, the farm appeared to be abandoned.

Before Crispin and Benny left the coaching inn, Crispin offered his companion another chance to bow out. Benny grunted, shoved his hat on his head, and stalked toward the coaching yard.

"I will take that as a refusal," Crispin said.

They rode in the direction of the farmhouse on fresh horses. As they neared the farm half an hour later, Crispin explained the plan.

"I will approach the house from the southwest. The thick undergrowth will provide cover. You search the outbuildings. Do not come in the house until I tell you it is clear."

"What if you yell for help?"

"I won't."

Benny's scrunched face said he lacked faith in Crispin's strategy, but he did not offer further argument. He led them to a neglected apple orchard at the edge of the property where they tied the horses and approached the farm.

"If you call for me," Benny said, "I will come to your aid."

Crispin didn't bother with a response.

Benny ran toward the barn, fast as a streak of lightening, and Crispin headed for the house.

Just as Benny had described, overgrown juniper bushes partially blocked the windows facing southwest, and the upper story window on this side of the house was boarded up. Crouching on the ground, he crawled toward the house. Anyone inside would be blind to his approach.

When he reached the stone structure, he stood and pressed his back against the wall. He listened for evidence of someone in the room. He heard nothing. Slowly, he leaned to peek through the window. The drawing room was vacant. No movement was spotted beyond the open doorways leading to a dining room and study.

Benny had been right about the windows as well. There were no locks. Crispin pushed up the lower sash, and the window opened a sliver before resisting. He retrieved the knife from his boot, found a flat rock for leverage, and pried the bottom sash high enough to get his fingers beneath it. With a bit of muscle, he was able to force the window open and climbed inside.

A layer of dust coated the heavy, dark wood furnishings and dulled the colors in the woven carpet. Spider webs were thick in the corners and draped the threshold like garland.

With pistol drawn, he listened at each doorway before proceeding with his search. He found no evidence that anyone was residing at the home. No embers smoldered in the hearths. No muddy footprints at the backdoor. Nevertheless, the hair stood up at the back of his neck. His instincts insisted someone was in the house.

After insuring the ground floor was clear, he eased up the staircase, taking care with his footing to minimize creaking on the treads. Each bedchamber he encountered along the dark corridor was empty. As he neared the end of the passage, a cough came from the last bedchamber. His heart slammed into his throat, and he froze, straining to hear movement in the room. A low groan carried on the air. On silent feet, he traveled the last few steps to the chamber.

The pungent stench of infection wafted into the corridor. A quick survey of the room revealed a large lump in the bed—a man with covers pulled over his head. He was alone and shivering hard enough to shake the bed.

"Garrick?" he called.

An answering moan came from beneath the quilt.

Crispin cocked the hammer on the pistol and aimed it at his adversary. "Show me your hands, slowly."

The blackguard didn't move. Crispin barked the order.

"I am unarmed," Garrick mumbled. "I need... a... doctor."

"Show me your hands, and we will talk."

Garrick slid the covers from his head, weakly pushing the quilt down to his waist. The back of his hair was matted and damp, and a dark stain had ruined his shirt.

Crispin rushed the bed, prepared to disarm the villain, but Garrick told the truth. He was without a weapon. His arms were splayed limply on the bed, and his face was pale and slick with sweat. Red splotches on his neck were the most telling sign. Crispin had seen it before. Garrick had blood poisoning from the wound he had sustained when he made an attempt on Sophia's life.

"Lord Margrave?" Someone was calling his name from the ground floor. "Are you still in the house, Lord Margrave?"

It was Benny.

"Above stairs," he shouted. When the big man lumbered up the stairs and appeared in the threshold, Crispin frowned. "I told you to stay outside until I gave permission."

"You found Garrick." Benny entered the room. "There is only one horse in the stable, and she hasn't been cared for in a while. I gave her some oats. I knew whoever was here was alone. Why is he in bed?"

"He is dying." Crispin saw no reason to soften the blow.

313

Garrick had to know his condition was dire. "Ride into Harlow and retrieve the doctor. Tell him to bring laudanum."

"Yes, milord."

While Benny set off on the errand, Crispin made a trip to the well for water. When he returned with the bucket, he helped his adversary take a drink from the dipper. Garrick gulped the water then glowered at him before collapsing on the pillow.

If their positions were reversed, Crispin wouldn't receive the same treatment, but the ability to show mercy set him apart from monsters like Garrick. Without it, Crispin's conscience would become too heavy to bear.

He pulled a chair close to the bed. Garrick drifted in and out of sleep, as well as reality. Sometimes his answers to Crispin's questions were clear, but more often his words were slurred and made no sense. He refused to speak of Farrin and Wolfe. Soon, he fell into a deep sleep, and Crispin couldn't rouse him.

He gave up. Perhaps the house held clues to where Farrin and Wolfe had gone. Crispin stood with the intention of searching the house. Garrick jerked awake with a loud snort. He blinked; his clammy forehead wrinkled as if he didn't know where he was. When his gaze landed on Crispin, signs of awareness filtered across his face. He sneered.

"Yer too late, Margrave. Everyone you love will die while you play nursemaid."

Dread seeped into Crispin's gut, acidic and icy. "Tell me where they have gone. Do they know Sophia's location?"

Garrick stared toward the ceiling with glassy eyes, lips parted.

"Garrick!" Crispin grabbed the front of his shirt and

shook him, but he had lost his ability to focus. "Answer me. Where are Farrin and Wolfe?"

The blackguard slipped under and did not wake again.

Benny arrived with the doctor a short while later. Crispin handed the doctor a purse full of coin. "See that he does not suffer and bury him in a pauper's grave."

He stalked from the room, heading for the stairs. Benny was on his heels. He kept stride with Crispin as they exited the house. When he broke into a run, Benny followed.

"Where are we going, milord?"

Crispin didn't answer. He ran faster, pushing himself until his lungs burned. When they reached the orchard, he forced himself to walk and lock away his fear. The horses would spook if they sensed his state of mind. He gathered the reins and mounted the gray mare.

"I believe Farrin and Wolfe have gone after Sophia and Beatrice," he said, still breathing hard. "It is another hard ride to Finchingfield, but I must reach them tonight." He tapped the horse's sides.

"I am coming with you." Benny swung into the saddle and urged his horse to follow.

TWENTY-SEVEN

As Sophia had poured over *Shakespeare's Sonnets* and Lord Geoffrey's letters earlier that morning, she had come to realize Crispin and the Duke of Stanhurst had underestimated the man. The cipher was more complicated than it appeared. In some instances, the first number coincided with the sonnet number—not the page like most book ciphers. Other times, it did refer to the page.

Once she made that discovery, she spent another couple of hours detecting a pattern. The first number in the first three groupings referred to sonnets, the fourth indicated the page, and the fifth reverted to the sonnet again. The repeating pattern of 3 sonnets, 1 page, 1 sonnet, 3 pages, 2 sonnets, 2 pages carried through all of the letters. Other times, the numbers seemed to correspond to the letters of the alphabet. It was an arduous task, but she was finally making progress. Unfortunately, the contents so far did not reflect favorably on the Duke of Stanhurst's kin, but she didn't wish to alarm him by speaking prematurely.

Thoughts of Stanhurst seemed to summon him. He strolled into the study where she was working at the large desk. "Your aunt is a delightful woman, Sophia. Her unpredictable conversation kept me entertained on our turn about the pond."

Sophia abandoned her task briefly. "I hope she did not say anything too shocking. She tends to speak her mind."

"It is a refreshing quality."

The duke perched on the edge of the desk. His cheeks were pink from exercise, and the apprehension that had seemed to weigh heavily on him, slumping his shoulders, was absent—at least temporarily. She expected his burden would become thrice as heavy soon.

"What progress have you made?" he asked.

"Only a little," she lied. Until she finished deciphering Lord Geoffrey's correspondence and was certain no mention of Stanhurst's father was contained in the letters, she didn't want to reveal too much. "I learned the identity of the letter writer. His name is Ulysses J. Roth. Lord Geoffrey encountered him in Geneva on his Grand Tour."

"It is a name not easily forgotten. Roth was Geoffrey's old classmate. I am surprised they corresponded after the chance meeting. I do not recall them being chums at school."

"Perhaps they found they shared more in common than they had previously realized," Sophia said.

The corners of Stanhurst's mouth curved down. "I heard rumors Roth made a fortune during the war smuggling goods into the British Isles and France. The magistrate suspected smugglers were responsible for Geoffrey's death. What if my brother was murdered because he reported on Roth? He could have been on the docks to gather evidence."

The duke seemed more hopeful than he had been since his arrival. Sophia hated to shatter that hope, but Lord Geoffrey's reason for being at the docks had been far from noble.

"Perhaps," she hedged.

Someone banged the knocker at the front door. Stanhurst tensed. "Stay out of sight. I will find out who is calling."

Curiosity pulled Sophia away from her task, and she moved toward the threshold to peek around the doorjamb. The duke blocked her view, but when he stepped aside, she spotted the housekeeper greeting a middle-aged woman. Two young ladies—adorned in their Sunday best, pretty bonnets, and shy smiles—flanked her.

"I have come to look in on Mr. Ness." The older woman smiled sweetly and lifted a basket she had brought with her. "It is an assortment of sweet breads."

Sophia suspected the trio was composed of mother and daughters. All three shared the same shade of auburn hair and high round cheeks that loaned them an air of robust health.

"The Nesses are indisposed, Mrs. Evans," the housekeeper said. "Shall I deliver the basket in your stead?"

When Mrs. Poindexter reached for the handle, the woman jerked the basket close to her chest and a glimmer of hostility flashed in her eyes. "Do not be ridiculous. Mr. Ness is in no condition to consume sweets. Would you have him choke to death?"

"No ma'am, but Mrs. Ness—"

"Oh, hush," Mrs. Evans snapped. "You know we have come to see Lieutenant Locke. Sweet breads are his favorite."

She barged into the house; the housekeeper quickly shuffled backward before her toes were trampled. The woman's eyes flared when she noticed the duke standing to the side of the foyer. Her hostility vanished and was replaced by the sweet smile she had initially aimed at the housekeeper.

318

"Oh, my! Forgive the intrusion. It must have slipped my mind that the Nesses were entertaining guests."

Stanhurst came forward to greet the ladies, supplying a false identity and stripping away his title. The woman's pleasure dimmed at hearing he was a mister, and a poor relation at that. She reluctantly introduced her daughters and barely suppressed a snarl when he lifted their hands to kiss the air above their knuckles.

Anne and Jane were less displeased by his attentions and grinned widely at him, showing too much teeth. The Duke of Stanhurst was a handsome man, and the girls were too young to realize they were not free to love whomever they chose—at least not if their mother had a say.

"Forgive my curiosity," Stanhurst said, "but how did you know the Nesses had guests?"

"Papa saw you passing by the other day," Anne blurted and blushed, averting her gaze.

Sophia turned to leave her post. She had work to do.

"Yes," Mrs. Evans said, "and my dear husband said nothing to any of us. I never would have known if those men hadn't come to the door this morning."

Sophia froze; her breath caught.

"What men?" the duke asked.

"No one of interest," Mrs. Evans said. "An older gentleman and his servant. They became separated from a hunting party. I did not recognize the host's name, but gentlemen come up from London all the time to let manor houses this time of year. They asked Mr. Evans if any strangers had passed through the area recently. Mr. Evans said he hadn't seen anyone except our neighbors' guests."

Sophia returned to studying the woman and her daughters as the duke questioned her further. Mrs. Evans had nothing helpful to add. The men had gone on their way and hadn't been spotted again.

"I will take the sweet breads to Cousin Alexander," Stanhurst said and plucked the basket from Mrs. Evan's hands before she could protest. "Good day, ladies."

The woman bristled when he walked away, dismissing her with the arrogance of a duke. As the housekeeper herded the woman and her daughters from the foyer, Mrs. Evans grumbled about Stanhurst's uppity manners for someone lowborn.

The housekeeper chirped a happy good-bye, interrupting the neighbor's complaints, and closed the door with enough force to be satisfying.

When Stanhurst walked into the study, he caught Sophia spying. He arched a dark eyebrow. "Did you overhear the conversation?"

She nodded and swallowed. "It could be anyone, could it not? There is no cause for worry."

"Yes, of course." He rubbed the tips of his fingers back and forth across his brow as if warding off a pain. "Nevertheless, we should practice caution. No more walks around the grounds until we are certain the men who questioned the neighbors are harmless."

Sophia took a cleansing breath. "Auntie will not easily be discouraged from following her morning routine."

"I expect it will be easier to convince her if she is provided a good reason to stay indoors. Your aunt deserves to know her life could be in danger." The duke's stern tone left no doubt he expected Sophia to accept his guidance.

She nibbled her bottom lip. Perhaps he was right. It had been well and good to shelter Aunt Beatrice when it seemed they were safe, but if Farrin and his men were close, the time had come to confide in her. "I will tell her tonight after supper."

"Very good," the duke said. "I will inform Lieutenant

Locke of the latest development while you return to deciphering the letters."

He made a shooing motion with his hand that would have irritated her under different circumstances. She resumed her place at the desk. Crispin had entrusted her with this task, and she would not disappoint him.

When the duke and Crispin's brother came to inquire into her progress an hour later, they found her slumped in the chair, staring at the papers and book on the desk.

"Are you unwell?" The duke's voice jolted her from the stunned trance she had fallen under.

She blinked the men into focus and gathered a stack of papers from the desk, holding them close to her chest. "I have deciphered all of the letters. Your Grace, perhaps you should sit."

Stanhurst pulled himself up to his full height and looked down his nose at her. "Do not treat me as an invalid, Miss Darlington. What did you discover?"

Her mouth was dry; she licked her parched lips. Her gaze strayed back and forth between the men. "Y-your brother was raising funds to hire a mercenary group—"

"The Black Death," he snapped. "I know about them. To what end?"

She frowned in censorship. Stanhurst was anxious; she understood his distress. Nevertheless, she would not abide becoming his whipping boy. Crispin's brother inserted himself into the conversation, acting as a peacekeeper.

"Please, Miss Darlington," Lieutenant Locke said gently. "Do continue when you are ready."

She met the lieutenant's gaze, shoring up her courage to deliver the news. "The Black Death has been hired to rescue Napoleon. Once he is liberated, he intends to drive the Spanish from their colonies in America and reward his supporters with land and titles in his new empire. Your brother and Lord Van Middleburg secured investors to pay the warriors' fee. Gentlemen, we might be on the brink of another war."

When she glanced at the duke, his eyes blazed with a fury that caused her to quiver. "You found evidence Geoffrey was a... *traitor.*" He spat the last word. "Give me the letters, Miss Darlington."

She hesitated a full heartbeat then placed his brother's letters and the deciphered messages into his outstretched hand. "Thank you for your service." He tucked the papers under his arm, spun on his heel, and marched from the study.

Sophia watched helplessly as the duke commandeered the only proof they had that England's interests were in jeopardy.

"What should we do?" she whispered. "What if he destroys the evidence?"

Lieutenant Locke grimaced. "He risked everything bringing the letters to Crispin, and his worst fears have been made real. Allow him time to recover. I believe the duke will make the correct choice."

She hoped Crispin's brother was not underestimating Stanhurst. Desperation caused men to take desperate measures. When the duke did not join them for supper, her concern grew.

If only Crispin was here...

Unfortunately, she couldn't devote her attention to solving the problem of how to recover the letters from Stanhurst. It was time to have a conversation with Aunt Beatrice—a task Sophia dreaded. When she and Aunt Beatrice retreated to the drawing room, Lieutenant Locke created an excuse not to join them as prearranged.

A jug of claret sat on the sideboard, and Sophia crossed the room to pour a glass for her aunt. When she returned with the wine, Aunt Beatrice waved it away. "You seem tense, dearest. Perhaps you should partake instead."

"I am afraid I would become a dismal companion if I did." Sophia placed the glass on the low table in front of the settee and sat beside her aunt. "I can barely keep my eyes open."

"I do not find it surprising. What were you working at all day in the study?"

"Crispin requested help with correspondence." How easily lies fell from Sophia's lips these days. She cleared her throat. "Auntie, I have not been forthcoming with you, and I am worried you will be disappointed."

Aunt Beatrice patted her hand. "You could never disappoint me, my sweet girl."

Sophia took a deep breath and started her story with the moment Farrin tried to steal the map from Wedmore House and ended with the real reason Sophia and Aunt Beatrice were staying with Crispin's family.

"I am sorry I did not tell you, Auntie. My sisters and I wanted to protect you."

Aunt Beatrice, who had held her tongue while Sophia was speaking, pursed her lips. Inwardly, Sophia cringed. She was in for a good scolding—much deserved but still unappealing.

"Sophia Anastasia Marietta Jane," Aunt Beatrice bit off each name as if barely restraining herself from yelling. "It has never been and never will be your responsibility to protect *me*. When Charlie asked me to help raise you and your sisters, I knew what was expected of me. I swore to him and to each of you that I would do everything within my power to protect you. That is my responsibility. Do I make myself clear?"

"Yes, Auntie."

"Furthermore, Lord Margrave has overstepped his

bounds greatly. He is your betrothed, not your husband, and he has no authority to take matters into his hands. He should have consulted with me, and I would have made the decision."

"I understand, but please do not fault Crispin. I begged him not to tell you."

Aunt Beatrice jabbed a finger in her direction. "It was not your place to make decisions either. I have been caring for you since you were a little girl, and I always kept your best interests in mind. I may not have given birth to you and your sisters, but you are my children."

"I know, Auntie."

As her aunt continued her tirade, Sophia's nose began to tickle and her vision blurred with tears. Aunt Beatrice stopped mid-sentence. Her mouth opened and closed a few times. Eventually, she asked, "Why are you crying?"

"I cannot bear the thought of losing you like Mama."

"Oh, dearest."

Aunt Beatrice's stern face softened. She gathered Sophia in a hug. Her aunt was thinner than she had been when Sophia sat on her lap as a child, but her hugs were just as strong. When her aunt released her and drew back, she cupped Sophia's cheek.

"I am not going anywhere anytime soon, sweet girl. Do not waste a moment fretting about it. I have too much to do. There is still Evangeline to see settled into marriage, baby blankets to knit, and Charlie's household to run."

"I thought you would live with Crispin and me."

Aunt Beatrice laughed. "I do not expect Lord Margrave would appreciate having me underfoot. Besides, Evangeline cannot be left on her own. Can you imagine the mess she would make of Hartland Manor? There would be even more holes to fall into around the estate, and the groundskeeper has already threatened to tender his resignation if she does not stop her excavations."

Sophia laughed too and swiped the dampness from her eyes. "She did find Roman coins one autumn."

"The import of her discovery was lost on the man, I think."

Sophia leaned against the settee cushion, more relaxed than she had been for a while. She and Aunt Beatrice reminisced about Sophia's childhood, recalling funny stories involving her sisters. She missed Regina and Evangeline, and she hadn't realized until this moment how much she had missed Aunt Beatrice. Being unable to confide in her aunt had created an unintended rift between them. Relief washed over Sophia, as comforting as one of Auntie's knitted shawls.

"Well, dearest," Aunt Beatrice said and yawned. "It is early, but I am ready for bed. Would you like to crawl in with me tonight like old times?"

Sophia was too old to snuggle with her aunt, but she couldn't resist keeping her close. "Yes, please."

They retreated to their respective chambers above stairs to ready for bed. Dressed in her night rail and wrapper, Sophia slipped into the corridor to make her way to her aunt's room next door. She glanced toward the door at the end of the passage. A light was burning in the duke's chambers. He hadn't made an appearance since he disappeared with the letters. She could only imagine the demons he wrestled tonight.

May you triumph over them, Your Grace.

Despite the early hour, Sophia was exhausted. Her eyes felt gritty and her back ached from too many hours spent bent over a desk. She did not recall surrendering to sleep, but a strident bellow jolted her awake.

"Fire! There's a fire!"

TWENTY-EIGHT

SOPHIA BOLTED UPRIGHT IN BED—EYES WIDE, HEART hammering. Interwoven with panicked voices were the sounds of people running outside the bedchamber door. A man shouted orders she couldn't make out. She grabbed her aunt's shoulder and jostled her.

"Auntie, wake up!"

Her aunt mumbled in her sleep.

Sophia shook her harder. "Aunt Beatrice, the house is on fire. Wake up!"

The racket in the corridor grew louder, and she heard her name. "Sophia, where are you?"

The bedchamber door flew open. The Duke of Stanhurst burst into the room with a handkerchief pressed to his mouth and nose. He dropped his hand. "Thank God! You were not in your chamber."

The interruption broke through Aunt Beatrice's deep sleep. She stirred and mumbled, "What is happening?"

"There is a fire. We must go." Sophia scrambled from bed. "She needs help, Your Grace."

Stanhurst stalked across the room and lifted Aunt

Beatrice from the bed, cradling her against his chest. Auntie was awake enough now to bark orders.

"Bring my sewing basket."

"There isn't time." Sophia grabbed her wrapper at the foot of the bed and found her slippers. "We must save ourselves."

"No!" Aunt Beatrice kicked her legs and made such a fuss that she almost toppled from the duke's arms.

"Stop! I will get it." Sophia found the basket near the chair where Aunt Beatrice had been working earlier and snatched it from the floor. She followed Stanhurst and her aunt into the corridor. A light haze hung on the air.

"Cover your face," the duke said.

She fished the baby blanket from her aunt's basket and shoved it into Aunt Beatrice's hands before balling up her wrapper to cover her own mouth and nose.

Taking the lead, she held onto the duke's arm to guide him while feeling the wall with her hand. Crispin's mother was sobbing from the floor below.

"Mother, let's go," Lieutenant Locke commanded. "They carried Father through the servants' wing."

A wave of heat rolled up the staircase.

"Get low," Stanhurst shouted.

Sophia dropped to her bottom and scooted down the stairs, dragging the basket with her. Aunt Beatrice and the duke followed suit.

Orange flames licked at the walls in the foyer. Sophia stood; her eyes stung.

"Stay down and go!" Stanhurst nudged her toward the front door.

Crispin's brother barged inside the house to take her elbow and pull her to safety. Sophia stumbled into the night, dropped the wrapper and basket, and gulped fresh air.

The duke burst outside with Aunt Beatrice in his arms. Once they were a safe distance from the house, he lowered her to the grass and collapsed on his knees beside her, panting. Aunt Beatrice doubled over, coughing.

Sophia walked on wobbly legs to reach her. "Auntie, have you been injured?"

"No," Aunt Beatrice said between coughs and reached a hand toward her. "Bring my knitting."

"What? *Now?*"

"Do it," her aunt snapped.

With an exasperated sigh, Sophia retrieved the basket and dropped it on the ground next to her aunt.

"Thank you." Aunt Beatrice shoved the baby blanket deep into the basket, taking care to arrange it just so.

Satisfied her aunt was well—despite her new obsession with babies—Sophia turned her attention toward the others gathered on the lawn. Mrs. Ness was sitting on the grass cradling her husband's head while two manservants stood close to the housekeeper. Everyone had escaped the manor house and gaped as the fire hungrily consumed the home.

Black smoke rolled into the night sky, obliterating the stars, and a relentless crackle filled the air. Occasionally, an eerie creak and echoing bang emanated from deep within the house. With so few of them and the nearest neighbors at least two miles away, there was nothing to do except become voyeurs to the destruction. Fortunately, there were no other buildings close, and no wind to whip sparks into the air.

Lieutenant Locke tunneled his fingers through his hair. Soot left it darker than natural. He cleared his throat and addressed the servants. "My father cannot tolerate the night air. Retrieve the handcart. We should get him to the groundkeeper's cottage. Teddy, carry a message to the Evans and tell them we need shelter for the night."

"Yes, sir," the young men said in unison, shaking off the shock that had kept them immobilized, and set off on their tasks. Lieutenant Locke was not finished issuing orders. "Mrs. Poindexter, I would like you to run ahead to the cottage and ready a bed."

The housekeeper hurried in the direction of the cottage.

The manservant returned with the handcart, and Sophia tried not to gawk while the lieutenant and duke loaded Mr. Ness into the bed of the cart. Dressed in only a nightshirt, his emaciated body was on display. It was her first time to catch sight of Crispin's stepfather, and her curiosity battled with the desire to help him maintain dignity by not looking. He groaned several times during the process and mumbled his thanks once he was settled on the hard cart bed. His bare calves hung over the edge of the handcart.

Sophia retrieved her wrapper and carried it to Crispin's mother. "Please, take this for Mr. Ness."

Crispin's mother accepted the once blue satin robe and covered her husband as best as she could. The duke shrugged out of his jacket and offered it as well. When the handcart rolled over a small knoll, Mr. Ness gritted his teeth. He didn't utter a word of complaint, however. Mrs. Ness walked beside the handcart, murmuring words of comfort for her husband. Lieutenant Locke excused himself to see his parents settled and promised to return shortly.

"Mr. Evans will send a carriage soon," he said. "He is a good man. He would not ignore a neighbor in need."

Sophia, Aunt Beatrice, and the duke were left alone. The blaze heated Sophia's back. She crossed her arms, newly aware her thin night rail was far from modest, but the duke was not looking at her or her aunt. His gaze was trained to the darkness beyond the circle of light created by the fire.

She nervously wet her lips. "I hope Lieutenant Locke is right about—"

"Quiet," Stanhurst hissed. "I hear something out there."

Her heart jumped into her throat.

Aunt Beatrice sidled up to Sophia. "We should join the others at the groundkeeper's cottage." When her aunt linked arms, Sophia looked down and gasped. Aunt Beatrice was cradling a small pistol in the palm of her hand.

"Auntie, how...where...?"

"My sewing basket," Aunt Beatrice muttered. "I protect my own."

Hysterical laughter bubbled up at the back of Sophia's throat. The situation was too ludicrous by half. Perhaps she was still safe in bed and dreaming.

"Your Grace," Aunt Beatrice said, "let us withdraw to the cottage with the others."

Stanhurst snapped his head toward them, blinking as if trying to claw his way through the foggy layers of a deep sleep. "Yes, very good," he said at last.

As they turned to go, a sharp voice split the night. "Stay where you are."

Two men appeared from the dark, like specters slowly taking solid form. Their faces remained in shadow. One man held a hatchet; the other pointed a pistol at the duke. A chill ran down Sophia's spine. Had Farrin and his men found them?

"I was always somewhat fond of you," the man holding the firearm said with a hint of mirth.

Sophia wrinkled her brow in confusion. Was he speaking to the duke? Did he know the men?

"As fond as one can be of a total bore," the man added. "I am almost sorry to reach this end."

The duke squared his shoulders and snarled. "You are a traitor, Van Middleburg. You will hang for your crimes."

Sophia experienced an odd rush of relief at discovering it wasn't Farrin. Even though the baron still posed danger, he was not a trained killer.

Lord Van Middleburg and his companion stepped into the light. Sophia made quick study of the man with the hatchet.

Filthy attire.

Gaunt face with sunken eyes.

The stench of alcohol and acerbic body odor wafting from him.

A poor sap down on his luck and desperate for coin.

If Sophia gambled, she would place her money on the baron's companion being a hired henchman—possibly a local man.

The baron clicked his tongue. "I see that you have deciphered your brother's letters. What a pity the evidence will be destroyed in the flames."

Stanhurst raised his fist, clenching and unclenching his fingers. "*You* set the fire. Have you no care for the lives that could have been lost? You are a coward and a traitor."

"You were the only one I hoped would perish, but here you are." Van Middleburg shrugged sheepishly. "My apologies, ladies. I take no pleasure in harming the gentler sex, but witnesses are a damned inconvenience. I beg your understanding." The baron's jaw firmed when he addressed his accomplice. "Take the women out of sight to dispose of them."

The man with the hatchet grabbed Sophia's arm above the elbow; his calloused fingers bit into her skin. Aunt Beatrice cursed him for a brute and swatted at him with the hand without the gun. Her aunt had managed to keep the single shot pistol hidden, which offered them the advantage of surprise.

"Leave them be," Stanhurst growled. "They know nothing."

"It is too late, Perry." The baron raised his arm and aimed the pistol at the duke's face. "You came here and placed them in danger. Ida and I will look after the girls. This is not personal."

"Wait!" Sophia jerked against the hired man's grip, but she couldn't break free. "The letters are not here. The duke sent them to his estate in Lancashire."

"She lies," Stanhurst spat and glowered at her. "They are in the house."

Sophia pleaded with her eyes for Stanhurst to trust her. He needed a fighting chance. "The duke wants to protect his sisters, but he is lying. He sent the letters north with the man who brought him here. If any harm comes to him, the letters will be delivered to the King."

Van Middleburg lowered his arm. "Why are you telling me this?"

"I want to make a bargain. Allow my aunt and me to go, and we will forget this night ever happened."

The baron laughed, taunting the duke. "Were you courting this one? She is prepared to drive a dagger into your back."

Stanhurst did not rise to the bait. He continued to glower as if he could rip her apart with his bare hands if given the chance. Van Middleburg seemed to derive immense pleasure from the duke's rage. He slapped his knee and cackled. His guard was down.

"Now," she shouted.

Stanhurst leapt on the baron, driving his shoulder into the man's stomach. They seemed to hang in the air before crashing to the ground with a loud thud and groan. The impact knocked the pistol from the baron's hand.

Sophia swung toward the thug trapping her arm and

drove the heel of her hand into his nose. He yelped, releasing her and dropping the hatchet to cradle his face. Sophia scrambled to reach the baron's pistol while the two men wrestled nearby. She dropped to her knees, crawling and fanning her hands over the dirt to find the weapon.

"Sophia!" Her aunt's panic-stricken cry pierced her chest.

She looked over her shoulder. The thug was standing over her, his hatchet poised overhead and prepared to strike.

Her breath caught in her throat.

A flash of light and a sharp retort came from Aunt Beatrice's direction. The shot from her small pistol missed its target, but served as a distraction. Sophia twirled and kicked, sweeping her assailant's legs out from under him. He held on to the hatchet.

She jumped to her feet and dashed toward her aunt. The thug was already pushing up from the ground. "Run, Auntie!"

TWENTY-NINE

AN ORANGE-TINTED CLOUD HUNG OVER THE HOUSE IN THE distance. Crispin leaned forward in the saddle, galloping his horse along the straight stretch of lane between the neighbor's home and his mother's. Every muscle tensed and trembled with a single-minded determination to reach Sophia.

Benny stayed with him as best as he could, but he fell behind. As Crispin neared the drive, he eased back on the reins. A shot rang out. The sound ripped through his gut as if the lead ball had struck *him*.

He raced the horse onward. Two men were wrestling on the grass in front of the house, their faces in shadow. They were alone.

No Sophia.

No Beatrice.

No brother or mother.

His gaze locked onto the burning house. The inferno hungrily consumed the walls, causing them to implode. Fury and fear co-mingled inside him, indistinguishable from one another. He shouted at the men, but they were clenched in battle.

The man on top rose to his knees, lifted his fist, and slammed it into his opponent's face. Flames illuminated his profile.

"Stanhurst!" Crispin jumped from his horse.

The duke struck the man twice more. His opponent collapsed on the ground, unconscious.

"Stanhurst!" Crispin grabbed the duke's shoulder and blocked his fist when Stanhurst swung at him. "It is me, Margrave. Where is Sophia?"

The duke startled and swung his head side to side, searching. "She was here with her aunt. Van Middleburg's thug is after them. Check the cottage!"

Crispin dashed toward the back of the house, shouting Sophia's name. Benny had arrived and dismounted his horse. He shot past Crispin and was swallowed by the dark. When he rounded the house, a lump lay beside the path close to the pond. *A woman.* Benny spotted her, too, and reached her side first.

"I found Aunt Beatrice."

She moaned as the big fellow helped her sit up. Her forehead was smeared with mud and her arm hung limply at her side. "Sophia lured him away," she muttered. "You have to help her."

Crispin reached Beatrice. "Where did they go? Are they on foot?"

She nodded, winced, and pointed with her uninjured arm. "He chased her into the field. He is armed with a hatchet, no pistol."

"Stay with her," he ordered Benny.

"Yes, sir."

Crispin flew past the pond and veered into the field. The ground was uneven; he couldn't see what lay beneath the overgrown grass. He stumbled but kept his balance. A scream came from the left, up ahead. He changed direction and topped a hill. Sophia's white gown was like a beacon in the sea of darkness. The blackguard sat astride her, gripped her shoulders, and slammed her against the ground, shouting insults. She fought him, jabbed him in the eye.

With a howl, he drew back and slapped her.

Crispin's vision turned red. He barreled down the hill, hooked an arm around the blackguard's neck, and dragged him off Sophia. Her foot kicked out and connected with the man's gut. He grunted.

Crispin shoved him face down in the grass and buried a knee between his shoulder blades to keep him subdued. A stream of curses poured from his captive, but he was helpless to do anything else.

"Come here, love," he said to Sophia. "I need something to tie his hands."

She pushed from the ground and hurried to assist. "What do you need?"

"Help me remove my cravat." Crispin settled his weight on the man while Sophia fumbled with the knot.

As he lashed the blackguard's hands behind his back, Sophia grabbed the hem of her night rail and ripped a strip from it. She waded it into a ball, knelt beside her assailant, and shoved the fabric into his mouth. Her hands landed on her hips.

"I have never heard such salty language in all my life. That should quiet him for a bit."

Not for long, but the act seemed to provide her with a hint of satisfaction. She stood. "I must find Aunt Beatrice."

"Benny is with your aunt, darling. She is all right. Are *you* hurt?"

Her hair was down around her shoulders, and her night rail was dirty and ruined, but she seemed less rattled than he was.

"I am more furious than anything." She jabbed a finger in the thug's direction. "That man has the manners of a goat. The way he handled Aunt Beatrice was deplorable."

The brute slapping Sophia flashed through Crispin's mind. He quivered with suppressed rage. He could tear the blackguard apart with his bare hands for what he had done, but it was best to leave his punishment to the authorities. A larger risk was present, perhaps waiting to pounce from the dark.

"Benny is taking Beatrice to the cottage. We should not linger. There is a chance Farrin and Wolfe have discovered your location." He removed his pistol from the holster and passed it to her. "Do you remember how to use this?"

She stared at the firearm in her hand as if seeing one for the first time. "Uncle Charles made us practice. It was so loud."

"I know, darling." He stood and hauled his captive to his feet. "I need you to keep guard, and if I tell you to take a shot, do not hesitate. Can you do that for me?"

Her wide eyes sought out his. They glittered like obsidian in the scant moonlight. Eventually, she nodded.

The man spit the cloth on the ground and changed tactics. "Please, it weren't personal. I didn't mean any harm to the lady. T'was only a job."

"Quiet," Crispin snapped and nudged him in the direction of the cottage.

As they traipsed through the field, Sophia remained close at Crispin's side. He listened for any sounds out of place in the night. Aside from the distant rumble of crumbling timber as the fire destroyed his mother's home, everything was as it should be.

Alexander was standing in the cottage doorway, looking out as they approached. He left his post, coming out to intercept them and stopping in the middle of the path. He glowered at Crispin's captive; the blackguard shrank away.

"Miss Darlington," Alexander said kindly, "your aunt is sick with worry. She will be relieved to see you are unharmed." He shrugged out of his jacket and offered it to her. She passed the pistol to him, donned the garment, and thanked him.

"I should go reassure her," Sophia said to Crispin.

"Of course, see to Beatrice, love."

She scooted around Alexander and hurried toward the front door. Cries of joy spilled from the cottage when she entered.

"Did everyone in the house escape the fire?" Crispin asked his brother.

"We were fortunate." Alexander glared at the man before him as if it might have been a mistake to hand him the pistol. "I sent a man to retrieve the magistrate, and your man Benny went back to assist Stanhurst."

His brother relayed the tale he had heard from Sophia's aunt about the arson and ambush.

"Van Middleburg failed to kill the duke," Crispin said, "but I suspect he achieved his other aim. I take it the letters were lost in the fire."

His brother grimaced. "We barely escaped with our lives. There was no time to take anything. Do you need the letters as evidence? Miss Darlington was able to decipher them. They point to treason. Couldn't she testify to the contents?"

"Possibly."

Crispin's stomach soured at the thought. A trial could take months, and Van Middleburg would see to it her character was maligned and her credibility called into question. The ordeal would be trying for a man of Crispin's experience, but to subject an innocent young lady to the pandemonium a trial like this would generate was beyond cruel. He would find another way.

"Van Middleburg will be held accountable for his crimes tonight. There will be time to search for more evidence to use against him."

Crispin refused to take his prisoner into the cottage, so he and Alexander waited outside until the magistrate arrived. Van Middleburg had already been slapped in irons and tossed into a prison wagon. Crispin surrendered his captive to a guard and sauntered to the wagon to peer between the bars. The baron avoided meeting his gaze—although it was possible that he couldn't focus after the blows he had sustained to the head.

"I hope you enjoy this view," Crispin said. "I expect it will be similar to the one awaiting you."

Van Middleburg closed his eyes and kept quiet. As the wagon pulled away with the two prisoners, a carriage came around the bend closely followed by a wagon.

"It appears our neighbor has responded to my request for assistance," Alexander said.

Sophia and her aunt were ushered to the carriage for the ride to the neighbor's manor house, and Crispin's stepfather was carried to the wagon and placed on a pallet. His mother grabbed Crispin's hand and squeezed it. "I am relieved to see you safe."

"Likewise, Mother. Did you sustain any injuries?"

She shook her head. "I am well, and Mr. Ness is no worse for the experience. We were blessed this night."

She climbed into the wagon with her husband and smoothed his hair away from his forehead, murmuring words of comfort to him. A memory of her sitting with Crispin through a fever came back to him. Her soft, cool hand on his forehead. The sweet crooning of a lullaby.

In his anger and bitterness over being abandoned, he

had forgotten the best parts of his mother. He might never fully forgive or trust her again, but he knew with certainty he could no longer hate her.

Crispin joined the ladies in the carriage and assumed the seat next to Sophia. He placed his arm around her, and she laid her head on his shoulder. Benny and the duke arrived on horseback in time to follow the caravan.

Mr. Evans greeted their party when they arrived while his wife fussed over the ladies and insisted on showing them to the chamber that had been prepared for them. The servants had taken the wagon around to the servants' entrance, and four large men carried Mr. Ness to a room prepared especially for him located on the ground floor.

Once Sophia put her aunt to bed, she came below stairs. She had changed into a clean gown one of the ladies of the house had provided, and she had donned a pair of slippers that were too big for her. They slapped against the marble floor as she followed a footman into the drawing room where Crispin and his brother were discussing plans to protect the house and its occupants through the night. With Farrin and Wolfe still out there, they couldn't afford to relax their guard. Alexander, Benny, and Crispin would take turns keeping watch until morning. The larger man was at his post now.

"We must return to London in the morning," Sophia said without preamble. "Uncle Charles has a hidden safe at Wedmore House where he keeps valuables. Aunt Beatrice thinks if he is in possession of a map of St. Helena, it will be in the safe."

Crispin shook his head slightly, uncertain he had heard correctly. "What is this about St. Helena?"

Sophia dropped onto the sofa next to him and swiveled in his direction. Her knee brushed his, and he was overwhelmed by a desire to wrap her in his arms to reassure himself that she was unharmed. Instead, he laid his hand on the sofa between them, the edge of his little finger touching her thigh. How was it possible to miss her so completely when they had barely been apart? How could he ever leave her again?

Sophia's tongue darted across her dry lips. A light sheen caught the candlelight. "I forgot you do not know; I deciphered Lord Geoffrey's letters."

He sensed his eyes flare in surprise. "Already? You have only been at it two days."

"Your betrothed is a clever young lady," his brother said. "It took her little time to determine the book Stanhurst's brother used for his cipher."

"She has always been twice as sharp as me." Crispin smiled with fondness for the woman he loved and her incredible mind. "What did you learn from Lord Geoffrey's letters and diary?"

Alexander downed the rest of his brandy and stood. "If you will excuse me, I am already aware of the details and should look in on Mother."

Crispin inclined his head. "Please convey my regards and reassure her all will be well."

"She will be relieved to learn she and Father have a place to go." Sophia watched Crispin's brother exit the room and pull the door closed before swinging back to face him.

"Where will they go?"

"I have offered my mother and her husband shelter at the manor house. It is Alexander's home, so he will take up permanent residence. Alexander will travel with them at first light, see them settled, and hire a nurse to care for Mr. Ness."

Sophia reached for his hand, hers cool and small in his. "Are you certain you are prepared to have her close? This is all very sudden, and the relationship is still tentative."

"My father did not provide for her and my brother like he should. I have an opportunity to right the wrong. She might prefer the dowager cottage; she and Mr. Ness are welcome to make use of it." He shrugged. He did not possess the wherewithal to maintain a grudge formed before having all the facts. "Thank you for thinking of me, love. It will take time for me to grow accustomed to someone caring about my thoughts and feelings on matters."

Sophia smiled softly. "We have the rest of our lives."

Crispin laced his fingers with hers and raised her hand to his mouth to brush a kiss across her dainty knuckles. He inhaled, savoring the scent of her skin and longing to feel it pressed against his—to bury himself in her and banish the fear that had seized him when he thought he might never see her again.

His throat squeezed as the truth of how close his fears had come to being realized closed in on him. If he lost Sophia, he would lose his laughter, his joy, his ability to breathe.

"I love you," he murmured.

"I know, and I love you."

"No, darling, you do not understand."

He cradled her hand between his larger ones and struggled to find the words to explain the depth of his sentiment. It defied definition. It was vast and ever expanding. He was drowning in it and yet, its power over him no longer frightened him.

Loving Sophia did not make him weaker, more vulnerable. His determination to reach her tonight had been forged in iron. He was stronger—unstoppable— because he was in possession of something of value that he'd never had in the past. He had someone to lose.

"I am finished with the Regent's Consul," he said. "Your

uncle was right; I was too hasty, but I never anticipated having *you* in my life. Now I cannot imagine how my heart could keep beating if you were gone."

She leaned her forehead against his. "I will never leave you, Crispin." Her breath—mint-tinted from her tooth powder—whispered across his heated skin. "I will never stop loving you."

He closed his eyes and inhaled. Her promises were a balm to his heart, a slow cure for an old injury he hadn't wanted to acknowledge.

"I wish we were home," he murmured. "I would strip you bare and show you how much I love you."

"Law, now I will not sleep a wink tonight." She drew back; her breathy laugh caused him to smile. "I wish we could follow Aunt Beatrice's suggestion and run off to Gretna Green, but duty calls. You cannot leave the Regent's Consul until England's future is secured."

He cleared his throat and put distance between them. "You deciphered the letters."

"Yes, the letters." She propped her arm on the back of the sofa, still facing him. "From what I was able to piece together from Lord Geoffrey's diary, his association with Farrin began after a chance meeting at a gaming hell. Lord Geoffrey found him insufferable, but he also recognized an opportunity.

"I know from Claudine that Farrin began to dine regularly with Lord Geoffrey and the duke at Claudine's town house shortly after the men met. Claudine remembered the men barricading themselves after dinner while the Duke of Stanhurst retreated to his study. I imagine the plotting began during these meetings."

"Are you sure Old Stanhurst was not involved?"

"Lord Geoffrey took pains to keep his father in the dark. He wanted to become a man on his own terms and break free of his father's control." She pursed her lips. "Of course, he intended to break free at the expense of his country, so I have no sympathy for him. The letters are from an old school chum living in America—a supporter of Napoleon. Apparently, there are still a number of Bonapartist followers in America, although his brother does not appear to be involved in the scheme."

"From all reports, Joseph Bonaparte is content providing counsel to politicians and entertaining dignitaries and Philadelphia's upper class," Crispin said. "Restoring his younger brother to power could disrupt his new life. I imagine he is keen to keep the peace."

"I hope for all of our sakes we are able to keep the peace. It seems Farrin provided the solution for rescuing Napoleon since his brother was taking no action."

Crispin frowned. "The Consul has been aware of the Black Death's existence for ten years, but the mission has been to keep the warriors as far from England as possible. Not even Farrin could want them descending on the country. When he murdered Lord Geoffrey, he couldn't have known a man had already been sent to engage the group."

"Perhaps that is true, but he provided Lord Geoffrey with a map of St. Helena with details about the guards' locations and indicating where there are vulnerabilities. Farrin was looking for this map at Wedmore House, I am certain of it. I cannot figure out how Uncle Charles came to be in possession of it, though. Aunt Beatrice thinks he might have discovered the plot and stolen the map before it could be delivered to the warriors." Sophia puffed her chest, appearing quite proud. "Auntie says Uncle Charles is an excellent spy. I cannot wait to tell Regina and Evangeline."

"I did not realize Beatrice knew."

"Of course she did. She said Uncle Charles couldn't keep

his involvement a secret. He required her help in keeping my sisters and me safe. I wish you had told me."

"It was not my place to tell."

"No, that should have been Uncle Charles's doing. It does explain his frequent absences from home." She nibbled her bottom lip as if considering this new information she had in her possession. "Without the letters, we cannot prove any of this, can we?"

"It would be your word only. Perhaps Stanhurst's testimony would add weight to the accusation, but it would not be to his benefit to come forward. With Farrin free, I cannot allow you to assume the risk. Your uncle would not allow it if he were here. I intend to take you and Beatrice away from England as soon as possible, to Athens to reunite with your family."

"I will be happy to see them." Sophia sighed. "I am relieved for Stanhurst if I am being truthful. I would not like to see him suffer for his brother's actions. He is a good man."

Crispin agreed. The Duke of Stanhurst was more than he had seemed, which His Grace proved late the next morning.

THIRTY

THE DUKE OF STANHURST SLAPPED A PIECE OF PAPER ON THE low table placed in front of the sofa where Crispin was seated, waiting for Sophia and her aunt to come below stairs so they could depart for London. His newfound partner, Benny, would accompany on horseback, helping Crispin keep guard on the journey.

"The letters were lost, but we have this," Stanhurst said. He paced the carpet as if his life depended on remaining in motion.

Crispin eyed the paper and bent forward to retrieve it. "What is this?"

"Read it."

Crispin read the words aloud while the duke continued to pace. "I, Cyrus Finlay James Jacobson Van Middleburg, do hereby confess to being under the influence of my treacherous wife, Lady Margaret Ida Carolyn Van Middleburg, and her deceased cousin, Lord Geoffrey, son of the late Duke of Stanhurst, and unknowingly participating in a plot to rescue the Emperor Napoleon Bonaparte from exile." Crispin glanced up from the page. "How did you come by Van Middleburg's confession?"

"I borrowed a horse and rode to the village at dawn. Van Middleburg is eager to be released and believes testifying against Ida will allow him to escape culpability."

Crispin frowned. "Farrin and Wolfe might not have made an appearance last night, but I believe my orders were for *everyone* to remain watchful. You should not have ventured out alone."

"The only danger posed to me comes from my cousin and her husband. Van Middleburg has no contact with Farrin. Geoffrey never shared his name. As far as I have been able to deduce, Farrin's involvement was limited to suggesting Geoffrey hire the Black Death and providing information about St. Helena security. He has no connection to Geoffrey's American conspirators, the Van Middleburgs, or the merchants funding the venture."

Crispin considered Stanhurst's hypothesis. It made sense. If Farrin could be linked to the Van Middleburgs or the merchants, he would have targeted them as well. He was fastidious when it came to covering his crimes, and he would not allow anyone to live who could implicate him.

"Does Van Middleburg believe claiming ignorance and casting blame onto his wife will excuse him from charges of treason?"

The duke smiled grimly. "I may have hinted he would be shown leniency on the charge of attempted murder and his other crimes if he confessed. He chose to betray his wife to save himself."

"He is a fool *and* a coward."

Crispin returned to the confession, skimming over the parts he already knew to gather missing pieces of the story. Van Middleburg's testimony confirmed Farrin's map had been stolen soon after he had delivered it to

Lord Geoffrey, but Lord Geoffrey was able to reproduce it for the emissary hired to negotiate with the Black Death.

Lord Geoffrey hadn't wanted to alert Farrin, and since he knew the thief's identity, he had tried to handle the matter himself. The thugs he had hired to kill the thief did not fare well in the encounter, and the man fled England on a ship sailing to the Mediterranean the next day.

Crispin suspected the thief in question had been Charles Wedmore. It seemed likely Wedmore left England to stop the emissary before he could engage the Black Death. He was not the sort to abandon his family to save his own skin. Wedmore hadn't mentioned his mission to Crispin, however, which was puzzling. Crispin would have a chance to ask for an explanation once he, Sophia, and Beatrice arrived in Athens.

After Wedmore left the country, Lord Geoffrey had gone to Farrin to admit what had happened and asked for his assistance in cleaning up the mess.

"Security on the island is a well-guarded secret," Crispin said. "Farrin and high-ranking military officers are the only men with knowledge of the island's vulnerabilities and the strategies put in place to defend it. If Wedmore has possession of the map, he can prove Farrin's part in the scheme."

The duke dropped into a chair across from Crispin and rested his head in his hands. "Telling Farrin about the stolen map was a mistake, wasn't it? Geoffrey condemned himself to death."

Crispin did not point out that Geoffrey's treasonous actions could have only come to one end.

At the conclusion of Lord Van Middleburg's confession, he named every British merchant involved. There was no mention of Old Stanhurst or the current duke in the confession, and therefore, did not clear either duke of any wrongdoing, which Crispin found concerning.

He folded the confession and tucked it into his jacket pocket. "The evidence was destroyed in the fire—nothing to incriminate your family. Why did you urge Van Middleburg to confess? Why do you risk having your title and lands stripped away?"

Stanhurst lifted his head; his gaze was direct, fierce. "Without loyalty to country, one is not fit to call himself a duke."

Crispin inclined his head. "I will vouch for your honor when I present the confession to the Lord Chamberlain."

"I intend to be present for the audience, but your testament to my character is appreciated." The duke's hard face lost its sharp angles. "Thank you, Margrave—for everything. I will never forget you saved my life."

"Thank my protégé when you return to your sisters at the end of this all. Kane is the hero." Yet, he was no match for Farrin and Wolfe alone, and Crispin could not delay his, Sophia's, and Beatrice's departure. The sooner they were on their way to reunite with Sophia's family, the easier he would breathe.

Crispin cleared his throat, hesitating a beat. "May I ask a favor, Your Grace?

"Whatever favor you ask, I will grant it."

"Would you take Kane under your employ while I am away? Mind you, I will insist on having him back when I return. I *am* fond of the whelp."

"I understand." Stanhurst smiled. "You have my word. Kane will be looked after in your absence, assuming I am not locked away at the conclusion of this mess. Shall we convene at the carriage when the ladies come below stairs?"

The duke had no hat and his borrowed attire was ill fitting at best, but he was every inch the aristocrat as he walked toward the door with his head held high. Crispin called to him; Stanhurst turned.

"Thank you for what you did last night." His throat constricted, and he couldn't utter another word. Dwelling on what could have happened last night would overwhelm him. Sophia was alive. Nothing else mattered.

"You are welcome, Margrave."

Sophia never would have thought to look for anything beneath the floorboards in Uncle Charles's study, especially with his heavy oak bureau bookshelf sitting atop the hiding spot.

The shelves had been cleared of Uncle Charles's treasures, and they were crowding the top of his desk. Crispin eyed the behemoth piece of furniture, his head moving up and down as he surveyed the situation. "Is Beatrice certain this is the location?"

"She insists it is. Uncle Charles showed her the safe after she came to care for my sisters and me."

Sophia could go above stairs to ask again, but she didn't wish to disturb Aunt Beatrice. Her poor aunt had fallen asleep on the chaise in her chambers after Dr. Portier treated her arm. Fortunately, the injury was a sprain and not a broken bone, and the doctor had cleared Auntie to travel as soon as she felt up to it.

Cupid, content to have his owner back in residence, had curled up on her lap while Joy packed Aunt Beatrice's trunks. Crispin said it was best to be prepared, even though he could not predict when they might be allowed to leave.

"Would you like me to summon footmen to move the bureau?" she asked.

"Thank you, but I can manage on my own."

With a fabricated huff of annoyance, she moved to the other side of the bureau and grabbed the edges. She and Crispin locked gazes. She raised her eyebrows. "You do realize you mustn't do everything alone. I am helping."

His hazel eyes appeared greener this afternoon, sparkling with what she assumed was delight. "Need I remind you that I provide the brawn and you the brains in this partnership?"

She sniffed. "I am not a weakling, Lord Impertinent."

"You have proven you are far from weak, darling, and *you* do realize you will be Lady Impertinent soon. Are you certain you do not wish to bestow another moniker on me?"

"Hmm... You do raise an interesting argument. I shall give it more thought."

Crispin counted to three before tugging the furniture toward him while Sophia pushed. The bureau resisted with a groan of protest, but they were able to move it together. Sophia was stronger than she realized.

Once the area was clear, she and Crispin knelt on the floor while he wedged a knife blade between the boards. The first gave way with no resistance, and he lifted the others out of the way. Just as Aunt Beatrice had reported, a small safe was sunken into the hollow between the floor of his study and the ceiling of the lower level. Sophia dangled the key between them that Aunt Beatrice had provided. Crispin trapped it in his fist and kissed her cheek.

"To new beginnings," he said.

She echoed his sentiment as he inserted the key into the lock. It turned with a clank. Crispin grabbed the handle and lifted the door, allowing it to rest against the opening. Inside, among Uncle Charles's treasures was a single scroll. Sophia retrieved it and rolled it out on her lap, smoothing and holding the edges. Crispin's hand was hot on the small of her back. Her breath caught and her heart fluttered as the markings came together on the page.

"We have found it," she murmured. "This is the proof we need to rid ourselves of Farrin, isn't it?"

He leaned closer to inspect their find. "This is it." He stroked her hair and leaned close to place a lingering kiss at her temple. "This map is my freedom, my chance to start over and give you what you deserve."

She slanted a glance at him. "I do not understand."

He took the map, rolled it into a tube, and stood, offering her a hand up. "No one has ever resigned from the Regent's Consul. Farrin made certain everyone knew the commitment was for life. Those who attempted to leave met with mysterious ends."

Sophia frowned. Membership in one of Lord Seabrook's silly clubs looked more appealing all of a sudden.

Crispin placed the map on Uncle Charles's desk. "I thought I only had one way out. Can you understand I did not want that sort of life for you? Why I pushed you away?"

"Oh, Crispin." Tears misted her eyes; she cupped his cheek. The horror of his situation cut her deeply. "Why didn't you tell me sooner?"

"It no longer mattered, because I had already made a decision." He captured her hand where it rested on his cheek. Hooking her around the waist, he urged her closer. "Nothing will ever tear us apart," he said with the fiercest gleam in his eyes. "I will not allow it."

"Do you know what I have decided?" She slipped her arms around his neck, toying with the blond locks brushing his collar, and aimed a flirtatious glance at him from beneath her lashes. "Your commanding side is most attractive."

A wicked smile spread across his face. "Is it now?"

She nodded, widening her eyes and attempting to appear most solemn.

"In that case, I demand a kiss, darling."

"With pleasure, Lord Margrave—as many as you wish."

Sophia was more than delighted he did not limit himself to one.

EPILOGUE

THE SOLDIERS IN THEIR RED COATS WITH RIFLES PROPPED ON their shoulders created quite the spectacle at the London docks. A drumbeat rose over the din of the crowd and heads swung around in confusion as the soldiers marched in formation. The sea of people scrambled out of their path. When the armed men reached the *Cecily,* they formed a wall in front of the ship. No one who didn't belong would be stowing away onboard.

"If our departure was printed in the morning newssheet," Crispin grumbled to his old school chum where they stood at the bottom of the gangplank, "it would draw less attention."

"Fireworks would have been a nice touch," Ben Hillary teased. "I must admit their presence eases my mind."

"It is an unnecessary precaution, I assure you."

Farrin and Wolfe were not foolish enough to launch an attack in daylight, but even if they were, neither man was in the vicinity. A new leader had been named to the Regent's Consul, and every man was under orders to bring in Farrin and Wolfe, dead or alive.

Three days ago, the Consul received a report two men meeting Farrin's and Wolfe's descriptions were spotted on the Great North Road en route to Scotland. That had been before Garrick's appearance at the Seabrook estate. It seemed the great leader of the Regent's Consul had abandoned his man and was running with his tail tucked between his legs.

Nevertheless, he was pleased the Consul was keeping watch over his brother, mother, and stepfather, too. Alexander decided he would stay at the dowager cottage with their mother for the duration of Mr. Ness's illness, for which Crispin was glad.

"I cannot fathom how you kept this part of your life hidden for so many years," Ben said. "You were eighteen when you were recruited, for heaven's sake. You had plenty of time to confide in me."

Crispin shrugged. "I suspect you were too preoccupied with your own interests to notice what I was up to."

"Yes, because it could not have anything to do with you being tight-lipped."

"In my line of work, that was a requirement."

When Crispin had approached Ben about booking passage on one of the ships owned by Hillary Shipping, Crispin was honest about his situation. He was tired of lying to those who would never betray him.

Besides, the papers were already filled with stories of Lord and Lady Van Middleburg's arrests as well as those of their co-conspirators. The truth would be revealed in time. Miraculously, there was no mention of Lord Geoffrey's involvement or his murder in the papers—only tales of the Duke of Stanhurst's heroic rescue of several people from a house fire.

Stanhurst was either very lucky, or he had befriended every editor in Town. Whatever the case, Crispin was pleased for him. The duke had been cleared of any wrongdoing by the authorities, and his reputation seemed to be on the mend.

"Socializing with kings often results in unwanted attention," Ben said. "If His Majesty insists on an armed escort, you will have an armed escort."

Crispin grunted. "I would not classify our meeting as a social occasion. I am his servant." Albeit, Crispin's duties were no longer beyond what was expected of every other loyal subject.

After Crispin's audience with the Lord Chamberlain, he had been called before the King. Crispin had expected to be questioned thoroughly, and with prejudice. His Majesty had discovered Farrin and promoted him to head of the Regent's Consul, after all. In the end, however, the King had simply thanked Crispin for his service and granted his request to be released from the Consul.

Ben shaded his eyes and looked toward the ship's railing where Sophia, her great-aunt, and their lady's maid were viewing the fanfare with wide-eyed interest. "You should grow accustomed to attracting attention, Margrave. Your betrothed is breathtaking."

Crispin turned to admire his brave little bride-to-be. The sun hanging on the horizon lit her hair and created a halo around her that made her appear very much like the angel after whom she was named.

"Sophia is beautiful," he said, his chest puffing with pride, "but she is more than she appears."

Ben chuckled and clapped a hand on Crispin's shoulder. "As a happily married gent, I feel qualified to say the best ladies always are."

Crispin smiled at his oldest friend. "Thank you for allowing us the use of one of your ships." He hadn't expected to be the only travelers onboard the cargo ship, but Ben had insisted.

"My brother assures me Captain Emerson and his crew are to be trusted. He was Daniel's first mate for many years." Ben called to the captain on deck. "Patch, come allow me to make introductions."

The man's barrel chest was as broad as a bull's, and he descended the gangplank with powerful strides. Ben presented the captain and asked him all the questions Crispin had posed to Ben earlier. Once the captain answered to Crispin's satisfaction, Crispin bade his friend good-bye and joined the ladies onboard.

As he approached, Beatrice's devil-hound wiggled free of her arms, landed with a thump, and tore across the deck.

Beatrice yelled for the little dog to come back, but he paid her no mind as he dashed between the seamen's legs and barreled toward Crispin. Sophia and her lady's maid gave chase.

"He is going to escape," Sophia shouted to Crispin. "Stop him!"

The blasted troublemaker ran straight to him and jumped, but Crispin wasn't fast enough to grab him before he crashed back to the deck. The dog ran circles around him, yipping loudly and causing a general ruckus. Sophia and her lady's maid tried to catch him, too, but he evaded their outstretched arms.

"Cupid, look here!" As if by magic, Beatrice conjured a piece of fatty ham from her reticule and waggled it back and forth in front of her face. "Come get your treat, precious."

At the sound of the word 'treat', the poodle stopped in his tracks and cocked his head. He spied the meat in Beatrice's hands and shot in her direction. Safe in her arms again, she hugged him to her bosom.

"I should take him below deck," she said. "Joy, will you help unpack my trunks?"

"Yes, ma'am." The loyal and most certainly patient lady's maid hurried after Sophia's aunt.

Crispin sighed and offered his arm to Sophia. They moved to the railing to watch the men unmoor the ship.

She tipped her pretty face toward him, her blue eyes like glittering gems. "Thank you for agreeing to allow Auntie to bring Cupid. I know he can be trying, but she loves him so."

"This is going to be a long journey," he muttered, knowing he would endure the little dog's antics because it made Sophia happy.

"It could be." Sophia chuckled softly and rested her head on his shoulder as the ship drifted away from the dock. "But I will endeavor to make it an enjoyable one."

"You already are, darling." He brushed a kiss across her silky hair and smiled, savoring the warmth of her body close and her sweet scent. "You already are."

BOOKS BY SAMANTHA GRACE

THE DUKE OF DANBURY: HALLIDAY SISTERS SERIES
Twice Upon a Time
One Less Only Earl

NOVELLA
Charming a Scoundrel

BEAU MONDE BACHELORS SERIES
Miss Hillary Schools a Scoundrel
Lady Amelia's Mess and a Half
Miss Lavigne's Little White Lie
Lady Vivian Defies a Duke

RIVAL ROGUES SERIES
One Rogue Too Many
In Bed with a Rogue
Kissed by a Scottish Rogue
The Best of Both Rogues

ABOUT THE AUTHOR

RITA-nominated historical romance author, Samantha Grace, discovered the appeal of a great love story at the age of four, thanks to Disney's "Robin Hood". She didn't care that Robin Hood and Maid Marian were cartoon animals. It was her first HEA experience, and she never wanted the warm fuzzies to end. Now that Samantha is grown, she enjoys creating her own happy-endings for characters that spring from her imagination. *Publisher's Weekly* describes her stories as "fresh and romantic" with subtle humor and charm. Samantha describes romance writing as the best job ever. Part-time medical social worker, moonlighting author, and a lover of history, Samantha lives in the Midwest with her family.

www.samanthagraceauthor.com
samantha@samanthagraceauthor.com

Made in the USA
Middletown, DE
08 June 2019